Tryin' To Sleep
In The Bed You Made

Tryin' To Sleep
In The Bed You Made

DeBERRY GRANT

BANTAM BOOKS
LONDON · NEW YORK · TORONTO · SYDNEY · AUCKLAND

TRYIN' TO SLEEP IN THE BED YOU MADE
A BANTAM BOOK : 0 553 50556 4

First publication in Great Britain

PRINTING HISTORY
Bantam edition published 1997
Bantam edition reprinted 1998 (three times)

Set in 10/12pt Linotype Plantin by
County Typesetters, Margate, Kent.

Bantam Books are published by Transworld Publishers Ltd,
61–63 Uxbridge Road, London W5 5SA,
in Australia by Transworld Publishers (Australia) Pty Ltd,
15–25 Helles Avenue, Moorebank, NSW 2170,
and in New Zealand by Transworld Publishers (NZ) Ltd,
3 William Pickering Drive, Albany, Auckland.

Printed and bound in Great Britain by
Cox & Wyman Ltd, Reading, Berkshire.

For
Valerie DeBerry, Arlene Hamilton, Lawrine Childers,
and sisters/friends everywhere

WE GRATEFULLY ACKNOWLEDGE

Hiram L. Bell III – Thank you for lettin' me be myself . . .
again.   D G

Lawrine A. Childers, for opening the door.   V D B

Jeanette F. Frankenberg, for so much more than can be
listed here.

Loren Johnson, Talisha Miller, and Gloria Frye, our
readers – your questions, opinions, enthusiasm, and eager
requests for more pages kept us moving toward the finish
line.

Kim Allen Mayfield, who turned us on to Kim Jones who
provided invaluable information about our folks on the
Vineyard.

Ken Harris and Stephen Gronsky, for the baseball scoop.

Dolores Fisher and Laurie Prosper, for some nitty gritty
on the ad agency business.

Max, our favorite loving, awful, orange tabby and muse,
and the Fishes of Brunswick, for keeping us laughing.

André T. Browne, for being in the right place at the right
time.

Andrea Cirillo, our agent, for believing we could.

Charlie Lafave, who turned us on to Jody Hotchkiss who turned us on to Andrea.

Jennifer Enderlin, for taking a chance.

The late John L. DeBerry II, for being there each and every day, and to John L. DeBerry III, M.D., for being there for *his* daughters.

Always Gloria Hammond Frye and Juanita Cameron DeBerry, for the right stuff.

Alexis, Lauren and Jordan, Brian and Christine, the future.

And all of our friends and family members whose love and support is surely the grace of the Creator at work.

PROLOGUE

'What happened to my life?'

1989 WESTCHESTER, NEW YORK

This don't make no kinda sense! Gayle plucked a wet towel from the bathroom doorknob and flung it toward the white terry cloth mound on the gold-veined marble floor. *This heifer just checked in last night and already used every towel in the place!* She wiped her hand roughly against her thigh to dry it, then shuddered, still feeling the unidentifiable, orange-scented goo she'd palmed while changing the sheets in the room next door.

From the moment Gayle entered this room and eyed the expensive clothes tossed on the bed, spilling onto the floor, she knew this woman had money, or at least liked to look like she did. Some of those same pricey designer labels, neatly arranged by color and style, used to hang in her own walk-in closet. *Humph . . . at least that made it easy to organize 'em for the consignment shop.* She stooped to retrieve a soggy washcloth wadded up in the middle of the tub and felt so tired she could have curled up on the hard cold enamel and been asleep before her eyes closed. *Snap out of it!* She straightened up and went to the sink.

Mocha makeup streaks stained the hand towels balled up next to the basin. *So, it's a sister.* Gayle pitched the towels into the pile. *It don't take long to become just like 'Miss Anne.' I know her momma didn't raise her to be this*

9

nasty. It reminded Gayle of how her husband used to fuss when she dusted and neatened up at home, before the housekeeper came, but he didn't grow up listening to her momma go on about cleaning up behind filthy people. She had hated those stories and any other reminders her mother was a cleaning woman, but determined not to be the subject of similar tales, she always ignored his wisecracks and kept on dusting.

When we stayed at hotels like this, I never left such a . . . Stop it, Gayle, just stop it! That was another life, and every day she vowed to stop reliving it . . . reliving him, at least in the daytime. The dreams were bad enough. *I gotta let him go.*

Gayle spritzed the expansive mirror and vigorously polished, erasing the hair spray cloud and toothpaste specks, without once catching her own reflection. She didn't need a mirror to tell her she looked 'like somebody sent for and couldn't come,' as her daddy would have said. It was the one good thing about this job. As a part-time hotel maid she didn't even have to pretend she cared how she looked.

The shapeless gray-and-pink uniform hung like a potato sack, hiding her curves, but it was better this way. At least most of the men who stayed one drink too long in the hotel lounge had stopped calling her 'girlie' and asking what she charged for extra room service. *If I'd stopped caring how everything looked a long time ago, I wouldn't be in this sorry mess now.* She picked up a still-slick bar of hotel soap with the abandoned shower cap and threw them in the trash.

The long wavy brown hair Gayle had pampered and gloried in all her life was carelessly twisted into a frizzy knot at the nape of her neck. For the first time in her life Gayle avoided mirrors. The golden glow of her skin had sallowed, and sooty crescents had settled beneath the eyes he used to love to gaze into. 'I put the fire in your big brown eyes,' he'd say. 'And I'll always keep it burnin'.' But after he vanished, the flame dimmed and flickered, and now it was ash-cold.

Gayle held her breath and fought the tears that threatened every time she poured the pungent disinfectant in the toilet. *I need this job. Vanessa and Momma need me to have this job.* She swished her rag around the seat, folded the toilet paper edge into a perfect triangle, then poked her head into the bedroom and checked the clock. *Only ten-thirty.* Gayle sank to her knees and scrubbed the tub. *Lord, what happened to my life?* Before she finished she was startled by palsied rattling of the door.

'Shit! I hate these damned cards . . . Money! He asked if I wanted money!' The woman's muffled voice quaked with rage. 'What the hell is wrong with a key?' The shaking intensified, punctuated by sharp kicks.

What is wrong with this girl? Gayle rose to open the door.

'What are you doing in here? I'm checking out!' the woman snarled as she shot angrily through the doorway. 'Doesn't anybody in this damned hotel know what they're doing?'

Heat seared Gayle's cheeks. To keep from saying what was on her mind, she looked down and felt in her apron pocket for the list of rooms to clean she was given when she started her shift, but when the woman flung her folio on the desk and sent a vase of roses crashing to the floor, Gayle nearly jumped out of her skin.

'Would you leave? . . . *Now!*'

Oh my God . . . it can't be. Gayle was dumbstruck, riveted in place. *But that voice.* It was clipped and commanding now, all traces of the down-home drawl long

11

gone, but she could almost hear that rich alto singing from the back of the choir loft. Gayle stared as the woman yanked open her suitcase, snatched clothes from the bed, and stuffed them into the black leather bag. She noted the woman's hair, styled in a sleek, sophisticated cap. *No more nappy kitchen, much less those wiry pickaninny braids Momma used to frown at when we were kids. She's still on the round side, but a lot thinner than before. And that outfit would pay my rent for the next two months. It's been . . . ten years at least.*

'Are you deaf or just plain stupid? I said get the hell out!' The woman wheeled from the closet, clenching a red chiffon dress like she would rip it in two. Her eyes blazed right through Gayle.

It really is Patricia. Gayle looked dead in Pat's face, opened her mouth to speak, but clamped it shut again, silenced by the scalding stare. *I have to say something.* She tried to find words, but this time choked on the memory of their last stormy meeting and how shamefully she had treated Pat, her best friend, the closest thing to a sister she ever had. Suddenly, Pat spun around and continued packing.

Anger and embarrassment enveloped Gayle in a hot, musty, airless, haze. She backed slowly from the room, daring Pat to see her. A film of sweat coated her body and anger seeped through her uniform. *Miss High-'n'-Mighty thinks she's too good to know me. Humph! She lived in my house when her own mother wouldn't own her.*

Gayle pulled the door to, then sagged against the wall and shivered with a fevered chill, her head in a daze, her heart in an uproar.

'Damn you! *I hate you!*' Pat's anguished wail pierced the quiet. Gayle was drawn toward the cry, reached for the knob, but she knew there was much more than the door still between them. Then, a torrent of sobs from Pat's room flooded the impenetrable, carpeted silence of the hall.

All the years we were together . . . everything that happened . . . I never heard Pat cry . . . not even that day . . .

Part One

MAKIN' THE BED

1

'. . . an invisible crack in the world.'

'I gotta pee . . . bad,' Gayle whispered to Pat. Fat snowflakes had settled on Gayle's rabbit fur hat and on her bangs, framing her small almond face like a halo.

'You went before we left school!' Pat knew Gayle was stalling to keep from facing her parents with dismal grades. Pat pulled at her green knit cap, trying to keep her hair dry. Her straight-A report card was tucked inside the folded newspaper cover of her math book, but she'd have hell to pay if Aunt Verna had to get out the pressing comb before Saturday.

First thrown together in kindergarten by the random selection of alphabetical order, Patricia Reid and Gayle Saunders were as different and as inseparable as day and night.

Pat had been raised by MaRay, a cake-baking, opinionated woman with immense bosoms and fat, hugging arms, in Swan City, a hiccup near Raleigh Bay on the North Carolina coast. Lil' Daddy had passed, soon after Pat's hello holler to the world, 'But MaRay's here for you, Sugar.' Then, when Pat was six, MaRay passed, too. Pat went north to live with her Aunt Verna, a hard knot of a woman with no space in her heart or her life for a little girl.

17

Her first week in the small dark second-floor flat, Pat learned not to mention MaRay and to be very quiet, especially after her aunt's late nights on her job at the Easy Street Bar & Grill. Luckily fall came soon. Since Pat was from the South, which to teachers up North meant she was at least borderline backwards, she was put back a grade, but starting school meant that for at least half a day she didn't have to be quiet, and she wasn't alone.

Pat was chubby and chocolate brown with a wise, wide-eyed face she would 'grow into' and hair that resisted the taming of heat and grease. Her classmates called her 'Aunt Jemima on the pancake box' and made fun of her accent, which was thick and slow as the molasses MaRay had laced in her infant bottles. The madder they made her, the more determined she became not to show it. Gifted with keen intelligence nurtured by the strong mother wit of MaRay, Pat quickly proved she was smarter than she looked. In class she always had the answer, which impressed the teacher, but not the students, except for Gayle.

Dainty and honey-colored, with long, wavy 'good' hair, Gayle was the answered prayer of Joseph and Loretta Saunders. They married late, past the point when anyone at the venerable Mt Moriah Baptist Church thought they'd bother. To make up for lost time, they worked hard, saved money for a house, and soon moved from Harlem to St Albans, Queens, the home of Count Basie, James Brown, and other important people Loretta was happy to tell you. It was a two-bedroom frame house, with a brick front, pale green siding, a bay window, and, best of all it was detached, a fine thing to all their apartment-living friends. The lot was even big enough for a carport and a brick barbecue pit in the backyard.

Joseph and Loretta were all set for a family, yet after twelve years and three cruel miscarriages folks said they

18

were too old and ought to stop. Goodness, most of their friends' children were nearly grown. But ever since she was little, Loretta, the ninth of ten in a family where nothing seemed new or enough, had dreamed of being grown and having a daughter. Only one, so she could dress her in pretty clothes bought just for her. She'd have a pink room with dainty white furniture, a room like Shirley Temple must have had, a room of her own.

Just when Loretta and Joseph were beginning to think their friends were right, praise the Lord, their prayers were answered and Gayle Denise Saunders arrived, crying and hollering and demanding to be noticed. Although Loretta was thrilled, she worried that Joseph might be disappointed since she knew men wanted sons, but Gayle landed like an arrow, smack in the bull's-eye of her daddy's heart. He worked for two days with no sleep, laying carpet, hanging Peter Rabbit wallpaper in the nursery, and putting the finishing touches on the new dresser and canopied cradle.

Gayle was their pretty, pampered prize, loved and spoiled by her parents every day, so kindergarten was a rude awakening. She was unhappy to find herself surrounded by dozens of children clamoring for the teacher's attention. Gayle's long hair – worn loose, not braided – her clothes – Sunday-best for other children – and her stand-offishness marked her as someone who thought she was too cute, and she was isolated accordingly.

Gayle was so miserable that her good Baptist parents considered enrolling her in Catholic school. But on a day the class had to choose partners for an outing to the park, Gayle decided not to be left alone again. She chose Patty, the other girl nobody ever picked, and a friendship began. To Gayle, Pat seemed like she knew things, and she never seemed lonely or worried, even when she was by herself.

And Gayle let Pat into her fantasy world, where anything was possible and it was okay to be a child. They shared finger paints and animal crackers and the hand clap-slap of 'Miss Mary Mack, Mack, Mack, All Dressed In Black, Black, Black.' They played dolls and blocks, but they always played together, and by first grade, each declared the other her best friend.

Loretta, however, did not approve of Pat, or 'her people,' meaning she didn't like Verna Reid's job as a barmaid. She kept trying to convince Gayle she could find a nicer girl to be her best friend. Gayle didn't care what Loretta thought on the subject and persisted in inviting Pat over. Lips pursed and nose out of joint, Loretta would complain to Joseph that Verna and her ilk were exactly what they left Harlem to avoid. 'Patty's only a child, 'Etta,' Joseph had said over the sports page. 'Smart one at that. Gayle can learn a thing or two from *her*.' Loretta was so put out with Joseph, she put him out of her bed for a week.

Verna thought Gayle's family was uppity, for no good reason. 'Her daddy's a damn janitor and her momma does day work!' Pat sat in silence, playing with a bowl of Trix and pretending to watch *Soul Train* while Verna ranted. 'They treat that silly-ass girl like she somethin' special, always tossin' her hair like she White.' Verna couldn't figure out why the hell Pat, with her flat face and eyes like a walleyed pike, wanted to be around somebody who made her look even more homely, but if Pat wanted to be a fool, that was on her.

Now in fifth grade, the unlikely twosome was inseparable. The very children who had disliked Gayle because she was so pretty were eventually drawn to her for the same reason. Pat had all but lost her Carolina drawl, but brains didn't make you popular. She was quiet and a little too bookish, but she could be funny sometimes, she always had the right answers to math homework, and her inexplicable closeness to Gayle sealed her acceptance.

And the girls' walk home was ritual. By three-forty they would reach Pat's street. She had orders from her aunt not to let 'any little bastards in my house.' Verna called most days at four o'clock to make sure Pat was home alone, so rain or shine, the girls talked outside until three-fifty-five. They discussed schoolwork, sang songs from the radio, and sometimes said things they didn't want anyone else to hear, like how Pat wanted to be a doctor or lawyer, somebody important so she didn't have to work at night like Aunt Verna or wear those clothes that made men click their tongues and talk to her out the side of their mouths. Gayle couldn't wait to be old enough to wear makeup, date, and get married, probably to a prince, because her daddy always had dirt under his nails and her momma's hands were so rough they snagged her stockings. Besides, they worked all the time and didn't seem like they had any fun. Pat inevitably asked the last time she saw a Black prince. 'That doesn't mean there isn't one, and I plan to marry him! I'll find a prince for you, too, and we'll have a double wedding!' Gayle would announce, then stroll home daydreaming about gowns and weddings, which she would draw until her mother made her get her homework.

The snow was falling double-time, and car tires whined, spinning for traction. Gayle stomped the caked snow off her boots. 'Just went doesn't help when I gotta go now, Patty!' To show the urgency of the situation, Gayle passed up their daily stop at J&T Candy Corner, where she would check for new hairstyle magazines and Archie comics because she loved that Veronica Lodge. Pat would buy a chocolate chip cookie the size of a 45 record to knock the edge off until she warmed the dinner plate Aunt Verna always left her.

'You are the peeingest girl in the world. If there was a peeing contest, you'd win.' Pat giggled, and Gayle held her stomach and tried not to laugh, but she did anyway.

'Shh!' Gayle chided Pat, as she glanced back and saw Marcus Carter climbing to the top of an icy gray mound, piled high by a snowplow. 'Going to the bathroom is girl stuff. Don't let him hear.'

Last year, Marcus had moved around the corner from Gayle and appeared in their class and on their walk home. At first they ignored him. He was, after all, a boy, but when Gayle developed a crush on Marcus's eighth-grade brother, Freddy, Marcus became the first male member of this very exclusive club.

Marcus leapt off the bank with a whoop and grinned like a fool as he landed on his butt in the fresh snow. 'Everybody pees!' He got up, galloped past them, and snatched Gayle's hat. Trotting backwards he added, 'I can pee and write my name in the snow at the same time!' Freddy had just taught him this miraculous feat.

'That's nasty, and gimme back my hat!' Gayle squealed and ran after him.

They arrived in front of Pat's house, and, hat in hand, Gayle shifted her weight from foot to foot, looking pitiful. She knew Pat wasn't allowed company, but three C's, two D's, and an F in geography meant she'd have to listen to a lecture on how important education was so she could take care of herself and not have to scrub other people's floors and toilets.

'Come on, Pat-ty, I can't hold it. I gotta go . . . *now!* I can't walk another step.' Gayle crossed her heart and her legs.

'You mean if I tickle you, you'll pee all over yourself,' Marcus said, his fingers wiggling in anticipation.

'Marcus Garvey Carter, I'll scream if you touch me,' Gayle threatened.

Pat hemmed and hawed, yanking at a drooping kneesock. A resounding 'whap' interrupted her debate as the frozen sparks of a well-aimed snowball exploded off Marcus's head. His books fell and skittered across the snow as he spun to face his attacker.

'*Steeerrrriiike!* Right in yo' bean head,' shouted Freddy, bounding up to the trio. At thirteen Freddy, a cocoa brown length of budding muscle and energy, viewed tormenting Marcus as his brotherly right, secure that he was big enough to call the shots. 'Freddy "Fastball" Carter wins the World Series! Roberto Clemente eat that! Tell me I ain't bad.'

'Baseball is lame!' Marcus yelled, then barreled into Freddy, knocking him to the powdery pavement.

Ignoring the melee, Pat continued, 'You only live four more blocks, Gayle. You could make it if you stop talkin' and start walkin'.'

'*Pleazzzz!* It's too cold, and I can't wait!' Gayle looked near tears.

'All right! . . . But you gotta hurry up.' Pat swung open the chain-link gate and felt under her scarf for her keys, which dangled from the braided orange lanyard Gayle had made for her last summer in vacation Bible school.

Gayle followed, but a howl stopped them before Pat unlocked the door.

'Aw, Freddy man, you busted my lip. Look, I'm bleedin'.' Marcus triumphantly pulled his lower lip down to display the blood collecting around his teeth. 'Wait 'til I show Daddy. He's gon' whip yo butt. He tol' you to quit messin' wit me.'

'Eeeyew!' Gayle moaned, as Marcus spit out a mouthful of blood that dotted the snow like Redhots.

'Don't be no sissy, man. You ain't even hurt.' Freddy lifted his drawstring gym bag and gingerly dusted off the snow. 'Besides, I got somethin' in here I was gonna show you, but I can't be showin' no sissy,' Freddy said, baiting his hook.

'You ain't got nothing in that stupid bag but s'more a them stupid motorcycle magazines,' Marcus said, trying to resist the enticing lure.

'That's what you say. Not what I know.' Freddy dangled the bait in front of Marcus.

'What's he got in there?' Gayle whispered to Pat.

Marcus, unable to ignore temptation, bit. 'Okay, okay, I won't tell.' He prepared to spit again.

'Don't you spit no more blood out in front of my house,' Pat yelled, knowing that somehow she'd be blamed for it.

'What I'm s'pposed to do?' Marcus tried not to swallow.

'You could come up to wash your mouth out, and Freddy could come, too . . . so you act right,' Gayle offered.

'Gaa-yle.' Pat shot her friend a scalding glance, which was answered by Gayle's 'Oh come on, just this once' smile. Pat sighed and reluctantly opened the door. 'But y'all have to be outta here by four. No kidding.' Everybody could do their business by then.

They rumbled up the steps and into the apartment. Pat hurried Gayle into the bathroom and tried to confine the others to the narrow hall, except that meant they were right outside the bathroom and Gayle wouldn't pee until they moved. The boys were remanded to the living room.

'Dag, you sleep on the couch?' Marcus poked the pile of clumsily folded sheets and blankets.

'None a your business and keep your ole nasty hands offa my stuff.' Pat emerged from the kitchen and handed Marcus a napkin for his mouth. She missed her bed in

Swan City. It was near a window, and she would lie at night counting the stars beyond a clutch of scruffy pine trees except when there was thunder and lightning. Then she would take her covers and hide with MaRay in the pantry, where there were no windows and nothing electric. Ma would tell stories about when she was little while they waited out the storm. The sofa was comfortable, though, and she could watch TV in her pajamas with all the lights out when she was by herself at night.

'What'cha gon' show me?' Marcus zeroed in on Freddy, forgetting his injured mouth.

Freddy knelt on the parquet linoleum and carefully loosed the drawstring of his bag. The hood of his jacket fell forward, obscuring most of his face. 'You gotta swear not to tell. You hear me. . . never. . . nobody.' Freddy hunched over like a wizard fiercely protecting the secret magic hidden in his pouch. Pat's curiosity drew her closer. 'You too. You have to swear.' Caution, fear, and excitement tinged his solemn voice. Good sense told Pat that Freddy should take his bag, its contents, and his brother and get out because Aunt Verna was going to call any minute, but her eleven-year-old need to know made her slowly nod yes as she crossed her heart and swore not to tell.

Freddy milked the anticipation. 'I shouldn't be showing you this. Y'all just kids, but . . .' He reached inside and slowly, reverently, withdrew his secret by its black, plastic handle.

Patricia's mouth dropped open as she backed away. 'You gotta get outta here. Now . . . you gotta leave. . .'

Marcus swelled with an excited intake of air. 'Where'd you get it? That's a toy, man. That ain't no real gun.' Marcus looked skeptically at the Saturday night special.

'This ain't no toy, chump. I found it. On the way to

school . . . next to a garbage can in Baisley Park.'

'You lie . . . Lemme hold it.' Marcus sprang toward Freddy.

Time oozed in thick oily seconds. Pat wanted to be outside again, waving good-bye to Gayle, but she couldn't alter the past or grab hold of the present enough to change it.

'Naw man . . . it's dangerous.' Freddy moved to tuck the gun away.

Dense and slippery, the time slick spread.

'I bet you never saw lips like these.' Gayle sashayed from the bathroom, her mouth painted with Verna's lipstick in a plum so deep it looked crude. She stopped cold when she saw the melee.

'Come on . . . lemme hold it.' Marcus reached around Freddy, grabbing at the pistol.

'Stop, Marcus!'

But he couldn't, and the boys locked, struggling over the weapon.

'Marcus, cut it. . .' A crackle, no louder than a finger snap, stopped them all. Pat saw Freddy fall through Marcus's arms and land on the floor in slow motion. Then the shrill ring of the phone cut the thick silence. Pat knew it was her aunt, and she couldn't answer.

'Get up,' Marcus commanded, standing over his brother. 'Quit playin'.' He took hold of Freddy's shoulder and turned him faceup. Gayle screeched. Freddy's mouth opened and closed, opened and closed, but no words escaped. Marcus pleaded, 'Come on, get up,' but then the scarlet trickled from the corner of Freddy's lips. Pat knelt and unzipped his parka, revealing the small hole and the big wet spot on the front of his striped velour shirt.

Stumbling clear of hearing and the sick, greasy knot in her throat, Pat found the phone and called for help.

Time blurred and focused. In the lucid moments Pat said just tell the truth, you didn't do it on purpose, but Gayle ranted they would all rot in jail if they told that Marcus and Freddy had fought over the gun. 'Freddy tripped over his books. It was an accident,' she insisted. Marcus paced, not uttering a sound, like something wild that was cornered.

Sirens blared. Paramedics worked feverishly on Freddy as a cop ushered the children outside past the crowd that had gathered and bundled them into a patrol car. A quiet man in a brown tweed coat squatted next to the open door and asked what happened. Without hesitation Marcus told about coming upstairs to wash his bloody mouth, what Freddy said about finding the gun, and heaping the lie on the pile of truth, about how Freddy stumbled over his books and fell on the gun and it went off. Pat and Gayle nodded their agreement. After a few more questions Tweed Coat left them alone.

They knew it wasn't snowing anymore. They knew there were no handles on the inside of the police car doors. They knew they were scared. And they knew they would keep Marcus's secret.

'But what happens when Freddy wakes up? He'll tell the truth,' Pat asked.

Gayle and Marcus looked startled by this thought, but before they could answer a cop got in the car and started the engine.

'Freddy's okay, right?' Gayle asked.

The cop sighed, tossed his cap on top of a clipboard in the front seat, and ran a hand through his hair. 'I'm sorry, kids.'

And then they knew that Freddy was dead. Gayle wailed like a banshee. Pat tried to comfort her. Marcus clutched his arms around himself like a straitjacket and

27

stared out the window, clenching and releasing his jaw, the salty taste of blood still in his mouth.

Gayle's parents arrived at the precinct house first, and as soon as Gayle saw them she dissolved in tears. Loretta gathered her daughter into her lap. She wiped Gayle's eyes, cleaned the lipstick smeared around her mouth, and rocked her. Joseph watched, looking pained and sucking so deeply on a cigarette, he barely exhaled any smoke. Eventually Gayle calmed down enough to answer questions for the detective. When she explained what she was doing at Pat's, Joseph said, 'But you know to come straight home after school.'

'Hush, Joseph. The child's been punished enough,' Loretta said.

When Tweed Coat finished with Gayle, Joseph and Loretta tried to take her home, but she got hysterical, refusing to abandon Pat and Marcus, so they stayed.

Booker Carter appeared, still wearing his blue-gray postal uniform and thick-soled black shoes. Ethel, his wife, was too upset to come, so he had a neighbor stay with her. Booker's shoulders always listed to the left to mark the place where his mailbag hung, but now they both slumped, the weight of his sons a heavier burden than he could bear.

Marcus sat, head bowed, silent, wedged in the corner of a wooden bench. He saw the black shoes, polished to shine like patent despite the snow, and raised his eyes to meet his father's, but the pain he saw in a split second was blinding, and he lowered them again.

Booker T. Washington Carter, Jr, had a government job. That meant he had done better in life than his father, but he felt that the prophecy of his great name had not been fulfilled. When his sons were born, he decided to give them each their own great name legacy, and with it

28

their own chance at something more. But now that hope, that wish for better lives for his sons, leaked like tears from the corners of his heart.

Tweed Coat escorted Booker to an office and spoke to him in sympathetic official tones. It was terrible about his son. The police had reason to believe the gun was ditched after a liquor store robbery, and by the way, where was Freddy last night?

'My son ain't robbed no liquor store,' Booker said with finality.

After more questions and paperwork Tweed Coat told Booker he'd have to go to the morgue and identify the body, then he brought Marcus in. The boy told his story, showing his bloody lip and telling the tale of Freddy's fall. When they were done father took son lightly by the arm. Booker walked like his legs wouldn't carry him much farther, and when they got to the door he gave way, slumped against the frame, and sobbed open and unashamed. His shoulders heaved, his face glistened with tears. 'Oh Lawd, why did you take my boy?' The hustle bustle of the room quieted to an embarrassed, nervous murmur. And Marcus, who had never seen his father cry, wished with all his heart he was dead, too.

In a minute Booker collected himself, mopped his face with his handkerchief, and took Marcus home to his mother.

Verna came in the door, black leather coat flapping, cussing, the sour malt smell of Johnny Walker Red punctuating every word. 'Where the shit is she?' A Salem dangled from her lips and wagged as she spoke. Pat, who sat staring at her fat knees, still shiny from this morning's greasing, flinched when she heard the gritty voice. She steeled for the harangue.

'Goddam police draggin' me down here 'cause this little

bitch decides she's gon' have a party while I'm out workin' my ass off. Knew from the git-go you wasn't never gon' be nothin' but trouble.'

Gayle tuned up to cry again. Pat tried to explain, but went silent when Verna raised the back of her hand. The blow landed with a resounding whack on Pat's cheek. Joseph rose from his seat, but Tweed Coat intervened and led Pat and Verna, still fussing, to his office.

Pat answered questions the best she could with Verna's commentary in the background. Tweed Coat seemed nice, and Pat wanted to tell him she was a good girl and show him her report card as proof, but she just told him what he needed to know and told it the way they all promised they would. When he was done with her he asked her to wait outside on the bench. He wanted to talk to Verna alone.

Verna's outbursts periodically interrupted the hum of the station house. 'None a your damn business what time I get home,' or 'Ain't nobody give me nothin' 'cept her, and I *didn't* want that.' With each outburst Gayle and Pat huddled closer, Loretta cringed and gave Joseph her 'I told you about that woman' look. Pat stiffened when she heard the furious tap-tapping of Verna's high-heeled boots against the green-and-gray tiled floor. Hand jammed into waist and disappearing into a roll of flesh, Verna posed in front of her niece. Pat stood automatically.

'Don't be too hard on the girl,' Joseph said, gathering his family to leave.

Verna cut her eyes. 'Maybe you ought to stop mindin' my business and ask your child what she and them boys was doin' in my house.' She pinched the shoulder of Pat's coat, snapped, 'Come on,' and propelled her into the night.

The day of the funeral Pat and Gayle clutched hands in their pew of the storefront Temple of the Lord, trying to be brave. Loretta and Joseph sat beside them, looking weary.

Pat listened to 'Just As I Am,' played low on the organ, and tried to ignore her stinging legs, a reminder of the extension-cord whipping she got the night of the shooting. In Swan City, church was part of every week, but Verna didn't hold much with religion, so Pat hadn't been to church since MaRay's funeral. Now, Pat heard Ma's alto singing, '. . . Without one plea, But that thy blood was shed for me.' That's when she saw Freddy in his blood-soaked shirt and closed her eyes to stay the tears.

Frightened, but unable to look away, Gayle stared at the array of flowers guarding the white casket. She thought the ruffly lining looked like Reddi Whip. Then she saw the arm of Freddy's white suit, and a vision of Marcus and Freddy, caked in snow, flashed in her mind. She shuddered and faced Pat, whose lids fluttered open. Silently Gayle asked, 'This all happened, didn't it? Freddy's really dead?' Pat's eyes answered back, 'Yes.'

Just then the Carter family entered the church. Booker supported Ethel, who moaned helplessly, 'My baby . . . oh my baby . . .' Marcus followed solemnly, wearing a baggy blue suit. He looked vacant. Holding-back tears hung at the corners of Pat's eyes when she saw him. As he passed their pew, Gayle began to sob, and Marcus paused long enough to give her his handkerchief. Gayle peered at it, then timidly looked at him. *He doesn't hate me.* She clutched the starched square as he continued up the aisle.

The preacher worked the congregation until he dripped sweat, and their misery flowed in anguished sobs and shouts. Freddy's baseball coach spoke movingly of the wasted potential and promise. As the soloist sang 'His Eye Is on the Sparrow,' ushers signaled each pew to file by the

31

casket and say good-bye to Freddy. By the time their row was called Gayle was crying so hard that Joseph stayed behind and cradled her as she clutched the now sodden handkerchief. Pat followed Loretta to the front of the church. On either side of Freddy's head were white satin pillows, lettered in gold, one 'Son,' one 'Brother.' His skin looked chalky to Pat. *Just like MaRay did*. When she stood opposite Marcus, she didn't know what to say. There was nothing *to* say. He reached out and took her hand in a dry-cold grip, and she leaned in and kissed him on the cheek, then moved on.

When it was time for the family's farewells, Ethel Carter tried to climb into the coffin. 'Leave him be. He's just restin',' she wailed, and had to be restrained until Marcus spoke. 'It's okay, Mom. It'll be okay,' he said, but in her mind it was Freddy talking, and she calmed down, saying, 'See, I told you he was just asleep.'

Gayle's folks decided not to go to the cemetery, afraid the scene would be too hard on the girls. After a lunch they all picked over, they left Pat at her door as Verna had instructed, looking small and frightened despite her valiant front.

Pat dragged upstairs, wishing she could have gone home with Gayle, but grateful her aunt was already gone. She just wanted to lie down and wait for the pounding in her head to stop. Her breath rose in puffy clouds, which meant the landlord had let the oil tank run dry again, so she tried to light the oven. Holding the match over the hole and turning the knob at the same time proved a greater challenge than Pat was up to, and each time she bent over, her head throbbed harder, so she gave up. Still wearing her coat and hat, she lay on the sofa, swaddled in her blanket, and wished for MaRay. Then, she bolted up and rummaged through the plaid fabric suitcase that still

32

held everything she had brought with her from Swan City until she found it.

After MaRay was buried in the old cemetery behind the church, everybody had come back to the house. They ate and drank, and people started taking things, knickknacks or the silver cream pitcher, 'something to remember her by.' Pat wanted something, too, so she sneaked into MaRay's bedroom while the others were busy reminiscing. It was strange being in the dark, crowded room. It still smelled like her, like lavender soap and sassafras tea. Pat reached way in the back corner of the mahogany chifforobe, behind the shoes, avoiding the mousetrap, and found the bergamot tin where MaRay kept her good jewelry, the jet cluster earrings, the Sunday strand of just-like-real pearls she bought at the Belks in Raleigh, a cuff link with fancy letters Pat liked to trace with her finger, and the one lacy gold hoop earring. Ma had laughed 'til she cried when Pat asked if her daddy was a pirate.

Holding the tin made it seem that Ma was with her, and Pat settled back into the blanket and closed her eyes, clutching the box in the hand she shoved in her pocket.

That siren sounds like it's right outside. Pat thought only minutes had passed, that the clanking she heard was still her headache. *But at least it's a little warmer. Good, I won't have to hear Aunt Verna cuss the landlord when she gets home.*

'. . . a few more blocks.' '. . . not gonna make it . . .' *Who's talking?* But the voices were jumbled and unfamiliar . . . *I musta left the TV on.* Pat tried to open her eyes, but her lids felt leaden. *Ma, I dreamed about her . . . back in Swan City . . . I was following her down the dirt road and she turned around. 'Go on back chile, you can't come with me. Not now . . .'*

'Hey, I think she's comin' 'round!' Pat felt like she was hurtling through space, but when she tried to move she was stunned to find herself firmly strapped in place. Forcing her eyes to open a sliver, she saw a plastic bag of clear liquid suspended in the air and swinging like a manic pendulum. Fear gripped her, but she tried to speak and found her mouth was covered. 'That's right, just keep breathin' . . . Pat . . . that's your name, right? We're pulling in right now, you're gonna be okey-dokey, Patty.'

The rest was a banging of doors, a blur of doctors, nurses, needles, questions. 'What?' 'How?' 'When?' 'Who?' And answers; 'I don't know.' 'Yes.' 'No.' 'I don't know.' *What did I do wrong?* Voices hovered nearby. '. . . gas on . . .' '. . . so thick your eyes watered . . .' '. . . could be a suicide, but she's so young' '. . . thank God for the neighbors . . .' 'Where are her parents?'

Pat heard her name. Slowly, the fog lifted. Pat still didn't understand what had happened, but she knew it was bad. Then a woman who smelled vaguely of mothballs started asking questions again. Before Pat could answer, she heard it. Tap-click. Tap-click. Tap-click.

'What the fuck she do now?' Verna never did get those raggedy boots fixed. The steel shank had worn through the rubber lift and sidewalk-shredded leather curled around the heel. 'First she let some boy get offed in my house . . .' The rings holding the pale yellow curtain around Pat's cubicle trembled noisily against the rod as the drape flew open. The Ambush Verna had generously dabbed behind her ears and poured down her cleavage mixed with Johnny Red, cigarettes, and her own musk, creating a heady, unique perfume.

'Mrs Reid?' The woman who'd been questioning Pat stepped forward into the scented smoky air that surrounded Verna.

Verna stepped back. 'The only Mrs Reid's my momma, and she's dead.' Her head and shoulders rocked and rolled, an indignant choreography for each word.

Pat watched helplessly from her bed.

'Who the hell are you? You a cop like him?' She nodded toward the policeman who stood by the doorway. 'Bein' stupid ain't no crime, las' time I checked!' Chuckling at her own humor, she looked at Pat. Then, momentarily distracted, dug feverishly in her purse.

Pat wished she could melt right into the covers. She didn't know how any of this had happened, but Aunt Verna, who finally found her pack of Salems, was definitely drunk.

'I'm not a policewoman, I'm with the Department of Social Services.'

'That's the Welfare. I ain't on no Welfare!' Verna huffed drunkenly, and put a cigarette to her lips.

'It's better if you don't smoke in here,' the officer said.

'Better for who?' Verna retorted, and struck a match. 'Fuck you, naw come to think of it a cop's a lousy lay. The only thing they shoot off is they mouth and they gun!'

Pat closed her eyes and silently inched down until the sheet covered her mouth.

'Please put that out. There's oxygen in use.' He indicated the sign.

Verna touched the match to the end of her cigarette. 'It's a free country.' She took a drag. 'They can take that sign and shove it up they . . .'

The policeman snatched Verna by the sleeve. The rip under the arm of her black leather coat sputtered farther along the seam as Verna drew back her arm and landed a punch on the cop's nose. Pat wanted to explain that her aunt didn't mean it, she just got mad sometimes. But a swarm of guards pulled Verna away in a cloud of cussin'.

The next day, Pat was surprised when the social worker arrived and helped her dress. Undershirt and socks accompanied questions about Pat's home life, which she answered as best she could. Yes, she was alone sometimes, but she didn't mind. Aunt Verna was nice enough to take her in, and she promised not to be any more trouble.

'Why do you call your mother Aunt Verna?'

Pat looked puzzled. 'My momma's dead.' She wasn't sure of much right now, but she was sure of that. She reached for her coat, pulled MaRay's bergamot tin from her pocket, and pried open the lid. 'See. This stuff was hers.' *If MaRay was here now, she'd fix everything.*

Then, the woman sat her on the bed and slowly, like she was talking to a three-year-old, proceeded to rewrite the story of Pat's life. Verna went from the aunt who rescued her to the mother who threw her away. *MaRay was my grandmother?* Pat lost her grip on the bergamot tin and it clattered to the floor. She couldn't make her arms move to get it. Putting those things back in the box wasn't going to help. She wanted to stomp the beads and earrings into dust, but the woman got down on all fours and continued talking while she picked them up.

'. . . only assault' '. . . But the cocaine possession . . .' 'jail.' '. . . custody.' 'Hearing . . .' '. . . group home.' 'Foster parents . . .' '. . . court order.'

Finally the social worker placed the small metal box in Pat's palm, folded her fingers around it, and asked if she understood everything. Pat nodded yes mechanically, but she hadn't heard much above the roar of her own thoughts. *They wouldn't all lie to me? She must be wrong. Aunt Verna can't be my mother.* Pat put on her coat and sat in the wheelchair. *And where am I going now?* She felt her throat constrict against the bitter taste biting at the back of her tongue. *I won't throw up.*

Outside an icy gust whipped candy wrappers and newspaper scraps into a motley whirlwind on the snow-clogged street, but Pat didn't feel the cold. She climbed into the battered green Dodge and rested her head against the frosty car window. The last thing that made sense was waving good-bye to Gayle as the Saunderses drove off. *I won't cry. I won't.*

Pat felt like she'd entered the Twilight Zone, and from the moment she'd crossed her heart and promised Freddy she wouldn't tell she'd slipped through an invisible crack in the world and landed ir another dimension.

2

'. . . the last stop before freedom
and the rest of your life.'

'But I don't have a home anymore . . .' Gayle awakened
from a fitful sleep with Pat's words echoing in her head,
singsong, like a schoolyard taunt.

'She's your mother, Pat. She has to come for you.'
Gayle's logic had no time or space for gray. Mothers and
fathers take care of their children, period. But Pat knew
different, and she would not be swayed.

After the nightmare of Freddy's shooting, Pat's life had
become a daymare. Eight foster homes and six schools in
three months and not one word from Verna. Pat called
Gayle whenever she could.

How could your mother not want you? Gayle shivered and
pulled her pink-and-white comforter snugly around her.
*Mommy and Daddy would never let anything bad happen to
me. It's not fair. It's not Patty's fault.* The empty desk
where Pat used to sit seemed to blame Gayle for everything
that had gone so wrong, and she could hardly concentrate
in class. *If I had just gone home with my stupid report card,
none of this would have happened.*

After two weeks Marcus had returned to school. She'd
wait for him at three o'clock, and they would walk home
together, but always as far apart as the sidewalk allowed,
as if they were leaving enough room for Pat or Freddy.

Gayle threw off the cover and padded across the plush rose carpeting. Whenever she tried talking to Marcus about Freddy or Pat, he'd change into Spider-Man and dart off in search of evildoers or cut her off with some stupidness about spring training or motorcycles, so she stopped trying. *He never even liked baseball before. How can Marcus act like nothing happened? Everything is different, and everything is wrong.* She started downstairs for a glass of water, but heard her parents talking and sank down on the steps to listen.

'I don't know the last time I saw my baby girl smile,' Joseph said. 'She don't eat. She hardly talks. We have to do something, Loretta.'

Gayle couldn't believe her parents were inside her head. She barreled down the stairs and into the kitchen. 'Daddy, I know what we can do. She can live here. We'll share my room. We won't be any trouble, Mommy. I promise.' Gayle crossed her heart. 'You can't let her keep living with strangers.' Then, pulling out the heavy artillery she said, 'Isn't that what Reverend Hobson always says? "If we don't help ourselves, who will?"'

Joseph looked at his wife, then at his daughter. His eyes were full, and his heart was heavy, but when he took a deep breath and squared his shoulders before he spoke, Gayle knew he was on her side. 'We sure can't change what happened to the Carter boy, but we can do somethin' about this.'

Gayle had seen her mother's frown often enough to know it meant the discussion was closed until later, but she kept pleading until her mother ordered her to bed without one more word. She could still hear them arguing though.

'We got problems of our own. Now you lookin' for somebody else's mess to drag in here. You don't know

40

what can a worms you openin',' her mother said sharply.

'You the first one talkin' 'bout the Word of the Lord, and what folks should do. Now you got the chance to do more than say amen and bake pound cakes, and you can stand here and tell me no, we can't help that child through somethin' that's not her fault? That girl deserves a home as much as Gayle does,' her father answered.

Gayle squinched her eyes shut, muffled the angry voices with her pillow, and prayed like never before. *Dear Lord, let them stop fighting, let Daddy win and Mommy not be mad, but please God let Patty come here so she won't be all alone.*

For days Joseph maintained a weighty silence. Loretta huffed and slung grits and eggs at the breakfast table until the afternoon she answered the phone and heard hopelessness through the bravery in Pat's voice. The cost. The time. The space. No matter how much she wished otherwise, all her arguments paled because nobody's child should sound like that. And since Gayle wanted it so badly, she guessed she could put up with it.

Making the decision was the easy part. Joseph and Loretta filled out applications, then endured months of meetings, screenings, and background checks. Hurry up. Wait. Loretta wanted the whole mess over with, one way or the other. They had certainly tried – anybody could see that – but she couldn't keep her family all shook-up forever.

Gayle sent Pat letters and cards she drew herself, with dimes and quarters taped to the bottom for ice cream sandwiches or bubble gum. She wrote and illustrated several installments of 'The Adventures of Gayle and Pat,' and she fretted and cried for ten hot days in July when she hadn't heard from Pat and a paperwork error meant nobody in authority knew where she was either.

By the time Gayle's parents, with the help of Reverend

Hobson and the Mt Moriah Community Assistance Board, got through the labyrinthine tangle of Social Service agencies and arranged to take Pat into their home, she had given up any hope of being rescued.

The social worker assured Pat there was no reason she couldn't live with Gayle a long time, but on the car ride Pat clasped her hands tightly in her lap and counted Beetle cars as they inched through traffic. She didn't want to get her hopes up in case something went wrong and she was disappointed again. She'd learned that nothing was what it seemed and believing in people too much only made you a sucker. Everyone had lied to her. MaRay used to quote from her Bible, 'The truth will set you free,' but she'd lied, too, every single day they were together. When Pat realized that, the foundation for all she believed in heaved and cracked, leaving her on seriously shaky ground. And unlike Verna, at least her father, whoever he was, had the decency not to lie – he just left.

The car had barely stopped in front of the neat brick and siding bungalow when the screen door flew open and Gayle ran, full out, yelling, giggling, laughing, surrounding Pat with her arms. 'I love you, Patty!'

They spun in a dizzy circle, hugging harder than Pat had ever hugged anyone, finally letting herself be happy, at least for a moment. 'I love you, too.' She couldn't think of anything else to say, but Gayle talked for them as they headed inside, arm in arm.

The rhythm of the household changed to accommodate the new member, but the song remained harmonious. Uncle Joe and Aunt Loretta, they said Pat could call them that, squeezed a new twin bed and chest of drawers into Gayle's small, cluttered bedroom. The girls got matching pink chenille spreads, and Gayle divided her dolls and the menagerie of stuffed animals that lived on her bed so Pat would have some, too. There was barely an aisle to walk in, but Gayle and Pat liked the closeness, and at night they whispered across the darkness until somebody gave in and fell asleep.

They never mentioned it, but Pat's old street was avoided on their route to and from school, and just like before, Marcus still pestered them. People quietly marveled at how well he'd adjusted after Freddy's accident.

At first Pat was spooked by the nightly dinner table debates. Uncle Joe, who Pat thought was all bones and joints like a gangly, brown prehistoric bird, would tap a long skinny finger on the table and start, 'They ain't on the moon no more than I am. They in some desert, tryin' to fool folks!' Aunt Loretta, a five-foot-nothing bit of copper wire whose slenderness fooled those who didn't know her into thinking she was fragile, would fuss back. 'We'd still be ridin' a horse and buggy, let you tell it.' Then Uncle Macon, a Sunday dinner regular, who wasn't really anybody's uncle, would tell some crazy story, and everybody would nod and 'uh-huh' like he was making all the sense in the world. Gayle always threw in her four cents and eventually Pat tossed in a penny or two. The girls cleared the table, and they'd crack up on the nights Joseph chased Loretta around wanting to see her knees or elbows or something silly, and she'd whack him with the dish towel and tell him to stop.

Every other Saturday morning the aroma of Aunt Loretta's buttermilk doughnuts filled the house. She'd be gone to Della's Beauty Den for her shampoo, press, and curl by the time the girls scampered down to the kitchen to find a platter, piled high with golden brown rings iced with her special vanilla cinnamon glaze.

At Mt Moriah Pat joined the Youth Choir where her rich, strong alto, a gift from MaRay, set many a hand to clapping on second and fourth Sundays. While Pat all but disappeared under the voluminous ruby choir robe, Gayle chose the Junior Usher Board because it gave her the opportunity to sashay up and down the aisles with the offering plate.

For Pat the regular pulse of the Saunders home was comforting, especially Uncle Joe. While Gayle and her mother went clothes shopping, Pat and her Uncle Joe, wearing their matching Mets caps, cheered their favorite team on TV and drank red Kool-Aid out of big plastic tumblers from the gas station. She'd smile when he told her she looked pretty in her blue velvet Christmas dress even though Aunt Loretta fussed that she was getting big as a house. And she was always a little embarrassed, but very proud when he'd carry on over her good grades. The only spanking he ever gave her and Gayle was for getting into the brown box hidden in his sock drawer where he kept the neatly folded canvas apron and white gloves he took with him to Masons' meetings. Seeing him upset hurt Pat much worse than the few licks he gave them.

Gayle loved to tell people she and Pat were sisters. Pat went along even though it made her a little uneasy. She loved Gayle like a sister, but no matter how nice life was in the Saunders house, Pat never once forgot that these were not her parents.

By junior high, where every forty-one minutes the bell signaled a four-minute parade of hyperhormoned bodies through sweat-scented halls, Gayle, with her long hair, clear golden skin, and high, tight curves, was, no contest, the finest girl. She made it her business to look cute every day so she'd be noticed by the boys and envied by the girls.

Pat, intent on being no trouble, camouflaged herself in jeans and T-shirts because they were cheap and easy. She gave up the pressing comb in favour of a mid-sized Afro, which Joseph shaped up with his barber shears. She did her homework, her chores, and sometimes Gayle's just to keep peace, but a voice in her head whispered, 'This can't last,' and to keep it quiet she fed it Baby Ruths, bologna and cheese heroes, or slice after slice of toast with butter and Alaga syrup.

Art was Gayle's best class. In eighth grade she even won a citywide poster contest, got a certificate from Mayor Beame, and her winning entry was displayed on subways and buses for a month.

Pat was in the special progress class with the students officially identified as smart. Other kids called them kiss-ass freaks cause they talked 'like they White,' but because Gayle was 'Miss It,' she made sure Pat was invited to the hip parties, too. Besides, Gayle always felt bolder when Pat was around. Pat mostly felt like a tuna fish sandwich on Thanksgiving, unwanted and out-of-place, but she'd go because Gayle wanted her to. Besides, Joseph and Loretta felt better when the girls went out together.

And Marcus was always there, always in motion, as if he were trying to keep from catching up with himself. Some part of his body was always stitched, bandaged, or encased in plaster because he never went half-speed, and he never backed down. His grades were decent, girls liked the way he did the Funky Four Corners, and people were starting to say he and Gayle looked cute whenever they were together.

Marcus played killer handball, shot hoops with the bloods, but when he had a bat in his hands, he was all business. Pat accused him of sleeping with his mitt, which he didn't actually deny, but they were always fussing. It almost came to blows once when she wouldn't do his book report on *The Pearl* and he flunked English. He went to summer school and missed summer league baseball, but she helped him study and pass the makeup exam.

Ninth grade brought the promise of high school, the last stop before freedom and the rest of your life. Right after Christmas vacation, Pat's English teacher, Miss Cooke, who quoted Nikki Giovanni and actually wore pants to school, encouraged her to apply to Southridge Academy. The exclusive girls' school had scholarships meant to offer a few inner city kids an excellent education and, if they could read between the lines, the rules to a whole new game. 'It's an open ticket, Pat. The destination is up to you,' Miss Cooke said.

Being accepted seemed so remote, Pat hadn't mentioned it to anyone, not even Gayle, but now they wanted her to come to the Princeton campus on Saturday for an interview. Pat lay on her bed trying to read her algebra book and gnawing on the hunk of ham she had slapped on a hot dog bun. *I have to tell them about Southridge.*

Gayle leaned against her headboard, jabbering on the phone while she doodled on the sketch pad propped against her knees. Her pastel renditions of *Ebony* and *Teen* covers fought for wall space with the Mets posters Pat saved from the Sunday newspaper. The room that had once seemed cozy was now just too crowded. Neither girl had space to think or stretch or grow, but they never talked about the crunch. When Gayle needed room, she absentmindedly pushed aside whatever was in the way. Pat, who didn't complain or admit even to herself she resented it, would squeeze into a smaller space.

I could just not say anything and go to Jackson. But Pat took a bite of ham and thought of Southridge and that open ticket.

'Are you deaf?' Gayle held a sky blue poorboy sweater and a matching hip hugger skirt in front of her. 'I asked

46

you if I should wear this to Brenda's party or my plaid bells?'

'Uh-huh,' Pat replied distractedly. *I've been living here for four years. How much longer can it last?*

'What kinda answer is uh-huh? What's up with you?'

Pat sighed. 'I can't go to Brenda's on Saturday.'

'How come? Didn't you and Marcus make up?' Gayle remembered Pat was mad with him for saying she looked like Gumby's fat-assed sister, Gumbyisha, in her green gym suit.

'It's not that. . .' Pat got up and rearranged the books on their desk as she told Gayle about the scholarship. The words spilled in a steady stream, fueled by only one breath.

'But it's all planned. . . us goin' to Jackson and all! We been talkin' about it for a year, and you never said different!' Gayle grew louder and more hurt with each syllable. 'How could you?'

'I didn't think I'd get in, Gayle. I still don't know if I will, but I want to go for the interview,' and, as she spoke, Pat realized how much she wanted this scholarship. Because she could begin to make a life of her own and stop living other people's hand-me-downs.

'Why, so they can decide if you're hard up enough to make you a charity case?'

'You mean like I am here?'

'Nobody here ever called you that.'

'No, but I have to make a place for myself, and I may as well start now. Would it kill you to be happy about something *you* didn't plan?' Pat asked angrily.

'Would it kill you not to eat everything in the refrigerator?'

'What the hell is going on in here?' Joseph appeared in the doorway.

47

Pat sheepishly explained about the scholarship. With every detail Joseph's admiration swelled and Gayle's scowl deepened.

'This is beautiful! Shows you're usin' your head. Gayle Denise, you need to learn from Pat how to look out for your future.'

'My art teacher said *I* was good enough to get in Art & Design High School. I could still put a portfolio together.' Gayle folded her arms across her chest and pouted.

'I'm talking about an education, Gayle, not something to *play* with!' Joseph said.

'But, Daddy . . .'

'Ain't no but about it! This Saturday we goin' to Princeton.'

'But Brenda's party. . .'

'It's not the first, and it won't be the last. You'll survive.'

Gayle and Pat put on their pajamas in silence and turned out the light. There was no chatter across the aisle. Pat stared into the darkness, worried about the interview, and hot, mad tears rolled onto Gayle's pillow.

By 8.00 A.M. Saturday Pat and Gayle's parents had gone for the interview. Gayle didn't even get up to see them off. *She thinks she's so daggone smart. How could she decide to move out, just like that?* Gayle's anger propelled her out of bed and down to the kitchen, where she did the first grown-up thing she could think of and made herself a cup of instant coffee, which she drank even though it still tasted nasty after five spoons of sugar.

If Pat can think only about herself, so can I. Brenda was her main competition for cutest girl in school. Gayle *had* to show at this party, even if her parents expressly said no. *What can they do? I'm too old to spank.* Fueled by defiance, she blasted the radio and painted her fingers and toes with the seventy-nine-cent bottle of red nail polish she'd bought with her allowance and was promptly forbidden to wear. Then she posed with one of her father's Kools waggling, unlit, between her fingers. *I can't wait 'til I'm grown and outta this house.*

A single red lightbulb colored the rhythmic vibrations pulsing in the body-heated darkness of Brenda's basement. A bunch of boys Gayle didn't know were hanging by the stairwell. She switched by, trying to be nonchalant, as they grunted approval of the coral double-knit number she finally put on because it showed off her shape and looked good with her torrid nails.

Gayle passed the punch fountain and three girls dancing with make-believe partners and singing, 'Love Jones . . . I Got a Love Jones,' struck a slightly bored pose. *I wouldn't be standing here looking stupid if Pat were here.* Just then a high-school guy wearing sharkskin pants and high-topped Cons bopped over and held out his hand for a dance.

The next song was slow and Gayle begged off, but he pulled her close, and she struggled against his strength. Marcus, who had watched them from across the room, strode over. 'Why you gon' be like that, man? She said she didn't want to dance.'

'Who you, her father?' The boy let go of her wrists.

'Naw, it ain't about that.'

The tension of the moment coursed through Gayle. She was surprised how much she liked the way it felt.

Marcus and the older boy glared cold-eyed at each other. Couples inched off the dance floor, and the room held its breath. Gayle took a step back, too, but her eyes were locked on Marcus. He never flinched or blinked. Gayle thought he looked bigger every time he inhaled, slow and deep, and that gave her a rush.

Finally, the other boy rolled his shoulders back, clicked his teeth, mumbled, 'It ain't worth all that,' and re-bopped across the room and up the stairs.

Gayle trembled slightly as Marcus guided her to the side. He filled a paper cup with fruit punch spewing from the mouth of a slightly tarnished cherub and gave it to her. 'Thought you couldn't come.'

'That's what you get for thinking!' She peeked at him over the rim as she sipped.

'Then I guess I shouldn't say I think you look nice.' He checked out her dress, including how it hugged her butt in the back, and nodded appreciatively. He remembered how Freddy used to say, 'Gayle's gonna grow into a nice piece a tail someday.' He guessed that since she had, Freddy would approve.

Gayle felt flushed and cool all at once, like the shock of goose bumps in July. 'Then I won't say thank-you.' She ignored the strange tingle and sailed off.

Gayle and Marcus traveled the room in different orbits, always aware of the other's gravitational pull. Brenda declared Marcus was fine and asked Gayle point-blank if she was going with him. 'Practically,' she answered, looking at old stupid Marcus in a new way. Marcus was taller than most of the guys, and his dove gray Blye knit hung casually from broad shoulders. He was a sweet liquid brown, like a soda-fountain Coca-Cola, with dimples and a devilish smile edged in a fuzzy preamble to manhood.

After turning down offers to dance because she hadn't found anybody worth the perspiration, she knew she wanted Marcus to ask. Finally, he did.

Marcus pulled her onto the dance floor. The pungent citrus-cinnamon cologne he had splashed everywhere that didn't sting filled Gayle's nostrils and made her dizzy. She leaned into his chest, closed her eyes, and felt his hands travel lightly from her shoulders, hesitate half a breath at the place where her bra hooked, and come to rest at the small of her back. 'Gimme Your Love, Gimme Your Love,' Curtis Mayfield pleaded. Instinctively Gayle tightened her arms around his neck, his thigh wedged between hers, and they surrendered to the dip, swivel, and rise of the grind. Slow dancing usually felt like too much sweat and hot, onion-dip breath on her neck, but not now. Marcus lightly kissed her temple, grazed her cheek with the surprise of prickly whiskers sprouting from the satin smoothness of his face. And then she felt it, hard and urgent, nudging her. *That's . . . his . . . thing!* The realization shocked her, but she never lost a beat.

When the music stopped, Marcus whispered, 'Thanks,' his voice husky with the longing he struggled to control. He escorted her from the floor. 'How you gettin' home?'

It was the first time Gayle had thought about it, and, glancing at her watch, she knew it was time to make that move and deal with the consequences. As they walked home, their hands brushed awkwardly against each other until Marcus finally took hers, and her heart skipped a beat. It was perfect and at that moment Gayle couldn't imagine feeling like this with anybody but him, ever. *This is how it's supposed to be.*

On the ride back from Southridge, Pat realized she wanted to go there so bad her head ached. The grand ivy-covered buildings, the statues dotting the campus, all were impressive, but more than that it was the attitude of the people she met. Miss Cooke was right. They spoke as if nothing in the world was out of their grasp. They expected to succeed, and from the list of illustrious alumnae, that's exactly what they did. Pat wanted confidence like that and the power to decide her own future. She couldn't dream

Gayle's dreams in Gayle's room in Gayle's parents' house anymore.

Anxious to tell Gayle about the day, Pat raced to their room to find clothes flung all over and an empty bed. *Brenda's party! I should let her sneak her butt back in here the best way she can.* They had barely spoken six words to each other all week, but the thought of Joseph and Loretta's wrath was too horrible. She quickly put on her pajamas and her lavender quilted robe and joined them in the kitchen, where Joseph was eating ice cream. Pat nodded when they asked if Gayle was asleep and yawned a lot to help them realize how tired they were. Soon they got the hint and went off to bed.

Pat posted herself by the living-room window, holding the rusty flashlight that had lived behind the sofa since the '64 blackout, until she saw Gayle and Marcus skulking in the shadow of the Dutch elm in front of the house next door. Pat signaled them with her light, pointed toward the side door, but before Gayle tiptoed away Pat watched, bug-eyed, as Marcus kissed her, *on the mouth.*

That they managed to unlock the door and tiptoe upstairs undetected was amazing, because once the bedroom door was closed they exploded. Wild squeals erupted from girl hearts and breathy half sentences fluttered from woman lips that had dined and kissed.

'They called me Miss Reid . . .'

'Marcus almost had to fight 'cause this boy wouldn't get offa me.'

'The dean said she was almost sure I'd get in . . .'

'When I was grindin' with Marcus . . .'

'When you were what? Ooooh girl, you so nasty . . .'

'I could feel . . . his . . . *thing* . . .'

'Marcus's? You lyin'!'

'Yeah!!! Cross my heart!'

They were dumbstruck. Until tonight the subject of boys and kissing and what it made you feel had only been gossip, titillating hearsay. After a moment the dizzying knowledge was too much to contain and exploded in pillow-muffled screams which finally brought Loretta and sent Gayle diving under the covers.

They talked into the night, their conversation peppered with, 'I wish you were there when . . .' and for the first time the future they each wished for, when they'd be grown and free, didn't seem so far away.

'I'm sorry for what I said before . . . you know about the refrigerator and stuff,' Gayle said quietly.

'I'm sorry I didn't tell you about school,' Pat said.

'What am I gonna do without you? I miss you already.' Gayle rolled onto her stomach, hand propped under her chin.

'It's only school, Gayle. Everything else will be the same,' Pat replied.

The spring skipped by quickly. Marcus gave Gayle his silver ID bracelet and they became a 'thing,' although not in earshot of Gayle's parents. On the day Pat received her letter of acceptance from Southridge, Loretta cooked a big dinner, got out the china and tablecloth, and Joseph, who had no buttons left on his shirt to pop, made a toast, which they drank with grape juice and ginger ale in the 'for company only' stemmed glasses. It was only when Pat mentioned she needed her birth certificate that the celebration quieted.

'Honey, your mother must have your birth certificate.' It was like a cold slap out of the blue. Verna's drug possession and assault charges had been plea-bargained to five years' probation. She only showed up on the odd Christmas or birthday, always with a present that would fit somebody else's child, not hers. Their visits were always chaperoned and rarely lasted more than an hour, just long enough to twist Pat's guts.

Joseph promised her they'd take care of it, call, send Verna a special delivery letter, or something. That night Pat lay awake, thinking about the official record of her birth, which had been promptly ignored by everyone involved in favor of whichever story suited them best. Here she was, sixteen years old, and she'd never seen it. That made her mad. *It's my right!* She wanted to read it, see what else it said that nobody bothered to mention, like maybe who her father was. *What if Verna lost it or tore it up?* A string of questions wound into a knot around Pat's stomach and she wanted answers, to her face, not by mail.

So next morning, on the way to school, she would not be dissuaded by Gayle's arguments. Pat was going to Verna's at lunchtime, and she was going alone.

Pat hadn't walked past her old house in years. The front yard was now patches of brown grass and bare earth, the awning above the steps was gone, and the blinds in Verna's front window hung lopsided. Pat reached through the storm door where the glass should have been and pressed the bell for a good long time. No answer. By the third try the blinds rattled as the window slid open.

'Who the fuck is it?' Verna yelled.

'Patricia Ellen Reid, and I'm your fucking daughter, in case you forgot.' Pat had spent her life avoiding trouble, but this was a fight she was going to start. 'And you ought to let me in 'cause you don't want to have this conversation in front of the neighborhood.'

The window slammed shut and, shortly, the door opened. Pat followed Verna silently up the stairs. Aside from a new orange crushed velvet sofa and matching chair, everything was as Pat remembered, only smaller and sadder.

'I know this ain't no social call.'

'I want my birth certificate.'

'How come?'

'Because it's mine, *that's* how come! Because I've never *seen* it, and it's about time!'

'Who the hell do you think you're yellin' at! You act like you think you grown.' Verna reached in the pocket of her food-stained quiana bathrobe and took out her Salems.

'And you act like you think you're my mother!'

Verna raised her hand back in a slap, but Pat gripped her mother's wrist and glared. Verna's watery eyes were bloodshot brown, her face waterlogged and blotchy. Last night's Scotch had fermented into something rank on her breath. Nappy gray roots emerged below last month's Gleaming Ebony, and remnants of red polish dotted ragged broken nails.

'Just give it to me, and I won't bother you again.'

Verna snatched her hand away and fumbled with her lighter. 'Shit. I don't even know where the damn thing is. Probably in some of MaRay's junk. I'll look for it and send it.'

'I need it. I'll wait.' Their eyes locked again. Pat's stony resolve couldn't be misread.

'Shit.' Verna took a deep drag on her cigarette and coughed as she exhaled a big smoky cloud. 'Wait here a minute.' Verna rummaged in the hall closet, dragged out a large cardboard box, and pulled out stacks of papers and envelopes.

'I'll help.'

'No thank you.'

Pat was agitated just standing around waiting. The last time she was there she was carried out on a stretcher. She stared at the spot on the floor where Freddy had died. Marcus's mother still wasn't right, still wandered off sometimes looking for her son. The air, thick with Renuzit over stale cigarettes, was too dense to breathe, the dingy walls edged closer and closer, and when Verna said, 'Here,' Pat jumped.

The certificate was folded into a small rectangle and she opened the brittle paper, careful not to rip it. She had been born in Richmond, Virginia, not North Carolina like she thought, and weighed six pounds two ounces at birth. It was jarring reading about herself because the details were no more familiar than a stranger's, so she folded it back and looked at Verna. 'I need it 'cause I'm going away to school,' she volunteered.

'I know I ain't kept up much, but ain't you a little young for college?'

Pat rolled her eyes. 'It's not college. It's a boarding school, Southridge Academy in. . .'

'Who's payin' for that?' Verna asked.

'I have a full scholarship.'

'Humph! Just like him. All that high-fallutin' fancy-assed shit.'

'Just like who?' Pat demanded.

'None a your business.'

'It is my business! You talkin' about my father, aren't you?'

'What business there was, was between him and me. Now I gave you what you came for. Don't think you gon' come here and arrange things to suit you, 'cause this is my house.'

'I was born in Virginia?'

'Is that what the paper say? Then I guess that's what it is.'

'Why do you hate me?' Pat wanted her voice to sound cutting, but the hurt little girl came through.

'Don't ask me no sorry-assed question like that 'cause

my luck ended the moment you drew breath and ain't nobody feelin' sorry for me either. I was trying to save a little money so I could buy into the bar when you went and had your little accident. Now I got a record, and I can't have a liquor license, so all I got was a couch. Are you losing sleep over that?'

Pat couldn't speak.

'I didn't think so. So why don't you carry your ass on outta here, 'cause I can't do nothin' else for you.'

Pat jammed the birth certificate into her pocket and stormed out. She wanted to sit on the steps and boo-hoo, but she wouldn't give Verna the satisfaction. Outside, she was glad to see Gayle leaning on a car fender. Pat flung open the gate.

'Did you get it?' Gayle asked.

'Yeah, but she acted like she was doing me some kinda favor. Well she don't have to worry about me askin' her for anything else 'cause I'm never gonna see her again. Never.' They headed down the block. 'As far as I'm concerned, she's dead.'

3

'. . . shared thoughts and separate dreams.'

Marcus raced his bike through the rain-slick streets, dodging buses, weaving between cars. Horns honked, and drivers cussed in his wake. *He can kiss my ass!* Yeah, Marcus had accepted a baseball scholarship to Mississippi State, but then the Baltimore Orioles offered him a spot in their farm system and changed everything. He tried to discuss it with his father, but Booker didn't see anything to talk about.

Since the day of the funeral, the echo of Freddy's 'potential and promise' rang in Marcus's ears, drove him to excel. Baseball wasn't a game. It was a debt Marcus had to pay.

And when his mother wandered the streets, asking strangers if they'd seen 'Freddy, Freddy Carter. I'm gon' beat the devil out that boy when I find him,' Marcus would search for her because he knew that what was wrong with her was his fault.

The first time she disappeared was in the middle of cooking smothered pork chops, Freddy's favorite dinner. Marcus came home from baseball practice and found the kitchen smoky and the meat scorched to the pan. Fear, anger, and guilt that weighed on him like a ball and chain made his heart thump wildly as he searched the house, then the neighborhood. He found her staring in the window of Linden Photography Studios. 'They musta took it down,' she had said, a little peeved. And Marcus realized she meant the portrait taken the Christmas Freddy was ten and he was seven. Marcus looked at the space where the picture had been, but now he saw the reflection of his mother, hair uncombed, still wearing her fuzzy blue house shoes and holding the gravy-caked wooden spoon. He wanted to take his bat to the window, smash it with all his might, but he knew that wouldn't change anything, so he talked to her, became Freddy for her long enough to lead her home.

Now Ethel Carter lived more and more in her own world, but Booker still called cancer 'C' and believed she'd come back to herself, so there was no point in discussing it.

By the time Marcus got to Gayle's house he was soaked and had replayed the fight with his father a dozen times. *I'm no kid! I'm man enough to know what I gotta do.*

By junior year the *Daily News* took notice of Marcus in the high-school sports column. Booker would wear out his paper showing it to everybody, even people along his mail route. When Marcus was named to the all-city team, and scouts appeared to watch him, baseball became more than a game for all those people, too. He represented their best chance to leap from the familiar but unremarkable same old–same old, to the shimmering fame they longed to feel, even from a distance. And Marcus added the weight of their dreams to his burden, because he deserved to carry the heaviest load.

Marcus ducked under the carport, chained the ten-speed to the handrail, wrung the water from his T-shirt, and laid on the side-door buzzer.

'No one in this house is deaf.' Pat opened the door, and he strode past her.

'Gayle here?' Water from his shirt trickled onto the hall floor as he paced.

'You could at least say hello.' Pat reared back, crossed her arms, and waited.

Marcus stopped pacing and faced Pat. *She sure looks different*. Still on the round side, but packaged better. *Definitely more Deuce-and-a-Quarter than 'Vette, but she used to look like a surplus tank from the Salvation Army*. Instead of husky-boy dungarees and those ugly navy-and-mud-striped T-shirts she used to wear, she had on khakis and a pink Izod.

'What are you staring at?' Pat asked.

'How come you cut your hair so short?' Marcus reached for her head, but Pat sidestepped him. 'Ain't long as dust on a jug,' he teased, but he kind of thought it suited her.

'And since when did you become a beauty consultant?'

'I was just askin' . . . I guess it looks okay.'

It had taken some time for Pat to get used to it herself, but she'd had no choice. Her first night at Southridge, she sat on the side of the bed, jar of Afro Sheen between her knees, cornrowing before she went to sleep. Beth, her perky blond roommate from Connecticut, breezed in from the shower and stared at Pat's braids like she was watching an episode of *National Geographic* and wondering what native ritual came next. Pat felt like dirt, and by the next afternoon found the one Black barber near campus, had her mid-sized Afro trimmed teeny-weeny and vowed never to be caught so completely exposed again.

Pat touched her hair self-consciously and glared at Marcus, waiting for him to crack on her again.

'What?' He glared back.

'Nothing!' Pat snapped, and walked into the kitchen.

Marcus shrugged and followed her.

In the rarified, uptight, buttoned-down atmosphere of

Southridge, Pat's brains ceased to be a liability. She had some catching up to do when she arrived, but it didn't take her long to get up to speed. The school was filled with second- and third-generation 'Ridgies,' but she'd always been the odd one out and adjusted quickly to the awkwardness of being one of a handful of Black girls in the school. *'Patricia? She's so nice, not like some of them. She's the one whose parents, Dr and Mrs Reid, were killed in a boating accident off the Chesapeake Bay.'* Verna, thankfully, had abandoned even the occasional pretense at motherhood, so Pat was free to concoct a family history she felt was more acceptable.

Most of the scholarship girls stayed to themselves and ranked on the spoiled, flat-assed, Prell-using, White girls, who made them feel like having a butt that hiked up the back of your uniform made you some kind of mutant and parents who didn't work in offices, travel frequently, or play golf weren't trying hard enough. Pat figured she could have hung out with poor Black girls in Queens, so she mingled freely and soaked up the Southridge ways. She mimicked the crispness of Ridgie speech and dress, resurrected MaRay's like-real pearls to wear casually with oxford-cloth shirts, and sometimes heard 'Oreo' whispered in her wake.

Edwina Lewis, who transferred in her junior year, was a misfit, too, because there was no category at Southridge for rich and Black. The Lewis family maid had preceded Edwina's arrival, and she thoroughly cleaned Edwina's room before the dorm director found out and asked her to leave. Edwina's parents had parlayed a five-thousand-dollar Model Cities grant into the largest commercial cleaning service in Connecticut. Pat showed Edwina how to make hospital corners and do hand laundry and taught her the ins and outs of boarding-school life. Edwina accepted Pat's help through the rough spots, but they never became really close.

Pat's eagerness to fit in was rewarded with invitations to White classmates' homes, however, where she received a whole other education.

On weekends in Old Greenwich with Beth, Pat knew she was a novelty act, but she enjoyed the surprised looks on the faces of the Morgans' guests when they met 'Beth's friend from school.' Pat picked up a fine game of tennis, played on the family's courts, and perfected her poker face, learning to act like she'd grown up socializing with families who owned banks. When classmates went on about the debutante season she pretended she knew what they were talking about, then looked it up later. Pat kept her eyes in her head even when she realized the art on the walls was by painters she read about for art history.

Never mind that she had nothing that resembled a date while she was at school. She figured things wouldn't have been any better at Jackson and refused to acknowledge the achy emptiness that embraced her when she saw others holding hands or making out in shadowy doorways. While secretly craving Teddy Pendergrass, she swooned along with the rest over Paul McCartney and eventually she lost track of the Soul Brothers' Top Twenty.

Pat hadn't seen Marcus in almost a year. *He looks the same, just bigger.* 'No one's home but me. Gayle's getting her hair done for the prom tonight.' Pat swung open the refrigerator door. 'You want . . .' she stopped, noting the low growl of thunder in the distance. 'You want a soda?' She held up a root beer in one hand and a cola in the other.

'Root beer.' *Gayle said Pat was acting seddity, but she don't seem boojy to me.*

She grabbed a handful of ice cubes from the freezer and poured the soda into a glass, remembering how she would have given anything for ice during her stay in France.

The second semester of her junior year Pat studied in Paris, where her fluid, well-accented French made her popular with both French girls and Ridgies who needed a translator, while her brown skin and American passport made her quite the celebrity. On the night of her eighteenth birthday a bunch of girls treated her to a rowdy dinner at Bachimont, a crowded noisy bistro where she ate steak-frites and sipped her first Bordeaux. Smoke from the Gitanes she puffed nonstop merged into the blue-gray cigarette cloud that made the joint seem magical, and she felt liberated, as totally jazzed as the saxophone's euphoric exclamation in the background. Coming of age in this foreign place, with people who knew only what she wanted them to know about her, made her feel unique and special instead of just odd, and she, too, abandoned the little girl nobody wanted to claim.

And now, after three expansive years, she couldn't seem to make Gayle understand why she didn't want to hang out at Green Acres Mall. Instead she rode the 'F' train into Manhattan and browsed in Rizzoli, wandered through the Met, and drank café au lait in the Village. She couldn't say she'd grown, and St Albans didn't fit anymore. She couldn't say she wished she'd accepted Miss Cooke's offer of a summer on Martha's Vineyard to help her finish work on her book. If it hadn't been raining, she wouldn't be here today.

Pat handed Marcus the soda and sat back at the kitchen table. 'What are you doing out in the rain anyway? Shouldn't you be home checking your tux or polishing your shoes?'

The mention of home relit Marcus's fuse. 'He acts like I'm a damn kid!'

'What are you talking about?' Pat asked.

He told her about the Orioles' offer. 'But all my father could say was, "Nobody in the Carter family been to college, boy, and you gon' be the first." Shit! I ain't a damn boy, and it ain't his life. He spent his draggin' a mailbag and dodgin' dogs, and he ain't gon' run mine.' The furious tattoo of raindrops on the aluminum carport underscored Marcus's anger.

'At least he cared enough to drag that bag around for you . . .'

'I know that, but he think he know it all and he don't. Not about this.' Marcus straddled a kitchen chair backwards and took a swig of soda.

'What do you want to do?' Pat propped her elbows on the table.

'See! How come he couldn't aks me that?' Marcus slammed down his glass, sloshing foam onto the table.

'Marcus! If you still sayin' "aks," you need to go to college, quick!'

'Don't you get on my case, too. I been dreamin' baseball since I was a kid. Now the big boys say, "we want you." How'm I supposed to say no? I could break my leg in college, and then I'm screwed.'

'You could break your leg in the minors.'

'At least I'd be trying to get where I wanna go. I could go to college and play ball and when I get out nobody would be lookin' for me. They lookin' for me now. I got the chance now – I don't know 'bout later.'

'Nobody knows about later, Marcus. But a baseball player with a broken leg and a college degree probably has a better shot in life than a plain old broken legged almost big-time baseball player.' Pat flinched as a silent spike of light flashed outside.

'Yeah, and you get shit-assed odds on a sure thing. Sometimes you gotta gamble, but you can't tell my father that. He only sees what he wants to see. Hell, he still acts like there ain't nothin' wrong with Ma.'

Pat had heard Mrs Carter wasn't any better, but she and Marcus never brought it up, and she of all people knew when not to ask questions about someone's mother.

A booming thunderclap shook the house, and Pat jumped up and flicked off the light.

'Whatchu do that for?' Marcus asked.

'I . . . I gotta go,' Pat stammered, her heart pounding. She tried to control it, but electrical storms still made her tremble just like when she was a four-year-old in Swan City.

'You scared?' Marcus was amazed. He'd never seen Pat act afraid of anything. She was the one who stayed calm and called for help . . . that day. A bolt of lightning lit up the room. Pat muffled a whimper and dashed down the hall and into the basement.

Marcus followed. He groped along the wall and inched down the dark stairwell. When his eyes adjusted to the ashy gray light filtering through the frosted basement window he saw Pat huddled against the flowered bolsters on the studio couch, her knees drawn up to her chest, rocking. For a second she looked to him like the scruffy kid with stick-figure hair and sad eyes, and he had the urge to protect her.

'Remember the time we found that kitten and hid it in the storeroom.' Marcus slid onto the couch and chuckled. 'It was okay 'til Miz Saunders went lookin' for a jar a tomatoes.'

'Oh Lord.' Pat let the memory replace the fear momentarily. 'When that cat rubbed up against her leg she hollered and dropped the jar. Then the cat screeched, and she knocked all the jars off the shelf getting out of there. Gayle and I cleaned up tomatoes and chowchow for a week, with her fussing the whole time.'

'Yeah, man, my daddy made me go to bed at seven o'clock for longer than that.' Marcus leaned into the cushions.

Pat stretched her legs. 'You were almost as mad at him then as you are now.'

Marcus thought for a second. 'I know he wants what's best for me but—' The crackle of thunder and lightning interrupted him and Pat balled up again. Marcus put his arm around her shoulder. 'Ain't nothin' comin' down here for you,' he said gently.

Pat, always embarrassed by this fear, was more ashamed in front of Marcus, but she couldn't control it, so she leaned into the unfamiliar curve of his arm and sat quietly, trying to calm herself. Aside from an occasional hug, no one had really held her since MaRay, but beyond the comfort, she felt an excitement that was different. She stayed still, afraid if she moved, the feeling would go away.

The gurgle of rain rushing through the downspout filled the silence.

Regaining some composure, Pat said, 'You never answered me, Marcus. What do you want to do?' Marcus idly massaged her arm, vaguely aware that he liked the dense softness against his palm and the fresh smell of her hair. He started to answer, but when she looked up at him, his brain stalled, and his eyes locked on her mouth, full, brown lips that he had never noticed before, and the next thing he knew he was kissing them.

The instant his mouth brushed her own, it was like he tapped a root Pat didn't know was at her core. Marcus's grip on her arm tightened, she closed her eyes, cupped his cheek in her hand, and, as they kissed again, a warm syrup oozed through her body. Pat let her eyes flutter open, but was horrified when she realized she was making out with her best friend's boyfriend, and, before she lost herself completely, in a place she had no business being, she jerked away and stood up while she could still find the door.

'I think I'm okay now. The storm's letting up,' she said, adjusting her shirt.

Marcus sprang up, too, and thrust his hands deep in his jeans pockets.

'Yeah . . . I gotta get home.' *What the hell did I just do?* Pat hadn't ever been like a girl to him. She was just Pat, somebody he could talk to and who didn't expect him to be anything but what he was. *I ain't no dog, so what were my lips doing all over her face?* He stared down at his Pumas, unable to look at her. 'I'll talk to Gayle later.' He took the stairs two at a time and reached the top just as Gayle unlocked the door.

'Marcus, what are you doing here! You're not supposed to see me!' She quickly unwound the dry cleaner's bag that protected her hair, revealing a tower of curls laced with pearls and ribbon just as Pat appeared in the hall. 'All that high-class education and you still hidin' from thunder and lightning? Well, now that you're here, check out the hair!' Gayle twirled to give them a full view.

Feeling trapped and wrong, Pat mustered a compliment and headed for the bedroom.

Marcus pulled a damp envelope from his hip pocket and handed it to Gayle, only half-looking at her. 'I came to show you this.'

In a moment Gayle shrieked and danced, waving the paper. 'We did it! Oh, Marcus, you're gonna be famous.' She threw her arms around his neck and bounced excitedly.

Gayle wasn't an academic star, but she was a quick study, and she recognized early in her tenure as 'Marcus's thang' the relative ease and enormous power of reflected light. She basked in it, and she liked it, a lot. With the help of its glow, Gayle became the prettiest, the most popular, and the captain of the cheerleaders. At games, especially away games, she would slip on his jacket between cheers like she was cold, but it was really to make sure everybody knew she belonged to the star, Number 23. When he made a hit or scored a run she cheered extra hard and felt charged, like she'd done something special, too.

'You'll win the World Series! I knew it! I told you!' She kissed his cheek. 'What's it like in Baltimore?'

'Whoa!' Marcus unhinged her from his neck. 'I don't even know if I'm gonna take it. I did say yes to that scholarship.'

'What are you talkin' about, not gonna take it? This is all you ever wanted. I can't *wait* to be at Yankee Stadium and hear them say your name over the loudspeaker. I'll be screaming and waving. Oh Marcus, I'm so proud of you.' And she was, but as she hugged him she got a flash of the wives sitting in their box during World Series games she watched with him. They were decked out, wore big diamonds and the occasional fur on a chilly night. She had imagined herself there, and now she was on her way.

For Gayle it was perfect. Marcus was talented, popular, fine, and he gave her the respect Loretta told her she had to demand. Gayle heard other girls talk about their boyfriends and what they had to do to keep them and, truth be told, some of them bragged about being *real* women, like giving it up ever made anybody grown. She also saw them disappear from school and turn up five months later buying Pampers at the Key Food. She told Marcus that wouldn't happen to her, and he didn't tell her she had to give him the cherry or he'd find himself another pie. Not that he didn't have the appetite. He'd been close enough to smell it, had nibbled around the edges, content for the time being with the gropes and feels Gayle permitted above the waist, but she wasn't cutting him a slice and so he had agreed to wait on dessert. Her girlfriends said she was lucky, and maybe she was, but she intended to take lucky all the way to the altar.

Gayle's once-mentioned thoughts of art school and developing her talent were long forgotten, stashed in the back of a closet stuffed with the latest, most stylish clothes her parents could afford. She still sketched, even did some artwork for the yearbook, but she'd decided that wasn't really her calling. She was meant to be appreciated by someone who could afford to, just like the women who her momma cleaned for and who lived in the building Daddy kept scrubbed and spit-shined. Gayle read *Ebony* and *Jet* religiously, devouring each word of social chit-chat and every picture of the parties, celebrity weddings, and famous homes they featured, planning for the day she and Marcus would be among the prominent couples. For Gayle, it had never mattered what team or what city. That was up to Marcus. Black princes might be scarce, but they were going to be royalty.

Marcus grinned for the first time all day. His father had deflated him, but Gayle's exitement pumped him up. She believed in him the way he wanted to believe in himself, and her vision of the future filled in the blanks, making it seem possible that his sweat and sacrifice would be enough. 'I ain't made the Orioles yet. It's a rookie league in the boonies.'

'Yeah, yeah, yeah. It's gon' take you about a minute.'

'You really think so?' Marcus asked.

'I know so, Marcus. It's perfect. I can't wait to tell Brenda! She's always braggin' about her boyfriend Dexter and how he's a Specialist Fourth Class in the army, like that's a big deal! We'll tell *everybody* tonight and celebrate . . . but you have to go. I gotta get ready. I'm gon' be so pretty for you.' She kissed him on the lips, marched him toward the door, and ran up to the bedroom.

'Patty, it's happening.' Gayle picked up a hand mirror and checked out her prom 'do from all angles in the mirror above the dresser. 'I knew it would. This is just the beginning. Soon Marcus and I will have a fierce wedding, with a white Rolls Royce, or maybe a carriage and horses, and then we'll have a big ole house built, with marble bathrooms and chandeliers . . .'

'Gayle Denise Saunders, do you hear yourself?' Pat sat on a corner of her bed. 'Did you think he might be throwing away his education? Have you even once considered what's best for Marcus?' She hadn't meant to say that. She was planning to joke around while Gayle got dressed, like they used to, but she heard Marcus's name and something that was still too hot exploded.

'And you know what's best for everybody, right?' Gayle yanked open a dresser drawer and pitched a strapless bra, ivory lace panties, and a package of panty hose on the bed. *She met all those rich people, and it's like I'm not good enough for her anymore.*

'I didn't say that, but all you're doing is counting his money and what he can buy you with it,' Pat snapped.

When they were girls the small bedroom had been plenty big for shared thoughts and separate dreams. But they were almost women now. Pat's dreams stepped on Gayle's toes, and Gayle's hopes just rubbed Pat the wrong way.

'And suppose Marcus doesn't marry you. What are *you* gonna do?'

'He's gon' marry me 'cause we're in love, but I wouldn't

71

expect you to know what that means 'cause it's not in a daggone textbook.' Gayle tied a nylon scarf around her hair, carefully tucking in stray curls.

'Believe me, I know more than what's in a book. For instance, I know bein' cute won't get you over forever.'

'What would you know about bein' cute or havin' a boyfriend? You dress like a bulldagger and you act like you know more than anybody. No man is gon' want you makin' him feel stupid all the time. It's gon' be hard knowin' so much and bein' all by yourself.'

'I may be alone, but I'll be able to take care of myself. What are you plannin' to do between the time you graduate and when you become Mrs Marcus Badder-than-Reggie-Jackson Carter, huh? Or are you just gonna sit on your lazy behind and wait? And what if he never makes it? You still gonna marry him then?'

'Oh, he's gonna make it all right. I know Marcus will do it, and I'll be right there with him.' Gayle snatched her underwear and her robe. 'Look, I don't have time for this.' A ray of after-storm sun sliced the space between them. 'I have to get ready 'cause I'm not gon' let you spoil tonight.' She stormed off to the bathroom.

Pat's hands shook and she felt like her head would burst. *Why the hell did I start that? What Marcus and Gayle do is none of my business.* But Marcus had been her friend as long as he'd been Gayle's. She threw herself on the bed, head under the pillow, tasting the salty sweat of his lips, feeling his hot, wet, hard body. *I can't stay here this summer.* She wanted to stuff her clothes in a bag and go right then, but she went downstairs because she couldn't think in that room, and she didn't want to be there when Gayle finished her shower.

In a little while Joseph and Loretta came home looking like two cats who just finished a canary sandwich. 'We got it,' Joseph whispered to Pat. 'It purrs like a kitten, and it's red.' They'd told Gayle they were going to look for drapes, but they really went to Hempstead to look at a Mustang they'd seen in the classifieds. It was used, but Joseph said Macon had a buddy who detailed cars and he'd clean it up like new before graduation. A bunch of Pat's school friends got cars for graduation. Beth even got a new Fiat. After commencement, Uncle Joe and Aunt Loretta, gleaming and proud, presented Pat a box, wrapped in glossy white paper and tied with a gold satin bow. In it she found a calendar watch with a black snakeskin band and the date engraved on the back. Then Joseph handed her an envelope with two hundred-dollar savings bonds. 'A little something for you to build on,' he said. It was the most wonderful present anybody ever gave her, and she nearly cried, because she was happy and because she'd had the nerve to keep them away from her prep-school friends, ashamed of these people who had made her family.

'Let me see your knees. Come on, 'Etta. Just a peek.' Uncle Joe chased Aunt Loretta around the kitchen table. She giggled and told him, 'Get on 'way from here, Joe,' but she let him catch her. Pat hadn't seen them so silly in a long time.

Fortunately Loretta went up to fuss and primp with Gayle, and Joseph followed them both around, taking pictures, so nobody noticed that Pat made herself scarce.

Marcus arrived on the dot of six, corsage in hand, looking handsome in his white tux. Neighbors gathered as driver and white stretch, a present from Uncle Macon, waited at the curb to whisk the couple to their first ever evening of dinner and dancing.

Gayle wasn't about to let her fight with Pat ruin this night. Arm in arm she posed with Marcus, lovely in her slinky white halter gown. 'And what if he never makes it?'

echoed in her mind, but she smiled sweetly, looked at Marcus adoringly, and, as Loretta dabbed at tears and Joseph snapped away, the question faded.

Despite Pat's protest Joseph pulled her into a picture with the couple. Marcus stood behind Gayle, his arms wrapped around her, and Pat was at their side, an awkward appendage with a brittle smile. 'Have fun,' she said, a little too brightly, as she faded back into the woodwork.

'Just one more. So Uncle Macon can have one.' Joseph could barely focus. When he looked at Gayle through the lens, dressed in an evening gown and all made up, he realized she wasn't his baby girl anymore. As much as he tried not to, he saw a woman, and he wasn't ready. He worried about Gayle. What was she going to do after high school? She had applied to York Community College because it was close and because he and Loretta insisted, but he knew the next graduation she was planning was from Marcus's girlfriend to his wife. There was nothing wrong with Marcus. He'd grown up to be a fine young man even with all his troubles, but that wasn't the point. Sometimes, late at night when there was nothing to interrupt his thoughts except the occasional creak of the house, he wondered if they'd done right by Gayle. Yes, they spoiled her, but they had wanted her so badly. Yes, they kept a lot of cruel reality as far from her as they could, but what was wrong with protecting her? Yes, there was something they needed to tell her. He thought there'd be time, but here she was looking grown and he wanted to tell her to go back in the house and wash that mess off her face because he wasn't ready for her to be a woman. He wasn't through raising her yet. Joseph blinked back tears and took the picture. Then he kissed Gayle, palmed Marcus an extra fifty dollars in a good-night handshake, and said,

'Don't do nothin' foolish and make sure she has a good time.'

Loretta and Joseph reminisced over pound cake and ice cream, then, still giggling and jiving, excused themselves and went up to their bedroom. Pat spent the evening on the phone, tracking down Miss Cooke on Martha's Vineyard and was glad she still needed help with her manuscript. She felt guilty because she had promised to spend the summer with Gayle, but this was an emergency.

Pat wandered through the house like she wouldn't be back for a long time. She examined the cuttings rooting in old jars on the kitchen windowsill. Stray coupons cluttered the countertops and, stuck in every cranny, were the pairs of salt and pepper shakers Aunt Loretta collected. Pat went to the ceramic pumpkin cookie jar, lifted the lid that she and Gayle had cracked and tried to glue together with Elmer's, and got two Fig Newtons.

In the dining room she stood behind Uncle Joe's chair and remembered her first Sunday dinner there. Reverend Hobson was their guest, and his blessing had lasted about forever. The floor creaking upstairs interrupted Pat's thoughts. *So that's what seeing her knees means*. As kids she and Gayle just thought it was Uncle Joe's way of annoying Aunt Loretta. She smiled and moved on to the living room. The plastic slipcover crackled as she sat on the sofa and pulled two photo albums from the shelf under the end table. Loretta had made a point of telling everybody about her new French Provincial living room suite when they bought it, but Pat hadn't seen anything like it in France.

Pat leafed through the pages and the years, remembering outings and holidays. She planned to select a few pictures, but even though she was in many of them, she felt like they weren't hers to take. She'd been a welcome guest for many years, but she was eighteen, and it was time to leave so she didn't overstay her welcome. She turned out the lamp and curled up on the couch to rest a minute. She'd already packed and checked the train schedule. In the morning, she'd tell them her plans and be on her way.

Keys rattling in the front door awakened Pat. Gayle sailed in, dangling her shoes in her hand. She was startled when Pat sat up.

'Looks like you had a good time.' Pat knew it sounded lame, but she wasn't looking for a fight anymore.

'Uh-huh. We had a ball.' Gayle wasn't sure if Pat was being sarcastic, but she wasn't in the mood to care. 'Marcus gave me this.' She crooked her hand, the slender oval nails manicured red, so Pat could see the pearl with two diamond chips on her left ring finger. 'He said it was to hold the place for something bigger.'

Neither of them seemed to know what to say or do. The squeals and hugs that used to be so natural just didn't come.

'It's beautiful, Gayle,' Pat said quietly.

'I know you don't believe I love Marcus.' Gayle put her hand on her hip.

'I believe you. I'm really glad you're happy, Gayle.' Pat stood and massaged the creases the plastic covers had left in her cheek. 'By the way, I talked to Miss Cooke. She really needs me to help her finish the book, write the index, and stuff, so I'm going to Martha's Vineyard for the summer. I'm leaving this morning.'

'This morning! . . . That's not what you were gonna do yesterday! Dag, why'd you even bother comin' home?'

'Things changed, that's all.'

'Yeah, well, whatever.' Gayle scurried upstairs to show her parents the ring, and Pat sat in the chair near the picture window to wait for sunrise.

4

'hot fun in the summertime,'

Pat marched to the bow of the hulking white whale of a ferry. *I'm old enough to drive, vote, drink, and I got my own damn self into Princeton. I don't need their damned permission.* After hours of stewing in her own juices on the train and bus, she was still hot.

Aunt Loretta, breathing fire, had laced into her good about leaving so suddenly. 'Like we don't deserve *no* kind of consideration!' Pat tried to apologize, but nothing came out the way she wanted because random shock waves from Marcus's kiss still jolted her brain. Aunt Loretta however, had no trouble expressing herself. 'Just because you got yourself a fancy diploma don't give you the right to be ungrateful! Forgetting where you came from is the surest way to end up with nowhere to go, young lady.'

I'm sick of acting like grateful is my middle name. The boat lurched on its way. Pat gripped the rail and studied the homes that dotted Wood's Hole harbor like Monopoly hotels. *I don't need help every time I get a hangnail, like Gayle. I'll show them.* The taste on Pat's tongue was as salty as she felt. Cool spray coated her skin, raising goose bumps on her bare arms. Goose bumps, just like when Marcus caressed her with his hot hand. Suddenly, she was back in that basement and her insides flash-melted again.

Stop it! She dug the Princeton sweatshirt out of her bag and yanked it roughly over her head. *What is wrong with me?* Pat fastened her eyes on the mainland, which receded like a dream at dawn.

And the answer came like it was written on the surf. Yeah, she was legal, but aside from dry, closed-mouth kisses from boys who acted like she was the spin-the-bottle booby prize, nobody had kissed her until Marcus. *It's time, that's all! Time for a man.* After her revelation she went down to the concession stand believing she had it all under control.

'You look like you're headed for the firing squad.'

'What?' Pat was startled by the raw-silky voice. She thought she had on her poker face, but this stranger had just read her like the comics.

'Two Benson & Hedges Menthol 100s. Fresh packs, not the dusty ones, okay?' She winked at the clerk, then turned to Pat. 'Whatever it is, they won't shoot you.'

Pat smirked and ordered coffee, not the cheese curls she'd been thinking about. She felt rumpled next to the woman whose crisp, copper safari jacket complimented her bronze-brown skin and her just-so figure.

'Just for you.' The clerk pulled the cigarettes, straight from the carton.

'You're terrific!' She leaned close to Pat. 'Like I didn't know the others were old as dirt.' She pointed at Pat's shirt. 'You go to Princeton?'

'Uh-huh. Starting in the fall.'

'A freshman! So this is your breakout summer!'

'I hope so.' Pat was intrigued by the sparks that seemed to shoot off this woman. She wanted to know more. 'What do you do?'

'I influence people's lives, thirty seconds at a time. In other words, I produce commercials.' She held out her hand. The short, neat nails were manicured deep russet. 'Althea Satterfield.' Her gaze was friendly, but direct.

Pat felt like she was being committed to memory for future reference. 'Patricia Reid.' She extended her hand, which was grasped firmly, shaken twice, and released.

'Who are you staying with? Maybe I know them.'

Pat prayed she did. 'Ruth Cooke; she's one of my old teachers. She hired me to help her finish work on a book.'

'Hmmm, we haven't met, but you got yourself a working vacation. Smart.'

Pat wasn't sure why, but she was pleased Althea approved of her summer plans. They headed downstairs and settled on an empty bench. 'What's advertising like?'

Althea laughed. It was rich and deep, and Pat made a note to practice sounding like that. 'Like having a heart attack on a roller coaster, but I like the ride.' Pat soaked up the details of Althea's career. Right after college she started at Comstock Gravitt Greene as a receptionist who made it known she was far too talented to answer phones.

'You told them that?' Pat was amazed.

'You gotta ask for what you want. How else will you get it?'

Within two years she was a producer. 'Not bad for a Brooklyn girl from the Albany Projects, and I'm far from through!'

'You grew up in the projects?' Pat was fascinated.

'Yes ma'am. Proud of it.'

Until now, Pat had never thought about advertising. The scholarship alums who returned to Southridge were always doctors or lawyers. Pat had pretty much decided to be premed because she liked the approving looks she got whenever she revealed her plans. But late-night sessions to meet impossible deadlines, travel to exotic locales, office intrigues, and seeing your work on TV, it sounded too exciting and glamorous to be work.

A scratchy announcement instructed car owners to return to their vehicles. 'That means me. Have yourself a good summer and don't work too hard without playing harder.'

'Maybe I'll see you 'round.'

'I'm in Oak Bluffs, just the weekend this time, but who knows?' Althea winked, and she was gone, leaving Pat feeling a little giddy.

Miss Cooke, in her tan polyester pantsuit, was a letdown, like watching the black-and-white portable after you've seen the color console. When Althea tooted and zipped by in her platinum 240Z, Pat sighed and climbed into Miss Cooke's pale blue Opel Cadet. During the ride she listened politely as her host showed her points of interest. *My breakout summer? Maybe I will find a man!* Her ears only perked up when Miss Cooke said, 'We're in Oak Bluffs.' *I wonder where Althea is staying.*

Pat spent the weekend trying to spot Althea. After that she gave up and concentrated on her work, indexing and verifying photo captions for *Each One Teach One*, a biography of twenty African-American educators. After two weeks she was bored senseless. She wrote Gayle to say she was sorry, not for having her tongue in Marcus's mouth, that was unspeakable, but because their summer together didn't work out. She even sent Aunt Loretta lighthouse salt and pepper shakers for her collection as a peace offering. And she thought about Althea and what excitement she was probably up to. '*If you work hard, play harder,*' but so far the breakout summer was a snooze.

After a morning in the library, Pat passed the Town Tennis Courts on her way home for lunch. She hadn't found the nerve to pick up a game yet, but she lingered at the fence watching a match. A languid heat rose in her belly when she noticed the muscled thighs and bulging forearm of the player as he returned a serve. And she could feel Marcus's touch again. *I gotta stop this! I need to find a . . .* Then she eyed the pretty, butterscotch sweeties with long ponytails and short tennis skirts prancing on the sidelines. *Who am I kidding?*

When she got back to the cottage, Pat was startled to find Miss Cooke still in her bathrobe, staring out the kitchen window. 'What's wrong?'

'My sister. . .' She turned and Pat saw her red, puffy eyes. 'They're not sure she'll make it.' The last words were garbled in a failed attempt to choke back tears. Her sister and brother-in-law had been broadsided by an eighteen-wheeler that had lost its brakes. 'I have to go home . . . to Detroit. . . She's the baby. She can't. . .'

'I bet you can get a flight today out of Boston.' Pat led her to a kitchen chair.

'I can't leave you here by yourself. It's not right.'

'I'll be fine. I survived prep school, didn't I?' Miss Cooke always seemed to have it together. It felt weird to Pat to be taking care of her teacher like this. 'Besides, I'm not a minor. I'm eighteen, so don't worry. I'll keep working. You go see about your family.'

Miss Cooke composed herself a moment. 'This book has to be done before my sabbatical ends this fall. I have the house until Labor Day. I can pay you in advance for the rest of the summer, leave you money for groceries. I'll be back as soon as I can.'

'I can mail you stuff when I finish it. Everything's gonna work out. You'll see. Why don't you pack while I check the ferry schedule and phone the airlines.'

Miss Cooke was off island and on her way by late afternoon. Pat was sorry about the accident and prayed everybody would be okay.

The next day, as a symbol of her newfound freedom, Pat stayed in bed until ten. She showered, dressed, coasted the Schwinn out of the garage and left to explore the island. Tufts of sea grass danced in the breeze along Nantucket Sound, and a deep breath of piney wood and salty sea grabbed Pat like a welcome home hug. Overhead a gull squawked, and the sound carried her back to Swan City. She was a four-year-old prancing in the yard making faces and yucky noises while MaRay shucked oysters. This place felt more like home than anyplace since North Carolina. She wanted to find her niche here.

Pat doubled back to town, parked the bike at the edge of the old Methodist Campgrounds, and went in search of the Littlefield sisters. In the early forties they founded a private school in Boston for 'Colored Young Ladies,' and they had more photographs for Miss Cooke's book. Pat wandered the maze-like paths lined with ornate Victorian cottages that looked like dollhouses dipped in Easter egg dye then iced in swirling butter-cream. *I'll never find it again*. She was ready to give up when she spotted their purple-and-green house.

The front door was open. Pat mounted the two porch steps and Dorothea looked up from the coconut cake she was about to slice. 'Look, Minnie, it's Ruth's little helper.'

Pat saw another lady seated on the doily-covered floral sofa. 'I didn't mean to intrude. I can come back later.'

'Nonsense. Come in,' Minnie said, and stood next to Dorothea. Never farther apart than their eleven-month age difference, the sisters wore identical shirtwaists, one pink, the other green. Both had their hair in neat curls tinted Roux Minx blue.

When Dorothea introduced Pat to their guest, 'Mrs Henry A. Jackson, wife of the Honorable Henry A. Jackson of Philadelphia,' Pat felt like she should curtsy.

Mrs Jackson gave Pat the once-over, then zeroed in disapprovingly on the fuzzy dome of her Afro.

Pat explained Miss Cooke's unexpected departure, then tried to escape the tea party, but the Littlefields insisted she have some cake.

'This is Patricia's first time on the Vineyard.' Minnie handed Pat a cup of tea.

'Well, there's no place like it. And so many fine young people! If my son were here he could introduce you, but his father, the judge, arranged an internship with our congressman, so he won't be on island this summer,' Mrs Jackson said smugly. 'Where are your people from, dear?' she probed with the bluntness of a double-edge razor.

Uh-oh. Pat had planned to retire the 'tragic boating accident on the Chesapeake' charade after Southridge, but now didn't seem like the time to admit her mother was a barmaid and her father was anybody's guess.

'You poor thing. All alone in this world,' Dorothea offered sympathetically after Pat's rendering of the orphan saga.

Mrs Jackson stirred her tea thoughtfully. 'So did your father go to medical school at Meharry? Of course not! You said Chesapeake Bay. He must have been Howard then?'

Minnie scooted to the edge of the sofa. 'Oh my! He would have been there after Nathaniel, that's our brother, but I bet Natty knows of your father. When did he graduate?'

Pat felt panicky, like the little girl at the 113th precinct answering Tweed Coat's questions and trying to keep her story straight.

'I don't really know. I wasn't even two when they died. There was no other family.'

'And no one gave you any more to go on than

that?' Dorothea huffed. 'They have robbed you of your heritage.'

Pat didn't know which was worse, lying about her heritage or not having one. She was still shaky from the grand inquisition when she emerged on Circuit Avenue to claim her bike. She wanted to stop having to explain who she was and why she belonged wherever she happened to be. 'Just because' was obviously not a good enough answer. Dead Dr Daddy and Mommy was no skin off anybody's nose, and if it made people think she was somebody, so much the better. *One day I will be.* She walked into the convenience store and surprised herself when she asked for a pack of Benson & Hedges Menthol 100s.

For days she worked at the kitchen table and smoked like a brushfire. Crammed in a stack of papers she came across a yellowed envelope, and inside she found a portrait of a woman whose face was brown and plain. Her eyes, magnified by wire-rimmed glasses, looked determined. A stern black hat covered her hair and her sober, round-collared blouse had a slim silver brooch at the throat. There was no name penciled in shaky print or penned in graceful script to identify her. Pat studied the woman a long time before tucking the picture in her suitcase. If she remained unclaimed by the end of the project, Pat decided she would become a great-great-aunt on her father's side, because it wouldn't hurt anybody.

Bolstered by her newfound family, she knocked off early, put on her navy tennis skirt, and left for the courts, determined to pick up a game. When she arrived groups of people who obviously knew each other laughed and jived around. They looked like *Ebony* goes to Wimbledon and Pat felt like a step-child. *What am I doing here?*

'Patricia? . . . Patricia Reid? What are *you* doing here?'

Pat whirled to find Edwina Lewis, arms akimbo, sylphlike in a white middy tennis dress. *Yes! Somebody I know!* But as she approached her Southridge classmate and the girls she was with, Pat realized that Edwina looked like Godzilla had just invaded the city. 'I'm helping a writer I know finish her book.' *Why do I always have to explain?*

'A job? You're kidding, right?' A couple of girls snickered and whispered something Pat couldn't hear.

Edwina had depended on Pat when she had first arrived at school, but once she got the hang of things she went kind of crazy. She was frequently AWOL from the library. 'Mommy and Daddy's money will get me farther than anything I'm gonna learn here,' she would tell anybody who asked. The party was always in her room, complete with Ting Tang, her concoction of Tang and the vodka she smuggled into the dorm in empty shampoo bottles.

'Working isn't so bad.' Pat positioned her racket to hide her chubby thighs. 'I make my own hours, and right now I have a house to myself. So what are you doing up here?'

Edwina eyed her friends. 'Lookin' for "Hot fun in the summertime,"' she sang, and her girls chimed in, 'Ooohh Lawd!' like it was their theme song. 'The folks built here last year. It's pretty hip . . . the beach, lots of house parties . . . and fine dudes with attitudes!'

'You never told me your parents had a house here,' Pat said.

'I guess it never came up,' Edwina answered.

But Pat *had* asked Edwina about her plans for the summer and was told she didn't have any. *Bet.*

They did intros all around, then Edwina and her friends continued to talk about people Pat didn't know, places she hadn't been. She waited for Edwina to pull her coat, but it didn't happen and her notion of having found a friend disappeared.

Guys in a variety of sizes and shades buzzed by the hub, flexing their muscles and talking *mucho* trash, smooth as they wanna be. Pat felt like a toad in tennis shoes.

Then someone whispered, 'Oh no. It's Willie.'

He was built like a bulldog, wide and low to the ground, but he had a baby face under his terry cloth hat. Sweat beaded on his brow, and his shorts rode up between his thighs.

'Any of you ladies care for a game?' The delivery was more determined than suave.

'We were just leaving, Willie,' Edwina said.

'I would,' Pat said, and officially sealed her place as an 'Outtie.'

Willie Calloway was twenty. A *man*. His dad owned a pharmacy in Brooklyn. He was studying pharmacy so he could take over when the old man retired. Pat thought Willie seemed sincere if not exactly scintillating, but at least she had a tennis partner.

When they finally got a court they rallied for a while, not keeping score, just enjoying the play. With a racket in her hand Pat calmed down, felt more in control.

Willie bought her a soda when they were done and asked if she'd like to go out.

A *date!* Pat was so excited, she thought about calling Gayle, but she felt too stupid to admit she'd never been on one.

They caught *Star Wars* at the Island, which didn't really feel like a date because they went in the afternoon and they never actually touched, not even a handshake.

Two nights later, Willie took her for lasagna at Giordano's. Pat replayed their evening over cigarettes and strong coffee the next day. She decided Willie was nice, a perfect gentleman in fact. His hand was a little clammy when he finally got up the nerve to hold hers. And he chattered for fifteen minutes in front of her door before he took a deep breath and kissed her good night. It was more of a peck. Pat was in no danger of igniting. *But it broke the ice.* Pat heard the putt putt of the mail truck. She flicked an ash in her empty cup and went outside to get it. She was about to open the packet from Miss Cooke when she saw the pink envelope with Gayle's curly round script.

Dear Pat,

This is the best summer of my life! Brenda, you know Brenda from school, she was working at the record store in Green Acres. She said lots of stores were hiring so I went and got a job at the Feminique Boutique. Can you think of a better place for me to work than a clothing store! Girl, I wear my paycheck and I look GOOD!

Brenda wanted me to share an apartment with her up on Hillside, but I told her no way. When I move it'll be in with my husband, Baltimore Oriole star Marcus Carter!

I been thinking I could open my own boutique after Marcus and I get married. Lots of players' wives do stuff like that. I could call it Gayle Carter's Fashion Chateau. Do you think that sounds French enough?

So Marcus got this boss black Firebird with his signing bonus. He calls it Nighthawk cause there's a gold hawk painted on the hood. His dad almost had a stroke, but it is fly! He said it fits his image cause he's gotta look like a player. When he drives me around people look like they're trying to figure out who we are. They'll know soon.

Anyway he's sharing a place in a big old house in Erie, Pennsylvania with one of the guys on the team. He called me one night, after midnight so Momma was not too happy. He sounded kinda crazy, but he said they just got back from a game and he was still pumped up. First he sounded all happy and he invited me to see him play a real league baseball game next week. I haven't seen him in almost a month and I can't wait! After that he complained about how hard the schedule is and about riding for six hours on a broken down bus to get to a game. He said the food was lousy and he works like a dog, but you know he sounded so proud! I sent him this cute little teddy bear and some peanut butter cookies I made to cheer him up. Yes, I made them from scratch, before you have something smart to say. I guess he liked them. Oh and I sent him pictures from the prom. I sent you some, too.

I wish he'd write more, but he was so cute when he gave me instructions to get to the game, sounding all serious and everything. He made me write down the directions to the stadium and read them back so I wouldn't get lost. I'll take the bus to someplace called Pittsfield and he's leaving me a ticket to sit in the wives' box! Pat, I can see it now. I already got this sunflower yellow skirt and top, cause it'll be easy for him to find me in yellow. When they announce his name I can just see him run out on the field and look for me in the stands. I'll stand up and wave and blow him a big kiss which, of course, everybody there will see. And after he wins we'll go celebrate at some cute little restaurant. Maybe Italian. I like Italian. It'll be so ROMANTIC!

By next spring I bet we'll be planning the wedding, the biggest thing they ever saw at Mt Moriah. I'll try to plan it for when you're not so busy with school, but that depends on Marcus. Winter is best for him. Maybe around Christmas, but that's so long.

I really wish you were here with me. I know Miss Cooke needed you and all that, but you didn't have to leave so fast. Like you were running away or something. Any way, write me soon. Next time I'll tell you all about the big game!

Love, Gayle

At least she doesn't hate me. Pat plopped into the big stuffed chair in the living room and threw her legs over the arms. *And Marcus is doin' what he said he had to do.* The prom pictures fluttered into her lap. *The Three Musketeers.* Gayle looked pretty, as usual. But Pat thought she and Marcus looked like two stiffs who hardly knew each other, which was real different from the way they looked in the basement. The other photo was just of Gayle and Marcus. Pat could hardly remember when it wasn't Gayle and Marcus, like peanut butter and jelly. His arm was around her waist, her hand rested on his so you could see her wrist corsage, and she was smiling like everything was perfect, whatever that meant. Pat stuffed the pictures back in the envelope and forced her thoughts back to Willie.

In the dorm girls talked about sex all the time. A few even said they had some. The details were usually hazy, but the discussions used to make Pat light-headed and juicy. Willie was old enough to be experienced with women. *If I do 'it' with him, I can get this woman thing under control.* And Marcus off her mind. Something had to replace the quivers that came whenever she remembered his kiss, and it looked like Willie was as close as she was going to come this summer. She figured she could lose her virginity and clear her head, 'cause she needed her head for more important things. The sooner she could pull this off the better. With her sister stabilized, Miss Cooke was talking about returning sometime soon.

So when Willie invited her dancing at Atlantic Connection, Pat decided it was time to help nature take its course. At the club they were barely acknowledged by Edwina and her vipers, who held court from a table at the edge of the dance floor. Pat concentrated on starting her own Disco Inferno with Willie. On the slow songs he held her awkwardly in his arms and made wheezing noises that sounded more asthmatic than passionate, but Pat decided she was only looking for an excuse not to follow her plan. She had fresh sheets on her bed, Lancer's rosé in the refrigerator, and the condoms she'd biked across the island to buy stashed between the mattress and box spring for easy access. She couldn't say it aloud, but she longed for that rush again, this time without the guilt, and she was ready to prove the meltdown had nothing to do with Marcus.

Willie drove her home and parked out front. 'You're so quiet. You feel okay?'

'No. I mean yes. Why don't you come in?'

He looked quizzical as he trailed behind her up the walk.

This is it. Pat dropped her keys twice before she unlocked the door. 'Wine?'

She came back from the kitchen, gave Willie his glass, and sat next to him on the sofa. Silence. *He should get it by now.* 'Well, here we are . . . alone.' She sipped her wine.

'I'm glad I met you this summer, Pat. You're a great girl.'

They made small talk until Pat couldn't wait any longer for him to make the first move. She scooted closer and let her hand rest on his knee. He flinched, like it was hot.

'I like being with you . . . a whole lot.' Willie sighed. 'It's just that . . . well . . . This is embarrassing.' He looked like he was about to cry. 'I've never . . .'

Damn! 'That's okay, Willie. We can learn together.'

'I thought you were, I don't know . . . experienced.'

'Not exactly.' *What does he think I am?* 'Not at all really.' Finally Pat took his hand. 'Come on.'

Willie groped her breasts and his tongue felt like a hunk of raw meat in Pat's mouth. *This isn't happening!* But they fell into the bed and he rolled on top of her with a weight that made it clear this was not a mental exercise. Willie straddled her, humping like a V-8 engine and slobbering kisses all over her face. He raised up and started fumbling with his pants and suddenly Willie was free and heading for open water.

'*No!* You have to put this on.' She fumbled under the mattress, and Willie whimpered helplessly as he sheathed himself in latex.

As soon as they made contact Willie started vibrating like he was possessed, then fell back to the bed, panting. He thanked her profusely, but as soon as he left Pat got in the shower, feeling like she'd been struck by a mud slide, not a bolt of lightning. She decided that when she wrote Gayle she would omit her little sex-capade. It was just too gruesome.

'I'm Marcus Carter's fiancée! There *has* to be a ticket for me!' Gayle spit, ignoring the line that trailed behind her.

Not a thing had gone right since Gayle left home this morning. She'd argued with her mother before she even got out of the house. Loretta had packed a Channel 13 tote bag, cast off by one of her 'ladies,' with two magazines, a white cable knit sweater, a pair of Keds with clean white socks stuffed in the toes, a blue headscarf, a plastic rain bonnet, a wet washcloth in a Baggie, an apple, and a dozen vanilla wafers. *Like I'm on my way to daggone kindergarten.* Gayle was so mad she almost left it on the subway.

Marcus wouldn't forget to leave my ticket. 'Gayle Saunders, S-A-U-N-D . . .'

The bus ride was torture. Gayle thought they'd stopped at every town with a traffic light from Port Authority to Pittsfield. The diesel fumes made her want to vomit, and the two little boys behind her fought over everything from potato chips to matchbox cars until their mother would threaten to kill them. Gayle was ecstatic when the brat brothers got up to leave, but then they had a shoving match in the aisle, tumbled into her lap, and the Berry Punch lip gloss she'd been applying ended up in a purple streak across her yellow blouse.

'I can spell, miss! I get a couple like you every game, claiming to be girlfriends and such. Like I already said, there's no ticket. Either you pay for one or get out of line!'

At the bus station she had washed the lipstick stain, which made it worse, so she put on the sweater, which looked fine, but was way too hot for the muggy summer day. She emerged from the ladies' room to find she had missed all the cabs, waited an hour for one to show up, and now there was no ticket.

Realizing she had no choice, Gayle plunked down a crumpled ten-dollar bill.

'Upper deck only,' the ticket seller announced. Gayle nodded her head, not daring to speak because the tears would fall. Sweat dribbled down her back, not one pleat was left in her skirt, and the heat had made her hair rise like her mother's Sunday roll dough. As she left the window, the bombs were bursting in air and she had missed Marcus's introduction.

Gayle walked toward the gate, trying to compose herself. *This will all turn out right.*

The Orioles were up first, but Gayle knew Marcus would never see her up in the stands. She found her seat, next to an old man who offered her a taste from the pint of rotgut he had lamely concealed in a sticky paper bag. His ripe aroma was enhanced by the relentless sun, and Gayle held her breath, convinced he hadn't bathed in a month. He shouted obscenities at the Orioles and Gayle tried to ignore him, but then he'd hunch her to make sure she was involved. On her other side, a couple who had been liplocked since she sat down had now draped the man's windbreaker across their laps and proceeded well past first base. *This is not how it's supposed to be. I should be in the box seats with the wives.*

It was the third inning before Marcus came up to bat. His team had a man on second and one out. They were down four to zip, and Gayle had to go to the bathroom in the worst way, but she couldn't leave now. She stared hard as he came to the plate, hoping she could will him to look in her direction. To her left the woman moaned and panted, to the right the old man belched, and wine-scented spittle dribbled down his stubbly chin. Gayle wanted to go home, but she scrunched in her seat and prayed for Marcus to get a hit.

He tapped the bat on the plate three times, just like Freddy used to, shifted his weight side to side, and glared at the pitcher. Two strikes and two balls later the resounding crack of bat to ball brought Gayle to her feet, heart pounding, but the center fielder caught the fly ball and fired it to second, catching the runner off the bag and retiring the side. Gayle expected a comment from her vocal neighbor, but found him snoring peacefully. She slid past him, not even looking at her other neighbors, and went to find the ladies' room.

The line snaked out the door and down the hall. Silent tears streamed down Gayle's cheeks and she fought to control the sobs that wanted to accompany them.

'Hey, it can't be that bad,' said a voice behind her. 'It's always smarter to go at the beginning of an inning than at the end, but the line moves pretty fast.'

'No . . . it's . . . it's . . . just that . . . I . . .' Gayle fished in her purse for a tissue.

'You oughta find another form of recreation if you're this broken up over the game.' The young woman tossed her shaggy blond hair and laughed at her own humor. 'Or . . . it's a guy isn't it? It's always a guy. Shoot, cute as you are, there's always another guy!' She dug a pack of Juicy Fruit out of her shoulder bag and handed Gayle a stick. 'Be grateful, hon. What's lethal is a guy who makes a living from the game. Trust me, I know!'

'That's why I'm here.' Gayle sniffed. 'My boyfriend's with the Orioles but . . .'

'Mine's the assistant manager,' the woman interrupted. 'Well I guess he's technically still my boyfriend. We're getting married next week. I'm Marianne, by the way. So how come you're not sitting with us? Our box is usually pretty empty for away games.' She adjusted her red-and-white-striped tube top as they finally reached the bathroom door.

By the time they emerged from adjoining stalls, Gayle and Marianne were laughing about the narcoleptic wino and the lovebirds who had nested next to Gayle.

'The wedding is in a week, and you're here! Don't you have a million things to do?' Gayle tried not to stare at her minuscule diamond ring as they left the bathroom.

'Naw. We're doing it on the field, right before Saturday's home game. Sunday they play a doubleheader, then they're back on the bus, but I'll be his Mrs. Most couples wait 'til the winter, but I'm twenty-six. I've been waiting for the right time in Billy's career for eight years' worth of long-distance phone calls, bus rides to nowhere, and crummy motel rooms by the hour. I told him he had to shit or get off the pot, so he finally shit.'

Dag, eight years! That's pitiful. Gayle stood aside while Marianne spoke with the guard at the entrance to the wives' box. He grinned, then nodded them past.

The other women in the box, home team spouses, paid Gayle and Marianne no attention as the Orioles gave up three runs in the bottom of the eighth. But Gayle was close enough to see Marcus's dimple pulse as he worked his jaw when the umpire called the second strike on him in the top of the ninth with runners on first and third. And if it hadn't been for the cheers nearby she would have heard his differing opinion when the ump called strike three and his team slogged out of the dugout under the weight of their eleventh defeat in a row.

'Looks like you came for nothin',' Marcus grumbled when he saw Gayle waiting outside the locker room. 'We leave for Oneonta in two hours. You wanna get some food?'

Gayle's heart sank. He didn't act like he cared whether she was there or not. *This isn't how it's supposed to be.* 'Why didn't you leave me a ticket?'

Marcus hoisted his duffel bag. His bare arms bulged bigger than when he had left St Albans, straining the sleeve of his black T-shirt. He looked so strong and handsome that Gayle almost decided not to pout. After all, he had a rough game. 'I did. Frankie, he's the shortstop, said he'd take care of it when he made arrangements for his girl's ticket.'

If you really cared, you'd have done it yourself. 'Well he didn't and I had to sit next to a smelly drunk and this couple that was practically doing "it" out in the open and I . . .'

'Yeah, well, I'm sorry. And we're wasting time. I need a

beer. You comin' or not?' Marcus headed out of the park, his long strides leaving Gayle trailing behind.

You don't act like you're sorry. 'You don't drink beer.' She remembered his speeches about staying in condition and how alcohol hurt your performance.

'I do now.' He didn't say there were other things he did now, too. They walked in silence for a couple of blocks until Marcus spied a sign that said Pizza, Burgers, Cold Beer.

Gayle was horrified when he stopped. 'We're going in here?' Inside, there were four booths, a smattering of red Formica tables with mismatched chairs, a long counter with six stools, and, from an old Wurlitzer jukebox, Elvis crooned 'Love Me Tender.' A man wearing a sauce-stained apron over an a-shirt and blue work pants, appeared from the back and stared at them long enough for it to feel uncomfortable. When he spied Marcus's bag with the team logo he shrugged. 'Sit anywhere you want.'

'Two beers,' Marcus said, as he and Gayle slid into the booth in the front window.

'I don't want beer. Thank you,' Gayle said tersely.

'Suit yourself.'

'Well then you only need one.'

'You won't give me what I really need.'

''Scuse me?' Gayle knew what he meant. He was on the road, away from home, feelin' man enough to call his father Booker T. when the old man wasn't looking. This was a test, but she wasn't givin' up any of her good stuff.

'Nothin'.'

The beer was delivered with the menus. Marcus snatched Gayle's glass and downed it in two gulps. Gayle noticed the glimmer of gold peeking from the neck of his shirt.

'When did you start wearing a gold chain?' Gayle asked. *And where's mine?*

'What is this, the third degree? Damn, you sound like my father. I got it on the road 'cause I liked it. Is that okay with you?' Marcus sucked his teeth, flipped open his menu.

This was not the quaint café Gayle had imagined. Instead of the flicker of candles, a fluorescent bulb buzzed overhead. She wanted to complain. Ask how he could take her to a place like this and why he was acting this way, but she decided to try a different tack.

'I'm sorry you lost,' Gayle ventured.

'What do *you* have to be sorry for? I made a goddam ass of myself with everybody countin' on me, and *you're* sorry we lost!'

'I only meant . . .'

'Two more.' Marcus waved a glass at the counterman. 'And a pizza with the works.'

'Do you really think you need more beer?'

'I don't have to think about it! I just want the damn beer! I ain't had a fuckin' hit in two weeks! I need anything that'll keep this shit outta my head for a while 'cause I'm tryin' to get to the next level, winter league ball in Florida, then spring training, but at this rate my whole career will be the fuckin' rookie league! What the fuck you do to your hair?'

Tears seeped from the corners of Gayle's eyes. 'It's humid, in case you didn't notice!' She angrily wiped at her face. 'And I don't like it when you talk like that! Like you're in the gutter!' A few locals drifted in just as the pizza arrived at Marcus and Gayle's table.

'Didn't know you had Oriole on the menu, Joey!' chided a man with long sideburns. 'It musta been pretty cheap today! I might have to try some.' He stared directly at Marcus.

Marcus stirred in his seat and Gayle could see his jaw tense and flex like it did when he struck out this afternoon.

'I seen better ballplayers in Little League.' The hairy heckler lit a Lucky and stared directly at Marcus.

'I don't need this shit . . .' Marcus grumbled, and slid to the outside edge of his bench.

'Marcus don't . . . please,' Gayle pleaded. *This isn't happening!*

'My sister plays better than that bunch a pussies,' the guy in a tie-dyed T-shirt added.

'Is that cause your sister's got bigger balls?' Marcus muttered.

'You wanna say that so we can hear it this time?' The man with sideburns dropped his cigarette in his beer bottle, slammed it on the counter, and faced Marcus.

Gayle buried her face in her hands as Marcus stood up, fists clenched at his side and inched closer to the counter. 'I said your sister's . . .'

'Damn, we've been lookin' all over for you.' Frankie and three other Orioles plowed through the door. 'The manager's been reamin' us out for the last hour! He's on the bus, and you don't wanna keep him waitin'.'

'I got somethin' to take care of,' Marcus said.

Frankie looked across at the men glaring at Marcus and sized up the situation. He grabbed Marcus by the arm. 'I'm tellin' you, it has to wait.' He nodded toward Gayle. 'You got your girl here and all. We'll be here again and we'll kick Mets butt!'

Marcus sucked his teeth, then relaxed his stance. The locals took a step back. Gayle, who had been peeking through splayed fingers, finally dropped her hands from her face.

'I guess you heard. I gotta go.' Marcus saw the tears in

Gayle's eyes, waiting to fall. 'Listen, I gotta take her to the bus first,' he said to his teammates.

'We'll all go, cause if we show up without you, he'll have a shit fit. Oh . . . excuse me,' Frankie said to Gayle.

The owner called a cab, and, while they waited out front, Marcus introduced Gayle to the guys, but she didn't hear their names. She was too busy hoping the car would come before the crew inside decided to leave. As he talked with his teammates, Gayle kept her eye on Marcus. Something was different. He seemed angry, spoiling for a fight.

When they piled into the rickety green-and-white cab, Gayle ended up on Marcus's lap. Her head rested on his shoulder, she could feel his heart thumping against her, and it was the only moment of the trip that she enjoyed. It was also the only moment she would paint accurately when she wrote back to Pat.

'It's Turner's annual Illumination Day affair. Be there or be square, two until.' Althea paid for her groceries.

Pat couldn't believe her luck, running into Althea at Our Market. 'I'll be there.'

'You can't miss the place. It's green, with gables and a wraparound porch.'

Of course Pat knew which house. It was the biggest one on Ocean Avenue, and people who didn't know better assumed the brass nameplate that read 'Hughes House' meant it was an inn. That group had included Pat, too, until Dorothea told her otherwise.

Pat had been on the hunt for the platinum Z, but by August she felt like she'd hallucinated her encounter with Althea. Then she asked the Littlefields if they knew her.

'That *woman* from New York who stays with Turner Hughes?'

Pat didn't miss the disparaging tone, but she was floored anyway. *The* Turner Hughes, former civil rights attorney, advisor to presidents, foreign leaders, celebrities, and corporate giants, and chairman of The Hughes Companies, the largest Black-founded business traded on the stock exchange! After some digging, Minnie told Pat that Hughes was separated, not divorced and his relationship with Althea was 'premature and inappropriate,' but Pat was still impressed. Now Althea was inviting her to a party! At Turner Hughes's house!

'Bring a date if you want! The more the merrier and we *will* make merry!' Althea winked, pocketed her change, flashed her megawatt smile, and sauntered out. Pat watched as she slid behind the wheel of a monster midnight blue Mercedes and drove off. *I bet that's Turner Hughes's car.*

Pat ambled along Lake Avenue, glad she'd run out of coffee. *Althea made it from the projects. I can make it, too.* It was a chant Pat had repeated often. Until this summer her only exposure to summer homes, boats, and people who could change lives with a phone call had been with her White classmates. To her surprise she found the Vineyard was filled with Black folks who were accustomed to money and class. She expected to have an easier time fitting in, but finding a niche proved tricky. By listening between the lines of Dorothea and Minnie's chatter she began to decode 'how we do things.' The rules were passed on like a secret handshake that confirmed membership in a very exclusive club. But Pat deciphered most of it and discovered that if she peppered her conversations with 'When I studied in Paris,' or 'my roommate's house in Newport . . .' certain things were assumed.

When she reached the harbor, Pat watched a sailboat ease into the berth next to Willie's father's boat. They'd gone out a few more times, even tried 'it' again before Miss Cooke got back, but the earth didn't move for Pat. He had stopped by last week to say he was going home early. She was kind of relieved at the time. *But at least I'd have had a date.*

Pat decided she had to get a new outfit for the occasion, so the next morning she got up the nerve to go into a boutique she'd been window-shopping all summer. Two hours later, as she examined herself in the mirror, she thought the kelly green poplin skirt and short-sleeved jacket looked okay. It was practical, and it was on sale, but . . .

'If you're trying to impersonate a scout leader, you need a beanie and a sash!' Pat looked up and over her left shoulder and saw Althea. 'I saw you through the window. I don't know if you want any advice, but that doesn't usually stop me!'

'Do I really look like a troop leader?'

'On my honor. There must be something less . . . uniform.' Althea combed the racks, felt fabrics, checked price tags. She quizzed the saleswoman, sent her scurrying for a size, and fifteen minutes later, Pat couldn't believe her reflection. The aqua cap-sleeved dress looked great against the molasses of her skin, which glowed red-gold from the sun. The bodice hugged the bosom Pat tried so hard to hide and scooped to show a little cleavage. Layers of sheer gauze in shades of blue-green floated down to just above her ankles. Althea had tied a scarf in the same colors like a headband, and the ends draped over Pat's shoulder.

'But . . .' It was so flirty, feminine, pretty . . . not like her. She shook her head and the waterfall of tiny silver beads Althea had picked out dangled from her ears, tickled her neck.

'But what?! You look *mah-velous!!*'

101

'It's so . . . it shows my . . .'

'You know how much women pay to have tits like that? Be proud of your assets.'

'I've never worn a dress like this.' Pat swung side to side so the skirt fluttered around her legs. 'I'm sure I can't afford it.'

'My guess is you're good at doing things you've never done before. I was.' Althea leaned in close. 'Look, end of the season markdown starts tomorrow, but I've convinced them to be sporting and give it to you today. These included!' She dangled a pair of turquoise-and-silver thong sandals between her fingers.

Pat gave in. She wouldn't have dared pick it for herself, but she liked the dress. And after Althea's bargaining the outfit cost less than Pat would have paid for the boxy suit.

Outside, Althea dug into her purse and handed Pat a bottle of nail polish. 'Don't forget the toes! See you tomorrow!' She dashed across the road and melted into the swarm of shoppers. Pat had never seen anyone appear and disappear so fast. *Like a mirage*.

Miss Cooke was a little startled by Pat's getup. 'It seems like just yesterday you were in my ninth-grade English class. Now, you're a young woman!'

That was a good sign, but Pat was still so afraid she looked ridiculous that she stared at her fuchsia toe nails all the way to Hughes House. *I'm going to the most important party of the summer with my boobs on display, and I won't know a soul, except Althea*. She smoothed her hand over her dress and resisted the urge to run. She had planned to go with the Littlefields, but when she stopped by earlier to help them get the house ready for tonight's celebration, Minnie wasn't feeling well and Dorothea decided to forgo the party, too.

Cars circled the avenue and jammed the side streets.

Music and laughter floated out to greet her as she headed up the walk. Clusters of people dotted the sweeping lawn and banked the wide porch that skirted the entire house. Minnie told her longtime Vineyarders were always invited, and Turner prided himself on all the famous people who accepted his invitation. Pat tried not to stare at the silver-haired anchorman relaxing on the steps, chatting with a young woman. *He sounds just like that on TV.*

She collected her nerve and walked inside. A long curved staircase marked the center of the foyer. Looking down from the walls were Hughes family portraits, dozens of faces who had witnessed the last two centuries of American history. Pat noticed that the women looked sturdy and determined, like the picture she had lifted from Miss Cooke's archives, but these women wore lace, velvet, and pearls. The men, some suited and spectacled, others with clerical collars, looked stern and strong.

In the rooms on either side of the hall guests mingled for all they were worth. Pat popped her head in each one, looking for Althea, anybody she knew. Even Edwina would be better than walking around alone. In the dining room a circle of men all but drooled over the legendary lady of jazz who had just been cast in the film version of a Broadway hit. Pat admired her pixie cap of hair and chiseled features. *Boy, Gayle would love this!*

'Glad you made it.' Althea materialized, dressed to the nines in bronze, black, and gold, very Egyptian from head to toe.

Pat thought she looked great, but sounded subdued. 'It's all so . . .'

'Yeah, I know.' Althea signaled a waiter. 'Campari and soda and make it fast.' She turned back to Pat. 'Turner likes . . . no he *needs* all this.' She glanced around the room. 'It's like oxygen to him.'

Why is she telling me this? Pat didn't know what to say, so she smiled and nodded.

Althea took a long drag on a cigarette and flicked her ash at a parlor palm. 'You look fabulous by the way.' No wink. No glimmer. No clever remark. *I wonder what's wrong.*

'But I still feel . . .'

'Listen to me. Don't *ever* let on you feel self-conscious.' Althea took hold of Pat's arm as she spoke and squeezed so hard that Pat felt her nails. 'Always act like you belong, because if you believe in yourself, other people will, too. Then you can do anything. *Anything!* Do you hear me?' Her dark eyes had an edgy, almost angry glint.

'I do believe in myself . . . mostly.' Pat was startled by the intensity of the lecture. It was hardly cocktail chatter.

'Althea, I've got a job for you.' The resonant baritone demanded attention, and Pat looked up to see Turner Hughes filling the doorway. She turned back to Althea in time to see her new friend's stony mask slip firmly into place.

'The congressman has to make a phone call. I need you to take him up to my study.' Turner's shirt, monogrammed on the pocket, gleamed blue-white against skin that was black like a moonless night sky. His taupe trousers broke perfectly over oxblood tassel loafers. He never registered Pat's presence.

'Of course.' Althea threaded her arm through the legislator's and smiled coolly as Turner walked away. 'Excuse me, Pat. Do enjoy yourself.' Then she escorted the portly politician upstairs. Pat recognized the congressman not just from the news, but from his election year Sunday morning visits to Mt Moriah.

On her way out to the gardens, Pat stopped by the bar and ordered a Campari and soda. The drink had a bitter bite, *but if Althea can take it . . .* She spoke to Mrs Henry A. Jackson, who was refreshing her bourbon and had to be reminded that they'd met. *She knows good and well who I am. I had to tell her my whole life story, the witch.*

Pat ran into Edwina's parents by the rose arbor. The Lewises, Indianola, a mountain of flesh under a tropical flowered pup tent, and William in a baby blue leisure suit and white patent shoes, were proof that money couldn't buy everything. When she found out Edwina hadn't been invited, Pat gloated and spoke about her good friend Althea Satterfield. She sent her best to Edwina and sailed off bravely on a sea of confidence. *Act like you belong.*

Servers worked the long buffet tables laid end to end with an overwhelming array of food. Two men in white aprons and toques oversaw a brick barbecue pit the size of a toolshed, but Pat was too excited to eat. She eased closer to a table where a best-selling author captivated his dinner companions, just like the griots in his book, with tales of his recent trip to West Africa. Pat eavesdropped until she spied several men in suits weaving cautiously through the crowd. Then she saw Turner Hughes shaking hands with the senator from the Commonwealth of Massachusetts and felt power surging through her body, like she had plugged herself into an electrical outlet. At that moment she realized that if she had made it this far, just to be here, then her dreams were possible. *I'm not crazy. I* can *do it.*

At dusk the crowd thinned as folks left for the Tabernacle. Pat wanted to say good-bye to Althea. She went back inside and checked the rooms off the main hall and was drawn through the open double doors into the library. She fingered the gilded spines of books that lined the shelves and had just stopped in front of an 1847 copy of the *North Star*, displayed in a glass case along with manumission papers for a James Hughes, dated 1823, when she heard Althea. Pat started toward the voice, but stopped when she saw them through the partially opened door of a smaller room that adjoined the library.

Althea abruptly turned to walk away. Turner spun her around by her shoulders and kissed her roughly, his hands groping at her body. She wrestled free and wiped her mouth in disgust. Pat backed along the walls, but her eyes remained glued to the scene.

'I've done everything the way you wanted it, Hughes.' Althea spit the words. 'It's never enough, is it? Well, you don't own me, and nobody ever will!'

Pat didn't stop moving until she had joined the stream of humanity headed for the Campground celebration. She caught sight of the platinum Z roaring out of sight and wondered what had gone wrong. And when she would cross Althea Satterfield's path again.

5

'. . . if I give you my stuff . . .'

Marcus was right! Gayle locked the apartment door behind her and pressed the key to her cheek. He left it under the mat because he said there was nothing to steal.

I can make it cute though. Oranges and recent sweat scented the air. Gayle put down her overnight case and set a grocery bag on top of the copy of the *Sporting News* that lay open on a card table just outside the closet-sized kitchen.

In the living room drawn shades blocked the April sunlight, and Gayle made a note to measure for curtains. The brown tweed sofa looked like something had chewed the cushions, but she decided a nice throw would fix that. The stereo and an old TV with foil balls at the tips of the bent antenna sat on green milk crates filled with magazines, records, and books. Actually the place looked neat considering he'd only moved in two weeks ago, just before the beginning of his second season in baseball.

Marcus had sounded blasé when he phoned from Florida, but Gayle did the boogaloo when he said he'd be playing for the Suns, the Orioles' AA team. His progress was taking longer than she figured, but with only one more step before the majors, Gayle decided it was time for some steps on the home front, like a proposal, a diamond engagement ring, and a wedding.

This morning Gayle navigated turnpike traffic, fantasizing her escape from home and the dinky room with the pitiful little twin beds. She was so involved in choosing between traditional and modern furniture for her first house as Mrs Carter that she almost missed her exit and would have ended up in Princeton, where her folks thought she was this weekend anyway. She'd visited Pat a few times, but Gayle couldn't stand those Princeton people, with their noses in the air, and Pat was getting just like them, acting like she knew everything worth knowing. It was a great cover, though. Her parents told her to drive carefully, call when she got there, and have a good time. And Pat would never be the wiser.

Gayle felt a shiver when she tiptoed into his bedroom. Marcus had weights and a training bench in one corner. Their prom picture, propped against a bottle of English Leather on top of the battered oak dresser made her smile. Lightly, she fingered the other things he'd piled there: a Suns season schedule, a carved ebony Afro pick, cherry Chap Stick, and a box of Chiclets. Her hand froze when she came to the Polaroid of Freddy, faded and creased, like it had once been folded very small. Now it was mounted between two pieces of glass with shiny black tape pressed around the edges to seal them. Freddy leaned against a handball court where he had written 'Ready Freddy' in black spray paint. His hands looped over either end of the baseball bat he had balanced across his shoulders and he smiled in that sly way she used to think was cute when she was a little girl. She hadn't thought of Freddy in a long, long time. It was like he had been part of somebody else's life. His gym bag . . . *that* gym bag, lay at his feet. She turned away.

Across the room, set on the floor, was a double mattress and box springs, neatly spread with a red chenille cover. *I guess that's where it'll be*. Sometimes she imagined their first time would be in a shiny brass bed, lit by the golden glow from the fireplace. Deep stares would lead to long kisses, then the music would swell. The next morning the birds would sing, and they'd awake in each other's arms. Gayle never really thought about naked flesh. Their bodies together would do a graceful, perfectly choreographed dance.

Brenda told her she was crazy. 'Sex is *not* some damned ballet. It's about the boogie fever. There's some gruntin', and some lickin'. Some sweatin', and a whole lot of funky stuff. By the time he turns you loose your hair be standing all over your head, and, girl, you feel so good you know why your momma tried to keep you from knowin' about it!'

That might be how she does it with her Sergeant Dexter, but not me and Marcus. But finally Gayle decided it was time to do 'it.' To prove to Marcus she was serious.

Brenda had been blunt. 'He ain't never gon' marry your ass if you ain't even give him a sniff. Would you buy a car you ain't *drive* yet? Besides, fine as he is, with them long eyelashes and that sweet basketball butt, I'm sure he gets his breakfast of champions regularly, and I don't mean no damned cereal! . . . Unless he into Queerios.'

Gayle had convinced herself Marcus wasn't doggin' around. He had discipline, that's why he was an athlete. And Gayle always remembered the day she first got her 'girlfriend.' Her momma brought her tea and toast with her homemade apricot preserves in bed along with her own lavender box of Kotex. Loretta told her, 'You been pretty since you were my baby, Gayle, and you gon' be a beautiful woman. Now if you carry it right, hold yourself like a lady, you can have whatever you want. I see 'em all the time, the ones who are pretty and smart, and they get fancy apartments, summerhouses, jewelry, trips all over the world, and you know why? 'Cause they hold out for prosperous husbands. I never had that option, but you do, baby. You do.' Every so often Loretta would show her a wedding announcement from the *Times* to prove her point.

So Gayle had kept her legs closed, not because she was a prude, but because she believed she could exchange her virtue, like books of S & H Green Stamps diligently saved and not wasted on cheap junk, for the biggest premium of all, the right kind of husband.

Still, Brenda had a ring on her finger that said she knew what she was talking about, at least about getting a man to say 'I do.' Last Christmas, home on a three-day pass from Fort Sill, Oklahoma, Dexter surprised Brenda with a half-carat diamond solitaire. By Valentine's Day Gayle and Brenda had pulled together the wedding. It was on the tacky side for Gayle's taste. Brenda looked like a three-tiered wedding cake in her elaborate ruffle and lace gown, topped with a white rabbit jacket and matching muff, but Brenda was a bride, and Gayle was miserable. By the time the minister presented the newlyweds, Gayle had vowed the next wedding she attended would be her own. That's when she hatched 'the plan.'

She went to Brenda's doctor and endured the poking, prodding, and questions she looked away to answer. She took her tiny white pill every morning before she set foot on the floor, even though it made her nipples hurt like they'd been clamped in a vise, and she'd put on seven pounds. She had the pink plastic case and a white lace peignoir in her overnighter, but thinking about it made her nervous. Besides, she still had dinner to make.

Gayle unpacked the tablecloth and the silver casserole with the Pyrex lining that she had sneaked out of her house. *Please Lord, let Marcus win.* She figured she'd taken care of the other details. The recipe she tore out of one of Brenda's bridal magazines promised a one-dish feast that took thirty minutes to prepare and an hour's cooking time. 'Guaranteed to wow HIM without spending all day in the kitchen. So good he'd say "I do" all over again!'

'Mmmmmm, Mmmmmm, sure smells good in here!' Marcus swung open the door and startled Gayle, who was slicing carrots for the salad.

He's not supposed to be home yet. Gayle had changed into her new blue-and-white wrap dress because she knew Marcus would like the skintight fit, but the matching navy sling backs killed her feet, so she had kicked them off in the middle of the hall.

Marcus posed in the doorway, arms outstretched, like Samson at the temple gates. 'Smells almost good as victory!' His lips curved into his easy, one-dimpled smile, and his eyes danced slow mischief. The gold chain peeked from the open collar of his burgundy ribbed sweater, which fit like a body mold, tracing the firm curve of his chest and his powerful arms. Marcus's thighs bulged beneath the taut denim of jeans which were pressed to knife-sharp creases.

Gayle should have been happy. The Suns had won, and Marcus was smiling, but at that moment she could feel tears damming up behind her eyes. 'What was the score?' She had to say something and 'If I give you my stuff, can we please get married?' didn't seem like a good way to start the conversation.

'We're tied in the bottom of the eighth, a runner on second, two outs.' Marcus crouched in his stance. 'Carter stares down the pitcher's throat and makes him cough up a fastball that's screaming, *"Hit me!"* So, I cocked my bat and stroked that sucker long and hard . . .'

111

Gayle could hear Marcus talking, acting out his hit, but 'stroked that sucker long and hard,' reverberated in her head. Brenda said that meant it felt good. Even so, Gayle didn't want to think about Marcus cocking his bat.

'. . . then I dig in and slide home, just in front of the tag.' He scooped her up and swung her around.

'Marcus, stop!'

'Turned out to be the winning runs!'

'Put me down. You're getting me all wrinkly!'

'You don't look all wrinkly to me. You look pretty good standing at my stove barefoot!' He put her down. *Damned good as a matter of fact*. He wanted to taste the tender spot at the back of her neck that was hidden by the wavy, black curtain of her hair.

Marcus hadn't been home much in the last two years. Being in Queens meant he wasn't playing ball, and that was a waste of time he couldn't spare. Spring training went good. Real good. He could hear it in the coaches' voices. Feel it in the way they spent extra time with him, like he only needed a little more polish and he'd be ready to shine. He'd pass through St Albans long enough for Booker to make him mad and his mother to make him feel like a fugitive who needed to get back on the road, so he didn't see Gayle much either. He'd drive her around in Nighthawk and take her to a movie and dinner at Cooky's with the all-you-can-eat salad bar. She'd find a reason to stop by the store where she worked, but he knew it was to show him off, and he liked it. And sometimes she'd drag him to the furniture store in the mall and make believe they needed things for their new place. It felt stupid, but it made her happy, so he went along, because then he'd be gone again.

He looked forward to the 'MajorLeague Marcus' cards she drew, where he was a cartoon character, slugging homers to the moon and fielding cannon shots without breaking a sweat. They spurred him on even when he was too busy to answer her, because it meant Gayle believed in his dream, the dream that would wipe out that blot on the past. If he could erase it for her, maybe Freddy's long shadow would be gone for him, too, and he needed that more than anything.

When she called and said she wanted to come down to his crib, Marcus was shocked. He asked if her folks or Pat were coming, but she said no, she'd be alone, and she could stay the weekend. He said 'sure' like it was no big deal, but that meant there'd be nights involved. He tried not to think about it because he was batting .367 and he needed to concentrate. Gayle had made the 'no wedding–no bedding' rule so long ago, he'd stopped pressing, and when she visited he half expected she'd sleep in his room and he'd take the couch. Still, early in the mornings when he dragged out of bed, mixed up a couple of raw eggs, some milk, and orange juice and hit the weight bench, the other half wondered if he'd finally get to kiss the scar, high up on her left thigh, where she fell off the handlebars of his banana bike. He was glad he had some experience 'cause he'd know how to treat her right, and it had to be right for her first time. He just didn't expect it now, with the season going so good and everything.

Marcus yanked open the refrigerator and swigged some OJ straight from the carton. *He'll have to use a glass at our house*, but Gayle let it pass, stepped into her shoes, and went to set the card table.

Having Gayle cook for him made Marcus feel warm and special. But watching her tip gingerly on high heels, hearing the swish-swish of her stockings made him hot and horny. He came up behind her and folded his arms around her shoulders.

'You sure look fine. Can I have dessert *before* I have dinner?' He brushed her hair aside and kissed her neck.

Marcus's hands felt rough against her skin. She looked down, and his knuckles, scraped raw, gave her the willies. 'We have all night for dessert,' Gayle said sweetly and wiggled out of his grasp. *How come he has to rush everything?*

All night for dessert! Marcus would have eaten all his vegetables and the folding table with gravy if that's what stood between him and that juicy slice of cherry pie.

Gayle brought the food to the table and Marcus tried not to drool as she leaned over, and he glimpsed the curve of her breasts cupped in ivory lace. He wanted to get through the meal fast so he scooped a heap of the steaming dish on his plate and put a big forkful in his mouth.

'I knew this was gon' be good. What is it?'

'Honeymoon Casserole . . .'

The food in his mouth became a wad of tar, hot, thick, sticky, and impossible to swallow. Then Gayle started babbling about Brenda's wedding and what she would have done different.

'I thought you liked it.' Gayle looked disappointed as Marcus put down his fork and stared at the plate.

'No . . . No . . . it tastes great . . . I'm just not real hungry. Happens all the time after a game.' *What's all this wedding shit about?* He wanted to change the subject, but decided to keep it mellow and let it ride, so he picked and chewed, hoping the food wouldn't strangle him.

Gayle brought out wedding pictures and gave him a blow-by-blow of how Brenda just about put the bouquet in her hands. 'The rest of the night people kept asking when *our* wedding is gonna be.'

'Guess they'll be waitin' a while,' Marcus answered.

The hollow clack of forks on Melmac filled the silence,

then Gayle erupted. 'How long do you expect me to wait, Marcus? Am I supposed to follow you around forever . . .'

'Look, Gayle, we talked about this.' His voice dropped and got edgy. 'I'm not marrying you or anybody else 'til I make it to the show.'

'Anybody else! What's that supposed to mean?'

'It's not *supposed* to mean anything. I told you from jump street this was gon' be hard, and you *said* you were down for that.'

'But we could at least set a date.'

'Do you know the date I'm gon' be in an Orioles uniform? 'Cause if you don't, we can't set no date! I gotta stay focused so I don't blow it.' Marcus got up, went to the living room, and turned on the TV.

Gayle chewed her bottom lip and fumbled with the place holder pearl and diamond chip ring on her third-finger-left-hand. She'd been going with Marcus since seventh grade. Guys still flocked to her like bees to a rosebush, always hovering, buzzing, trying to get the nectar. She had turned down the dates and ignored all the raps, 'cause she knew she was supposed to be with Marcus. All she needed was a more definite status because, after two years, fiancée sounded tired.

Gayle stood resolutely, got her overnight bag, and slipped into the bathroom to change into her peignoir. She anointed her temples with tea rose perfume, freshened her lip gloss, and opened the door. At that moment the fear of finally giving it up was knocked out of the box by the sheer terror that Marcus wouldn't propose.

Deep, slow breathing accompanied the TV voices. Marcus sprawled on the sofa, asleep. Gayle struck a Hollywood pose and whispered, 'Marcus,' until his eyes fluttered open.

'Hope you like this better than dinner,' Gayle cooed.

Marcus sat up slowly with Gayle locked in his laser gaze. 'Ain't this some shit!' He rested his elbows on his knees. 'Where the damned bridesmaids, Gayle? You got a preacher in the closet, too?'

'But Marcus, I thought . . .' Tears pooled in her eyes, and she pulled the filmy coat around her like it would shield her from his harsh stare.

'Thought what? Am I *stupid* or somethin'? You cook up some shit called Honeymoon Casserole . . . *Honeymoon Casserole!* Come on, Gayle. Now you standin' here lookin' like here comes the damned bride! In a nightgown! I ain't never even seen you in flannel pajamas! You been telling me "not 'til we're married" so long I don't even aks you. Now you think "I'll give him some and he'll be on his knees proposin'"? Do I look like some kinda chump? . . . I don't need this shit!' Marcus looked away in disgust and strode to the bedroom.

'It's always about *you*.' Gayle followed him. 'You and your precious baseball! What about me? What am I supposed to do?'

'Do? Do whatever you want! I'm not your daddy!' He picked out his hair with short angry stabs.

'Don't you want me, Marcus?' Her voice quivered, and a swollen tear rolled from the corner of her eye.

'It ain't about that.' He turned to her. 'You know, I could take what you wavin' in my face. Tell you "Yeah baby, let's get married." And what you gon' say if I come back later and say, "Too bad. I changed my mind"?'

Gayle couldn't even part her lips.

'That's exactly right. You couldn't say or do nothin'. But it ain't about that. It's about what I gotta do first. If you can't live with that, it's on you.'

'I been living with that, Marcus! You're away for months and you only call when you want me to feel sorry for you. Did you ever once think how hard that is on me? On Saturday nights, when everybody else is goin' out, I'm home watching *The Love Boat*. And it's not 'cause nobody asked. They ask me all the time.'

'Is that supposed to be a threat? Huh? 'Cause I got enough pressure, and I don't need no more from you. You want to go out on Saturday night? Go!' Marcus threw the comb on the dresser.

'You think I won't? Check this out, Marcus Carter, either we set a date or . . .'

'Or what?'

Gayle swallowed hard. 'Or it's . . . over!'

They glared at each other for a heartbeat, then Marcus shrugged. 'Bye.' He brushed past Gayle into the hall.

'That all you got to say? "Bye"? I wasted all this time waitin' on you, and you tell me "bye"? Well, you know what? It's a good thing. 'Cause I woulda wasted a bunch more years, and you'd still be playing Little League until you're too old and end up dragging a mailbag like your daddy!'

Marcus stopped stone-cold in his tracks. His arms hung heavy at his sides, weighted by his fists, balled up rock-hard. Only his jaw moved, clenching and unclenching, working to dissipate the fury that rose in him, slow and hot, like lava. Without looking at Gayle, he snatched a black leather jacket from the hall closet. He yanked a beer from the refrigerator door, popped the top and chug-a-lugged to the bottom, then tossed the empty in the sink and put another in his jacket pocket.

'Where do you think you're going?' Gayle blocked his path.

'Get out my face, Gayle,' his voice rumbled, low and threatening. Gayle retreated and watched his back heading to the door.

'You can't just . . .'

Slam!

'. . . leave.'

He'll be back. He wouldn't walk out like that. She stood, stupefied, until the engine roar and the screech of tires woke her, heart thudding wildly, from her cozy dream like a big, rude alarm clock early on Monday morning. *This isn't the way it's supposed to happen.* Great sobs rained a flood of tears down her face. *What should I do now?* This afternoon she was decorating a love nest, but now it felt like a house of horrors with dingy walls and shadows that lurked in the corners. Then, she got the lightning bolt. *I'll fix him. I'll leave.*

Gayle tore off her gown and got dressed. She dumped leftover casserole in the kitchen sink, shoved the dirty dish and the balled-up tablecloth in her suitcase, and split. *He'll be sorry when he gets back. Tomorrow he'll be begging me to forgive him.*

Gayle was on the highway when it occurred to her she didn't know where she was going. Her folks weren't expecting her until Sunday. *Shoot, I never called them.* But she wasn't in the mood to go home anyway. What could she say? I stole your dish and tried to get Marcus to sleep with me 'cause I'm tired of waiting to get married, but it didn't work out? She couldn't even say that to herself. Besides, she was supposed to be with Pat.

Pat. Gayle remembered the Princeton signs from her drive down. *I'll go see Pat.*

After two stops for directions, she finally arrived at Pat's dorm feeling tight as a rubber band, just about to snap. '. . . Not in her room. It's after eleven o'clock. Where could she be?' Pat's absence hadn't entered into Gayle's plans.

'Out having fun is my guess.' The desk monitor doodled

eighth notes in the margin of a chemistry textbook. 'You've heard the term "weekend"?'

Gayle about sucked the filling out of her left rear molar.

'You can wait or leave a message.'

And you can take your butt off your shoulder. 'I'll wait.' Gayle half read bulletin boards, paced the lobby, and dredged up the agonizing details of the day. Finally, she saw Pat strolling up the path and raced out to meet her.

Pat froze, and Gayle plowed into her, knocking the backpack off her shoulder. 'Where the hell have you been? Your parents have been calling here all day, and I've been lying to cover your ass!'

'I know. I gotta call them . . . I was gonna stay with Marcus, but we had this big fight . . .'

'Shit, Gayle, don't scare me like that! I didn't know what the hell was going on. I was beginning to think something was really wrong.'

'It *is* really wrong!' Gayle shrieked. 'We broke up!'

Pat shut her eyes and traced circles on her temples. *I got a lab report and a paper due next week. I don't have time for a damn soap opera.* 'Shit . . . I need some damn coffee for this.'

Gayle launched headlong into the day's events as Pat led her down Nassau Street to PJ's Pancake House, grabbed a booth in the back, and ordered a double espresso. Gayle got hot chocolate.

'I thought you were gonna quit,' Gayle said, as Pat unbuttoned her navy blue blazer and removed a pack of cigarettes and a Zippo lighter from her shoulder bag.

'Yeah, well . . .' Pat tapped the pack against her index finger and withdrew a cigarette with her lips.

Gayle shrugged. 'It's your life.'

'Uh-huh.' Like an often-repeated ritual, Pat flipped the steel lid with her thumb and flicked the flint wheel, igniting a blue-white torchlike flame. She lit up, then snapped the cap closed. 'First of all, are you using anything? You know . . . birth control?'

'Of course, Patricia. Do you think I'm stupid? I can stop now though, since . . .'

'Aw right, aw right, let me get this shit right. You actually thought if you dropped that quarter you been squeezing between your knees, Marcus would be so grateful, he'd marry your ass?' Like most sophomores, Pat took her first amendment rights seriously and freedom of speech meant the right to curse without restriction. She pulled hard on her cigarette, leaned into the corner of the booth, and slowly exhaled.

'Do you have to put it like that?' Gayle asked.

'If it's the truth, wear it.'

'It's just that we've been going together forever. You know that. And I thought . . . if I . . . if I . . .' Gayle misted up again, took a napkin from the chrome dispenser, and blew her nose quietly as the waitress placed their mugs on the table. 'I was really gonna do it, Pat. I was. You know . . . gonna have sex with him . . . I really was.'

Fast Willie flashed through Pat's mind. Her next couple of sex-plorations were pretty lame, too. She was starting to believe that kiss in the basement with Marcus was a fluke since nothing had come close to the charge she felt then. That afternoon had cured her fear of thunder and lightning, though. And since nobody had made the earth move for her yet, she had decided that maybe sex was like electrical storms, a big, noisy show that just left a wet mess.

'Is that what *you* wanted? To have sex? With Marcus?'

'That's what I *said*, isn't it! I *do* know what I want.' *To get out of this rut or I'll die.* But she wasn't going to admit to Pat that she was in exactly the same place she was the day after graduation. 'It's just that . . .' *Momma and Daddy never shut up about how well you're doing and how you met Turner Hughes, like he's a movie star or something. Brenda had her stupid no-class wedding. Now she's pregnant and moving to Germany! Marcus gets his name in the papers and he's even been on TV! But* nothing *is happening to me!* '. . . it's just that I'm tired of waiting.'

'So what are you gonna do now?'

'When he calls looking for me . . .'

'Why should he? You told him marry me or else and he said "else."'

'He's gonna call.'

'And if he doesn't?'

'He *will!' Why does Pat have to pick things apart.* Gayle was tired, prickly, and unwilling to entertain the idea that 'Bye' was the end to her dreams.

'Fine. Keep waiting, but if I'm not mistaken, you just told me you were tired of waiting.'

Gayle rifled the packets of Sweet'n Low.

'Uh-huh.' Pat grabbed her backpack and handed Gayle the check. 'Let's go. If I drink any more coffee, I'll be awake 'til I graduate.'

Gayle lay awake in the sleeping bag on the floor. Used to be they'd both have stayed up clearing the air under cover of night, but, despite the caffeine, Pat fell asleep in minutes, her roommate snored, and Gayle wouldn't have conceded her doubts anyway. In hopeful moments she imagined Marcus coming home, probably with flowers looking all sheepish. He'd be shocked when she wasn't there. But the vision would dissolve into the shadows and big white letters like skywriting across the darkness asked, *'What if he doesn't call? What do I want to do?'* She tossed and turned, doing mental somersaults to avoid the obvious answer. She didn't know, because since seventh grade she hadn't imagined the future without Marcus.

By morning Gayle felt like death on rye. The constant drone from the shower across the hall, accompanied by shouts, door slamming, and a phone somewhere that rang nonstop, drove Gayle out of bed. *How can Pat live like this?* While rummaging through the clothes piled on Pat's chair, Gayle noticed an old-timey picture in an ornate wooden frame on the desk. She wondered who the woman was as she pulled on a rumpled Princeton sweatshirt and went out to look for a pay phone. Her mother answered and fussed at her for not calling sooner. No, Marcus hadn't phoned, and when was she gonna bring her tail home. *I hate it when they treat me like a child. He hasn't even checked to see if I'm all right.*

Pat was sitting up in bed, with the window open, blowing lazy smoke rings and removing the pink sponge curlers from her hair when Gayle got back. 'When's the execution?'

'Come on, Pat.'

'He didn't call yet?'

'No.'

'It's early. Give him time.'

'I guess.' Gayle wanted to change the subject. 'Who's that in the picture?'

'You haven't met Great-Grandma Reid?' Pat's roommate, Jill, a redhead with braids that crisscrossed on top of her head like handles, was stuffing a month's worth of laundry into a dingy canvas bag.

Gayle raised an eyebrow. This was definitely not MaRay, and, to her knowledge, the rest of Pat's family tree was a stump.

'It's the most amazing story. Even though there'd be no role for me, I keep telling Patricia she should write a play about her family, especially her.' Jill nodded toward the picture. 'Working her way through medical school as a laundress. I couldn't do it. I hate laundry.' She pulled her sack out the door. 'See you.'

'You told her that?'

'Helps level the playing field. Who'll know?' Pat lit another cigarette with the butt of the first one.

'Uh-huh. What happened to your Afro? You know all that Black pride stuff?' Neat rows of tight shiny curls sprang from the grid left by the rollers.

'There's more than one way to make a point, you know. And I have to think about my future. "Dress for Success" and all that. Anyway, I tutor this kid from Lawrenceville in math twice a week. His mother's a hairdresser, so instead of the lousy four bucks an hour, I get a retouch every six weeks, shampoo and set every two.'

Gayle only half listened. 'So, you think he'll really call?'

'Ever again? Probably. Will it be the same? I don't know. Is that what you want?' Pat scrubbed out the butt against the bottom of her clamshell ashtray.

'I think I want to go home.' *And not talk about this anymore 'cause you just wanna be right.* For the second time in twelve hours Gayle dressed quickly.

'Next time I'm your cover, let me know. Okay?'

'Yeah, okay.' Gayle headed out the door, but Pat yelled down the hall. 'Call me when you get home!'

'I'm not a daggone baby. I can get home.' *I got myself here, didn't I?* But Gayle's bravado didn't last until she got to her car. Everywhere she looked couples strolled, arms casually draped around waists, mocking her. *This is supposed to be the morning after we . . .* Gayle slammed the car door. *Later for him!* The Mustang sputtered before it turned over so she gunned the engine, which sounded like she felt, then nosed onto the congested two-lane road that ran through the center of town. She wanted to be far from

123

the ivy-twined campus, but traffic crawled, stopping for pedestrians who crossed at will like they owned the road. *Dag, they can't even cross the street like other people!* A gang of students jogged off the curb. Gayle slammed on the brakes, laid on her horn. They looked at her like she was uncivilized. 'I'm supposed to wait while you take your sweet time?' she yelled, but Marcus wasn't there to hear. She made a beeline for Route 1, wiping tears, replaying snippets of the fight, and adding what she *should* have said to Marcus.

After ten miles of clear road she was convinced there would be a remorseful message from Marcus waiting when she got home, so she put on some speed, but a half hour into the trip the car sputtered, and she barely made it to the shoulder before the engine died. She turned the key, and prayed, but the engine coughed in reply. Then she scanned the gauges. *E! It can't be empty. I filled up . . . before I left Queens.* She'd been too distracted to notice gas stations along the route, and the auto club card her father gave her was useless without a phone. Even she didn't believe she had another tear left, but the burden of all that had gone wrong in the last twenty-four hours settled on her shoulders, and she couldn't carry it anymore.

'Are you all right?'

Gayle flinched and sucked in her breath to hold down the scream that was lurking. She didn't know how long she'd been hunched over the wheel.

'I didn't mean to scare you. Do you need a doctor?'

'No.' Her father had given her the drill. 'Lock the doors, roll up the windows.' Her eyes darted side to side. *They are.* And, most important, 'Don't open up for nobody but cops, and then only if they look right.' She saw a big platinum Lincoln parked in front of her.

'Are you having car trouble?' Even though he had to

shout, his voice was rich and warm as hot buttered rum.

'No,' she yelled back.

'So you're stopped by the side of the road for fun?'

'It's none of your business.'

'I'm not gonna hurt you. Why don't you try and start it?'

'You could be another Son of Sam for all I know! And who said my car won't start?'

'Do I look like I'm packin' a gun?' Arms akimbo, his hands rested on his waist holding open his silvery gray suit coat.

Gayle's eyes traveled up the black turtleneck, finally reaching his face, and a sigh escaped through her lips. His skin was the glossy, golden brown of peanut butter, kinda salty, kinda sweet. Smoked amber shades, resting on a wide pyramid of nose, obscured his eyes and brought her attention squarely to his mustache, a thick, silky black canopy that curled luxuriously over his top lip. He smiled and revealed even rows of the prettiest teeth she had ever seen. *He is fine! I shouldn't be thinking that.* 'Looks can be deceiving.'

He chuckled, 'You're a pretty tough customer. You know the nearest gas station is about five miles down the road . . .'

'*Five miles!?*'

'So, I was right. It won't start!'

'It would if I had some gas . . . but I'm waiting for a tow.'

'And you called them from where?'

'You are very nosy!'

'Okay, since you have things under control, I'll be on my way.' He laughed again and walked back to his car.

That was really smart. Now what am I gonna do! She watched as he pulled off. *I can't walk five miles in heels.*

She hadn't worn flats since she had graduated. They were for children. So she decided to wait a while and pray for a state trooper.

Fifteen minutes later she heard the crunch of gravel and saw the Lincoln pull in behind her. Silver Suit took a red gas can from his trunk and strode over. 'Still waitin' for the tow truck?'

'I'm not letting you in!'

'Lucky for you the gas tank is on the outside. But you need to pop the hood. My guess is the carburetor needs priming.' He pushed his sleeves up to the elbows and carried the can to the gas tank.

Gayle cracked the window and watched. He worked quickly, whistling the whole time, warbling really, like a songbird. Gayle knew the melody. *Everybody is a star. One big circle going round and round. Everybody wants to shi-i-ine* . . .

'That's beautiful the way you whistle.'

He made a particularly trilly run. 'Keeps me company and blows off the hot air. Are you gonna open the hood?'

Gayle eyed him a moment. *The car* is *locked*. She pulled the lever. He disappeared around the front for a while, then told her to start it up. The car was cranky, but after a few tries the engine came to life. 'That's the best sound I've heard all day . . . next to your whistling.' She smiled. 'What made you come back?'

He crouched next to the driver's side. 'My good deed for the day.'

'You don't look like a Boy Scout.'

'Weren't you the one who told me looks can be deceiving?'

'Uh-huh.'

'So, may I ask your name?'

She hesitated. 'Gayle. And yours?'

He got a business card from his wallet and pushed it through the cracked window. 'Ramsey Hilliard, President, Greener Pastures, Incorporated, Mount Vernon, New York,' she read.

'Well, Miss Nightingale, there's another gas station up the road on your right. You should stop and fill up 'cause this pony won't run without oats.'

'Thanks.' Gayle reached for her purse.

'This one's on me,' he said.

'Lucky for me you hadn't done your good deed already.'

'Me too. And if you really want to thank me, you should let me take you to dinner. You've got my card. Get home safe, Miss Nightingale, and I hope to hear from you.' He tapped the door twice, stood, and headed for his car. Ramsey waited until Gayle pulled off, followed her to the gas station, then honked twice and was gone. Gayle tucked the card in her purse, not because she intended to call. Just because. *Wait 'til I tell Marcus.*

By Wednesday, when she still hadn't heard from Marcus, Gayle fluctuated between hurt, anger, and worry. *He did leave driving crazy that night.* She dialed his number, not knowing if she wanted an answer or not.

'What's up?' Music played in the background and Marcus actually sounded happy.

Click. She cradled the phone, chewing her bottom lip. Then she dialed again.

'Mr Hilliard, please. Tell him it's Miss Nightingale.'

6

'. . . just seein' stars . . .'

'Be sensible, Gayle. The man says he owns a business. You're a salesgirl. Now, what does he want with you?' Joseph yanked the paper napkin from his shirt neck and tossed it in his egg-stained plate.

'I'm assistant manager, Daddy, and you don't know what you're talking about.' Gayle tore a biscuit into jagged bits and dropped them in her dish.

'I know there's only one reason a thirty-one-year-old man is sniffin' around you, Gayle Denise Saunders.' He rubbed the flat of his hand over his bald head. 'Soon as he gets what he came for, he'll be waggin' his tail and headin' on down the road.'

'Ramsey's not like that. He's been a gentleman, and he treats me like a lady. You just don't know him like I do.' Gayle flipped the pages of the *Sunday News* that lay on the table.

Since their roadside rendezvous Ramsey Hilliard had shown Gayle a New York worlds away from the one where she grew up. He would arrive at her door with a charming greeting for Loretta, a firm handshake for Joseph, and one perfect pearly rose for her. Then he would escort Gayle to that big, silver car, and, once she was ensconced in plush, leathery comfort, Gayle felt transported to another galaxy.

Over a candlelight dinner, 104 stories in the sky, with Manhattan a jeweled carpet, twinkling below, Ramsey held her hand and told her about his business, commercial and residential landscaping. Gayle hung on every word like it was ancient truth and relished the procession of waiters who seemed to anticipate her every need.

Perched on a barstool at Sardi's after *Ain't Misbehavin'*, Gayle loved the caricatures of celebrities on the walls and the way people noticed them and nodded, like they *must* be *somebody*. Ramsey sipped Southern Comfort and mesmerized her with his story of growing up in Kentucky, on a dirt road in the shadow of horse-country wealth. After he scraped together enough money for an old car he moved to Louisville, lucked into his landscaping business, and moved north. Gayle wondered how he was so lucky, but she didn't interrupt his storytelling. Ramsey's rich baritone loitered over words, and his eyes lingered over her. When he brushed her hair away from her face, Gayle felt the heat from his palm sear her cheek, and although she barely sipped her wine, Gayle felt intoxicated.

Gayle had dismissed Billy Eckstine as some relic of her parents' youth, but pressed up next to Ramsey, enveloped in the smoky haze of the Blue Note, 'Body and Soul' spoke to her. When that velvety voice crooned 'I am yours, for the taking,' Gayle melted inside.

'The man is a con artist or a simpleton one if he can't find a woman his own age.' Joseph turned up his coffee cup and peered at Gayle over the rim.

She met her father's gaze. 'You just don't think your little girl could *possibly* have anything to offer a man, do you, Daddy?'

'Yeah, you got something to offer. That's what I'm worried about.' Joseph reared back in his chair. 'What about Marcus?'

'What *about* Marcus?' Gayle got up and stacked dirty dishes. He called a week and a half after the blowup, acting like nothing happened and like she really cared that the Orioles first baseman was out with tendinitis.

'He called again yesterday. Said you didn't call him back.'

'That's because I didn't. Marcus is still a child, Daddy. He plays a game for a living!' *Pat was right. I needed somebody to compare him to.*

'All I know is Marcus didn't make you forget how you was raised. After two weeks you come home wearing jewelry from this man! For cryin' out loud he wears a diamond pinkie ring, Gayle! You didn't go to church *last* week 'cause you were out too late Saturday night. Now you're goin' to . . . what d'you call it? Champagne brunch? What kinda man takes a woman drinkin' on Sunday mornin'? You answer me that!'

'I guess the kind I like!' She unconsciously fingered the gold star suspended from a delicate filigreed chain around her neck.

'Humph!' Joseph rifled the paper for the sports section.

Gayle piled dishes in the sink and turned on the hot water. *The kind of man who always knows exactly what to say, and do.* Suds filled the sink and she poured bacon drippings into the old Crisco can next to the stove. Ramsey was a man, not an awkward, insecure, unsophisticated boy. Every movement, every decision was quick and sure. Most of the time it was like magic. As they walked crowded city streets, his arm would slip around her waist and make her feel secure. He seemed to know what she would like and ordered for her in restaurants. He'd open doors, guide her through, and whisper something funny all at the same time. The warm, moist, clove-scented voice in her ear always caught her off guard and made her breathe in tiny, shallow ripples that left her dizzy. And when she was with him, he made her feel like she was the only thing that mattered in the world.

'You fixin' to wash the floor, too?' Joseph asked.

Bubbles slipped quietly over the edge of the sink, and Gayle jumped to turn off the water. 'Why didn't you say something?'

'Are you two still at it?' Loretta appeared in the kitchen door dressed for church. 'Joseph, leave the child alone. She's young. She should have some fun, and Mr Hilliard seems like a fine man.'

'Havin' money and fancy ways *don't* make him a fine man, Loretta. And just because he kisses *your* hand and tells you how pretty *you* look don't mean he ain't a scoundrel.' Joseph stood and pressed his hand to his chest. 'What do we have for heartburn?'

'I told you not to put hot sauce on your eggs, Joseph . . . And all that slab bacon!'

'I'll get it.' Gayle was happy to have an excuse to leave.

'You look mighty fine this mornin', Mrs Saunders. New dress?' Joseph said.

'What do you want, Joseph?'

'Exactly. When *I* pay you a compliment you're suspicious. That's how I feel about this Ramsey character.'

Gayle returned, plopped two tablets in a glass of water, and handed the bubbling concoction to her father, who drank it straight down.

'Let's go.' Joseph got his suit coat from the back of the kitchen chair and walked out the back door.

Loretta secured her blue straw cloche hat with a pearl-topped pin. She turned to Gayle, smoothed her thumb over her daughter's right eyebrow, and started to speak, but instead cupped Gayle's chin in her hand for a long moment, then headed out the door.

Gayle watched through the window. *They're getting old.* When she was little she asked why they were older than her friends' parents. 'God blessed us a little later,' her father said. He still had spring in his step, but he used to eat whatever he wanted and then some with no complaint. And Gayle had noticed the gray roots sneak up on her mother's auburn curls if she missed her 'special' appointment at Della's. Gayle just hadn't thought about it much.

Gayle watched her father back the car into the street. *It's always the same.* Most Sundays for her whole life, they rode into the city with her father fussing about finding a parking space. When she and Pat were kids, a ride anywhere promised adventure. But Pat was gone, Gayle was grown, and riding to church with her father complaining about his indigestion and her mother retelling hairdresser gossip was boring.

They've been doing this almost thirty-five years. They were planning to renew their vows for their anniversary, and they were both excited about the 'wedding' and reception because they never really had one. *When was the last time they had anything to be excited about? When they bought the house? When I was born?* But it would be different for her. Thanks to Ramsey Hilliard, it already was. She trotted upstairs to get ready. *Won't everybody be surprised when I show up at the anniversary party with him?*

When the doorbell rang Gayle raced to answer. She smoothed a hand over the full skirt of her ivory silk shirt-dress and turned the knob. Marcus leaned against the banister.

'I thought you might be at church, but I stopped anyway 'cause I ain't got much time.'

'Then don't spend it here, 'cause I don't have much either.' Marcus had to be gone before Ramsey showed up

133

because she hadn't rehearsed this scene yet and didn't know how it would play.

Marcus frowned. 'Yeah. Can I come in, or we gon' talk through this screen door?'

Gayle shrugged and let him in. 'Make it fast, Marcus. I'm on my way out.' She crossed her arms and waited. Everything about him annoyed her. His gum chewing, the tired leather jacket, his sneakers, and, most of all, his attitude. Like just showing up would make her day. 'Well?' Gayle tapped her foot impatiently.

'I'm movin' up to AAA . . . Rochester. I report today.' He shoved his hands deep in his pockets.

'That's nice. What does this have to do with me?'

'Like you don't know?' Marcus eased toward her and put a little sugar in his voice. 'Why you wanna act like this? It means that maybe before the season ends, I'll make the show. And then . . . you know, what we always talked about.'

'I'm through talking about *you*, Marcus. And' – she looked out the door and saw Ramsey pull up – 'and I think you should go.'

Marcus examined her closely. 'What's that around your neck?'

'What does it look like?' Gayle touched the star at her throat.

'I know what it is. Where did it come from? And how come you not wearin' the ring I gave you?'

'How's m'lady today?' Ramsey stood at the screen.

'Uh . . . um . . . I'm fine, Ramsey.' Gayle opened the door and Ramsey leaned over and kissed her on the cheek.

'What the . . . ?' Marcus sputtered.

'I told you I was on my way out, Marcus.'

'So when were you gon' tell me, Gayle?'

I don't know when I was gonna tell you. She didn't even

know what she was going to tell him. She hadn't planned to have to make that move so soon. 'Marcus . . .'

'He gave you that necklace, didn't he? So this is how it's gon' be?'

'Is there a problem, Youngblood?' Ramsey asked.

Marcus looked Ramsey up and down, checking out the expensive pin-striped suit and well-shined Florsheims. 'Not until now . . . Pops.'

'I'm ready, Ramsey.' Gayle felt like all the blood in her body had rushed to her head and pulsated between her ears. She grabbed her jacket from the doorknob. 'Let's go.'

'You gon' act like I'm not here?' Marcus tightened his jaw until his dimple twitched.

'Fine. Ramsey, this is Marcus Carter, an old friend of mine. He plays *minor league* baseball and he just stopped by to say hello.' Gayle's voice echoed in her head.

'Ain't this some shit!' Marcus threw up his hands and paced in the small hallway.

Ramsey stepped in Marcus's path. 'You should watch your language.'

'And I don't need *you* tellin' me what to do.' Marcus and Ramsey stood too close to blink. The next ten seconds felt like an hour to Gayle. Beads of sweat dotted Marcus's forehead, and fire blazed in his eyes. Ramsey stared back, cool, confident, immovable. Then, Marcus backed up slowly and faced Gayle. 'Is this how you want it?'

Gayle swallowed hard. *I don't know!* '. . . Yes.'

'Bet!' Marcus punched the screen so hard the restraining arm snapped and the door banged against the railing. Halfway down the path he turned back toward the house. 'I *thought* we had a dream, Gayle, but *evidently* you was just seein' stars!' Marcus stabbed the air with his index finger.

Gayle felt every word pierce her skin. Part of her wanted to run to him, say she was sorry, but she'd made her bed. Marcus screeched off in Nighthawk, burning rubber. Without looking at Ramsey she said, 'He was my boyfriend. He left to play baseball for the Orioles. We broke up. Before I met you.' *And a month ago I was planning to marry him.* 'Can we go?' An instant of panic washed across her face.

Ramsey could see she was on the verge of tears. 'Let's get outta here, pretty lady.'

Gayle jabbered nonstop to ward off Ramsey's questions and her thoughts about Marcus. Occasionally she'd sneak a glance at him, noting the way his sideburns curled slightly into his ear, or the way he drove, steering with only a finger looped casually over the wheel. *Of course this is where I want to be! With him.*

They drove way beyond the Bronx. When Ramsey parked in front of a run-down warehouse on a desolate-looking block and opened the car door, Gayle hesitated to get out.

'You trust me, don't you?' Ramsey held out his hand.

'I don't know. Should I?' Gayle tilted her head down and peeked up at him.

'Without question, Nightingale.' Ramsey winked and looked into those sparkling almond eyes. Gayle swung her legs out of the car and Ramsey eyed those sweet feet, perched on dainty black patent sandals. She took his hand and he led her carefully over the gravel and broken glass that littered the sidewalk and rapped four times on the battered steel door. It creaked open slowly and a hulk of a man in a white dinner jacket, with a nose that hooked like an eagle beak and a head as shiny and smooth as an eight ball, nodded to Ramsey and graciously waved them inside.

Gayle was astonished. The sugary scent of magnolias

136

and barbecue sauce filled her first breath, and bouncy ragtime piano accompanied laughter and the tinkling of glasses. White shirred draperies obscured the rusty barred windows and a massive chandelier, dripping crystals, dangled two stories above their heads.

'You looking mighty prosperous today, Mr Hilliard. Business must be good!' His waxed and curled handlebar mustache broadened his already wide grin.

'*Everything's* good, and I'm plannin' on keepin' it that way!' Ramsey clapped the center of the man's back exuberantly and turned to Gayle. 'Bessie, I'd like you to meet Miss Gayle Saunders.'

Gayle smiled and offered her hand, which Bessie took by the fingertips as he bowed low. 'It's always my pleasure to have a beautiful woman grace my humble establishment.'

Gayle thought that being greeted by name in a restaurant only happened in the movies. But it was like that with Ramsey all the time. Not like with Marcus, when people looked at them like they didn't have enough money to pay.

The hostess, a full hourglass with time to spare, knew Ramsey, too. Her red-fringed flapper dress shimmied dizzily as she led them past the carved mahogany bar overseen by two snowy cockatoos in a gilded cage, snaked through tables crowded with well-dressed brunchers, and stopped in front of a pair of lush emerald velvet drapes. She pulled a golden cord, which admitted them to the almost illicit ambience of a private booth.

Once they settled into the curve of the richly upholstered banquette, a waiter in black tails and spats appeared. Ramsey ordered vintage champagne. 'The stuff that comes with brunch tastes like swamp water. Lots of folks don't know the difference, but I know quality.'

137

He knows so much. And Gayle felt primed to learn. In all the years with Marcus, what had she learned? That a tie on the bases went to the runner. Who cared? Ramsey taught her about champagne and secret places. He didn't just promise, he delivered, and she wanted it all. He made her feel like a woman.

'The man at the door, is his name really Bessie?'

Ramsey stroked his mustache with his fingertips. 'His grandma's name was Bessie, and she ran a speakeasy during Prohibition. You know, gangsters, bootleg whiskey, whatever your hand called for, you could find it at Bessie's. Her daughter Bessie turned the place into a legitimate nightclub and when she had a baby boy instead of a daughter, they called him Bessie, too. You know he named *his* son Bessie! Nobody laughs when they say it either, and Bessie makes the best ribs and potato salad you ever put between your lips.'

'How'd you find this place?' Gayle asked.

'The same way I found you. Just lucky. But I always have my eyes open for good things.' Ramsey fanned Gayle's napkin open and draped it across her lap. 'Actually, I don't live far from here. But I drove past this place for a couple of years and had no idea. And you have to know. Anyway, I met Bessie at the Urban League, gave him my card. Been sending a crew to his house twice a week ever since. Now that's a house!'

Gayle loved the way Ramsey talked. He still had a hint of a drawl, but instead of sounding country, like she thought other people did, Ramsey's voice lapped over her like a warm bubble bath, and he always had a story to tell.

'Hmmm.' *I wonder what Ramsey's place is like.*

The waiter tinkled the small brass bell suspended at the drapery opening to signal his arrival. Then he pulled the drapes, and, with well-rehearsed ceremony, uncorked the champagne, poured two glasses, rested the bottle in a silver cooler, and withdrew.

'To luck and the lady who brought it.'

They clinked glasses and sipped. The taste, a tangy, effervescent sweet and sour, surprised Gayle. *I'll have to get used to the good stuff.* She put down the flute glass and focused on the delicate bubbles rising to the top. 'I'm sorry . . . about what happened.'

'Forget about it, Nightingale.' Ramsey caressed her cheek and drew her so close his mustache tickled her lips as he spoke. 'I have.' First he kissed her between the eyes, which she closed, waiting for his tingly touch. Then he kissed her chin. Gayle's breath hung with anticipation. Finally he found her mouth and kissed her, just long and deep enough to leave her wanting more.

They ordered and ate in a kind of languid luxury. Gayle had Eggs Bessie, two poached jumbos and big rounds of country ham on huge buttermilk biscuits, smothered in a hollandaise spiked pink with Tabasco. She could eat it and remain ladylike. Ramsey had it all. Barbecue, collards, corn bread, and more, piled high on a platter-sized plate. He fed Gayle a taste of the spicy pork, wiped a spot of sauce from the corner of her mouth with his pinky, and relished the sauce he licked from his finger.

While they drank coffee Bessie stopped by the booth and Gayle excused herself to the ladies' room. 'That's quite a little filly you got with you today. Still looks kinda young and skittish. You think you can ride that?' He rested his hand on Ramsey's shoulder.

'Just leave that to me.' The men chuckled.

'Anything I can do for you today?' Bessie asked.

'Naw. I'll be by later in the week.'

Bessie smiled and retreated when Gayle got back. She and Ramsey finished their coffee, and by the time they emerged from the booth only a few stragglers remained, conversing in murmurs around cluttered tables. The dusky colors and amber light of their private chamber had lulled Gayle into a sense of time and space that gelled around them like sweet, thick blackberry preserves. She was startled by the brilliant sunshine when she stepped out of Bessie's world and back onto the street. Everything seemed hollow and so far away. Her parents, St Albans, the Feminique Boutique, even Marcus. Everything but Ramsey seemed like distant, dusty recollections. She heard the crunch of gravel beneath her feet, but she felt like she was floating, and she didn't want the feeling to end. 'Ramsey, I'm having such a good time. I'm not ready to go home yet.'

'We could go for a drive up the Hudson.' He unlocked the car and ushered Gayle in. 'We could stop by my place . . . listen to some music.' He closed the door and walked around the other side. The piney musk of his aftershave lingered. Gayle inhaled so deeply, she could taste it, and could hardly wait for him to get in beside her.

'I'd like that,' Gayle said. And when he settled behind the wheel and covered her hand with his, she felt as if she'd stopped breathing until he pulled into the cool darkness of the garage beneath his building. As they rode the elevator to the fourteenth floor she had no plan, only an achy longing for the next sensation. Then Ramsey unlocked the door and led her into his domain. The rest became a blur.

They did some talking, about the dusky Hudson River panorama, framed by ceiling-scraping ficus trees that bracketed the far wall of his living room. About the furniture, all burled wood and clubby comfort just the way he'd seen it in the showroom. Just like the rooms he was forbidden to enter when he was a boy sent from the stables up to the house with some message. He'd even bought the painting of horses grazing in a paddock. It hung above the tufted saddle leather sofa where Gayle perched, trying to listen to what he said when he went to the kitchen for ice, but she couldn't hear him because she couldn't breathe. There was no air until he sat next to her. She leaned in close because she couldn't help it – she was dizzy from the yearning and wanted Ramsey to breathe life into her, now.

Ramsey traced the star at the hollow of Gayle's throat. 'You know I want you, Nightingale. I don't know how much longer I can hold out.' His index finger meandered up to her chin, lightly traced her lips. 'But I'd never take you someplace you don't want to go.'

Gayle inhaled him with her eyes, her ears, her skin. 'I want . . . you . . . I want you to . . .'

Ramsey lifted her onto his lap. 'First time, isn't it? Are you using something?'

'Uh-huh.' Last week she'd started back on the pill, just in case.

'Umh, umh, umh, look at them eyes. Like a thousand fires burnin' just for me.' He memorized her body with his hands. Outlined her face, the slope of her neck, her shoulders, and Gayle closed her eyes and traveled with him. He unfastened each of her buttons, slowly, reverently, then continued on his journey. Gayle's whole body felt new to her in a man's hands, and she shuddered, reached out for him, held his face in her hands, and looked him eye to eye, so close they breathed the same air, in and out. In and out. Until she was drunk with it. Until he raised her in his arms and carried her to his bed like something precious that he was damned lucky to find. He cherished her tenderly, pleasured her slowly, judged by her gasps and whimpers when she was ready for more, until she had it all.

And when it was over, and she clutched the sheets and cried, Ramsey held her, rocked her until she was quiet. Until she exhaled a breath both satisfied and exhausted, then turned and looked at him, eyes shining, and he knew she was his.

The next day, while she logged in a shipment of gauze tunics at the store, she savored her entry to womanhood. *Maybe I'll call Pat.* But Gayle decided to wait. *Patty'll be home in a few weeks anyway for Momma and Daddy's anniversary party.* By then Gayle was sure she'd have even more to tell about Mr Ramsey Hilliard.

7

'. . . always put a little on a filly.'

'You can't be serious!' Pat stopped, midpuff, and the balloon at her lips sputtered across the basement. 'Are you sure?'

'Yes, I'm sure. Do you think I'd say it if I wasn't sure.' Gayle stomped on a balloon and the loud bang let her know this wasn't a dream. It was all she could do to keep the words from spewing out of her mouth, like the eggs she had tried to eat for breakfast. She didn't think her folks would ever leave so they could talk. Pat was going back to her summer internship in Princeton right after the anniversary festivities, and Gayle couldn't say the word pregnant yet while her parents were in the house.

'You tell Marcus yet?'

'It's not Marcus.'

'Okay . . . this is a joke, right? I'm supposed to laugh now.'

'I'm not playing with you, Pat.' Gayle sank to the new sofa. After years of false starts and delays her father had finally remodeled the basement – his consulting room he called it. The old daybed and snack trays were replaced by tweed Herculon and white Formica Parsons tables, delivered just in time for the party after the cake and punch reception at church. 'I'm just into my second month.' Gayle liked saying that. Like the flutter she felt when she thought of the baby, their little angel, floating inside her.

At the clinic, when the test came back positive, they had asked her what she wanted to do. The question made her laugh. She giggled out the door, all the way to her car, where she couldn't remember what 'D,' 'R,' and 'P' on the gearshift meant or which pedal made the car go forward. Howled 'til the tears rolled down her face.

'I thought you were on the pill.'

'I was. But I'd stopped after Marcus and I . . . didn't, then I started again, because Ramsey and I might . . .'

'Who?'

Gayle painted Ramsey in flowers and candlelight. Pat wanted black and white.

'Have you told him?'

'Yeah.' Gayle had called, said she needed to see Ramsey, right away. Had something to tell him, but not over the phone. Yeah, she knew it was summer busy season, but it wouldn't keep.

Ramsey was preoccupied when he picked her up. They drove in silence for a while, then he parked by a playground, asked what she had to say that couldn't wait. Gayle swallowed. She noticed that moonlight on the monkey bars cast jagged shadows on the ground. The words 'I'm pregnant' dropped like deadweight from her lips. Ramsey muttered something that sounded like, 'Shit,' then got out, and leaned on the hood. Gayle's heart was in her mouth. She wanted him to come back, say something, anything, but she sat, waiting.

When he got back in the car he drove her home without a word. 'I'll be in touch,' he said, and stared through the windshield 'til she got out. Then he was gone.

'That's it. That's all he said, "I'll be in touch"?'

'He will. It was just such a shock, he needs some time to get used to it. He's coming to pick me up for this thing on Sunday. By then he'll be back to normal.'

'Are you crazy? You've known the man what, two months, and you get pregnant and expect him to be normal? He's not gettin' used to anything but leavin' your ass.'

'Not everybody leaves.'

'Right. So what do you want him to do? Marry you or pay for the abortion.'

'I'm *not* having an abortion.'

'Gayle, how are you gonna raise a baby? You can't even say you're pregnant 'cause you'll be in trouble with your momma and daddy.' Pat reached for her cigarettes, then looked at Gayle and put them away.

'Can't you just be happy for me?'

'You are crazy! No, I'm not happy. You're knocked up. You're twenty years old, you live with your parents. You can't even remember to put gas in your own damn car! How's this supposed to make me happy?'

'Just because I want something different than you doesn't mean I'm crazy. I always wanted to get married and have a family! I'll be good at it, Pat.'

'You need to stop watchin' *Gidget* reruns. *The man has not proposed. He's gone!*'

'I'm in love with him, Pat.'

'I thought you loved Marcus.'

'I thought so, too, but this is different. I can't explain it. It just is. Me and Marcus were kid stuff. Ramsey's not like that. He'll be back. You'll see.'

'Don't do it if you don't mean it, Gayle. This isn't a hairstyle you can change or a dress you can give to the Goodwill when you're tired of it.'

She's talking about herself! Pat hadn't mentioned Verna

in years, so Gayle thought it was 'case closed' on the mother who didn't want her. Gayle never for a moment felt unwanted, and she'd love her baby just the way her parents loved her. *But what about Ramsey? What if Pat is right?* Panic rode in on a wave of nausea, and she ran to the bathroom.

When she emerged Pat was sitting in the dining room with a plate of saltines. 'Whatever you decide, I'll be there for you. But you've got to think this through.' Her voice was calm, strong.

Gayle took a cracker and rested a hand on Pat's shoulder. 'I know,' she said quietly.

Loretta left early Saturday morning for the beauty shop, and Joseph got busier than a one-armed paperhanger. He mowed and edged the lawn and made a vat of his special Memphis Mashed Potato Salad before he left for the barbershop; then he went to a lodge meeting. Pat and Gayle spent Saturday cleaning, cooking, and not mentioning Ramsey's name. Every time the phone rang, Gayle's heart fluttered, then sank again when it was one of her parents' cronies. At ten that night she started calling, every half hour. She'd let the phone ring fifteen, twenty times, praying he was just coming in the door, that he would pick up, out of breath, on the next ring. At two A.M. Pat made her stop and go to bed.

'One,' Ramsey barked. His hand wasn't worth horseshit, but he pushed the seven of spades, facedown, toward the dealer and snatched the replacement. *Two a clubs. Pitiful.* But he arched an eyebrow, just enough to look like a hopeful glimmer that he mistakenly let slip, but he meant for them to see it. Wanted them to go for the bluff. It's what he liked about cards. There were fifty-two of them in a deck and even when you didn't have the best ones in your hand, you could still win if you could make the other guy believe you did.

After he had dropped Gayle off, Ramsey drove home in a stupor. He fell asleep on his sofa with all the lights on, still in his clothes, and woke up the next day, feeling like somebody had beaten on him all night. *What the hell am I supposed to do?* Nobody walking the earth ever had a claim on Ramsey Hilliard, and he liked it that way. He was too damned smart to get corralled by the oldest trick known to *man*. 'I'm having your baby.' *Shit!* Like that made a difference. There were a whole lot of little pickaninnies running around the world and any six of them weren't worth a colt who liked to run, but Ramsey didn't like it when anybody had something that belonged to him, even if he didn't want it.

He went to the office without checking on any of the crews in the field. He didn't ask Mrs Banks if she'd heard from the garage about the truck that had been without a transmission all week. Ramsey opened the safe, gave her the paychecks to hand out at the end of the day, and left.

He cruised around for hours, like he was looking for something. *I shoulda known things were goin' too good.* He liked Gayle. She was sweet and ladylike, not bossy like most of the women he'd met since he left Louisville. They were stone foxes all right. Looked like a damned fashion show, but they were hard-ass bitches on a mission. Their little ears would perk right up when he said he owned a business. Some of them even had the nerve to ask him out, like they had bigger balls than he did. The others would let him make the first move, then they'd proceed to take over. They picked the restaurant and movie because they had heard how *fabulous* it was. They wouldn't eat a steak because it might cause cancer, but they did a little cocaine now and then. *And* they told him what to do in bed.

147

But nothing made Ramsey madder than when they stuck their noses in his business affairs. He didn't give a shit about their 'expertise' or how some 'friend' with a jive-ass title on a business card thought he should run Greener Pastures. Ramsey had no use for their opinions. His business card said 'president,' and as far as he was concerned, that was his ace.

On the other hand, Gayle liked him to take charge. He didn't want this little girl under his skin, but she did do something to him. Made him feel so good, *like a natural man*. And she did little things for him. Things nobody ever thought of, like presenting him with a whole stack of *Superman* comics, wrapped up pretty like Christmas, after he told her he used to go to bed dreaming about them because he couldn't afford them as a kid. He didn't even know why he told her that, but she had remembered. And he was so tickled by the drawing she did of him, kind of a cartoon, like the ones they saw at Sardi's, right down to the black lacquer frame. He'd hung it right behind his desk at work.

And he had to admit that since he had spotted her broken-down on his way back from AC and decided she was worth the price of gasoline, his luck had turned around. Nothing had been this good in five years. He'd won some, but there hadn't been any magic in a long time. The problem was he wasn't in the daddy business.

After driving halfway to Canada and back Ramsey stopped by Bessie's to check the spread on Saturday's Yankees-Orioles game. Bessie took him aside and told him that Moses had an open seat in 'The Promised Land' if he was interested, and Ramsey took it as a sign. He'd only ventured upstairs for high-stakes poker a few times, and he'd left with only loose change in his pockets, but the invitation carried respect. The game was power with a high-risk rush. It wasn't a game – it was a contest that could last for days, a test of endurance and cunning, a process of elimination, and luck was always a deciding factor. This was a chance to see if his lucky charm was real. If he won, he'd marry her. If he lost, he'd say so long.

He liked slipping through the door at the top of the stairs. Ceiling-high cases of whiskey lined the scuffed brown linoleum hall that led to 'The Promised Land.' It was a windowless room that reeked of dirty ashtrays, coffee, bourbon, and money. A bare lightbulb dangled over the round, felt-covered table at the center of the room. Moses, an albino bullfrog in a black Kangol cap, with a cold, chewed-up cigar butt always knotted tightly in his right hand, sat on a high-backed stool in the corner by the door. He'd made a desk out of the old bar from downstairs and, from his lofty post, dispensed chips, advice, pity, and high octane coffee. He also guaranteed markers, settled disputes, and cashed checks.

Ramsey laid his cards facedown on the green felt. This was the worst hand he'd had since he sat down. *When was it . . . last night? Two nights ago?* But he was up nine thousand and they didn't know he didn't have shit. Ramsey felt good, too good to lose. He tossed a thousand in chips to the kitty and waited to see if his luck would hold.

When he was a little boy, his father told him never to forget that 'Knowhow without luck is like a car without gas. You can still push it and get where you're going, but if you got a full tank, you get to enjoy the trip. You just got to remember to keep yo' eyes peeled for them fillin' stations 'cause no luck is bad luck, boy.'

His parents weren't lucky. His ma died of cancer when he was nine. Then his papa stopped trying and took up sour mash full-time instead of as a sideline. He lost their little truck farm to the bank, and by the time his daddy was run over by another drunk driving a pickup truck, Ramsey was seventeen and had been working at Tripletree Stud Farms, mucking out stalls, cleaning the paddocks, and watching how rich people lived for four years.

Ramsey promised Mr Johnson that if he would give his father a decent funeral, he would give him half of his pay every week until the bill was paid. The first payday after the funeral Ramsey dropped off half his money at Johnson's Safe Haven Funeral Home just like he promised and went to get a haircut. On his way, the prettiest little brown-skinned girl he'd ever seen stopped and offered him a ride. Unless it was Saturday, Milton never cut more than two heads in a day. But he was open for all 'bidness,' as he called it, from six in the morning until midnight, every day but Sunday. When Ramsey finally got to the barbershop two hours later, the regulars were smoking Lucky Strikes, drinking Wild Turkey, betting on the last race at the Downs, and Ramsey was feeling like a man. They called him a fool, and a whole bunch of other names, but he bet the other half of his pay on the only filly in the race because he could still smell the filly in the red Mustang on his fingers.

He won sixteen hundred dollars, paid off Mr Johnson, bought himself a piece of car, and dropped by the barbershop more regularly. At Tripletree Ramsey worked the stables, helped the groundskeepers, and paid attention to everything. Sometimes at night men would come down to the tack room next to where he slept and play cards. He'd climb up to the hayloft and watch and listen. 'Are you in? . . .' 'Straight flush . . .' 'That foal will go for a hundred thousand . . .' '. . . call your thousand and raise you . . .' '. . . just bought five hundred acres . . .' '. . . Trip aces. Beat that.' Their golden rule was always keep a stake nobody knows about. Ramsey would listen for more words of wisdom, holding his breath, afraid if he dared to inhale he would miss something important. He never did see his Mustang Sally again, but he always wondered about her and always put a little on a filly, especially a long shot.

Sunday morning Pat worked to keep things under control. Gayle was ready to come out of her skin. She'd had no word from Ramsey, and why did her parents have to marry each other again anyway? Loretta was flighty as a June bride. She went through three pair of panty hose fresh out of the package before she managed to get into one without a run and worried the whole time about sweating the curl out of her hair before they got to church.

Gayle kept pacing and peeking through the curtains, straining to see the nose of that silver car pull up in front of the house. *He knows this is today.* And although Ramsey didn't hold much with church, he'd promised to show up. *But that was before . . .*

By nine-thirty it was time to leave and Ramsey was still in the wind. Pat trotted downstairs and found Joseph stretched out on the sofa.

'I thought you'd be outside polishing the car or something,' Pat said.

'Too much toasting brotherhood last night. Movin' a little slow this morning. Must be wedding day jitters.' He chuckled, sat up, and mopped his face with his handkerchief.

'The blushing bride'll be down in a minute.'

'We don't have a limousine. Thought we might have us a ride in a Lincoln, but looks like Nature Boy ain' comin'.'

'I'm sure he'll meet us at church,' Pat said, not believing a word of it.

'I don't know what happened with her and Marcus. You know I like that boy. I think he's gon' do all right, too. I saw Booker at the barbershop yesterday. Seems the Orioles brought Marcus up and he's gon' be playin' the Yankees today.'

'Already?'

'Yep. Booker was struttin' and crowin' like a rooster. Got him a box seat. Brought some other boy up, but he didn't work out so good. So Marcus got him a shot.'

It was Freddy getting a shot that started all this. 'It's what he's been working for since we were little.'

'Ol' Marcus on the TV! You kids . . . I remember when all y'all were just dyin' to be grown and now . . . You know, sometimes I worry about my girl, Patty Cake.' Joseph's voice got that father-ache to it. Pat sat next to him. 'It's like Gayle don't have a mind a her own. She goes whichever way the wind blows, like it's gon' take her where she wanna go. Maybe I shouldn't a let her think all stories have a happy ending.'

Pat was rescued from responding by footsteps on the stairs. She patted his arm. 'Let's go. The bridal party's coming.'

Mt Moriah was full, like an Easter Sunday. Loretta and Joe would renew their vows right after service, and a large contingent of visitors, including Joseph's Masons in their formal gold braid and fezzes and Loretta's Eastern Stars, their white dresses adorned with the elaborate breastplates that marked their degrees, had come for the occasion. Even before church started, Gayle wanted it to be over, but the Reverend Hobson was feeling touched by the spirit, and he preached a while on love and happiness.

True love, he said, was not the way Al Green sang it, making you do wrong and stay out all night long. *True* love was the way Paul said it in First Corinthians, the kind, patient love that endures all the joy and pain thirty-five years could bring. The congregation praised the Lord and hallelujahed, but Gayle felt the words wind around her, bind her like rope. She loved Ramsey, but it made her achy, impatient, and as far from happy as she had ever been.

One of the junior ushers signaled Loretta, Joe, Gayle, and Pat just before the last hymn, and they slipped out to get ready for the renewal ceremony.

Gayle just had time to bolt for the door and scan the cars parked in double rows along both sides of the street. The early sun had hidden behind damp gray, but there was no silver Lincoln, and she hurried down to the ladies' room to join her mother.

Pat kept Uncle Joe still long enough to pin his carnation to his lapel. He looked nice in his navy blue, twice-a-year dress suit. His shirt was starched 'til it wouldn't dare wrinkle, and his Masonic tie tack accented the new paisley tie Loretta had bought him.

'I didn't think there'd be this many folks.' His voice wavered with emotion. 'Sure is nice. Loretta deserves this, even as late in life as it is.' Pat moved the boutonniere, looking for the right spot. 'Careful now.' He patted his pocket.

'What you got in there?' Pat looked at him with mock suspicion.

'That's for me to know.' He winked.

Pat pinned his flower, then had him pose by the sanctuary doors for a picture. She'd just clicked the shutter when Uncle Macon came and got him. 'Boy, I got a few things to tell you 'bout married life.' He laughed at his own joke as he led Joseph inside.

At the first chords of the 'Wedding March' the congregation rustled to its feet. Hand in hand Loretta and

Gayle walked down the aisle. Pat thought Gayle looked almost serene, and she was proud of her. And for the entire walk down the aisle Loretta beamed Joseph a look that spoke the long, slow burn of a lasting love, and he returned the adoring gaze.

Pat noticed Joseph's eyes looked a little glassy. Then he fixed his mouth in a twisted sort of smile she hadn't seen before. Just as Loretta and Gayle reached the end of the aisle, Joseph pressed his hand to that breast pocket again.

What's he got in there?

And then he groaned and crumpled to his knees.

'Daddy!' Gayle's yell rang through the church, and she bolted toward her father.

The music stopped abruptly, replaced by anguished cries and shouts as people strained to see what happened.

Macon held on to Joseph's shoulders and eased him to the floor. Loretta knelt beside him. 'What is it Joe?' She put her hand to his cheek, and he buried his face in her palm.

'Pain like fire . . . in my chest . . . Lord, I can't . . . breathe.'

Gayle rocked and cried. Loretta sat on the floor with Joseph's head in her lap. Pat went ice-cold when she looked down at her uncle's ashen face. Pockets of whispered prayer rose up in the congregation. Reverend Hobson called out for a doctor and two women and a man rushed forward, loosened his tie, took his pulse. Sent someone to call an ambulance.

''Etta . . .' Joseph's voice was weak and thin.

'Is it the pain again?' Loretta looked as though she could feel it, too.

'My pocket . . . In my pocket . . .'

'Joseph hush and be still.' Loretta tried to quiet him.

'No . . . I want you to have it . . .'

Pat crouched down, slipped her hand into his jacket pocket, and removed a small blue felt pouch that she gave to Loretta.

Loretta shook the pouch and her old wedding band tumbled out into her hand, along with a sparkling, diamond solitaire on a delicate gold band.

'Joseph, what did you do?' Loretta flicked the tears away before they could fall.

'I wanna give you somethin' nice, 'Etta . . . put it on . . .'

She slipped both rings on her finger and held her hand where he could see it.

Joseph tried to speak, but instead nodded his weak approval. Then he screwed up his face against a flash of pain, clutched his chest, and closed his eyes.

Reverend Hobson stood and faced the congregation. 'Let us bow our heads in prayer for Brother Saunders . . .'

8

'Sometimes love is stronger than blood,'

Balancing three cups, Pat peered through the tiny window in the CCU door. She couldn't see Uncle Joe. Back in the waiting room, she gave a cup to Loretta, one to Uncle Macon. She took a sip of the muddy brew and glanced at Gayle, asleep on a vinyl couch.

A doctor had come around midnight, said the attack was mild . . . some damage to the muscle . . . needed an angiogram . . . maybe some blockage . . . they would schedule tests.

Pat and Loretta took turns checking for news at the nurses' station. All night they listened to the ding of the elevator, the wheezing of machines, coughs, whispers, and the scrunch-squeak of rubber-soled shoes. Now it was six-fifteen in the morning, and they waited, still in their wedding clothes. Uncle Macon looked worn-out, and his tie had long ago found a home in his pocket. He jabbered about the lodge picnic and every few sentences he'd say 'He'll be all right, 'Etta.'

Loretta tied and untied knots in her 'something blue' lace handkerchief, half-listening to picnic plans. She'd smile weakly at Macon or pat Gayle's hand and say 'Lord willin'.'

Pat was glad Gayle had fallen asleep. She was so

157

hysterical when they got to the hospital, they wanted to give her a sedative. Only Pat knew she refused the pill because of the baby. On one of Gayle's countless trips to the bathroom, Pat saw her hang up the pay phone. Most of the evening Gayle had cried quietly. Pat didn't know if the tears were for her father or herself, but if ever there was a time for crying, she guessed this was it.

At seven a nurse came in and asked for 'Saunders,' and Gayle awoke with a start. Joseph was stable and asking for his family. That was a good sign. She explained that one of them could go in at a time, but just for a few minutes.

'You go in, Gayle. I'll go next.' Loretta smiled.

'No, Momma. I'll wait 'til the next time.'

'It'll do him more good to see your pretty face than to see this old one.'

Gayle had never been in a hospital room, and this wasn't what she expected. Six space-age beds formed a semicircle in front of a glass enclosure that looked like Mission Control. She tiptoed to keep her heels from tapping on the floor as she crossed the room.

Joseph was sitting up. His green hospital gown was pulled low in front so she could see the wires and electrodes that tracked every beat of his heart on a monitor above his bed. An IV dripped in his right arm, a blood pressure cuff encircled his left. Gayle looked at the spikes on the tiny screen, then leaned over and kissed his cheek.

He squeezed her hand and smiled. 'Y'all been here all night? You shoulda made your momma go home, get some sleep.'

'We wanted to make sure you were okay, Daddy. Can I get you something?'

'I want bacon and eggs, but I'll settle for some water.' He nodded toward the pitcher on the nightstand. Gayle poured some into a plastic tumbler and inserted a straw.

Joseph took a few sips. 'Gayle, I have to talk to you . . . About something important.'

Gayle felt the lecture coming. *'What kind of man would stand you up for such a special family occasion?'* 'Daddy, I know you don't like Ramsey, but you shouldn't be worrying about that now.'

'Child, I know you got that man on your mind, but what I want to say ain't got nothin' to do with him.'

'There'll be plenty of time for talking later. You should get some rest.' Gayle was relieved. She didn't have the energy or the conviction to defend Ramsey this morning.

'There was always gon' be a better time, but yesterday scared me. It made me realize I can't wait around countin' on later no more.'

'Stop talking like that. The doctor says you'll be good as new. You won't like your new diet much, but you're gonna be okay.'

'Hush up, girl, and let me talk. You're as bad as your momma.'

'You should rest, Daddy, they said just a few . . .'

He squeezed her hand. 'I will as soon as I've said my piece. This is somethin' I shoulda said fifteen years ago. Loretta stopped me then, but I can't go to my grave without sayin' it, so you just listen to me, baby girl.'

Gayle placed her other hand on top of her father's. 'I'll listen if you promise to stop talking about going any-where.'

Joseph took a deep breath. 'First I want to tell you I love you. I ain't said it much, but I want to say it today. I love you more than I ever loved anybody 'cept for 'Etta, and that's different. The first day I laid eyes on you, you were screaming like a stuck pig and I wanted to fix it so nothin' would make you cry like that again . . . It just never was the right time to tell you.'

'I know you love me, Daddy.'

'Gayle, this is hard enough without you keep inter-ruptin' me.' He cleared his throat. 'Your momma and I . . . What I'm tryin' to say is . . . you're our baby girl . . . you're my heart . . . in every way a daughter can be . . . never could've asked for more . . . exceptin' . . . we . . . we ain't your real mother and father . . .'

'You're not making sense, Daddy. I'm gonna get a nurse.' The antiseptic smell of the hospital room suddenly made Gayle queasy.

Joseph's long brown fingers gripped Gayle's so tightly she felt them start to go cold.

'Your Uncle Macon, he was a super in a buildin' on 143rd Street, near where we used to live. He called me one day, just before we moved to Queens . . . said it was an emergency.' Joseph stopped to catch his breath.

Gayle could feel the chill in her fingers creep along her skin, seep through her pores, and settle deep into her bones.

Haltingly, Gayle's father told her how he hurried to the basement where Macon had his 'office,' thinking it was some foolishness, as usual, but in the midst of crates, stacks of cardboard, light fixtures, rags, mops, and brooms, Macon sat in an old wooden swivel chair holding an infant, wrapped in a clean white shirt. 'Found her a little while ago out back. Bundled up in old newspaper by the trash. Shoulda called the po-lice, but I know how much y'all been wantin' a baby. Y'all would sure do better by her than the city.'

Joseph couldn't believe their prayers had been answered. He knew it was wrong. Illegal even, but . . . a baby girl. A scrawny little thing not more than a couple of days old and somebody threw her away. He touched her cheek with a long leathery finger. She opened her tiny mouth and wailed. Macon wrapped her up again and handed the bundle to Joseph.

'Go on, get outta here . . . and Joseph . . . I ain't seen you today.'

Loretta nearly fainted when he walked in the door, stumbled past moving boxes, and handed her his package, but she quickly recovered and, as she heard Joseph's story, she made plans, plans for her daughter. The move couldn't have come at a better time. No one would know them. Gayle Denise, Loretta had picked out the names years ago, would be theirs. A cryptic phone call to Reverend Hobson and a late-night visit to Mt Moriah produced a baptismal certificate, and everything was official. Uncle Macon was the only visitor from the old neighborhood, and when Joseph and Loretta returned to Mt Moriah two years later, tongues wagged and eyebrows raised, but to their face, everyone oohed and aahed over their beautiful little girl.

'It's not true!' Gayle wanted to vomit. 'The medicine's making you talk crazy!'

'We shoulda told you before.' Tears slipped from Joseph's eyes.

Gayle swallowed hard against the pool of saliva collecting under her tongue. She realized her father had never lied to her, and she had never seen him cry. *Not my real parents. Left like garbage?* She wrenched her hands from Joseph's.

'I'm sorry, Gayle . . .' But she couldn't hear him as she ran from the room.

'How could you lie to me all this time?' Gayle screamed at her mother and Uncle Macon while Pat looked on dumbfounded.

'Oh Lordy, he didn't.' Loretta looked at Macon, who dropped his head. They both knew that what Joseph had done could not be undone.

Gayle snatched her purse and ran from the waiting room, down four flights of stairs and hailed the first gypsy cab she saw on the busy Harlem avenue.

The stale smell of pancakes and sausage from yesterday's breakfast still hung in the stuffy, hot air at home, just like Joseph's words hovered in Gayle's mind. She moved through the house opening windows, but fresh air didn't clear the memory.

Upstairs, she turned on the shower, undressed, and stared at her naked body in the bathroom mirror, wanting desperately to see a difference. This baby was her only flesh-and-blood link to anybody in this world, and she clung to that because right now she felt so alone. *How can I stay here? Where should I go?* Then she shivered from way deep inside, dropped to her knees, and retched, but only a bitter, filmy liquid was left. She dragged herself under the steaming water and scrubbed 'til her skin felt raw.

Gayle gathered all the photographs she could find. She ignored the ringing phone and examined every picture, looking for a sign, something she must have missed. But she couldn't find a clue in the tiny face peeking out of a fluffy pink blanket in Loretta's arms. There wasn't a hint of the secret in the picture of her tentative first steps, with Joseph standing behind her, proudly holding her arms. Every photograph was regular and familiar, but for Gayle they told a big lie. No, she didn't look like either of them. Loretta always said Gayle resembled her grandma Howard and left it at that, and so had she. Now she didn't even know what to call them because they weren't her mother and father.

Exhausted, she slumped on the stairs. She should have been at the boutique hours ago, but she couldn't worry about that now. Gayle clutched a snapshot of her and Pat in second grade, modeling the gypsy Halloween costumes

Loretta had put together for both of them because Gayle told her Pat didn't have a mother to make her one. *Pretty funny*. But she wasn't laughing, and when the doorbell rang she jumped like it hit a raw nerve.

What now? Then she heard the whistling and thought her heart would burst. She knew Ramsey wouldn't let her down. She flung open the door.

Ramsey had a long white box tied with a red satin bow tucked under one arm and a stuffed panda, the size of a three-year-old, under the other. 'There's my Nightingale. I went by the job, and they said you hadn't called. You had me worried.' Gayle threw her arms around him and nestled her face in his chest.

This was going better than Ramsey expected. He figured he'd have to tap dance around his no-show, and he had put on his dancing shoes, but ever since Gayle told him she had his bun in her oven it seemed like he could do no wrong.

He had played poker for thirty-eight hours straight, and he could have gone longer, but nobody had money left to lose. Ramsey had boo-koo green to line his pockets and he floated way past cloud nine, higher than booze, drugs, or sex could ever take him.

To add icing to his cake, the money he put against the Orioles had paid off, too. When Bessie slipped him his proceeds he said Marcus had gone hitless for the Saturday doubleheader and one for three on Sunday. He grinned long and low down because he'd already won Youngblood's woman; now Ramsey had him beat on the ball field, too. Ramsey tipped everybody at Bessie's, down to the dishwashers, went home and slept like a champ, and when he woke up on Monday he knew what he was supposed to do, because any fool could see she was good for him. Besides, he liked the sound of Ramsey Edward Hilliard, Jr.

There was nothing at the office that wouldn't keep for a week, so he called Mrs Banks, his secretary, told her to reschedule his meetings, and to tell the garage to forget about the rebuilt transmission because he was buying a new truck. Whenever he won big he put money into the business because it was a sure way to get ahead. 'Make sure the guys get out on time and don't run my business into the ground while I'm on my honeymoon.' He hung up before she could ask any questions.

Gayle sat on the sofa to open the box. 'I thought something happened to you, too.'

'Some unexpected business came up and I had to take care of it . . .'

'Ooohh, Ramsey, I've never seen flowers this beautiful!' Gayle held up one of the dozen pink roses with stems as long as her arm. 'And who's the bear for?'

He hitched up his pant legs and sat beside her. 'My son's gonna need lots a toys.'

Gayle's eyes sparkled. *I knew he wouldn't leave us!*

'Now, I have a question for you.' He took her hand and looked into her red-rimmed eyes. She looked tired, but she was still the prettiest little filly he'd seen. *Hope she don't get fat behind this body.* 'How would you feel about being Mrs Ramsey Hilliard?'

He's asking me to marry him. The words were like joyful music replacing the morning's blues and she sang, 'Yes!' with all her heart.

Ramsey fumbled in his pants pocket. He'd stopped by a jeweler, asked for the best diamond they had, and counted cash while they nestled it in a blue velvet box.

It was the biggest diamond Gayle had ever seen, a marquis perched high on gold prongs. She was speechless, and as she put the ring on her finger, Ramsey's euphoria soared a level higher because only a big man could afford to take care of his woman like this.

Ramsey was flying so high he wasn't ready to land. He couldn't tell her about the weekend. That was none of her business. But he wasn't out of gas yet, and he liked company while he touched the sky. 'We could get married today.'

'Today? We need blood tests . . . a license . . .' I need to tell Momma and Daddy was what she started to say, but she remembered that's not who they were.

Ramsey fingered his mustache. 'I got it all figured out, Nightingale. Leave it to me.' He'd drive down to Elkton, Maryland, shotgun wedding capital of the East. It wouldn't take long for a justice of the peace to say some words over them and give them an 'X' to sign by. Then they could head back to Phillie, hop a flight to Miami, and catch a commuter to Nassau. He'd heard the casinos were lively, and he was ready for a new challenge.

'But I need to . . . pack.' She wanted to say let's wait. Her wedding day was supposed to be the perfect event recorded with pictures in a thick white album with gold-edged pages. But she wasn't supposed to be pregnant either. And although she wouldn't admit it to herself, and especially not to Pat, she wasn't sure until he rang the bell that he was coming back. If Ramsey was ready to get married today, how could she say no?

Ramsey took her in his arms. 'Baby, just throw some things in a bag. Whatever you need we'll pick up when we get there.' He kissed Gayle like he would swallow her whole, then she hurried upstairs.

Gayle stuffed clothes and shoes into her overnight bag, the only luggage she had. She was still too mad to speak to Joseph and Loretta, and since they had omitted some very important facts when it suited them, she could leave them out of this. *They don't have to know everything I do.*

She moved quickly, hoping to get away clean, but she couldn't help glancing at her ring. *It's at least four times as big as Brenda's!* It was just like a dream. Everything that was happening. She'd never thought about eloping, but she never considered marrying anyone but Marcus either. Now running away with the man she loved seemed so much more romantic and exciting. *And this baby will know her real mommy and daddy and that we love her.* She put on the white lace sheath she'd been saving for a special date, because nothing could be more special than her wedding day.

Ramsey drove like a bat on acid. Gayle had never seen him like this. The scenery raced by so fast it made her dizzy, and the whole time he whistled, pieces of songs, not finishing one before he took off on another melody. When he cut off a VW so close she could read curses on the driver's lips she said, 'Don't you think you should slow down?'

'Don't ever think for me, Nightingale.' Ramsey's threatening tone cut Gayle to the quick, but she bit her tongue and stayed silent.

The stop in Elkton took about as long as an oil change. The town was plain, not quaint the way Gayle had imagined, but Ramsey led her to a jewelry store and made a big deal of choosing a diamond and emerald wedding band because green was his favorite color.

Ramsey trilled the 'Wedding March' as Gayle took her place by his side under a dusty, fake flower arch. Then, the voice in her head screamed, *What am I doing? I don't know this man!* But Ramsey took her arm, and she settled down again.

The justice stood barely higher than his scarred white podium. He then raced through the vows as fast as an auctioneer at a cattle sale. 'I do' replaced 'sold,' and they became man and wife. When they kissed, Gayle swelled with a love that Ramsey had never actually spoken, but there'd be plenty of time for that. Then they were on the road back to Phillie, and, by evening, she and Ramsey were eating conch soup and fried grouper on a patio surrounded by palms fluttering in the balmy, salt-sweet sea breeze.

'How's my bride?' Ramsey held her hand as they strolled along the beach toward their hotel, the ritziest on Paradise Island, Ramsey had assured her.

'Perfect. This feels like it was meant to be,' Gayle purred.

'I wanna stop and see what's going on,' Ramsey said as they entered the hotel lobby.

'But it's our wedding night!' Gayle pleaded.

'I'll only be a few minutes. Why don't you go up and get ready for me. I'll be there soon to tuck you in.' He kissed her temple.

'You promise.'

'Promise,' he whispered, his breath hot in her ear.

So she showered, dressed, and waited. And waited. For three maddening hours, until she heard the whistling in the hall and snatched open the door. 'Where have you been?' she hissed.

'Aw now, that's not how I like to hear my Nightingale sing.' He tried to put an arm around her, but she stormed across the room. Ramsey strolled over, one hand behind his back. He thought she was cute with her brow all furrowed and that angry squeak in her voice. He liked taming it into a purr again. 'Baby, it hasn't been that long.'

'You *promised* you'd be right up!'

'. . . and what kind of man would I be if I didn't get my wife a wedding present.' He handed her a box wrapped in silver.

Gayle didn't know whether to take it or knock it on the floor. She glared at him.

'Come on . . . open it,' he coaxed.

'It's our wedding night, Ramsey, and you left me all alone!' But her anger broke, like a fever. It wasn't gone, but the danger was over.

'There's plenty of night left,' he said. 'Now go on, open it.'

She snatched the box and turned her back while she ripped off the paper. It was a watch, with a gold bracelet and diamonds around the face.

'How do you like it, baby?' He was very successful at the poker table. And, jazzed because he still had the power, he'd spent some of the proceeds on a peace offering. Ramsey came up behind her and massaged his hands over her belly.

'It's beautiful.' She fastened it on her wrist. 'But all I needed tonight was you.'

His hands rose from her belly to her waist and came to rest over her breasts, kneading them, and she turned to face him in the embrace. 'And you got me.' He rubbed his hands along her hips and gathered up the fabric of her gown until he touched bare behind. Gayle was about to speak, but the look in his eyes silenced her. It was wild, and impatient with a hunger.

'I been waiting all day, Nightingale. I need you bad.'

Gayle was suddenly ignited by his need for her. They fell into bed, and she surrendered to his urgent groping, his ferocious thrashing. Gayle could barely keep up until he shivered in an agony of release. Then his body went limp. She felt stranded between arousal and confusion as she listened to his panting relax into the low deep breaths of sleep.

The week flew by in a sun-drunk haze of clear azure

water and lazy afternoons. Ramsey would disappear into the casino in the heat of the day. 'I'm as black as I wanna be. I don't need a tan,' he said. Gayle went once. She was about to drop some coins in a slot machine, but Ramsey told her only fools feed the one-armed bandits. She watched him play poker for a while, but he tossed hundred-dollar chips around like subway tokens, and it made her nervous. Besides, she felt trapped in the windowless deep green grotto of the gaming floor. So she'd lounge by the pool signing 'Mrs Gayle Hilliard' to restaurant checks with a flourish. She'd flip through magazines, make lists of what she needed to pack when she got home, and reflect on the secret her father had shared. The more time passed, the more she remembered about the people who taught her everything, gave her whatever they had, and demanded nothing in return. She realized that she wanted to be as good to her baby as they were to her and that sometimes love is stronger than blood.

Lounging on the deck of a sailboat, Gayle finally told Ramsey about the drama she'd left at home. He tried to get her to call, but she couldn't face them on the phone. She shopped for presents in the duty-free shops. *When I get home I'll put things straight.*

9

'I hope he makes you happy . . .'

'I don't know who's gonna be madder, Momma or Daddy.' The closer Gayle got to her street, the jumpier she felt. After a week her folks would be fuming, but they deserved to stew. They *did* keep something important from her. She knew it would be awkward at first. Her mother would hug her, then fuss about how much she worried. So would her father, but he'd fuss louder and longer. He was probably in a lousy mood anyway since his new diet didn't include bacon and ice cream, but he'd be glad to see her. Gayle had it all planned. She'd apologize for upsetting them, tell them she loved them and that she was glad they were her parents, her *real* parents. Then she'd show them her rings. Loretta would kiss Ramsey and welcome him to the family, then try to feed him. *Daddy will come around as soon as he sees what a good provider Ramsey is.*

'When you say their grandchild's on the way, they won't stay mad.' Ramsey parked in front of the house. He dreaded this in-law business. The sooner it was over, the better.

'You're right!' Gayle looked adoringly at Ramsey. *My husband.* She liked the way that sounded. Then she fluttered her fingers, admired her rings, and opened the car door.

After a week in the wide-open, blue-green of the tropics, the house looked dingy, and the block seemed crowded and dirty, but Gayle got a homesick pang when she realized she wouldn't live there anymore. She clutched Ramsey's arm and headed up the walk.

'Here goes!' Gayle turned her key in the lock. 'Momma? Daddy?'

'Gayle?' Pat rushed to the door, a dish towel still in her hand.

'What's with you? You look like you had nails for breakfast.' Gayle laughed. 'Besides, I thought you were going back to Princeton?'

'Where the hell have you been? I've been out of my mind tryin' to find you!' Pat sounded both hurt and irate. 'Your mother's half-crazy, prayin' you're alive. How could you just *disappear?* What were you thinking?'

'I really did it this time, huh?' Gayle talked faster, trying to smooth Pat's ruffled feathers. 'But wait 'til I tell 'em I'm married! Pat, it was so-oo romantic. I always thought you'd be standing next to me at my wedding, but this was kinda sudden. Oh, how could I be so rude? Patricia Reid, this is my husband, Ramsey Hilliard! Pat's like my sister.'

Ramsey made a move toward Pat, who glared at him just long enough to make it clear she couldn't care less who he was. 'Gayle . . .'

'Where's Momma and Daddy? Is all that stuff left from the party? The party that never was, I should say.' She looked at the dining table laid end to end with casserole dishes, platters covered in tin foil, and cakes wrapped with wax paper. 'We'll *really* have a party when Daddy's all better, for their anniversary and our marriage and . . .'

'Gayle, shut up and stop flittin' around like this is a game!'

Gayle didn't know when she'd seen Pat so upset. 'All right,' she said quietly. 'I'll go apologize. Are they in the basement or . . .'

'You don't get it, do you?' Pat looked at Gayle with sad eyes, trying to tell her. 'Gayle, your mother's upstairs lying down.'

'Ramsey, I'll be right back.' Gayle started up the steps. If she couldn't get them at the same time, she wanted to tell her mother first, so she'd help soften up her father. 'It's only seven o'clock! What's she doing in bed? Where's Daddy?'

'Gayle . . . your father . . . Uncle Joe . . . we buried him, yesterday.'

Gayle stopped midflight, instantly cold to the bone. 'No, uh-uh.' She shook her head. 'He was gonna be fine . . . coming home in a few days!' She turned to Pat, her eyes pleading for a different truth.

Pat took Gayle's hand and led her, past Ramsey, into the kitchen. 'He had a massive heart attack, in the hospital, early Wednesday morning. I called all over. I couldn't find you, Gayle.' They held hands tightly, like in kindergarten, when they only had each other. 'I don't know what upset her more' – Pat motioned upstairs – 'Uncle Joe, or you not being here.'

'Daddy can't be . . .' Gayle stared off into the distance. She had imagined him, holding his grandchild, looking silly in love.

'Mt Moriah was packed. Marcus and his parents even came.' Pat knew it was mean, but even in her grief she was so mad at Gayle, she didn't care. The starting first baseman was back in the Orioles lineup. Marcus was headed back to AAA. Pat hadn't seen the Carters in years. His father looked the same, but his mother looked old, like she could have been his grandmother. She'd stopped

173

wandering off, but she still wasn't over Freddy's death. Pat made a point of telling Marcus to keep in touch. Gayle or no Gayle, he was a friend.

'Oh Lord, Daddy died . . . thinking I was mad at him. Pat, what am I gonna do? Momma must hate me!' Gayle wanted to wail, but for once in her life the tears wouldn't come. All the stupid things she had cried her eyes out over, all the tears wasted on nonsense, and now, when she needed tears to water down the pain, there were none.

Ramsey stood on the fringes of the conversation. He had expected flak from Joseph, but Ramsey figured he'd use 'sir' a lot and ask his advice about buying a house and that would pacify him. He wasn't worried about Loretta. She'd see the rocks on her baby's finger and be relieved that Gayle wouldn't have to work herself to death like she had. But this was a whole other thing. He didn't know these people, and he was uneasy in the middle of their family tragedy. He had to go. 'Nightingale, your momma needs you. You ought to stay here, spend some time with her. Right now, I'd just be in the way.'

Gayle let go of Pat's hand, looked at him and nodded weakly. She wanted him to help her, do this for her, but she knew she had to face this by herself.

'If there's nothin' you need me to do, I'll go on. I gotta check on some things at the shop.' Gayle walked him to the door. He gave her a quick kiss – 'I'll call later on' – and he was out the door.

For Gayle, climbing the stairs was like scaling Everest, but there would be no glory at the top. She peeked through the crack in the door to her parents' room. The light was out, and Loretta lay with her back to the door, on Joseph's side of the mahogany double bed. Gayle tiptoed in and watched her mother for a moment. As a little girl she had run in here seeking comfort. She had sneaked in, with Pat standing guard, to find the Christmas presents she was sure were hidden in the closet. Later, she had bubbled with excitement about her first boy-girl party, but this conversation would be different.

She eased down on the bed beside her mother.

'Joseph?' Loretta called out as she woke up.

'Momma, it's me.' Gayle bent over and reached to put her arms around her mother.

Loretta sat straight up and slapped Gayle as hard as she could. Gayle's hand flew to her cheek. Loretta had never laid a hand on her before. Gayle wanted this slap to sting and burn, she deserved that, but instead she felt numb.

'Oh Momma . . .'

Loretta grabbed her daughter and held her so tight that Gayle could barely breathe, but she could squeeze back. They hugged and rocked in the dim light for a long time. Gayle started to speak, but there was no excuse, no apology, and no undoing. They would live with it, but talking about it served no purpose.

After a while Loretta took Gayle's hands and pulled back to look at her daughter, absently rubbing her thumb back and forth over Gayle's fingers. 'So where's my new son?'

Gayle explained where Ramsey was and where they had been, but she had sense enough to realize that all the little details she had been so thrilled about were best left to another time, if at all.

Loretta nodded as she listened. 'Well, I guess life does go on . . . I hope he makes you happy . . . your daddy and I were happy, you know. Leastwise most of the time.' Loretta smiled, swung her legs over the edge of the bed, and slipped on her house shoes. 'But the happiest he ever made me was the day he walked in the door with you, wrapped up in Macon's shirt. Lord, I wanted you to be mine, and I wanted you to be happy all the time. I spoiled you so. Joseph would fuss . . . it was my fault . . . that we never told you . . .'

'It's okay, Momma . . . Momma? . . . You know what you said about life going on? . . . Well, uh . . . We're . . . I'm pregnant. You're gonna have a grandchild to spoil now.'

Loretta's eyes filled with tears. *What would Joseph say?* Hesitantly, she reached toward Gayle's belly, toward a new life. *Is this really my grandchild?* Gayle took her mother's hand and placed it over the spot where she imagined the baby was. *'Course it's ours.'* She could hear Joseph clear as day. 'My, my, all this news . . . I was goin' to make some tea, but . . .'

'I'll bring you a cup, Momma.'

When Gayle got to the kithen, Pat was simmering and devouring a slab of pound cake. She had been ravenous since the day Joseph died. Friends and neighbors made sure there was plenty to choose from, but she never felt full.

The past week had been hell. When Gayle didn't come home, Pat dug around in her things and found Ramsey's card. After Pat did a lot of explaining, his secretary admitted he was off getting married, but she had no idea where. Pat put two and two together which kept Loretta calm enough to see after her husband, but they notified the police, just in case.

The last time Pat had stopped by the hospital Joseph looked chipper. He asked about Gayle. They didn't tell him she was missing, just home upset. He seemed to take it in his stride. Then he asked if the Mets and Orioles won and cracked Pat up when he said he was going to take up tennis for exercise so he could show off his legs. Pat left feeling confident he was better. The next morning the phone call came.

From one minute to the next, Pat hadn't known if Loretta would recall something Joseph had said and dissolve, beg Jesus to watch over Gayle, yell about her daughter being spoiled and selfish, or take the blame for not telling her the truth sooner. Every time the phone rang, Loretta jumped like she heard a shot, and when it didn't ring, she'd pick it up to check for a dial tone. So Pat coordinated the funeral, choking back the overwhelming sadness she felt every time she realized her Uncle Joe was gone. He had always been supportive, proud, and loving. Pat missed him terribly and was pricked more times than she cared to remember by the innocent and well-meaning for whom 'Are you family?' was a routine question, not a deliberate reminder that she was not.

The story that Gayle had run off to get married and couldn't be found was too awful and juicy not to spread like a flash flood, but Uncle Macon, who came every day, made sure that not one soul had the nerve to mention it to Loretta.

Now she shows up with a suntan, wearing a damn jewelry store on her hand. Pat heard Ramsey's sorry-assed good-bye and wondered what kind of husband would leave his pregnant bride when she'd just found out her father had died? *What does Gayle see in him?* Pat guessed he was handsome, if you liked that type, but he was too slick. *She didn't have to get married just because she was pregnant. I would have helped her. But getting married is all she ever wanted. Uncle Joe was right. Gayle thinks this is the breeze that'll take her where she wants to go.*

'Momma wants some tea.' Gayle headed for the stove.

Pat reached and turned the fire on under the kettle.

'I'll make it.' Gayle opened the cabinet for a cup and saucer.

'Yeah, well, I guess it's the least you could do.' Pat could understand being angry with someone for giving you away, disowning you. She knew what that felt like. And she had been upset when she found out MaRay had deceived her, but Pat couldn't imagine ever acting as ungrateful and inconsiderate as Gayle had.

'What's that supposed to mean? You don't think I would've eloped if I thought Daddy was . . .'

'What? Gonna die? Gayle, you were so pissed off all you wanted to do was hurt them. You could've called. But you didn't. I can hear you now. "It'll serve them right to worry about me." You didn't even *consider* the possibility your father might get worse.'

'How can you say that?'

'I know you didn't, Gayle. All you could think about was you, as usual.'

'I was wrong. I know that and I know I'll never be able to make up for what I did.' Gayle's whole body trembled, and she felt sick to her stomach, but still the tears wouldn't come. 'Momma knows how sorry I am. Tomorrow I'll get Ramsey to take me to the cemetery to see Daddy and . . .'

'All is forgiven? You know sometimes when we were little, I'd be so jealous because you had parents who loved you so much. And your father . . . I remember at Freddy's funeral when Uncle Joe rocked you like a baby. I wanted somebody to hold me like that, like MaRay used to. Gayle, I loved your father like he was my own. And you know, he was, at least in every way that counted. You weren't here, and I did everything I could, everything.'

'I know you did, Pat, and I'm glad you were here, for Momma and for Daddy.'

'Uh-huh. Look at this.' Pat handed Gayle the funeral

178

program that was left wedged in the napkin holder. The photo on the front was the one Pat had taken of Joseph in his groom suit. 'Open it.' Gayle did as she was told. 'Right there, read that.'

'Joseph Saunders is survived by his devoted wife of thirty-five years, the former Loretta Howard,' Gayle said. 'And one loving daughter, Gayle . . .'

Pat walked out the back door.

She lit a cigarette and started walking. Her brain was stuck in the last week, like a car in a ditch. Five steps down, seven out the gate. The harder she spun her wheels to get out, the deeper the ruts became, so she counted every step and sucked in smoke so she couldn't think of anything that hurt. Thirty-six paces to the corner, red light. She stopped. A bus, grunting and passing exhaust gas, rumbled by leaving a ghostly gray funk hanging in the humid July air. She threw her cigarette in the gutter and held her breath, *one Mississippi, two Mississippi,* until the smoke cleared, the light changed, and she continued, counting and walking, a zombie out for an evening stroll.

Three little brown stair-step boys approached her, seriously involved in a contest to see who could suck his Popsicle the loudest.

'The next one a you I hear is goin' to bed as soon as we get home,' the woman behind them warned.

'Ah Ma!' they wailed in unison.

Must be her children . . . I'm nobody's child . . . nobody's child . . . Stop it! Pat restarted the count and walked until the bottoms of her feet burned against the rope soles of her espadrilles. She stopped, looked up, and realized she was standing across the intersection from the Easy Street Bar & Grill.

Shit! What the hell am I doing here! She'd left the house with no place in mind and this was the last no place in the world she meant to end up, but she stared at the storefront with turrets painted on the stucco, like somebody might actually mistake it for a castle. *She probably doesn't even work here anymore.* The idea that Verna could still be slinging shots at the same gin joint seemed ridiculous, but where else would she be? *Dead for all I know.*

Pat crossed the street. A poster in the corner of the window announced a 'Boogie Down Summer Sizzler and Fashion Xtravaganza' at St Albans Plaza. She tried to peek inside, but dusty blinds blocked her view. *I have nothing to say to her.* She swiped beads of sweat from her forehead. *But I could use a damned drink and a seat.* She opened the door.

It was as hot inside as out. Jazzy organ music, laced with bourbon and payday, came from the jukebox to the right of the door. Pat saw her as soon as she walked in. Verna was at the far end of the bar, refilling the display of pork rinds and Lance peanuts. She looked up when she heard the barstool scrape the floor as Pat sat down.

'Be right with ya, honey,' she shouted over the music and wolf tickets being bought and sold by the glassful.

Pat watched her in the mirror behind the bar, collecting empty glasses and tips, wiping up spills, tucking the towel back in the waist of her black apron. Verna didn't look as bad as she had six years ago, the last time Pat had seen her. She wore too much iridescent eye shadow, false lashes, frosted lipstick, and a mess of curly, fake hair. *She looks like a reject from the Supremes.* Pat had no expectations when she'd walked in. She thought about her mother once in a while, but Verna had become like one of those books you start a few times because you think you should, but the story never grabs you, you don't care how it ends, and then you realize you just don't like it.

'It's hot as hell.' Verna blew into the low neckline of her

green tank top. 'Air conditioner's busted, but ain't nothin' stops them.' She nodded toward the noisy crowd.

Pat hesitated. 'Vodka and tonic.'

'You got it.' She poured a shot, added the mixer. 'Lime?' Verna looked at her customer closely for the first time, squinting, frowning. 'Pat?'

'Yep.' *Why does she always look at me like she's got a bad taste in her mouth?*

'You old enough to be . . .'

'Pretty much anyplace I choose. And yeah, I'd like lime.'

Verna added the wedge, took a napkin from a stack fanned in a spiral, and set the drink in front of Pat. 'I guess that's right. You must be what . . . twenty, twenty-one?'

She acts like she wasn't there. Pat took a sip. 'Is there someplace we can talk?' The only way to start this conversation was straight, no chaser. 'You wouldn't tell me anything the last time I asked, but I need to know . . . about my father.'

Verna emptied an ashtray. 'If you're old enough to buy a drink, I guess you can hear this.' She poured herself a Johnnie Red, neat, and called to the waitress who was fanning herself with a Ballantine tray. 'Lily, watch the bar for me. I gotta take care of something.' Verna led Pat to a booth in the back.

She took a gulp of her drink and fished in her pocket for cigarettes. 'It was summertime. I was nineteen. He was twenty-three. Come to North Carolina to register voters. Mississippi's what most folks heard about, but votin' fever was all over the South. They was concentratin' on all the little jackleg towns, and Swan City was one of 'em.' She peeled the cellophane from the fresh pack, tore an opening in the bottom corner, and tapped one out.

'I had a job at a dry cleaners in town, ironin' shirts. I

181

used to catch a ride with Lil' Daddy in the morning, but I walked home every night.' She lit up, taking a long slow drag. 'Turner, his name was Turner, drove the same road I walked just about every day, and he'd stop to offer me a ride. Asked three times before I said yes.'

When Pat lit her own cigarette, Verna raised an eyebrow, but said nothing.

Pat scrutinized Verna's features, beyond the wig and heavy makeup, looking for a resemblance, something that might connect her to this woman.

'He was good-looking, wore a tie every day . . . and the whitest shirts I ever saw, always with cuff links. Not them big flashy ones. These were refined, his initials in fourteen-carat gold. He was smart and talked all proper. Told me he just finished law school. Shit, I thought he knew more than all my teachers put together, but he said it wasn't nothin'. His whole family had been to college, even his grandparents. They were all doctors and lawyers, high muck de mucks in Virginia.' Verna looked past Pat, like she was reading words written in the air.

'He didn't act stuck-up, but MaRay told me not to mess with him 'cause he didn't want but one thing from a girl like me. I wasn't never pretty, but boys had been sniffin' around 'cause I had a big butt and big titties, well developed as they used to say.' She took a swallow of scotch. 'MaRay always did read people good, but I was young.'

Pat tugged at her blouse, trying to hide the gap that strained the buttons on the front, a gap that hadn't been there last week.

'He started ridin' me home every night, tellin' me about sit-ins and New York City, all kinds a shit I didn't know about. Gave me a fake gold necklace, a mustard seed in a little glass ball, probably from Kresges'. I acted such a fool, you woulda thought it was diamond. He read me poems and told me he loved me, and I was dumb enough to believe him.' Verna struck a match and let it burn down almost to her finger before she shook it out.

'Two weeks before he was supposed to leave, I told him I was pregnant. He looked me dead in my face, called me a stupid little country nigger. I grabbed his hand, and he snatched it away like he was all of a sudden too good to touch me. I was left holding a damned cuff link. He left the next day. Sweet MaRay said I had it comin'. I called. Even took the bus to Richmond, eight months pregnant. His momma called the cops on me. It wasn't long after, you were born. I figured MaRay already knew more than I wanted to about babies, so I left, moved up here.' She dropped the cigarette butt in her empty glass.

'So his last name is Turner. Does he have a first name?'

'Turner is his first name. He's one a them important Negroes now, the ones we supposed to look up to. His last name is Hughes. Turner Everett Hughes.' Verna dabbed at the sweat that trickled from beneath her wig.

Pat couldn't have heard right. *Not **THE** Turner Hughes?* 'You knew Turner Hughes?' *Turner Hughes from the Vineyard. Turner Hughes on the* Ebony *cover?*

'Oh, I knew him all right. Or at least I was stupid enough to think I did. The man had a silver tongue. I didn't figure out 'til too late it was forked.'

'Fine. If you don't want to tell me the truth, then say so, but don't sit here making up crazy bullshit and expect me to buy it.'

'You the one came in here askin' about your father. You think I picked his name out the paper and spent twenty years makin' up a story for you.' Verna examined Pat's face. She looked just like her and Turner, mashed up together, but that hurt too much to dwell on.

'I don't know,' Pat said. And that was the truth. Her drink was untouched, but she felt dizzy, like she was on the Coney Island ride that spins 'round and 'round, faster and faster until the floor drops out. And there she was, still spinning, stuck to the wall. 'I know him . . . I mean . . . I met him once.' *Turner Hughes can't be my father. He never would have been bothered with somebody like her.* She looked at Verna's cheap clothes and remembered how crisp and perfect Turner Hughes had looked. *Those white shirts.*

Verna struck another match. The fire faded from orange to blue as it worked its way down the match stem. 'Lovin' Turner was the worst mistake I ever made. If you see him again, tell him I said you're the real mustard seed.' The smell of burned popcorn filled Pat's nostrils. She leaned over and blew out the tiny flame on the end of Verna's thumbnail.

'There ain't no more to it.' Verna slid to the end of the booth. 'Take as long as you want, but I gotta get back to the bar.'

Pat sat a minute. She had expected Verna to say it was some boy from Swan City, or even that she didn't know who her father was. But the notion of a young and vulnerable Verna duped by a sophisticated stranger was as foreign and ridiculous to her as the idea that Turner Hughes could be her father.

Pat looked up when she heard Verna laugh, loud and raunchy. She was pouring a drink order for Lily and still chuckling at the joke. *Uncle Joe's dead. Gayle's pregnant and married, and Turner Hughes is my father?* On her way out Pat dropped three dollars on the bar. *Yep, I gotta get outta Dodge before shit gets any weirder.*

Pat wanted something to take with her to remember Uncle Joe by. Before she left Queens she dug in the back of the kitchen junk drawer, looking for his lucky rabbit's foot. He used to get it and make a big deal of rubbing it when he played crazy eights with her and Gayle around the kithen table. It was still there. Pat had given it to him the first Father's Day after she'd come to live in the Saunders house. He had laughed and hugged her and told her to remember there was no better luck than love.

When she got back to Princeton she decided to put the key chain away for safekeeping, so she unearthed MaRay's bergamot tin. Even though Pat had created a new history for herself, she hadn't thrown out that can of old junk. It was all she had of a past she wasn't ready to let go. It was her legacy, and she was going to add Uncle Joe to it.

Pat pulled off the lid, dropped the key chain inside, and was about to close it when she spied the small gold cuff link. She'd forgotten it was there. *'And I was left holding a damn cuff link.' That's what Verna said*. Pat picked up the oval. T.H.E. the initials read. *Turner Everett Hughes, Verna said*.

10

'. . . a long way from that little matchbox in Queens.'

1980 WHITE PLAINS, NEW YORK

'Go on, pick her up. You're not an official auntie until she spits up on you, so you may as well get it over with.'

Pat hesitated. *An auntie?*

During her pregnancy Gayle kept Pat updated with progress reports. They spoke more in seven months than in the last several years, but Pat always hung up feeling detached.

Vanessa Josephine Hilliard was born right after the New Year. Pat sent a silver-plated piggy bank, but she couldn't bring herself to visit. She had had a wicked case of the flu as an excuse. Then she was knee-deep in the spring semester, but school was out, Vanessa was sitting up, and Gayle threatened never to speak to Pat if she didn't get there soon.

And sometimes Pat wondered if that was such a bad idea. Gayle had gotten the life she always wanted with the husband, the house, and now a baby. Pat was happy for her, but this was Gayle's life with Gayle's family again, and Pat had the nagging feeling she'd always be the one left with no chair whenever the music stopped.

Then Gayle called and Pat heard Vanessa gurgling in the background. It hit her that Gayle, who used to mommy her dolls for hours when they were kids, actually had a daughter. It seemed amazing and wonderful, and Pat got a powerful urge to see this little girl, so she gave in and went to Westchester.

'You act like there's something to be scared of.'

Pat rubbed Vanessa's cheek, and the baby treated her to a gummy grin that gave Pat the courage to hold her. She was surprised by how warm and moist Vanessa felt through her terry cloth stretchy.

'Ramsey bought everything blue because he was so sure she was a boy. We had to take it all back, and I'm still not sure he's over it, but he says he is.'

'She's beautiful, Gayle.' On cue, milky spit dribbled from the baby's mouth. Auntie Pat wiped the sour spit with a clean diaper. In an alto whisper she sang '. . . and when you wake, you'll have some cake and five or six little horsies . . .'

'What's that?' Gayle asked.

'MaRay used to sing it to me.' A strong tug from a lonely place deep inside yanked Pat off-balance. 'Here, you better take her. Let's finish the rest of the tour.'

Gayle had described the house ad nauseam, which Pat took with a grain of salt, but the handsome Tudor lived up to the coming attractions. The lawn was Crayola green and plush as carpet, with precisely groomed hedges to mark the borders and flower beds down the walk. And the idea that all this belonged to Gayle blew Pat's mind.

'I wanted something lighter and more modern, but Ramsey said deep colors and oriental carpets looked classier. He insisted we get a decorator, who agreed with him.'

I'm bustin' my hump in college, and she's talking about damned decorators. Pat followed her into the living room, wrestling a creeping resentment. 'No plastic covers!'

'You *know* Momma said we should get some, with Vanessa and all. Ramsey informed her this furniture doesn't have to last forever. When it wears out he'll buy some more.'

'Uh-huh.' Pat trailed along, hearing what Ramsey liked, thought, did, and said until it came out her ears. When they returned to the sleek white kitchen Gayle put Vanessa in the high chair and the baby chewed on a rattle and gurgled in the light streaming through French doors that led to the patio.

'I wish it was warmer so we could go out by the pool.' Gayle spooned strained chicken, squash, and peas into a sectioned dish.

Pool. Right. Pat wanted a cigarette in a serious way. 'I've got an internship this summer at Comstock Gravitt Greene. They're one of the biggest ad agencies in the business.'

'I thought you were going to be a doctor.' Gayle retrieved the rattle from the floor, where Vanessa promptly threw it again.

'I told you I'd changed my mind a long time ago. After bio, chem, and anatomy and physiology I realized I didn't give a shit what the thigh bone was connected to.'

'No cursing, Auntie Pat,' Gayle admonished, and pulled a chair up to the baby.

Right. 'I switched majors sophomore year.' *If you ever listened to me, you'd know.* 'Anyway, I asked your mom if I could stay in Queens for the summer.' Pat leaned against the butcher-block kitchen island. Just like in St Albans, plants lined the windowsills, but there were no cuttings in jelly jars here, nothing taking root – just perfect, full-grown plants.

'I know. She told me when I went to see Daddy last week.'

189

'You what?'

'I go to the cemetery every month, on the fifteenth 'cause his birthday was the fifteenth. Ramsey makes fun of me, but I don't care.'

Pat had lots to say on that, like 'If you'd been home when you should have, you wouldn't be feeling so guilty and all the grave visiting in the world won't change that,' but she didn't. For a minute she considered telling Gayle about Turner, but there was no point since she didn't know what that meant yet herself, if anything. All she had right now was a scrapbook of everything she could find on Turner Hughes and the intention to make something of herself, so that one day, maybe, she'd be in a position to tell him she was his daughter. At that point it would be obvious she was nothing like Verna, that Pat was someone he would be proud to accept. *Gayle would probably tell me to send him some sappy Father's Day card, and then he'll welcome me with open arms. Right.*

After lunch Gayle put the baby down for a nap and put a roast she'd been marinating into the oven. Pat watched in amazement as she washed broccoli and shaped triangles of dough into crescent rolls, ready to bake. *Gayle barely made cereal at home.*

'So, do you like all this? It's what you always wanted.'

'What kinda question is that? This is the best thing that ever happened to me. It's like Marcus never existed. I love Ramsey and Vanessa, we have a great life, and Ramsey says it's only gonna get better. He says I'm his lucky charm.'

The speech came too quickly and straight from the can, but Pat didn't press the issue.

An hour before Ramsey was due home, Gayle fluffed sofa pillows, set the table with flowered place mats and napkins, and put the mail by Ramsey's plate. 'The

important mail, like bills and stuff, goes to the office,'
Gayle explained.

Like I care. Pat already knew too much about the
routine at the Hilliard house. She followed upstairs, where
Gayle changed from slacks and sweater to a blue-and-
white pin dot drop waist dress, heels, and hose, and
freshened her makeup.

'I thought you looked nice before.'

'Ramsey likes to see both of us looking pretty . . . even
though I'm still fat.' Gayle pivoted in the full-length mirror.

I'm gonna puke. 'Whatever it is, it's hardly an oink,
Gayle.' She looked as slim as always. They headed for
Vanessa's fantasy fairyland nursery, where Gayle got the
baby up. She wasn't through with her nap yet, so getting
her dressed was a struggle.

'You do this every day?'

'Uh-huh . . . Yes. Ramsey works hard, so I like to make
it nice for him at home.'

'Gayle . . . what do you do for money?' She'd been
dying to ask the question, and now seemed as good a time
as any.

'Ramsey gives me all I need, and I have credit cards.
What do you think I do? His money is *our* money.'

*No, it's his money. You get an allowance. It wouldn't be
me.* The front door opened, keys rattled. 'Where are my
girls?'

'Oops, I'm late.' Gayle grabbed the baby and headed for
the foyer.

Late for what? Pat followed downstairs, where she found
Ramsey kissing Gayle. It looked so strange. *I always
thought she'd be with Marcus.* Pat wasn't even sure Gayle
and Marcus were right for each other, whatever that
meant, but she always pictured them together. *I wonder
what he's up to.*

Pat offered Ramsey her usual, firm handshake, which he seemed to take as a challenge. 'You're the one with the big career plans. Gonna be a doctor, right?'

'Career yes. Doctor no.'

Ramsey wasn't listening. He played with Vanessa for about thirty seconds, while Gayle went to the kitchen and returned with iced tea, which she gave Ramsey in exchange for the baby. It was like a well-rehearsed ritual that Pat thought she shouldn't be seeing. Ramsey excused himself and went upstairs, and Gayle's next move was back to the kitchen to feed the baby and complete dinner.

'He likes to shower when he gets home, so I get Vanessa taken care of and the food hot so when he comes down we're ready to eat.' Gayle sounded proud of the routine she'd worked out.

The whole process gave Pat the creeps.

Vanessa wasn't interested in her dinner, and as soon as Gayle spooned it in, she spit it out. Then she squeezed a handful of carrots into her hair and wailed the whole time Gayle tried to clean her up. Pat watched the pots while Gayle, who was getting flustered, attended to the mess.

Pat could hear Ramsey trot downstairs and take his seat in the dining room. He opened mail and whistled, like a bird without a care, while Gayle brought the food in, served his plate, and set the baby in her mahogany dining-room high chair.

Pat was outdone by the dinner dance. She ate and searched for a neutral topic of conversation, but she couldn't find anything to say to them. Besides, Gayle was busy hanging on Ramsey's every bite. Then Ramsey started in. He complained the roast was too done, the rolls were doughy, and Gayle looked crestfallen. 'My baby's not the best cook in the world.' Ramsey patted Gayle's hand.

What are you, a damn food critic? 'I think dinner tastes

great.' *Be civil, Pat.* 'I don't know how you do it with Vanessa and all.' Pat's free hand was balled in a fist on the table.

'Some days it's really hard, but I couldn't do what you do either. Ramsey, she got herself an internship at the biggest ad agency in New York!'

'Internship? You said you weren't gonna be a doctor.'

'It's not a medical internship. I'll be . . .'

'Nightingale, get me some hot sauce, will you?' Gayle went to the kitchen. 'Your friend's done all right for herself. This is a long way from that little matchbox in Queens.' Ramsey pushed away from the table and nodded as he surveyed his domain. 'There's a pool you know.'

Pat wanted to throw daggers. Gayle returned and presented Ramsey the Tabasco. 'Pat, Momma fell in love with this place as soon as she saw it.' Just then Vanessa flung her rattle and it landed in Gayle's glass with a splash.

Ramsey frowned. 'As high as my phone bill to Queens is every month, it'd be cheaper to move Loretta in here. Then there'd be somebody else to keep an eye on that baby.'

'Oh, are you planning to go to work, Gayle?'

Ramsey stopped midshake, set the bottle down, and leveled an indignant look at Pat. 'My wife won't ever need to work. I'll see to that.'

Vanessa wanted out of her high chair, and she whined and wriggled.

'Can't you keep her quiet?' Ramsey grumbled.

Pat was ready to stand on the table and ask who died and made him king, but Gayle shot her a 'leave it alone' look, so she pushed food around her plate while Gayle tended to her daughter.

When Ramsey finished eating he gathered the mail and went to the den. Pat wanted to cheer. She helped clear the dishes and asked Gayle to call a cab because she had to go before she really said something out of line.

'Ramsey can take you to the train . . . or you can stay.'

'No really, a cab is fine.' Pat didn't even know when the next train was, but she'd rather wait at the station than risk another go-round with Gayle's husband. She had tried to like him. They met under funky circumstances, but she had planned to wipe the slate clean. If Aunt Loretta could accept him, Pat could at least try, but from the word 'go' he was on her wrong side.

When the taxi beeped, Pat hugged Vanessa for a long moment.

'You act like you'll never see her again.'

Deep down Pat knew it would be a while before she did. 'Don't be silly . . . I gotta go, the meter's running. Some of us aren't rich yet.' She handed Vanessa back, gave Gayle a quick squeeze, and was out the door.

Over the summer Pat saw Gayle and the baby a few times. Gayle would stop in St Albans on the way to the cemetery or drive out to bring her mother up for a visit. Gayle tried to get Pat to come, but she was too busy on the job. At least that's what she said.

Pat's internship was exciting and nonstop, and, at the end of the summer, her supervisor at Comstock Gravitt Greene took her aside, told her they liked her, and strongly suggested there'd be a position waiting at CGG after graduation. Pat couldn't believe it. Knowing at the beginning of senior year that she already had an offer from a top agency would take the pressure off.

She'd hardly seen Althea all summer, aside from an occasional shared elevator, but Pat ventured up to her office and asked what she thought it meant. 'It means you have a job if you want it. Don't think they say it to everybody because they're not that nice, and if you're smart, you'll get yourself a counteroffer so they have to pay you more.' They chatted long enough for Pat to ask Althea if she was planning to vacation on the Vineyard. 'I keep in touch with the Littlefield sisters, you remember, Dorothea and Minnie, blue hair and matching wardrobes. Anyway, they invited me up, but I can't go.'

'There's not a thing on that island that interests me that I can't find somewhere else,' Althea said, dismissing the idea.

Pat figured she should drop the subject, but curiosity wouldn't let her. 'So, what happened with you and Turner Hughes?'

Althea entwined her fingers and laid her hands down on the desk. 'Turner Hughes has a whole lot of money and a whole lot of power and when I was with him, he never let me forget it. That got tired in a hurry.'

Pat didn't know why, but what Althea said annoyed her, so she gathered her papers and left the office.

Pat didn't see the Hilliards again until Christmas, and she only went then because she couldn't think of an excuse not to. The house looked like a Yuletide spectacular on the MGM back lot. Garlands, wreaths, and red velvet bows decked the halls, doors, and every window. The towering Douglas fir, glittering with lights and decorations, was surrounded by enough toys to last Vanessa until puberty.

Pat and Ramsey got into it when her present for Vanessa was opened, a plastic airplane on wheels.

'That's no kinda gift for a girl.' Ramsey scowled.

'What does that mean? She can ride on it and push it around. I saw a little girl playing with one in the store, and she didn't want to let it go.'

'I don't care what you saw. That's a boy's toy.'

'And why is that? Because only boys are supposed to

grow up and fly airplanes? I suppose you'd like it better if I got her a baby carriage.'

Gayle tried to stay neutral and referee, but it was clear to Pat which side of the fence her friend was on. Finally Aunt Loretta told them it was the Lord's birthday and there would be no more fussing. Pat and Ramsey stopped arguing, but they glared at each other like sworn enemies. *If those are the house rules, I need to stay out of this house 'cause I'm not gonna bite my tongue off just to keep Gayle's man happy. She married this asshole, but I don't have to like him.*

When Pat woke up on New Year's Eve the sky was gray with the promise of snow. Nineteen eighty-one was going to be an important year, the real beginning of her life. Once in a while she wondered if she'd made the right decision about medical school, but she was ready to stop studying and live. Nobody with good sense and a place to be was on campus, but Pat decided it was exactly how she wanted to start the year, alone, with enough quiet to hear herself think, so when the phone rang she was surprised.

'Don't you ever leave school?'

'Marcus?' He was the last person she expected to hear from.

'I called Queens and got your number from Miz Saunders. Whatcha doin' tonight?'

'I don't know Marcus. I . . .'

'Good. I'm heading back to Florida, and I'll stop on my way down.'

'Did you hear me invite you?'

'Did you hear me ask?'

'Ask? Marcus Carter did I hear you say A-S-K? What happened to AKS?'

'You don't have to be in college to learn some shit, Miss Ivy League smart-ass. Listen, I wanna *ask* your opinion about somethin' since you do more readin' than anybody I know. I won't even be around long enough to get in your little bit a hair.'

'You already are.'

'Don't blame me 'cause you need dandruff shampoo. Now, you gonna give me directions?'

She hadn't talked with him since the funeral, and then barely for two minutes. *If he'd taken that baseball scholarship, he'd be graduating, too.*

'Damn, what they feed you to make you grow like that?' Marcus arrived a little after four carrying two grocery bags and a tooled leather satchel. His black cowboy brim had a generous dusting of snow, and the crown nearly brushed the top of the doorsill.

'Bullshit and promises.' The black leather trench coat he wore knotted tight at the waist heightened his imposing look.

Marcus set the bags on the floor. 'And you . . . turn around, let me see. You lookin' kinda slim and sassy in your jeans there, Miss Reid. You probably in love with some dude who wears tweed clothes and smokes a pipe.'

'Marcus, don't they teach you to step back before the balls hit you in the head?'

'Sometimes I let 'em hit me just to show what a mean mo fo I really am.' Marcus grinned and that dimple winked at her, then he took off his hat and coat, dug around the grocery bag, and opened two bottles of beer. 'What they got, around six Black folks in this town? I stopped at a store, and they acted like I'm a damned bandit. Suddenly stock boy is straightenin' potato chips and cans a creamed corn wherever I happen to be.' He handed Pat a beer and sprawled in her armchair.

'Yeah, well, welcome to university village, where you're

always the exception and not the rule.' She saluted him with her bottle, straddled her desk chair, and took a swallow. 'Besides, you look like the damned Cisco Kid. What's with the hat?'

'Just call me "Dark Rider." I always wear some crazy hat. It's an image thing. I dig 'em, and it gives people something to talk about. I gotta stand out from the crowd every way I can.'

'I thought you do that on the field.'

'That ain't all. I figured out it's not just numbers. I got decent numbers, and I been up and down to the show a couple a times. Part of it's luck, but somebody's gotta retire, get traded, or so broke up he can't hobble around the bases before there's a spot for you.'

'It's like that whatever you do, Marcus,' Pat said.

Marcus leaned forward, intense, fists clenched. 'Yeah, but it's not like civil service, where the next one in line moves up the ladder. You gotta act like you belong. Like you special enough to make a stadium full a people yell your name like they love you more than their mother. You start gettin' attention in rinky-dink ballparks with clowns running around the bases between innings and kids hangin' over the fence askin' for autographs. Now, if you give the sportswriters something besides boring-ass strikes and runs to write about, show 'em some personality, it makes 'em happy. Then management starts to look at you like they got something which makes 'em feel smart, so they play you more, and finally the agents start sniffin' around and you almost got yourself a deal.'

'And where are you in this chain of events?' Pat had never heard Marcus break it down like this, and she realized he was as driven as she was.

'Close enough to smell it. Keeps my damn mouth watering all the time.' He got a manila envelope out of his satchel and handed it to Pat. 'That's where the opinion part comes in, smart stuff. I had an agent offer to rep me. I like the guy 'cause he talks straight. He was a hotshot defensive end outta UCLA, but he busted up his knee senior year, right before the NFL draft.' Marcus shook his head. 'Damn. That musta hurt, to get so close. Anyway, he went to law school and became a rep with this big-ass sports management agency, but he just left them to set up his own. The good thing is that he knows what it's like to be a player, and he's really okay people, for a White dude. And the way I figure it, he's just startin' out, so he's hungry. I am, too, and two hungry people workin' together got a better chance of findin' somethin' to eat, but I want you to read the papers and make sure I'm not missin' somethin' important.'

'You need your own lawyer, Marcus. I've never looked at anything like this before.'

'I know a lawyer in Florida. I'll see him when I get down there, but I want somebody I can trust, who knows the way things should be, to read 'em, 'cause you'll tell me if you think it's stupid, or what questions to ask, without makin' me feel dumb. I tried asking Booker T., but all he kept sayin' was, "You gon' give somebody ten percent a yo' money? For what? Give me ten percent if you wanna give somethin' away." Shit, I can't make him understand nothin'.'

Pat felt honored that he trusted her, like when they were kids. She pulled out the papers, reached for her cigarettes.

'Don't tell me you sucking tar sticks.'

'Keeps my hands and my mouth busy.'

'I'd rather see you eat. Damn, maybe you not as smart as I thought.'

'Hush, Marcus. Don't you baseball players chew tobacco and spit all the time?'

'Not me. Makes your teeth look like you been drinkin' motor oil, and your breath stinks.' He reached for the paper bag. 'You want a sandwich or something to put in your mouth?'

'Never mind.' Pat dropped the pack and went through the contract while Marcus nosed around.

He picked up a thick volume from the top of her bookcase. '*Each One Teach One*. Damn, you read this whole thing?' He weighed the book in his right hand.

'Yep. Cover to cover.'

'Hey, your name is in here!'

'You remember Miss Cooke, from junior high? She hired me to help her finish it, the summer . . .' . . . *I ran away because you* . . . 'The summer you went to . . . Erie, wasn't it?'

Pat finished reading, then they went over the contract together. When she pointed to a paragraph she thought was unclear Marcus took the pages to make a note in the margin and his hand brushed hers. His skin was rough, but like flint on a match it caused a spark in Pat, and she got up and moved around to keep it from catching.

When they were done Pat handed him another beer to open for her. 'So, where are you going to ring in the new year?'

'I got nothin' planned. Mind you, I coulda been lots a places with some very talented young ladies.'

'Talented huh. That mean they play piano?'

'Not necessarily, but they're mellifluous in other ways.'

'Mellifluous?'

'Oh yeah.' He winked. 'In any case, y'all think if you're with a man when that clock strikes midnight it means you got him for the rest of the year, and I don't mean to give nobody the wrong impression.'

'Is that right?'

'Yeah, it's right. I need some TLC sometime, and I know where I can get it.' Pat looked at him with a smirk. 'Don't get me wrong. I don't dog nobody. I just don't make promises I know I won't keep. I can't let nothin' and nobody tie me down 'cause I got things to do.' Marcus rubbed his chin and grinned at her. 'And yourself? Anybody around to, uh, take care a bizness?'

'As much *business* as I got time to take care of.' *What am I gonna say, my love life sucks? Pity ain't pretty.* 'I get what I need, and getting back to this contract, will this get you what you need?'

'I've seen it before, Pat. A man gets an agent and all of a sudden he's playin' in a different league.'

'And if it doesn't happen?'

'I'll worry about that some other time.'

'Then I think you should trust your guts. It doesn't look like the contract sells you into slavery. If you think the guy will work for you, go for it.'

Marcus opened a beer and clinked Pat's bottle. 'To going for it.'

They ate heroes, drank beer, and talked, like they did this every week. Pat said things she hadn't said to anybody, like how she lied about her family.

'That's weird, Pat. It's like nobody who knows you, really knows you.'

'Yeah. And they'd feel a whole lot better about me if I told them about Verna, right? And my father . . .' She almost blurted out the Turner Hughes story, just to see if it made any more sense coming out of her mouth than it did swimming around in her head, but she wasn't ready yet. 'Who the fuck knows about my father.'

They were quiet for a while. 'Gayle still with that greazy son of a bitch?'

'Why you call him that?'

'Somethin' ain't right about it.'

'Yeah, I don't like him much either.'

'How come you don't say nothin' to her? You're her friend.'

'She didn't ask me when she married him. What am I supposed to say now? I think your husband's an asshole?'

Marcus shrugged, crumpled the foil from his sandwich, and banked it off the desk and into the trash. 'Anyway, this is the last night of the year. What are we doin' in this sorry-ass room? We should be out somewhere raisin' hell.'

'Not in this town. Hell won't raise here. It's a law.'

'What time is it?'

'Quarter to twelve.'

'We gotta at least go outside for midnight. No disrespect, but this room is not the first thing I wanna see next year.'

They put on coats and went out into snow that was past their ankles and still falling in slow, fat, flakes.

'Let's go to that big street that leads into the campus. Something must be jumpin' off there.'

'I swear there isn't.'

'We can at least go see.' Marcus walked quickly.

Pat, giddy from the beer, stopped and opened her mouth wide so she could feel the lacy cold flakes land on her tongue and melt. 'Wait up, Marcus. Some of us don't have stilts for legs.'

'Come on, girl . . . act like you got lead in your butt. Oh, excuse me. This is college, let me be proper. Lead in your buttocks.'

'You can kiss my buttocks.' She flung a hastily made snowball in his direction.

'Oh ho, is this the game? I can play this.' Marcus hurled one back that grazed her shoulder. They tossed snow at each other until he had her running for cover.

'I surrender! I surrender!' Pat was laughing so hard her stomach ached.

'Thought I'd never hear *you* say that. Come here. I'll get the snow off. You look like Frosty the Snowman.' Marcus brushed snow out of her hair, lingering a moment. Then they heard horns and noisemakers echoing in the distance.

'What time is it?' Pat asked.

Marcus checked his watch. 'Midnight, straight up.' They were standing so close.

Pat broke away and twirled like a top. 'Happy New Year!' Her yell repeated in the night.

'Happy New Year!' Marcus tossed his hat in the air and hollered.

They continued out onto the street, his arm around her shoulder, hers at his waist.

'What's that song people always get drunk and sing on New Year's? Old somethin' or other,' he asked.

'"Auld Lang Syne."' Pat trotted to keep up with him.

'What the hell does that mean?'

'It's about old friends never forgetting each other.'

'It's a dry-ass song.'

Pat sang at the top of her lungs. 'Should old acquaintance be forgot and never brought to mind.' Marcus howled along.

Just as Pat was about to drink a cup of kindness she saw the squad car pull across the street toward them. 'Shit!'

'I know that's not parta the song,' Marcus said.

The officer got out of his car, hand resting on his revolver. 'What's going on here?' He looked Marcus up and down. 'Where are you headed?'

'What difference does it—'

'Just for a walk. I go to school here,' Pat said quickly. She could see Marcus was angry, and she wanted this to be over, fast.

'Can I see some ID?'

'We gotta show identification to walk on a street? What kinda place is this?'

'Let it go, Marcus,' she whispered, feeling in her pocket for her student ID.

'Naw. This is some shit . . .'

'I could book you for drunk and disorderly, and disturbing the peace.'

'We're not drunk, and it's New Year's. We were singin' a New Year's song. Or were we singin' in the wrong part a town?'

Pat pushed herself between Marcus and the cop and shoved her card at the officer. 'He's visiting. We're on our way back to campus . . . just needed some air.' He perused the card carefully while Marcus paced.

'You don't have to tell him nothin'!'

'You got a smart-mouth friend. I could give him some time to learn to keep it shut.'

Before Marcus could say anything else Pat turned, grabbed the front of his coat, and hissed, 'I got twelve dollars and fifty cents to my name, and I cannot bail you out with that. So will you please shut up?'

Marcus yanked out of her grasp, and glared at her, his breath escaping in cold angry clouds, but he stayed silent.

The policeman gave Pat her card back. 'I don't wanna see you again tonight.'

'No problem,' Pat answered, and edged Marcus toward the gate. She checked over her shoulder until the black-and-white pulled away.

'Why didn't you just lick his damn boots!' Marcus threw his hat on the ground in disgust.

'And what good is yellin' him down gonna do? He's got the badge and the gun, so he wins!'

'Tell me he woulda said "boo" if I'd been some preppy motherfucker!'

'I don't know, but this is some stupid shit to get arrested over! Or is that part of your image, too?'

'Oh you don't know! Well, where is your damn head, Patricia? Or did you trade that in for a new one when you got yourself a new family! Shit, I gotta get outta here!' He kicked his hat and stormed away.

'You damn fool.' She meant to yell, but it came out a whisper. Pat watched until he got to his car. He swiped snow off the windshield, got in, and gunned the motor, then roared past her, through a red light, and out of sight.

11

'Ooooh! She bites!'

'I don't give a shit whether we only changed "the," "and," or "but" in the script. If we change anything, it goes back to legal for approval! Capeesh?' Tom Reynolds banged his three-hole punch through a stack of papers for emphasis. 'I won't have my ass hung on the moon for a technicality.'

'It won't happen again, Tom.' Pat fumbled with the folio on her knees.

The phone cradled on Tom's shoulder slipped and landed with a thud on the black rubber table. He'd set up shop for the morning in the 'Rubber Room,' where latex cushioned every surface, floor to ceiling. It was the preferred conference room for bouncing ideas around at Comstock Gravitt Greene. 'How long will this moron keep me holding?'

Not long enough you loud-mouthed, egotistical runt. Pat hated it when he yelled at her, but for Tom Reynolds 'good morning' was fightin' words. Every exchange was a conflict he intended to win. Right now she hoped he'd give her a long list of things to do by yesterday so she could redeem herself and be out of sight for a while. Tom ran a tight ship, but at twenty-seven he was one of CGG's young gun producers with a clear eye toward signed paintings on his office wall and executive vice president on his business card. Althea told Pat she was lucky to be assigned as his assistant producer. 'He'll get on your terminal nerve, but he's good.'

'Oh yeah, I got your budget numbers for the fifteen- and thirty-second Burger Hut spots. I need numbers on a ten-second, too . . . Yes, I'm still holding. Can you take a . . . shit! . . . And, Patricia, tell casting to keep looking for a principal for Vitahold hair spray. The client likes the green-eyed blonde and the hazel-eyed redhead . . . What the hell is wrong with these people? I've been holding a bloody hour!' He pressed the flasher and punched in the phone number again. '. . . But they really want a green-eyed redhead.'

'Will do, Tom.'

Tom pulled four videotapes off the credenza and handed them across the table. 'Hold on to these. They're from the cereal preference focus groups for Munchee Crunchee.'

'Uh . . . sure, okay.' Pat added the tapes to four she had from her last meeting. Since she had gotten to her desk, just after seven, Pat hadn't stopped moving. It was twelve-thirty, her next meeting started in forty-five minutes, the bagel and coffee she'd swallowed for breakfast were vague memories, and lunch would be yogurt at her desk. Although she still wasn't svelte, since she started the job she'd lost twenty pounds, and her crazy schedule would help keep them off.

'Make sure the Munchee creatives know the meeting's been rescheduled.' He made a note in the agenda lying open on his desk. 'So, what do you think of the singing flakes and dancing nuggets concept for the commercial?'

'I think it's fun and would appeal to children in their target market as well as . . .'

'Bull! Kids watch Smurfs, not dancing wheat flakes!'

'You've got a point.' Tom gave her a ton of grunt work, but she learned a lot from him, not the least of which was have an opinion about everything, and sell it with conviction.

'Damn straight! Besides, they're way over budget on animation. Tell Giles we need a new concept by first thing Tuesday . . . Hello! Do *not* put me on *hold*!'

Great. So Giles can yell at me. She had learned in a hot hurry that delivering bad news was an important part of her job description, but knowing that Tom counted on her made her feel part of the team. While he yelled at the unlucky soul who answered the phone, Pat took the opportunity to gather her cassettes and escape.

Pat trekked down the hall, past the main reception rotunda, a tranquil, vaulted space with slate suede walls and thick ash carpeting. The desk, an enormous brushed steel sculpture that spelled CGG, radiated power with a serious attitude. After her internship two summers ago, Pat decided this entryway was CGG's greatest ad because it masked the frenzy that drove the agency, but the workplace as insane asylum gave Pat a charge.

So during her senior year she got offers from two other agencies, like Althea said, so she'd have some leverage, but the whole time she had her heart set on Comstock Gravitt Greene. They were the hot shop, whose innovative approach and brash style, fostered by the inspired lunacy of creative director and founding partner Ian Comstock, got them plenty of ink in the trades. They cleaned up at the CLIO Awards, and several major advertisers abandoned established relationships with more venerable agencies for CGG.

That March, Pat bought a red suit for her interview because Althea told her to be bold. She met with Lloyd Zabriski, who was a production group head and several producers, including Tom, and the deal was done. She started the week after graduation. Assistant producer. It was so, well, so Madison Avenue. Pat arrived early, stayed late, and was flying high because this was the real deal, not a classroom exercise.

'Hey . . . hold that elevator!' She squeezed into the jammed midday express and noticed it was Chris Parker, an assistant producer who'd started a month after she did, who held the door. 'Nice suspenders, Chris.' Dressed in gray pinstripes, he looked the part of an adman.

'They are spiffy, aren't they?' He hooked a thumb in the paisley strap. 'Another solo working lunch? Patricia, you are turning into quite the martyr.'

Pat rolled her eyes. 'Spare me the speech, Parker.'

'But mine is a working lunch, too. I'm just having it at a cozy little restaurant. I feel I need to bond with my art director.' He smoothed a hand over his thinning brown hair.

'How nice for you.' Pat smiled sarcastically and edged to the front to get off at her floor. Bonding would have to wait since keeping up with her work felt like digging out of an avalanche with a teaspoon. She was almost at her cubicle when her phone rang, so she stepped over the books, magazines, and tapes on the floor and lunged for the receiver.

Althea was talking before Pat finished hello. 'Your ears shoulda been ringing this morning. I overheard your friend Chris call you a brown-nosed beaver.'

'What?' Pat cleared space on a file cabinet for the tapes, reached in her pants pocket for a cigarette, and plopped down on the sheaf of pink message slips taped to her chair. 'I just saw him.'

'I strolled by the viewing room and the boy had his feet all up on the desk, yakking with my assistant. According to him, you must live in the boiler room since you're here when he comes in and when he leaves. I'm sure there were other choice tidbits, but I had to go.'

'That slimy little rat.' Pat moved storyboards for the hair spray spot and reached under the stack of papers that lived in her 'in' box to grab the glass CGG ashtray Althea had given her as a welcome aboard.

'Don't sweat it. He's just dogging the competition, standard practice; but you need to remind him of something with a nastier bite, like a pit bull. Just make sure you watch your back, 'cause they will be aiming at it while you're movin' on up. Catch you later.'

Pat had hoped to be assigned to Althea, but they weren't even on the same floor. 'They'd never put two sisters together. Honey, they'd swear we were plotting insurrection.'

But Althea hooked Pat up with a hair salon on the East Side that catered to a high-profile Black clientele: celebs, execs, and old money. She showed Pat where to shop for sharp-looking outfits because although her job required too much bending, toting, and running to wear skirts every day, 'You can't show up in wrinkly chinos and deck shoes like they do, 'cause on you it won't be appreciated,' Althea informed her.

They ate haute soul cuisine at Jezebel and traded business cards during after-work network parties at Studio. 'You got to get out, be seen, and make noise,' Althea said, and if there was anything going on, Althea was in it, always accompanied by an escort of the power broker variety. Up-and-coming was nice, but Althea liked her men already arrived.

Pat didn't have the clothes or credentials to manhunt in that league yet. She'd collected some phone numbers, been taken out to brunch, but her door didn't need barricades because nobody was breaking it down. For now, romance was not a top priority. Pat had a career to build. She felt Althea kept an eye out for her at CGG and hipped her on the social front and Pat was grateful for a friend who understood her drive and ambition.

Pat finished Tom's budget figures after her one-fifteen meeting. Two casting sessions, three trips to legal, and one chewing-out for something-she-hadn't-done-yet later, and it was six-thirty. She would barely have time to go home and change before running to a staged reading her old roommate Jill had roped her into attending. Jill was in the city, slogging it out in the theatrical trenches and working in telemarketing so her days were free for auditions. Sometimes Pat got her into commercial castings, like the one for Vitahold since Jill was a green-eyed redhead. Jill promised to thank her in her Oscar acceptance speech, but in the meantime Pat said she'd go to the reading to support the cause.

Pat darted up Madison, weaving through the hordes released from their corporate cages, then took the bus across town to the West Side. When she'd moved back to New York, Aunt Loretta offered her the room in Queens, but Pat worked and played in Manhattan, so she wanted to live there, too. At first she rented a room at the Abigail Adams Residence Hotel for Women, but two months ago she lucked into a furnished sublet. Althea put in a good word for her with a copywriter who was getting married and didn't want to give up her rent-controlled apartment, 'just in case.' Pat loved saying she lived in the West Seventies, in a building with lots of 'character,' which meant the radiators clanged, the plumbing was ancient, but the rooms were huge. So were the windows. On Sunday mornings she'd lounge on the window seat, drinking coffee. With the skyline spread out in front of her she'd peruse the real estate ads, picking out her dream apartment in a high-rise, with a view of the East River, doormen, and a parking spot for her Jaguar, because a girl had to have goals.

A flip through the mail, some diet soda, a mad dash through the closet, and Pat was out the door, headed for an evening of culture.

Interface: First Intersection, Second Millennium, was an experimental theater piece. The cast, seated on folding chairs on a bare stage, would change roles and places at the sound of a dissonant piano chord. *This is the wildest shit I ever saw.* Pat couldn't find a plot, so she shivered in the church basement-cum-theater, wrapped in her overcoat, attempting to keep track of who was who at any given moment. So far Jill, her flaming hair piled dramatically on top of her head, had played a Manchu Dynasty herbalist and a sixties Chi-town radio DJ, but then Pat's attention shifted to the slender Black man wearing wire-rimmed glasses, a black turtleneck, and tight jeans. At first he played a first-century Mayan math prodigy. He seemed fragile and innocent in the role, but in his next incarnation, a fourteenth-century Timbuktu gold trader, Pat was intrigued by his commanding voice and his noble bearing. Sometimes she felt he was playing directly to her, looking through her. *Get real. It's called acting,* but watching him kept her alert through the second act.

After the performance Pat stood in back sipping coffee, reading a poster requesting donations and volunteers for the church's Thanksgiving food drive, and waiting for Jill.

'You looked downright frozen in there. I hope you've warmed up.' She turned to find the African gold trader at her side.

'I'm getting there.' His skin was creamy brown, like butterscotch pudding, and behind the glasses his eyes

213

were fiery amber. 'You're a very good actor.'

'I thank you, although I can only claim to be an amateur thespian. Theater is my love, and it was my undergrad minor, which is how I know the playwright. Now, I'm a common, boring, law student, down the road apiece at Rutgers.'

'That's not common or boring.' Pat wasn't cold anymore, and it wasn't the coffee.

'Ah, but it's safe. "There's a job at the end of that tunnel." My parents say that every chance they get, but they foot the bills, so, artistic expression be damned.'

His name was Peter Jackson, but he preferred P.J. He had been a senior at Princeton when Pat was a freshman. *That's what I get for living in the library.* P.J.'s voice was rich, like handsful of fertile earth, and there was a theatrical flair to his manner, but it didn't seem phony. Pat found he drew her in, the same way he had on stage.

'Who knows, you could still be discovered, and then you'd be able to interpret your own movie contract before you signed it.' Pat was glad she'd changed clothes. The amethyst silk blouse Althea had twisted her arm to buy looked suitably casual but chic. She shifted around to face him and cradled her coffee in both hands. 'You came just for this performance?'

'It was a good excuse to get away from some very dull research. Listen, Pat, would you like to get out of here and grab a bite?'

Pat was surprised by the invite. It was usually the Willie Calloways of the world who asked her out. Nice guys, but they didn't get her motor running. 'Sounds good to me.' P.J. already had her engine revving so loudly she had to concentrate to hear what he was saying. She caught Jill's eye and waved good-bye. Jill gave her thumbs-up when P.J. wasn't looking.

They exchanged vital statistics over sushi. She gave him the standard revised bio. He grew up in Philadelphia, an only child whose parents spent too much time arranging his life, according to him. 'I went to law school after a year hiatus that I spent traveling and arguing with them about whether or not I was going. This is my last year, which means we'll probably argue about what I do with the rest of my life.' He leaned in close, his chin in his hand. 'You sound excited about your career. Sure of where you're going. It's refreshing.'

'I don't know about sure, but I'm ready to go there and find out.' Pat felt all thumbs with her chopsticks.

'I admire your drive. So many women I've dated are content to follow where I lead. I much prefer someone who knows her own mind.'

Pat smiled. 'That's not usually called an asset. It's usually called a bitch.' *Prefer? What's he talking about?*

P.J. locked her eyes in a tempting invitation. 'Usual bores me.'

His hot stare warmed Pat's cheeks and thawed her cool. *Don't be stupid.* But his look was like spring sun after a long, cold winter. It felt really good, and at that moment Pat knew she was going wherever this led, so when he asked if she wanted a lift home, she accepted.

P.J. helped her with her coat and Pat could barely find the sleeves. Walking next to him along Broadway, even the glow of the streetlights felt magical to her. When they settled in P.J.'s shiny white Saab, she tried not to leap ahead and wonder about good night. Hoped she hadn't misread him and that he didn't just want a smart, platonic friend. She'd been that route often enough.

Traffic was light, and P.J. wound through city streets, like he was in no hurry to get anywhere. When he stopped for a red light, Pat faced him to say how glad she was she saw the play, but before she opened her lips, he kissed them, soft and light as a feather. A shiver trickled down her spine and floated up again. Sweet and gentle, he explored her mouth, and she floated outside herself, on a whispery breeze.

Pat didn't know how long they'd been kissing when the bleat of a car horn brought her back to earth. P.J. straightened and pulled off. 'Make a left at Columbus.' Her voice had a hot and bothered throatiness, and for the first time since that basement she felt her insides melt. *I didn't imagine it.*

P.J. lucked into a parking space and took Pat's hand as he walked her to the door. The voice in her head sang a round. *What's gonna happen? What do you want? I don't know this man. You're crazy.*

'I hate to say good night.' The look in his tiger eyes hushed the chorus in Pat's mind.

'Then don't.' Wrapped in his arms, she gave in to her body instead of her brain.

The next morning, after he'd gone, Pat had no memory of finding her keys, or the elevator ride to her apartment. The urgent fumbling with buttons, tearing at zippers was a blur, but their bodies, skin to skin, etched an imprint in her mind. Naked in the tangled sheets, she could still feel the curly roughness of his chest hair as she plowed her fingers through it, brushed her cheek across it. Her body recalled the weight of him against her breasts. His salty taste lingered in her mouth and, even now, she tingled from his licking, nibbling, sucking. And then the fluttering, like tiny butterflies, had come, faster and faster, from a secret grotto, until they lifted her, soared with her way up high. They let her go. She drifted weightlessly down again, and then she knew what all the fuss was about.

She swung out of bed, reached for her lighter. *He'll*

never call, but it was great. So when she answered the phone in her office and it was P.J., she had to concentrate to keep up her end of the conversation. Fortunately, P.J. had plenty to say, about how much he enjoyed her company. 'You're not like any woman I've ever been with. You're so . . . free.'

Not like any woman he's ever been with? Pat felt like she was levitating. P.J. invited her to his place in Camden the weekend before Thanksgiving for an early turkey dinner, and she mimed a celebration dance while she pretended to check her calender before accepting.

'I wish we could spend the holiday together, but I've got this family thing in Hartford that I don't want to go to, and I wouldn't put you through it.'

'I hear that.' Pat was looking for a graceful way to get out of dinner at Gayle's.

Pat kept busy every minute of the next two weeks, trying not to count the days. Fortunately, work went into overdrive. One of Tom's accounts, Tastea, had been around practically since the Boston Tea Party, but the competition caught them sleeping, first on herb teas and then on bottled iced tea. The company decided to spend some bucks to shake up their antiquated image and recapture market share. The first step was the summer launch of Tropical Quencher, a line of bottled, fruit-flavored iced teas. This campaign had the account execs beyond delirious because if it went well, Tastea planned to spend big on herb teas next winter and CGG would see a hefty increase in billings for the account.

Pat stayed busy attending planning sessions with Team Tastea, researching locations, reading marketing reports, and refiguring preliminary budgets. She was even a last-minute replacement for Tom at a meeting at Tastea headquarters in Indianapolis when he came down with laryngitis. The time flew by, but Pat did find a minute to buy a new black lace bra and panties, and a satin wrap robe, because this wasn't going to be a flannel weekend.

P.J. offered to come and get her, but since he was cooking, she took the train and brought the wine. Staring out at the wintry gray scenery she wondered if this adventure would be a bust. *Hell, we might not even get along. That night could have been one of those things.* But the savory aroma of butter and spices greeted Pat outside of his apartment, and when he opened the door he welcomed her with a kiss that picked up where they left off.

P.J.'s place was simple but sophisticated, in calming shades of taupe, beige, and black. *How did he do all this and go to law school?* She checked herself since she didn't want him to think she wasn't used to nice things. 'Is that a Cathlett print?' She admired the portrait hanging in the foyer.

'I'm not sure. My mother picked out the pictures and pretty much everything else.' P.J. hung up her coat. 'I'm glad you came down. You've been on my mind . . . frequently.'

I have? 'Have I?' She smiled, was it flirtatiously? It was a new part for Pat, but it felt right opposite P.J.

They ate by candlelight, and the Cornish hens stuffed with wild rice, glazed carrots, and spinach salad P.J. had made tasted as good as it smelled. They talked about his train trip across Europe and her six months in Paris. He kept her laughing with backstage misadventures from undergrad productions; she told him about wild times at CGG. The conversation was easy, the undercurrent unmistakably sexy.

After dinner they lounged on the twin Haitian cotton sofas. She eased into the languid pace of relaxing at a man's place with no agenda but the one you play by ear.

When the phone rang P.J. let the answering machine pick it up. 'Whoever it is can wait.'

Part of her wondered if this was just a sex thing, but the preparations were too elaborate for that. *Besides, if he just wanted to get laid, he could have found cuter local talent.* Pat wasn't sure what exactly he did want. She didn't even know what she wanted, but before they got into anything heavy she made herself go to the bathroom, because having him watch her bend into a pretzel and fumble around trying to shove a slippery rubber disk up her hoo-hoo was just too embarrassing to think about.

When she came back he poured her a brandy and joined her on the sofa, his head in her lap. The intimacy felt womanly. She rested her hand on his chest, wanting to unbutton his shirt and stroke his hairy chest again.

The first time they made love, it was on the sofa, and, just like before, Pat felt free, liberated from her so, so serious self. It was only after she peeled herself off the ceiling that she realized she was naked, the lights were on, and he could see her round brown body starkly silhouetted against the white sofa. She reached for his shirt.

'Aw, don't cover up. I like the way you look.'

You what? Nobody said that but Uncle Joe and that's 'cause he felt sorry for me.

'And I love the way you feel. Come on.' He led her down the hall to the brass bed that took up most of his bedroom. After making love again, they lay with their bodies spooned together, his breath on her ear, his hand idly massaging her belly. The actual sleeping part of sleeping with a man was so strange that Pat didn't doze off until long after his hand went slack and his breathing deepened.

In the morning she got up before he was awake and felt a tingle as she put on his white terry cloth robe instead of her silk one. After a stop in the bathroom because she couldn't face him first thing in the morning with her hair standing all over her head, she searched his refrigerator and cupboards to find breakfast fixings. The kitchen was stocked with all sorts of delicacies from artichoke hearts to chilled champagne. However intrusive mommy and daddy were, they were obviously generous, and P.J. knew how to live in style. She brewed coffee, sliced mushrooms for omelets, and checked to see if P.J. was awake.

'. . . I love you, too. Bye.' He hung up, hit the erase button on the answering machine, stretched and rolled over. 'You're up early.'

Pat hung back a moment. 'I love you, too?'

'My mother.'

'Your mother? The one you were complaining about?'

'She's a pain in my ass, but I still love her. That's who called last night, and if I don't call back within the allotted grace period, I'll hear about it.'

Pat looked him in the eyes, searching for telltale signs of a lie.

'What kind of insensitive rascal do you take me for?' He puffed up, playing hurt.

'An actor AND a lawyer.' She had to smile. He looked so cute pouting.

'Guilty as charged.' He held the covers up and she could see his bare leg and the curve of his hip. 'And right now we're both very cold and lonely.'

Moments from the weekend ambushed Pat without warning all day Monday. During meetings, on the bus, she'd struggle to suppress the shiver of pleasure they provoked.

That night he called. 'I just wanted to hear your voice,' he said. Pat curled up on her bed in the dark, and they talked for two hours, about the weekend, about what

P.J.'s life would be like after graduation. He debated about where he would practice, whether to take the bar exam in Pennsylvania, New Jersey, New York, or all three. Pat told him her life would get more hectic before it quieted down. They agreed the world couldn't stop for them to be together yet, but promised to make time for each other as often as possible.

'Think we'll ever end up in the same city?' Pat asked drowsily.

'Time will tell,' P.J. replied.

Tuesday and Wednesday evening and Thanksgiving Day Pat volunteered at the church where the reading had been, distributing bags of groceries to families who needed them and serving a holiday meal to those who had no place to cook one. It made her feel good, and it was a perfect reason to turn down Gayle's dinner invitation because Pat just didn't want to try that hard. She didn't feel like eating much these days, or having Aunt Loretta make some smart comment about why she wasn't. Ramsey would find a way to raise her hackles, and if she saw Gayle, she'd be tempted to tell her about P.J., but Gayle would blow it out of proportion. *She'll start planning a wedding, like I even want to get married.* The only one she really wanted to see right now was Vanessa. The last time Pat saw her was graduation. Vanessa was so intrigued with the tassel on Pat's mortarboard, she gave it to her. *Gayle still hasn't sent those pictures. Maybe this summer I'll make time to get to know Vanessa.*

The Monday before holiday break P.J. popped up to New York and picked Pat up at the office. He'd be in Vermont skiing with his family from Christmas to New Year's, so this was their only time to make merry. First he took her to help him choose a necklace for his mother. 'She's so hard to buy for,' P.J. said. Pat knew it was silly,

221

but examining the cases full of jewelry, telling each other which stones and settings they liked, trying on gold chains so he could see how they looked, it all made her feel light-headed. More than once she stifled thoughts about how much like a couple they seemed and what it would feel like to be picking out wedding rings.

P.J. took her to dinner with dessert back at her place. She was shocked when he gave her a little blue box with a white bow. Inside she found silver earrings shaped like swirls of ribbon. Pat assured herself it was a token of their friendship, but they became her new favorite earrings. When she wore them she looked in the mirror forty-seven times a day and smiled from lobe to lobe.

Pat had pretty much decided this was the best year of her life, until she was called into Lloyd Zabriski's office for her year-end review. Pat had done everything Tom asked, on time and to the letter, and she expected raves from the group head, but he pushed his glasses on top of his bald head and rated her solidly average.

'You can catch it as fast as Tom can sling it, which is no small feat. You're capable, you're accurate, you carry out instructions, but this is not the army. I want you to explore your hunches, turn the pieces upside down, shake the tree. Followers are useful, but basically expendable.'

Expendable? The word gave her an instant headache.

'I need trailblazers on my team. They bring chaos, but the results are fresh. You've got the potential, Pat. That's why I hired you. Don't be polite. Don't raise your hand and wait to be called on because I'll never see you. Just show me what you got.'

Pat shredded the edges of her desk blotter, trying to recover from the shock. She'd been a good girl with the right answers all her life, but good didn't count at all and right didn't count as much as unique, brash, and exciting.

'Knock, knock.' Chris poked his head in the door. 'You're looking a little grim. All that sacrifice not adding up with Zabriski?'

'Shut up and get the hell out, Chris!'

'Ooooh! She bites! . . . See ya.'

She hasn't started to bite yet.

12

'The doo-doo is knee deep . . .'

'The Quencher arrived in St Stephens safe and sound. Here's your ticket.' Pat handed Tom an envelope. 'I ordered you a car for six-fifteen tomorrow morning. I'll be down Monday with the director.' Pat waved at the cigarette smoldering in her ashtray, then stubbed it out. *Damn, this smoke smells nasty. They must be stale.*

Tastea was ecstatic with their improved sales figures after the first Quencher spots and ordered a new ad cycle in time for a late-summer debut. The client wanted Graham Maxwell, the flamboyant Hollywood darling, to direct again, even though his fees were killing their budget. Pat made it her mission to bring the numbers in line and stumbled on the little-known island of St Stephens as the site for the shoot. She negotiated rock-bottom hotel rates and got permit fees waived, earning her kudos from Tom and the account execs.

'Did you look at the director's reel I left you?' Previewing sample tapes was one of Pat's favorite duties. 'She's got great footage, zero attitude, and she's hungry. Her rate is dirt cheap.'

'Remind me when I get back. It's after six and I've gotta pack. Ciao!'

If I just sit here a minute I'll get a second wind. Pat still had marketing reports to read, but she'd been feeling queasy since she got a dirty dog from a street vendor for lunch. She rested her head on her folded arms. The drone of a vacuum cleaner woke her. *Eight o'clock!* Her limbs were leaden. *I don't have time to be sick. I'll go home and come in at seven tomorrow.*

Pat could hardly drag to the bus stop. She paused in front of a drugstore. *Maybe I need vitamins.* The flowery window display caught her eye. 'Feel Fresher, Longer, with Extra Protection.' *Maybe that's my problem. It's gotta be time for . . . When was my period due?* She rifled her bag for her date book, her pulse pounding like conga beats at her temples. *Two weeks ago?* April, May, June, she counted days in twenty-eights, all the way to the asterisk she made on the day she was due. She flipped forward two weeks and stared at the days she had marked in red 'P.J. N.Y. Bar!'

Pat hadn't seen P.J. since the week before his graduation. At the time she was on a tight postproduction deadline for Tastea, so attending the ceremony was out of the question, but he drove up for a private commencement exercise. The evening he left he was quieter than usual. They talked a lot about the decisions he'd made for the short term, like moving back home and accepting an associate's position with his father's law firm.

'Your father's a lawyer, too?' Parents were among Pat's least favorite conversation topics, so she hadn't asked many questions about the elder Jacksons.

'He was a judge for years, but a big firm offered him a partnership and he jumped at the bucks. I probably won't stay there long, but it's a check until I get on my feet.' Then he had pulled her into his lap. 'But I need your help.'

'Whatever I can do . . .'

'It's what I'm gonna ask you *not* to do. Until July I'll be cramming for the bar exam, or should I say exams, since I've decided to take both Pennsylvania and New York.'

New York! Pat tried not to read too much into it. 'How can I make it easier on you?'

'By not calling and understanding when I don't. Talking to you makes me want to be with you, and after I hang up, I'm hard-pressed to concentrate on torts. I have to focus, Patricia. I'll make it up to you, as soon as I hand in my last test booklet. I promise.'

Pat understood sacrifice for a worthy goal, so as hard as it had been, she didn't phone, but she missed him, terribly. Missed his impromptu visits when they could both steal the time. Missed the way her heart fluttered as soon as she heard his voice on the phone. In odd moments, snatched from the bedlam of her days, she thought she was in love with P.J. *It's my job. I'm under a lot of stress. It has to be . . .* But she passed up the bus stop, ducked into the bookstore on the corner, and headed for the 'Health' aisle.

'You should be refitted for your diaphragm if you gain or lose ten pounds or more.' The words shimmied on the page, mocking her. *I'd've remembered if they'd told me that at Student Health. I know I would. But stress can disrupt the cycle, too.*

She assured herself that's all it was, but as soon as she got home she checked the Yellow Pages and found a women's clinic close to the office. Twice an hour for the rest of the evening she trotted anxiously to the bathroom, hoping for even the faintest hint of pink on the toilet paper. When the doors at the clinic opened she was waiting, with her pee in a well-washed Stridex jar. *By noon at the latest, I'll know.*

Pat wanted to rip the hands off the clock by ten-thirty. She chewed out the bell lady because she never had any grapefruit juice left when she got to the fifteenth floor. On her way back to her desk she ran into an assistant in the art department, who showed her storyboards he just finished for Snuggables disposable diapers. *Diapers*. She almost lost it looking at the cuddly, gurgling babies. *I can't be . . .* and popped into the ladies' room to splash water on her face, check for the pink. Nothing.

Stay busy. Pat cashed her check at the bank, filed all the papers on her desk, and sharpened a box of pencils. Then it was time. *I did what I was supposed to do. I was careful. It has to be negative*. She walked her fingers to the phone. 'I'm calling for the results of . . .'

'. . . that test is positive. Would you like to make an appointment to see a doctor?'

Pat felt like she was drowning. 'Uh . . . I'll have to call back.' She slammed down the phone. *Positive. There's not a damn thing positive about this!* She remembered her last weekend with P.J., how happy she'd been. Now she wished it had been the day before, the week after, not at all, but wishing on all the stars in the sky would not change the fact that she, Patricia Ellen Reid, college graduate, good girl with a golden future, was knocked up. *What am I gonna do? How am I gonna tell P.J.?* She wanted to speak to him at that moment. *I can't tell him right before the bar. He's worried enough.*

She stumbled through the afternoon. On the way home she bought oatmeal cookies, a quart of ice cream, a roast beef sandwich, and a bag of potato chips. She dragged into her apartment, crawled into bed, and pulled the sheet over her head, feeling like a ticking bomb. *I live in a sublet. Counting today's paycheck I'll have 110 dollars after rent and student loans. I can't have a baby. Can I? What if P.J. wants it? What if he doesn't? Do I?*

She flipped her radio to the all-news station to hear

voices other than the ones in her head. Bits of murder and mayhem came over the airwaves. *My life could be worse.* That didn't help. Hazy, hot, and humid. *So what?* 'In sports, for the second day in a row, a run by colorful rookie Marcus "Cat-in-the-Hat" Carter boosted the Orioles past the Yanks.' In the spring, when she'd read that the Orioles brought Marcus up, she had hoped this time it was for good. Right now, the idea of him swatting at a ball with a wooden pole in front of fifty thousand fans at Yankee Stadium just seemed crazy. *As crazy as me being pregnant.*

The weekend passed in a haze of sleep, food, and agonizing self-torture. She dreamed about baby Gayle being thrown away like garbage and MaRay's fat hugging arms. In the middle of the night Pat got up and stared at her face in the bathroom mirror, searching for traces of either Verna or Turner. *They would be grandparents.* That was almost funny since neither one had been a parent to her. *It'll have to be different, or what's the point?*

By late Sunday she'd made up her mind to tell P.J. a week from Wednesday, after the New York bar. *We can talk it out then. What difference will a few days make?*

On Monday morning Pat arrived at the airport early and positioned herself so she'd see Graham Maxwell when he arrived. She personally arranged a car to pick up the director, but it was ten minutes to flight time and no Maxwell. *Don't panic yet. Check with the car service.*

When the dispatcher told her nobody answered at Maxwell's address she called his loft, then his studio. Finally, she reached his rep, who calmly reported that Maxwell had run into technical problems with his latest film on location in Manitoba.

'*Manitoba!* He has to start shooting in St Stephens tomorrow! When is he leaving?'

'I don't know. He won't talk to me,' the rep answered sheepishly.

Pat slammed the receiver down so hard that several people nearby jumped. *Think, girl, think!* She had a missing director, a missing period, and she wanted to crawl in a hole until she could talk to P.J., but she couldn't blow this. She took a moment to regroup, then called Tom in St Stephens, who lost it on the other end.

'Don't get on the damn plane! Go to the office. I need you in a central location.'

Pat found a message to call Tom on her desk. Maxwell had cried as he told Tom a stuntman was killed in a car rigged to explode. The set was under investigation, and he couldn't leave.

'We'll sue him for every dime he even *thinks* about making!' Tom rattled off a list of directors for her to call. 'See who can get here tonight and how much it's gonna cost.'

Chris posed at the door. 'Heard the doo-doo is knee deep. Care for a shovel?'

Pat shot him a lethal look, but she heard him snickering as he walked away. It took an hour to find out that nobody on Tom's list was available. Her work on this spot wouldn't mean squat without a director. Pat spied the card on her bulletin board. Tom hadn't seen her work, but what choice did they have? Pat had her reel rush messengered to the office.

Tom went ballistic when she called him with the update. 'Nobody knows this woman!'

'Look, we're past the twenty-four-hour cancellation on the talent, so we'll pay whether you shoot the ad or snapshots for your scrapbook. Fire me if I'm wrong, but do you have a better idea?'

'Get her reel for Zabriski and get back to me,' Tom said.

'It's on the way.'

Zabriski was silent as Pat ran the reel. When it was over she flicked on the lights. 'We come in at budget if we run into delays. If we make this on schedule, we come in under and impress the client with how well we handle a crisis.' Pat took a breath. 'I think her style is right for this project.'

'And you have years in the business and your reputation to stand on, is that right?'

'I've got one year and my intuition, but I'll stand by my suggestion.' *Followers are expendable huh? Okay. I'm leading.*

Zabriski pushed his glasses on top of his head. 'Have her here at one.'

Yes! The delirium of the moment took Pat's mind off her troubles.

Zabriski called a Team Tastea meeting in the Rubber Room. The atmosphere was like a four-ring circus with the snarling lions ready to devour the trapeze act. That's when Zabriski made Pat the ringmaster. She had no time to plan what to say or to be scared. Pat flattened her palms on the table and summoned her sonorous alto. She showed the reel, gave the spiel, and Tom, on the speaker phone, defended Pat's judgment. The director showed up on time, laid out her vision of the commercial like she'd been contemplating this shoot for weeks. By three-thirty Pat and her new find were heading to Kennedy.

It was a tough six days in the tropics. Pat was sick every morning, the client was edgy, and Tom yelled more than usual, but when they got back and saw the raw film, Pat's praises were sung on high. Althea treated her to dinner. Pat almost broke down and told her secret, but she wouldn't discuss it with anyone before P.J., and that talk was blessedly just two days away.

Pat spent most of Tuesday in postproduction meetings. When she answered her phone a little after five she figured it was legal returning her call.

'I didn't realize how much I missed you until now.'

When she heard P.J.'s voice Pat wanted to cry and blurt out her news. *Keep it together.* 'I've been thinking about you all day.'

'I wish I could say the same, but this test is a killer. I'm staying at the same hotel where the test is being given and I barely had the strength to ride the elevator to my room. But fortunately, there's only part two standing between you, me, and a happy reunion. Should I swing by the office tomorrow or see you at home?'

'Why don't we meet for a drink?' *He'll probably need a lot of drinks.* She wanted to start out on neutral territory. He resisted at first, but finally agreed to meet in the lobby bar.

'Five-thirty-ish. I can't wait to see you and lose myself in your arms.'

At the dot of five on Wednesday Pat was out the door. It was the first time in a year she'd left the office on time. She didn't know what to expect. Worse, she still didn't know what she wanted. It used to be clear as day that she was striving and sacrificing for her career, so she could excel and become someone her father would be proud to claim, someone exactly the opposite of Verna. Pregnancy, love, marriage, they weren't part of the blueprint she had so carefully drafted. But then she thought of P.J. and let the traffic sign flash 'Don't Walk,' then 'Walk' and back again before she remembered she had to put one foot in front of the other to cross the street.

She wanted P.J. to take her hand and make her feel as close to him as she did when they talked in whispers and their bodies melted together. She tried not to taste how badly she wanted him to look at her with love in those amber eyes. *Is that . . .*

'Patricia Reid! I haven't see you since Martha's Vineyard. How long has it been?' Edwina Lewis gushed, looking like the reigning 'Miss It.'

What is he doing with her?

'I can't believe it. Running into you right on the street. They do say New York is really a small town! You look so different!' Edwina caught Pat's eyes glued to P.J. 'I want you to meet my husband, Peter Jackson. You didn't meet on the Vineyard that summer, did you?' Edwina looked from one to the other, but nobody answered. 'No, you were working for the congressman that summer. Peter and I didn't meet 'til the next year anyway. He's an attorney in Philadelphia now. He's taking the New York bar so he can practice here, too. I thought I'd come up on the last day and surprise him since he's been working so hard! We got married right after his graduation and we haven't even taken a honeymoon yet!' She squeezed herself around P.J.'s arm. 'We'll fix that soon, isn't that right, honey?'

For a second Pat's world stood still. There was no sound, no air, just enough time to, please, let it shift back on its axis and make what she thought was real be a cruel mirage.

'Uh . . . nice to meet you . . . Patricia is it?' P.J. wore aviator shades that masked his eyes. He looked just past her, down the street, put out his hand.

Pat knew she would never forget this clammy handshake, because it infused every cell of her body with a hate like venom. *He planned to meet me tonight, like nothing had changed.*

'What adorable earrings, Pat.' She had on the silver ribbons P.J. had given her for Christmas. 'They're just like the ones Peter's mother and I got for the secretaries at his father's firm last Christmas.' So P.J. had given her secretarial leftovers, and around Edwina's neck was the necklace Pat had helped him pick out for his 'mother.' Edwina babbled a bit longer, about shopping for their new apartment, then she said something about getting together and nudged P.J. to give Pat one of his cards. 'Who knows. I'd really like to live in New York. That's why I pushed him to take the bar here, too.'

Pat wanted to rant and holler like she didn't have good sense. She wanted all the people passing to know that P.J. was a low-down, fork-tongued, spineless snake, but what would that make her? Stupid enough not to know a snake when she saw one? Fool enough to get bitten? 'It was good to see you Edwina. I'm meeting someone, so I've gotta run. Enjoy your stay.' Saying good-bye was almost easy, like the poison had already numbed her inside.

All night Pat sat up, putting the pieces together. No time, the family holidays in Hartford, 'I love you, too.' So P.J. was the son of Judge and Mrs Henry Jackson. The same Mrs Jackson who couldn't be bothered to remember Pat's name for a lousy six weeks on the Vineyard. *How big an idiot must he think I am?* By daybreak she was anesthetized to those passionate embraces, the tiger-eyed stares, and she knew what she had to do.

I can do this by myself. In her mind she checked off all the decisions she'd made, situations she'd handled, without assistance, advice, or support because she was no one's responsibility. She'd accepted that one night, lying under a scratchy blanket in a group home, feeling helpless and so scared she trembled. She got through that night, and from then on she only ever counted on herself. *Period. It's my mess. I have to clean it up.*

Pat got through the days by concentrating on work, but in the evening there were no distractions, and she felt her life slipping through her fingers. Like sand, it piled at her feet and threatened to bury her if she didn't reach out for somebody soon.

Call her. Call Gayle. There was not another soul Pat had let in, even a little bit. Certainly no one at work. They were too new. Althea could never know Pat had been this unforgivably stupid. And she had never trusted Jill or anybody else from school with her real, deep in the night feelings because she didn't expect them to understand. She was 'Pat the Invincible,' with no visible chinks in her armor, and that was how she liked it. It had been years since she'd confided in Gayle, but she needed someone to talk to now, someone to hear how sorry she was, how much this hurt.

'Well! Hello, stranger! What's goin' on?' Gayle said.

And the dam broke. Pat blurted her story, choking back sobs so she could talk.

Gayle listened in shocked silence. She had never heard Pat so desolate, not even when they were kids. Not ever. 'What do you need? I can come get you now.'

Pat squeezed her eyes shut to hold back the tears. She wanted to be rescued from the torture of replaying in her mind what she was about to do. 'No. Don't come now. It's late, and I know Vanessa's asleep.' *Oh God. Vanessa.* She couldn't think about those bright eyes, the little fingers reaching for her tassel at graduation, the warm body asleep in her arms. It made this too personal and it couldn't be. She felt weak asking this, but she had to. 'Will you go with me Saturday? I know it's short notice, but . . .'

'Isn't there any other way?'

'Like what, Gayle? I've turned this around every way I know how, and I get the same answer. I can't have a baby now.' A silence filled with 'buts' and 'ifs' and 'shoulds' hung between them. 'Look if you don't want to do it . . .'

235

'You know I'll be there. Momma can watch Vanessa . . .'

'Please don't tell her. Don't tell anybody.' Pat felt so ashamed.

'I won't tell a soul. Get some rest, and I'll see you Saturday.'

At eight-fifteen Saturday morning Gayle phoned in a panic. 'Ramsey was supposed to get Momma last night, but he didn't get home 'til after midnight. He's gone to get her now. I'll meet you there as soon as I can. I'm so sorry, Pat.'

Pat had been up and dressed since before dawn, sitting on the window seat drinking coffee, wanting a cigarette and tomorrow in the worst way. Now she wanted to crawl into a hole. *Dreading a thing is worse than doing it MaRay used to say, but she didn't mean this.*

Check-in, papers to sign, then waiting and pretending to flip through magazines. Pat looked past her pages at the room full of people, sitting in neat rows of yellow and orange canvas waiting room chairs. It seemed everybody else had someone to wait with. Mothers perched like stick figures, unable to look at their fidgeting daughters. Pat thought the guy wearing baggy jeans and a denim shirt looked too young to drive, but he clamped his girlfriend's hand in both of his. The girl's hair was slicked, patent leather smooth, and fastened in a ponytail. She bounced nervously against the back of her chair, chewing gum on the downbeat, wiping a tear with the heel of her hand. Occasionally her boyfriend whispered words that brought a weak smile to her face. *At least he's here.*

A toddler giggled in amusement as he removed pamphlets one at a time from the wall rack and let them flutter to the floor. When his father came to retrieve him he threw himself on the floor, rigid with anger, and hollered bloody murder. *Get him out of here!* Pat felt his screams like pins in her ears and dug her nails into her palms until they left crescent indentations. Finally the father hustled him out of the room.

Gayle will get here in the next five minutes. She looked from her watch to the big clock on the wall. *Ten max,* but by the time Pat heard her name called for the group counseling session, Gayle hadn't arrived, so she left word at the desk that someone would be coming for her and marched off with the others to a tiny room with big posters of female innards and birth control paraphernalia on the walls, to rap about what was going to happen. *She'll be here when I get out. That's when I really need her.*

Pat had tried to convince them counseling was unnecessary. 'I was using a diaphragm. It was an accident. It will *never* happen again.' But it was policy.

'We've found it's helpful to vent your feelings with women who know what you're going through.' *Right.*

For three endless hours she listened only enough to know when she was being spoken to and made up feelings when she was required to share some, because she was doing her damnedest not to have any. Yes, her boyfriend was supportive. Yes, the decision was hard, but they reached it together. *Like I'm really gonna say the lousy, lying bastard got married, to somebody he was engaged to the whole time he was fucking me. To somebody I know and don't even like. And I had to run into them on the street to find out 'cause he didn't have the decency to tell me to my face. Worse, I might actually still love him. No, I don't need that much pity.*

Myrna, the girl with the ponytail, sobbed and said she didn't want to do this, but her parents would throw her out if they knew, and she was scared her father would kill her boyfriend. The counselor comforted her, asked if she'd considered other options, if she wanted to think about this a while longer. Pat stared at her knees because she couldn't bear Myrna's sadness, too. Finally she settled down, said she wanted to go through with it.

After the birth control show-and-tell the counselor handed out plaid smocks, paper slippers, and told them where to find lockers. When they were dressed they waited, and one by one were called until only Pat and Myrna remained.

'Are you gonna be all right? You look real scared,' Myrna said.

That blew Pat away since she was trying hard as she could not to be. 'I'm fine.'

'I saw you by yourself out there. Your boyfriend's comin' to get you, right?'

'Uh-huh.' It was all she could manage, because her composure was slipping.

The counselor peeked in and called Pat.

Myrna squeezed Pat's hand. 'You let him help you, okay? Don't be no hero 'cause he shared the good; let him share the bad, too.'

Pat's paper slippers crackled as she shuffled behind the counselor, who led her to the procedure room. Two nurses tried to put her at ease. One scurried about checking equipment and singing 'Doe a deer, a female deer' in a high, tinny voice, the other helped Pat on the table, got her settled, patted her cheek with a warm, soft hand. Pat fastened her eyes on the white-tile ceiling, tried not to focus on the faces so they wouldn't be real, blocked out the sharp antiseptic smell, closed her lips tight so her teeth wouldn't chatter.

When the doctor arrived she was cordial and comforting, explained each move she made. But Pat only nodded, repeated over and over in her head why there was no other choice right now, but as the vacuum hummed and she felt the tugging deep inside, she clapped her hand over her mouth to hold in the gasp, not from the knot of pain, but from the profound loss. Logic fell away, and as tears flooded from her eyes she murmured, 'I'm sorry. I'm sorry.'

And when it was over the nurse with the warm hands helped her to a bed in recovery. Pat clutched the pillow and lay there, drained and utterly empty. Moans and gentle crying from neighboring beds filtered into her consciousness as if she was at the end of a very long tunnel. She accepted a can of apple juice offered by a gentle-voiced attendant who left a cellophane packet of peanut butter crackers on the bedside table. Pat had cramps, bad ones, but it hardly mattered. She just wanted to be steady enough to leave this place, to get out before Myrna, so she wouldn't see there was no 'he' to share this with. *If I can get dressed, Gayle will take me home. I just wanna go home.* She didn't know what she would say to Gayle about today, or if she could talk about it at all. She just needed a friendly face, a cup of tea, because this whole episode was so ugly.

So Pat pulled on her clothes with her last bit of energy. She glanced at a mirror, saw how lifeless she looked, and put on some lipstick and blush so Gayle wouldn't be so worried.

When Pat opened the waiting room door every head turned expectantly. The toddler slept in his stroller, Myrna's boyfriend paced by the window, and Gayle wasn't there.

Pat asked at the desk if anyone had come looking for her or called to leave a message, but there wasn't any word so she sat in an orange chair near the door and waited, because she had to be on the way. *She said she'd meet me. It's after one. She'll be here soon.* But by two she couldn't make any more excuses or sit still another second. *What* the hell am I waiting for? She's supposed to be here for me!

At four-thirty Pat's doorbell rang. She started not to answer, but she wanted to hear what Gayle had to say. Wanted to see her try and make this all right, because it wasn't. She'd planned to stay cool, but as soon as Gayle walked in Pat went off.

'You didn't even call. Not the clinic, not here . . .'

'I couldn't get here, Pat. Ramsey has . . .'

'What the hell made me think you'd be here when you went off and left your own damn father in the hospital "'cause Ramsey said"!'

'That's not fair! I tried . . .'

'Tried nothing! Shit, Gayle, it's four-thirty. I needed you this morning! I needed you to at least come get me! I stood up on the bus all the way home, but what the fuck do you care? You were probably out by your damn pool!'

Gayle recoiled, stung by Pat's attack, but she instantly went on the offensive. 'And if you were as perfect as you think you are, you wouldn't be in this mess in the first place. Ramsey's right. You think you're better than me, but I had my baby.'

It was like Gayle took a knife to Pat's belly, but she struck back despite the wound. 'Oh is that what Ramsey thinks? And I guess it's what you think, too, since you seem to have completely stopped thinking for yourself since you got *Ramsey* to do it for you! That's besides the fact you weren't going to tell anybody. I'd like to see where you'd be if you had Vanessa alone. Maybe then you'd understand how babies end up in the garbage!'

'Well your mother threw you away and *I* begged Momma and Daddy to take you in.'

'*Thank you, Gayle!* I've been in your debt since I was eleven, but you know what? We can call it even now, and

240

since the debt's paid, you can get the hell out of my life!'

'Excuse me!' Gayle stared like Pat was speaking in tongues. They looked at each other for a long moment. That used to be enough to say all that need be said, but not now.

'What's the point, Gayle? I'm not even sure I like you anymore, so let's not pretend.' Pat's voice was calm, relieved.

'So you can turn me off, just like a faucet?!'

'Call it what you want.'

'Fine, 'cause I'm not sure I like you anymore either!'

Pat's whole body shook after Gayle closed the door. She'd just dismissed her soul sister, the last link to the first two decades of her life. And who was there now? Certainly not Peter Jackson. Not only didn't he love her, but he was probably still laughing about just how dense she was to think he could. *Like a stupid little country nigger . . .* Verna's words came up in Pat's throat like curdled milk, but she choked them down. *No, this is different.* But then the horror of the afternoon and what she'd done brought her to the present, and she doubled in pain from the cramps and rocked to quiet the howl she was sure would never end if she let it past her lips.

The next morning Pat's whole body felt bruised, like she'd fought twelve rounds with Muhammad Ali, but her head was clear. As of today, she was officially shutting the book on the first part of her life. Whatever came before was no longer open for comment or consideration, and the future was yet to be written.

And two Sundays later she sat in the middle of her bed, with a ham sandwich and a glass of champagne watching the Yankees play Baltimore. Marcus had already hit a single and stolen a base. *Guess he was right about the agent. Looks like he left the past behind, too.* But the game was incidental. She was waiting for the debut of her Tropical Quencher spot.

They'd pulled it off, on time, under budget, the client loved it, and none of it would have gone down this way without her. Suddenly people who barely nodded in the elevator stopped by Pat's desk to talk. Chris couldn't find anything snide to say because he was too busy trying to save his ass since his Lush Lips commercial came in way over budget.

Zabriski took Pat to lunch and let her know Tastea was impressed with her, *big-time*, and he had a test spot for her. It was strictly low-budget, for focus groups only, 'But it's your baby.' He made it clear his door was always open. If she kept working this hard, he was sure she'd be promoted to producer in the very near future.

Baltimore was leading when they broke for commercial. When she saw the couple holding hands as they waded out of an aqua lagoon, she got goose bumps. In the thirty seconds it ran, Pat got a rush bigger than she got from anything or anybody. People in New York, Swan City, and Walla Walla, Washington, were looking at it just like she was. And she'd made it happen. *I can do this! I can be the best and nothing can stop me!*

Part Two

TRYIN' TO SLEEP

13

'Go head on with your rich self, Mrs Hilliard'

1988 WHITE PLAINS, NEW YORK

'I'm sorry, Mrs Hilliard, your card has been denied.'

'Pardon me?' Gayle cocked her head indignantly. 'That's not possible.' She'd used her platinum card here just last week. 'You must have done something wrong. Try again.'

Another swipe of the card and the saleswoman waited. 'I'm sorry, but . . .'

The heat of embarrassment rose in Gayle's cheeks. 'You're new, aren't you?' She removed another card from her wallet and thrust it at the clerk. 'Here.'

'Mommy?' Vanessa played an excited tattoo on Gayle's arm. 'Mommy, look!' She pointed to a display of glow-in-the-dark stars. 'Can we get those for my new room, too?'

'Not now, 'Nessa. Mommy's busy.' Gayle dug her elbow into the pile of linens they'd spent two hours selecting. *I know she made some stupid mistake. Wait 'til I tell Ramsey.* She twisted her rings impatiently around her freshly manicured finger. *But he's been in such a foul mood, if I mention it, he'll probably try to get her fired.*

With the increase in industrial parks and corporate headquarters relocating outside of New York City, Greener Pastures launched a commercial division and expanded into Connecticut and New Jersey. Ramsey had crews out seven days a week, and he worked killer hours, coordinating, supervising, and calling on prospective clients, because, like he always told Gayle, 'My company's like the shrubs I plant. If I don't tend them, they won't grow.'

Finally the slip chugged through the electronic register. Gayle signed the receipt with a flourish, only semiplacated by the clerk, who hurriedly bagged the purchases and apologized profusely for the delay. Vanessa, hands on hips, twisted from side to side, restless for the next adventure. At eight, she was tall and lanky like her father, but she was a honey-colored, doe-eyed fawn and the spitting image of Gayle.

Friday after-school shopping and dinner out became their mother-daughter ritual when a stroke forced Loretta to retire and move in with them two years ago. Gayle, still feeling guilty about her father's death, devoted herself to her mother's recuperation. Ramsey took care of selling the St Albans house and investing the proceeds for his mother-in-law.

Ramsey was glad Gayle had something to keep her occupied, and Vanessa thought her 'Gram' could do no wrong, so they never complained about the new arrangement. But when Christmas rolled around, and for the first time ever Gayle had no idea what toys made her daughter's eyes light up, she realized how little attention she'd paid to Vanessa.

Fortunately, Loretta approached her rehab with the same stubborn determination that carried her through life. She walked and talked a little slowly and forgot things sometimes, but she recovered to the satisfaction of her doctors. And when Loretta got up one morning asking about beauty parlors because her auburn hair had two-inch gray roots, Gayle knew her mother would be fine. Right then she decided that she and her own daughter needed some special time, just the two of them. Since Ramsey usually worked late on Friday, it became 'girls' night.'

'On second thought, I'd like this sent.' Gayle decided it was more than she wanted to carry. Besides, she looked forward to the delivery truck rumbling up the long driveway. She liked the surprised look on the driver's face when he realized *she* was Mrs Ramsey Hilliard, not the girl in to clean, and signed for her packages.

On a late-spring afternoon, shortly after Ramsey expanded Greener Pastures, he surprised Gayle by driving her farther up in Westchester County. He turned into an unmarked road and continued uphill along a meandering gravel path through the woods and stopped in front of a redbrick Greek Revival. The wide, pillared front porch was centred by towering double doors, decorated with enormous brass knockers. Imposing oaks and spruce trees shaded the rolling front lawn. Ramsey said it belonged to a client who was moving. If she wanted the place, he'd buy it.

Gayle loved their Tudor in White Plains, but this was a dream house, straight out of *Ebony*, complete with a small, separate suite intended for the maid, which would be perfect for her mother. 'Ramsey, can we afford all this?' she had asked.

'You leave that to me, Nightingale. I grew up looking at houses like this from the outside, trying to imagine how rich you had to be to live in one.' He smiled, slowly bobbing his head. 'Yes indeedy. You leave that to me.' Then he kissed her breath away, like he used to. Gayle hadn't felt that in a long time.

Maybe I won't mention the card trouble to Ramsey. It's

probably nothing. Gayle took her daughter's hand and led her out into the Galleria. 'Frozen yogurt?'

Vanessa grinned and pulled her mother in the direction of the concession. Gayle played with a small cup of strawberry and sat and watched her daughter enjoy the cone.

'Betcha Keisha and Monica are gonna be jealous of my new room.'

'You don't want them to be jealous, do you?'

'Only a little bit.' Vanessa's eyes sparkled as she licked her cone. 'Think Daddy will like it, too, so he'll play with me more?'

'We'll see about that.' It wasn't that Ramsey didn't love Vanessa, but aside from buying her presents he seemed not to know what to do with her. Gayle hoped he'd be more comfortable with Vanessa once she was older.

As it was he usually got in past Vanessa's bedtime, shoveled down his dinner, barely nodding to acknowledge Gayle's attempts to fill him in on her day or Vanessa's progress in school or ballet class. He'd be asleep before his head hit the pillow.

Gayle wasn't getting much of Ramsey's attention either. They used to get a sitter and go to Broadway shows, then end up at Bessie's for a nightcap. These days she knew Ramsey still went, but Gayle couldn't remember the last time they were at Bessie's together. She rarely complained though. She knew she was lucky, even when she was a little lonely.

A couple of times a year they'd still go to Atlantic City for the weekend. Gayle would get 'all dolled up' as Ramsey liked to say, and he'd play blackjack and tease her when she cringed at the stacks of chips he bet. Ramsey would call her his lucky charm and make sure all the other players knew she belonged to him. Gayle would squeeze his hand and close her eyes when the dealer turned up the last card, but they had fun and Ramsey never seemed to lose. Then he'd take her shopping for something expensive and the salesgirls would tell her how lucky she was to have a husband like Ramsey, who knew how to treat his wife.

Her mother agreed. 'Men have to have their own recreation. Every Friday your father went to his lodge meeting. Him and your Uncle Macon, God rest his soul. What you think they were meeting about 'til three in the morning? Ramsey's fun is little enough for all he provides. You live better than lots of folks I used to work for.'

At first Ramsey didn't see how Gayle could be lonely with Vanessa and her mother around. One day he complained to Bessie. Then the un-degreed restaurateur, whose shady past could have blocked his acceptance in 'certain circles,' showed Ramsey the ropes. The Hilliards joined the most prominent Black Episcopal church in Westchester County although Loretta complained that it was too snooty for her. 'Can't even say "Amen" without folks lookin' at you like you broke wind!' Ramsey only attended on Christmas and Easter.

Bessie showed Ramsey the importance of strategic charitable contributions. After Ramsey bought tables for political fund-raisers and donated Greener Pastures' services to charity auctions, Gayle was recruited for committees. She balked, claiming she didn't fit in, but Ramsey insisted Gayle start moving in the circles that would help the business grow. Besides, committee work kept her busy, and out of his hair.

And when their picture ran in *Jet* with a caption that read, 'Mr & Mrs Ramsey Hilliard attend Westchester's College Fund Gala,' Gayle knew she had arrived and mailed a copy to Brenda in Germany. But at the next planning committee meeting of the Phyllis Wheatley Scholarship Fund, Caribbean Splash Benefit Luncheon and Fashion Show, she got the same cool smiles and polite nods when the women clustered in their usual tight knots, bound by laughter and gossip. Most were older, belonged to the same sorority, shared alma maters, or friends who did. Gayle had never set foot in college except to visit Pat. Ramsey's checks couldn't buy their friendship, but she wanted Vanessa to belong to this club, so she ignored the slights, kept smiling, and hurried off like she had somewhere important to go.

'Mommy, it's dripping!' Melting strawberry cream ran down the cone, onto Vanessa's hands. Gayle got up to find more napkins.

As soon as he closed on the new house, Ramsey told her to hire an interior designer and gave her carte blanche on decorating. Fabric samples, paint chips, furniture showrooms, and antique stores became her job for nearly a year, which was perfect since it was Vanessa's first in school all day. Now the last phase, Vanessa's room, was almost complete. Her pickled oak country French furniture would arrive tomorrow, so everything would be in place for her first slumber party next week. With the house finally complete, Gayle told herself she should feel a sense of accomplishment, but all she felt inside was empty.

'Let's see those fingers.' Gayle wiped Vanessa's hands, and they left. On the way to the parking lot they cut through Neiman's. Gayle stopped at the fragrance counter, chose a bottle of Opium, gave the clerk her store charge, and waited, trying to look nonchalant.

'Thank you. Have a nice day, Mrs Hilliard.'

Good. No problem. Then she spied a pair of sunglasses she had to have. Charge. In the children's department they selected an outfit for Vanessa to wear the night of her party, and two new nightgowns because they couldn't decide which they liked best. Charge. Gayle was satisfied, but there was a sale in the shoe department. Two pair of sandals later Gayle and Vanessa were finally on their way.

'I have to get gas.' Gayle made sure Vanessa was buckled in, and she eased her Seville out of the lot. 'What would you like for dinner, Miss Hilliard? Mommy has a headache. Would it be okay if we got something and took it home?'

'Hamburgers! Yippee!' Vanessa knew fast food was mostly off-limits because her mother hated eating at those places, but she saw the takeout opportunity and seized it.

'Ugh! But okay. Burgers it is.' And since Loretta had gone to Cleveland for a weekend gospel festival with her friends from Mt Moriah, she wouldn't have to hear about 'those nasty cat burgers.' Gayle pulled up to the pump, told the attendant to fill it, and handed him her gasoline credit card when he was done.

'Sorry, ma'am. This won't go through.'

At home, Vanessa devoured her fries and cheeseburger. 'Aren't you hungry?'

Gayle's food remained untouched on the kitchen table. 'No, honey. I guess I'm not. But when you finish, go on up and get ready for bed.'

Vanessa slipped one of Gayle's fries out of the paper container and munched. 'Can we read in your bed tonight?'

'If you promise to go to your own bed when it's time. I can't carry you anymore.'

'That's 'cause I'm a big girl!' Vanessa scampered upstairs.

Gayle smiled. *That you are*. She took an aspirin since her head was still pounding, then got her wallet. Ramsey always made sure she had the new cards each year, but she checked the expiration dates anyway. He paid all the bills and she had seen him writing checks, so that wasn't it. *Ramsey will know what it's all about.* She fixed him a plate and left it in the refrigerator, ready for the microwave, in case he was hungry when he got in, then went upstairs without solving the mystery.

Vanessa was waiting in the king-size four-poster. Propped on a stack of ruffled pillows, she examined her bronzed baby shoes and the picture in the attached frame that sat on Ramsey's night table. 'How old was I in this picture, again?'

'For the five hundred and fifty-second time, you were fourteen months old and the shoes were . . .'

'The ones I took my first steps in.' Vanessa giggled as she finished the familiar story.

'And your daddy can't sleep without that picture right by his side of the bed.' Gayle nestled next to her daughter and read another installment of 'The Adventures of Ell Crawford: A Girl and her Magic Shoes.' Vanessa had invented Ell as an imaginary playmate when she was four, and Gayle started making up stories about her. Now she actually wrote them out and illustrated them, too. Before Ell had earned the eternal thanks of Mama Crocodile for rescuing her baby from the mouth of the Zambezi River, Vanessa was asleep.

Gayle worked hard at being a good daughter, wife, and mother, but every now and again, she thought it might not be enough. Ramsey spent almost every waking moment working. Loretta, determined not to be treated like an old woman, kept herself busy. She volunteered at the Red Cross and, in spite of Gayle's objections, insisted on helping the cleaning woman who came in twice a week. Gayle could always tell when her mother had been 'supervising.' She'd find one of her perfume bottles in the den or her pepper mill in the foyer, where her mother had absentmindedly left it, but the cleaning lady said she didn't mind the company, and it made Loretta feel useful.

And although Gayle knew Vanessa still needed her, every day she grew more 'I can do that myself, Mommy' independent.

When her daughter was four going on forty, Gayle started talking about another baby. Ramsey wasn't having it. Said he worked too hard to be kept awake at night by a crying baby, again. And she was lucky Vanessa didn't make her fat and flabby with ugly stretch marks. He didn't want to chance that. Did she? Then he made love to her and made her promise to stop thinking about it.

The next day he brought home a diamond tennis bracelet, two tickets to Hawaii, and told her to arrange for Vanessa's baby-sitter to stay the week. Gayle knew he was saying 'This can happen because we don't have a baby.' When they came back Gayle had her tubes tied, Ramsey bought her a Seville, and only once in a while, late at night, when she was alone, did she wonder 'what if?'

Gayle roused Vanessa enough to lead her to bed, tucked her in, smoothed her eyebrows, and switched off the light. Between school, dance, piano and riding lessons, and Brownies, Gayle was busy as a chauffeur. She talked to the other mothers in parking lots, at bake sales, on field trips, but didn't have any real friends. Ramsey didn't either, except maybe Bessie, but it didn't seem to bother him.

Brenda and Dexter had moved back to New York when he got out of the service. Ramsey liked Dexter right away, mostly because Dexter was very impressed with Ramsey's accomplishments. Vanessa and Dexter, Jr, enjoyed playing together, so the Washingtons had visited often. Brenda thought Gayle had hit pay dirt with Ramsey. She had walked through the old house with her mouth open. 'Go head on with your rich self, Mrs Hilliard!' *What if she could see this one*. Ramsey thought Brenda was common, but Gayle was thrilled to have her friend back, so he left it alone.

Then, Brenda found the wrong brand of panty hose in the trunk of Dexter's ride. She left him in a finger snap. At first Gayle called her regularly, but Brenda talked about her husband like a dog, and Gayle couldn't take it. As soon as the divorce was final Brenda moved to San Diego with Dexter, Jr, got herself a real-estate license, a new man, and decided California was heaven.

Divorce was unthinkable to Gayle. Ramsey, Vanessa, Momma, they were her family. Nothing was more important than that. Shortly before Vanessa was born, Gayle started to worry about carrying some rare genetic disease she knew nothing about and would pass on to the baby. She became so obsessed that Ramsey hired an investigator to track down her real parents, but all he found was a stone-cold dead end. Sometimes Gayle still wondered about them, but she'd feel disloyal to her mother, more like a traitor to her father than she already did, and she'd end up making an extra trip to the cemetery to ease her conscience.

Gayle turned the TV in her bedroom to *Dallas*, stretched out on the chaise, and reached for her sketch pad to work on a new Ell adventure for Vanessa.

She mostly tried not to think about Pat, but reminders lurked in unexpected places. Just last month, Vanessa found snapshots from Pat's graduation. Gayle remembered that she never sent them as she'd promised. And there was the woman at church who sounded like Pat. The first time Gayle heard her alto from the back of the choir loft, she got the shivers.

Ramsey was glad they'd lost touch and said as much.

When Loretta asked about Pat that first Christmas after she graduated, Gayle told her mother they'd had a fight, and to leave it alone. For once, Loretta did. Gayle never told her husband or her mother what had happened between her and Pat, but then there were lots of things she kept to herself.

When Ramsey tiptoed into the room, Gayle had been asleep for hours. He bent down and kissed her neck.

'Hi,' Gayle mumbled, stretched, and sat up. *What's it gonna be tonight?* Ramsey could come in bubbling with enthusiastic plans to expand the business or take a trip. Just as easily he could be withdrawn, or plain ornery like her father used to say. Gayle used to love Ramsey's whistling, but now, more often than not she used it as a mood-o-meter. Top forty soul meant he was cruisin' fine and dandy. Bluesy snatches of nothing in particular signaled a bad attitude, but she hadn't heard him come in, so she had no idea what to expect. Trying not to be obvious, she flipped on the light and glanced at the clock. She didn't want to start anything, she just wanted to know the time. It was three-fifty.

'How's my Nightingale?' Ramsey smiled and ran his finger along her arm.

'Glad to see you.' Gayle relaxed. She yawned and decided to tell him about her day. 'Something strange happened. With some of my credit cards . . .'

'Either Miss Banks forgot to mail my envelopes or there's some kinda computer mess up.' Ramsey peeled down to his underwear, sat on his side of the bed, and traced the bronze laces of Vanessa's baby shoe. 'I'll see 'bout it, first thing Monday.' He got into bed.

Gayle kissed his chest and glanced down at her hand to make sure her ring was off. After leaving a sizable gash in Ramsey's back one night, she stopped wearing the big

255

marquise stone to bed. She lifted her head and looked at him. Ramsey was one of those men who got better-looking with age, and Gayle, no matter how hard she tried, could never picture him looking old, like her daddy. The hair at his temples and his mustache were shot with silver, and the fine lines around his eyes and mouth added authority. He looked like a man who knew the answers. She snuggled up next to him, savoring the sweet moment, because she didn't know how long it would have to do her.

Ramsey slid his hand under Gayle's nightgown, massaged her thigh. He was feeling good, better than he'd felt in a long time. He'd hoped to get by without Gayle running into any problems with the credit cards, but it was all taken care of now. He'd mailed the checks himself yesterday. The first four months of the year had been touch-and-go, and he had to let a few bills slide, but two new clients just came through with sizable retainers and the ponies had been running his way all week.

'I don't like seeing worry in your eyes.' Ramsey kissed her lids. 'I put the fire in those eyes, and I'll always keep it burnin'.' He turned out the light, rubbed her breasts, and rooted around. Gayle squirmed and moaned a little to make it seem convincing, but it wasn't like it used to be. Mostly sex had become his need and her duty. It got so bad she had asked him point-blank if he was having an affair. When he stopped laughing he assured her there was nobody but Greener Pastures.

Every once in a while he would light her fire, but tonight she tilted her head to the side to keep from knocking the mahogany headboard with each mechanical thrust.

Ramsey twisted up his face and let his eyes roll back. Oh yeah, he felt real good. He fell over to his side of the bed. 'Your "Cat-in-the-Hat" ballplayer boy never knew what he was missing.' It was early in the baseball season, but

Ramsey had already won pretty big against the Orioles. *They mighta won the Series in '83, but they ain't doodley-squat now.*

'I *hate* when you bring Marcus into our bed!' A couple of times a year, especially since Marcus made it big, Ramsey dug him up, like squaring off in her front hall nine years ago didn't end the duel. 'I forgot about him the day I met you. Isn't that enough?'

'Yeah . . . Mr Big Stuff.' Ramsey scratched and raised up on his elbow, searching for the remote control. 'I betcha you read all about his sports cars and his girlfriends and wonder what the hell you doin' with a man who shovels cow shit for a living.'

Gayle sighed. 'Ramsey, I married you because I love you.' *I don't know what I felt for Marcus.* 'Marcus Carter plays games . . .' *I do wonder sometimes . . .* 'You're a successful businessman' . . . *what it would be like to be Mrs Carter?* 'How can you even compare the two?'

Ramsey channel-zapped in silence. 'He's goin' out with that model from Africa. You know, what's her name?'

'I don't know, Ramsey.' *Téa. Her name is Téa. Everybody knows that.* 'Any more than I know why you can't forget about him.' Gayle's head pounded like a bass drum. *I have a beautiful little girl, a gorgeous house, and a wonderful husband who takes care of everything.* She turned over. 'You wouldn't want to trade places with him if you could.'

'What does that mean?'

'Nothing, Ramsey.' She hadn't meant for that to slip out, she was just tired of this conversation. 'It's late.'

'It must mean somethin' or you wouldn't a said it.'

Gayle pretended to fall asleep, so he'd be quiet, but the next morning Ramsey worried her about Marcus, like a dog with a bone. Accused her of keeping secrets. He left the house in a mean mood, and it wasn't out of his system when he got home.

Nothing about that icy afternoon had ever passed Gayle's lips. They had promised, the three of them, never to tell another soul, but Ramsey kept badgering her, and Freddy had been dead so long she figured it couldn't matter anymore. She just wanted Ramsey to leave her alone and to stop envying Marcus once and for all. 'If I tell you, will you promise not to mention him again?'

'Yeah, all right.'

'When we were little, Marcus, Pat, and I, Marcus had an older brother . . .' Gayle told Ramsey about the gym bag, the gun, and the shot that sounded like corn popping. 'His mom hasn't been right since. It was Freddy who loved baseball. Marcus only started playing after his brother died, kind of in his honor, I guess.'

'Well, now. Mr Baseball is a stone killer. That's what he keeps under all those hats.' Ramsey's eyes glazed with satisfaction.

'I told you, you wouldn't want to be him.'

Gayle lay awake running slumber party preparations through her head, convincing herself she'd done the right thing, until sunlight sneaked around the edges of the window shades.

'Can we have pizza for breakfast, Mrs Hilliard?' Keisha smiled at her sweetly.

'Yea! Pizza!!!' a chorus of little girls chanted from the family room, where they sat cross-legged on the floor, in their pajamas, deciding whether to watch *Muppet Babies* or *Rainbow Brite* on the gigantic TV.

So far Vanessa's sleepover was a big success. Six of her 'very best' friends had given the room a proper christening. Last night a face-painting artist transformed the little girls into exotic birds and butterflies. Gayle hired a chef from the local pizzeria to supervise them in making their own pizzas, and she arranged for the sitter to help her keep the girls busy.

'What kind of breakfast is pizza? I'm making doughnuts. I haven't made doughnuts in a month of Sundays.' Loretta joined Gayle in the kitchen. Actually Loretta hadn't done much cooking at all. Originally, Ramsey planned to add a kitchen to her apartment, but her forgetfulness since the stroke changed his mind.

'Yea! Doughnuts!!'

They'd probably cheer for cauliflower. Gayle glanced at the ceiling, hoping they hadn't disturbed Ramsey.

Ramsey was enthusiastic when they had first planned the party. He even promised Vanessa he'd make her favorite, strawberry-banana pancakes, for breakfast. Gayle reminded him about it before he left for work yesterday, but he hadn't come home until nearly daybreak. Gayle knew he wouldn't show, but she had hoped anyway, for Vanessa's sake. Now she just wanted to get through the meal without incident.

'Pancakes. We're all having pancakes this morning!' Gayle said explicitly. It was as much for the benefit of her young guests as for her mother, who was in the cabinet, trying to drag out the big cast-iron Dutch oven she fried doughnuts in.

'Yea! Pancakes!' They cheered.

'I betcha my daddy makes better pancakes than any daddy!' Vanessa announced.

'Humph! Don't know what's good!' Loretta snorted, and sat on a stool by the island.

'We'll have doughnuts tomorrow, okay, Gram?' Vanessa got up and leaned on her grandmother's knees. 'When's Daddy coming down?'

'Honey, Daddy's not up yet. He worked really late last night, so we'll have to get by without his help.'

'He promised! He's always working. He never keeps his promises.' Vanessa pouted.

'You know he'll make it up to you.' Gayle disappeared into the pantry. Ramsey would bring her a new doll or whatever else was part of the biggest display in the toy store.

'I don't want a present. I wanted him to make us pancakes,' Vanessa muttered as she slunk back to the den.

Breakfast came and went disaster-free. By the time Ramsey appeared, shaved and dressed, they were back from the matinee, and the girls, lined up on the den sofa, swayed from side to side, singing 'Somewhere Out There' for the umpteenth time.

'Hi, Daddy!' Vanessa plowed into her father.

'I thought this thing was to celebrate your new room.' Ramsey nodded toward the chorus in the family room.

Vanessa grabbed his hand and smiled up at him, absentmindedly twisting the diamond ring around his pinkie. 'We did. I mean we are! We're having so much fun! You missed it!'

Gayle, watching from the kitchen, saw the tension lines around his mouth. 'Can I fix you something?'

'No. I'll eat when I come back. Stop it, 'Nessa.' Ramsey shook his hand loose and pulled his car keys from his pocket. 'I've got a run to make.' Vanessa sighed, and went back to her friends.

'Okay. I'll have a snack ready when you get back.'

'I wanna watch all the pre-race stuff.'

I forgot. It's Derby Day.

The first time they'd watched the race together, Ramsey told her stories about amazing horses, ponies he called them, and heroic jockeys. He explained in exacting detail the intricacies of racing. Last year Ramsey bought a horse, Dream's Girl, the first of his string, he told her. A colt with the same sire as Ramsey's filly was running this year, so she knew the Derby was important to him.

'I won't be long.' The door slammed and Ramsey was gone.

I hope these kids are gone by race time. Fortunately, mothers started arriving for their daughters, each departure triggering a long, sad good-bye, like they'd never have this much fun together again.

The drizzle that started when they got back from the movies had increased to an insistent shower. *Only Monica and Keisha to return to their rightful owners.* They rounded out the inseparable trio Gayle called the 'A-Team.' The way the three of them clung together always reminded Gayle of her and Pat and Marcus, but she kept that thought to herself.

Gayle, exhausted, sipped mint tea at the kitchen counter. The headache that had settled across her brow made her squint, and the jeers and boos coming from her mother's room didn't help. Loretta had the TV in her sitting room turned up to high heaven for her Saturday afternoon wrestling. *It's a wonder she's not deaf. Listen to me! She used to say that to me and Pat!* Gayle shook her head and got up to make a sandwich for Ramsey. *What if he wants something hot?*

Ramsey came in, whistling 'Heard It Through the Grapevine.' 'I brought pizza for my girls! It's wicked outside. But it's sunny and dry in KY!' He laughed at his rhyme as he put two boxes on the counter, then hung his wet jacket in the back hall.

Vanessa came in to investigate. 'But Daddy, we . . .'

'We love pizza!' Gayle chimed in, and signaled Vanessa

to leave it alone. Ramsey didn't remember they'd made pizza last night, and since he returned in a better mood than when he left, it was easier to pretend it was exactly what they wanted. Gayle popped one of the pies in the oven to warm.

Vanessa shrugged and went back to Monica and Keisha and their game of Chutes and Ladders. Ramsey followed Vanessa into the den and fiddled with the color on the TV until it suited him. Gayle debated whether to send the girls upstairs, but they were playing quietly and they'd be picked up any minute. In the background she heard a reporter run down a list of celebrities attending the Run for the Roses and daydreamed, just for a moment, of being there in a wide-brimmed straw hat, enjoying the festivities with Ramsey.

'It's almost post time.' Ramsey had settled in his favorite leather chair. Gayle moved a vase aside, set his tray on the table next to him, and perched on the ottoman. 'Do you know what it means for Dream's Girl if Shadow wins the Derby?'

Gayle figured it was good, but Ramsey didn't expect an answer anyway. Truth was she didn't care about all his horse talk, but she could see he was excited.

'I know he's twenty-five and one, but the favorite hasn't won this race since 1979.' As if to back him up the announcer said if the pace was fast, there was a strong possibility Shadow could finish in the top three. 'You hear that! What did I tell you!' Ramsey leaned forward, rubbing his hands together. 'I'll have investors lined up begging for a piece of my Girl.' And the way he figured it, he'd walk away with a big enough chunk of cash to put all his finances to rights and then some. He'd be flush again, and that didn't even count what he'd bet on the colt.

As handlers led the horses into the starting gate the

doorbell rang. Gayle jumped up to answer it.

Monica's mother stood dripping on the threshold. Gayle knew that Mrs Phillips was president of the Parents Alliance at school, ran her own catering service, and was married to the chief of police, but right now, dressed in a bright yellow slicker, matching rain hat, and red Wellingtons, the round, brown woman looked like a Paddington Bear.

Gayle smiled politely. 'Come in . . . I'll get . . .' The crash of exploding glass sent both women rushing toward the screams and shrieks coming from the den.

A smoky cloud and the acrid smell of burning plastic hung in the air. Gayle reached the room in time to see Ramsey disappear up the back stairs. The television hissed and sparked from a jagged gaping hole in the screen. Water dripped down the front of the set and pale yellow jonquils mingled with glass shards on the carpet. On the far side of the room the girls huddled and sobbed, Chutes and Ladders pieces at their feet.

'Mommy!' Monica attached herself to her mother's leg.

Gayle hugged Vanessa and Keisha.

'We . . . we weren't doing anything . . . just playing. Daddy just threw it . . . the vase, and it broke the TV,' Vanessa stammered.

'He did what?' Mrs Phillips snarled at Gayle. 'What kind of man would *do* that? And in front of children?' She scooped her daughter into her arms and pulled Keisha out of Gayle's grasp. 'Come on, honey, get your things. I'll take you home. You don't have to stay here another minute.' Keisha wiped her tears on her sleeve and went to get her coat. 'I can tell you this, Mrs Hilliard, Monica won't be back, and I'm sure once I talk to her mother, Keisha won't either!'

'We should have been upstairs . . . in my room.' Tears

streamed down Vanessa's cheeks when the others had gone.

'Shh.' Gayle held her daughter tight. 'You didn't do anything wrong. Nothing.' Gayle struggled to keep herself from trembling.

'That Tony the Terror is one mean . . . What happened in here?' Loretta emerged from her room and stared openmouthed at the smoldering mess.

'I'm not exactly sure, Momma.'

'The children did that?'

'No . . . No, but why don't you take Vanessa with you and finish watching. I'll clean up . . . okay?' Gayle turned Vanessa around to face her grandmother.

'Humph! You *want* me to take her back to watch wrestling?' Loretta knew something was up. 'Come on, Van.' Vanessa dashed into Loretta's arms. 'Tag team is next. Thor and Tommy Thunder versus Hook and Lockjaw.' They headed up Loretta's short flight of stairs.

Gayle unplugged the broken TV, then raced up to the bedroom.

He's never acted like this. Ramsey was moody, unpredictable, and often irritable, but this was insane. 'Well? What's the matter with you?'

Ramsey sat at the foot of their bed, his shoe shine kit open at his feet, rubbing paste wax on an oxblood slip-on. He had pulled up the spread and covered the ivory carpeting with an old towel just like he always did. He didn't look up, but he'd been expecting her.

She walked to the window. 'Have you gone crazy?'

In deliberate circles Ramsey massaged polish into the leather with a rag. He'd asked himself that question. Nothing like that had ever taken hold of him before.

Five O'Clock Shadow flew out of the gate and settled at the front of the thundering pack, running easy like a spring breeze. That's when Ramsey started shaking, down in his Kentucky bones. Shadow charged and Ramsey felt redeemed for all the shit he ever shoveled and all the times he was called outta his name by 'well-bred' gentlemen. His horse was coming home. He could feel it, and it was a sign his lucky star was on the rise.

'Do you know how much you scared 'Nessa? And her friends?' Gayle faced the rain-streaked window. She couldn't look at him.

Did she know how much he scared himself? Ramsey slipped his hand inside the shoe and started brushing. Shadow was in command, six lengths ahead. No prodding, no crop for him. Ramsey watched, spellbound. Then the horse dropped to his knees. Just like that. Keeled over, dead in his tracks. Ramsey knew it was a heart attack. He'd seen it happen once before, but it couldn't have happened to Shadow, and he couldn't have thrown that vase through the TV screen. Ramsey had relived the moment a hundred times since he came upstairs. Like that made anything different. The right side of his shoe gleamed from the vigorous strokes, but the left was still mottled with wax.

'Not to mention me. How could you do that?' She spun around to face him.

Of course he couldn't tell her he'd gone and broken his own rules. He hadn't been winning enough to keep out of the hole, and when he found himself in a tight spot, he had let the business invest in his hobby. Just for a while, until he got straight. He wouldn't tell her he'd used the retainers he got from the two new clients to clean up his stable and training fees for a filly that it didn't even pay to breed now. And it wasn't her business that he wouldn't dip into his private stash to fix this. That money was strictly a last resort, his last stake, and he didn't need the parachute yet.

Gayle waited, arms locked across her chest. She didn't look like his sweet Nightingale now. More like his mother, spiteful and cussing, meeting his father at the door when he stumbled in from a three-day drunk.

Ramsey kept brushing the shiny side of his shoe. He couldn't tell Gayle what happened. Of course he'd lost before. That's part of the deal, but this should have been a turning point. He'd bet on that. Now what could he say? *'Things haven't been going so good . . . I can't win for losin'. I'll make it up to you baby?'* That wasn't a man's way. He didn't realize he'd started whistling.

'Stop that and answer me!' Gayle glared at him, waiting for an explanation.

'I don't know.' He did still have a voice. He told her what happened to Shadow. 'It's just . . . I . . .' He dropped his head and stared. 'Well . . . the business, things haven't been going so hot lately. Some of my best clients left me for the big national chains. That's why I want to keep expanding.' He looked at her now, measuring the impact of his words before he continued. 'I hoped the money from investors in Dream's Girl would at least give me a fighting chance . . . I'd get some new equipment . . . I was stupid I guess.'

Gayle sat next to him on the bed. 'You should have told me. I know how hard you work, but you never let on . . .'

'I didn't want to worry you. I still don't. I just got real upset. I'll sell Dream's Girl, tighten things up a bit, and it'll be fine. I'll make this up to you and Vanessa. I will.'

Gayle thought she saw tears at the corners of Ramsey's eyes. 'How can I help?'

'I need you to forgive me, Nightingale.'

Need? He never said that before. 'Of course I forgive you.'

The next morning Gayle eased Ramsey's Mark VII into

a space in front of the Superqwik. The sky was bright and cloudless, a few oily puddles in the parking lot the only reminder of yesterday's downpour. Gayle didn't like driving his car because he always complained about having to readjust the seat and mirrors afterward, but he had blocked hers in the garage and Vanessa was worried about being late for Sunday School. *Orange juice . . . Half & Half . . .* Gayle turned the ignition off, opened the door, reached for her purse, and only then remembered it sitting on the kitchen counter. She checked her pockets. Eleven cents. *He's got to have change in here.* Between the seats, sixty-two cents. Map pocket, four dimes. Glove box, the coin slots were full. *Thank you, Ramsey!*

She didn't know why the book next to the lock de-icer caught her eye. The book was small and black, nondescript really, like a mileage log, but she opened it up. Names, dates, and numbers, written in Ramsey's small, cramped script filled the pages. Lots of numbers, underlined, circled in red. He pressed so hard that if you turned the pages over, it felt like braille. *He always presses too hard.* She tried to get him to stop, but he'd told her it was pretty near impossible to teach an old dog new tricks. Gayle's head started to throb and she pulled down the visor to block out the sun. She recognized the names, at least some of them. Sports teams. *The numbers. They couldn't be . . . dollars?* Thousands and thousands of dollars. There were multiple entries for almost every day. Football, hockey, basketball.

Gayle didn't remember the drive home. *'Things haven't been going so hot . . . buy some new equipment . . . I didn't want to worry you . . .'* She came to when she slammed the bedroom door.

Ramsey rolled over and lifted his head. 'Mornin', Ba . . .'

'How much have you lost, Ramsey?!' She knew he

gambled, but not like this. 'What did it cost you, or should I say us, when that stupid horse dropped dead?' She threw the book at him before he could deny anything. 'Tell me! Why did you lie?'

He raised up, pulled the covers around him. 'Where'd you get . . . It's not like that. This isn't . . . what you think.'

'And what is it I think, Ramsey? That you've got a problem 'cause you'll bet on anything?'

'Nightin . . . Gayle, I got a little carried away.' He tossed the covers back and got out of bed. 'But yesterday scared some sense into me.'

Ramsey stood in front of her in his white undershirt, his long spindly legs protruding from baggy boxer shorts.

'When we were away you always bet more than I thought you should, but what did I know? *Not* that you bet every day! Every day, Ramsey! Is that why you're so moody? You win, you're happy. You lose, you're miserable. Are we broke? Tell me! Are we?!'

'Broke?! No way . . . that'll never happen. I always have a safety net, always. Anyway, I told you I learned my lesson.'

'This is crazy, Ramsey. You can't do this anymore. You have to stop . . .' she caught herself before the 'or' escaped. *Or what Gayle? Or I'll leave? Take Vanessa and my mother and go where?* She had a checking account that Ramsey opened for her. He put money in it every month so she didn't have to bother him for minor expenses. *That should last us . . . how long? I don't even know how much is in there.* In an instant, the tears welled up, and Gayle realized that she didn't know what they owed or what they owned or have two quarters to rub together that didn't come from Ramsey. *What would I . . . we . . . do if . . .*

'I swear to you, Nightingale, it's over, finished.

Yesterday was it for me. Come here . . .' He opened his arms for her.

'It's just . . . I'm so . . . scared, Ramsey,' Gayle sobbed into his chest.

Ramsey held her tight. 'You don't have to be scared of anything. I promise, Baby. I promise.'

14

'You can't live your life worryin'
about some people.'

'Take a good, slow stretch. You've earned it.'

Damn straight! Pat sat on the gym floor, her legs straight out in front of her. She glanced at her watch as she reached for her toes. *Six-forty-seven. Almost over*. The class was jammed with hard-bodied corporate overachievers looking to start their day with a burn before they went to work and set the world on fire. Pat despised this predawn torture session, but when her determination flagged she visualized herself in that new, short, black leather skirt and cropped red leather jacket, size ten thank you very much. She wanted to keep the weight off, and this was the only way to fit in the exercise, because her days at CGG were long and her nights, many at the office, the rest on the town, were even longer.

Before the end-of-class applause she tugged her trench over her leotard and headed out the door to hop a cab. Pat preferred her own shower, with the fluffy towels and nobody else's funky wet footprints on the tile. Besides, she was home so seldom she looked for opportunities to enjoy her East Seventieth Street apartment. She paid enough rent.

Pat kicked her sneakers off, continued down the hall past the étagère that displayed her collection of carved

271

African combs, and heaped her sweaty gym clothes on the floor of her closet. *Cleaning lady is coming today. She can take care of it.*

When she first hired a woman to clean, Pat worried that her messiness would be dinner table talk the way Aunt Loretta used to complain about her clients. Once in a while she wondered if Aunt Loretta was still cleaning and funneling lifestyle tips to Gayle, but her former friend, her used-to-be sister, was still too hot a topic for her to hold on to, so she'd drop it. Pat got over her uneasiness in a hot hurry and quite enjoyed plumped sofa pillows, the tart smell of lemon oil lingering in the air, and neat piles of clean clothes that appeared at the foot of her bed like the laundry fairy had brought them. Her time was too valuable to spend on housework. Pat prided herself on fitting more in a day than anybody else could. Her agenda bulged at the sides, confirming she didn't have one moment to spare.

In the kitchen she flicked on the TV. When Pat was home a set was usually on so she could check out the competition's ads. She poured a cup of coffee from the pot that was timed for six-forty-five A.M., swallowed a vitamin with the first swig, tore the bready center out of half a bagel, then munched on the crust as she headed for the bathroom.

In the shower a blast of cold water and some peppermint suds cut the sweat. *I have to drop Susan a note.* Pat had met the editor last night at the Essence Awards, and she was ever conscious of building her network. Then she let a thought of Reggie dart through her mind while she loofahed her thighs.

Reggie Singleton was a stockbroker, and her current companion of choice when the occasion required a date or she needed to get laid. Strictly speaking he wasn't handsome, but tall and stringy with skin the color of Coney Island sand, he oozed success from the crisp collars of his custom shirts, to his hand-sewn, mirror-shined wing tips. Reggie had a son and daughter from a previous marriage and a vasectomy, a convenience Pat appreciated greatly. Reggie was as single-minded about his career as she was, so there were no misunderstandings about commitment. Neither of them wanted any.

The sex last night was good-n-plenty. She dragged out of Reggie's bed at five-twenty and was at the gym by six. Pat preferred sleepover dates at her escort's place because *he'd* have to deal with the sticky sheets. Reggie liked them because she was good at finding the door by herself. He was a decent roll in the hay, but last night he'd suggested they take a trip together. *I don't think I can take him for a week in Bermuda. He will bore me to tears.* But she had more important things on her mind than a vacation.

The announcement of which producer would be elevated to group head was expected any day. Lloyd Zabriski had become VP, director of Broadcast Production after a rift in the agency over whether to solicit takeover bids left the position open. In the last two years, so many independent shops had been swallowed by international, megabehemoth agencies, it was hard to know who was in bed together and who was on top. After bitter infighting, CGG lost a horde of key people to Trafalgar Trace, Worldwide, Ltd, their most widely rumored overtaker. Several accounts threatened to follow. Rumors wore running shoes at the agency, and morale wallowed in the gutter, but Ted Gravitt rallied the staff and stabilized the situation. Pat paid lip service to the shame of losing so many talented people, but she secretly cheered the shake-up. It made room for her to ease on up the ladder.

For weeks all the producers had been jockeying for

position and privately handicapping each other's chances to succeed Lloyd. Pat emerged as one of the favorites, but lots of folks weren't happy about that.

Pat had a reputation for being difficult and exacting. She knew that meant she was a bitch with big, brass ones, but she liked that and kept them polished. A tough negotiator, she kept the budgets down on her projects by examining every detail and finding ways to do it for less. Scouting new directing talent was her trademark, and she had developed a stable of competent, no-name directors who worked their asses off on a shoot instead of the big-name, bigger-budget directors with egos to match, who the creatives always fought for. Pat trimmed the production schedules to the bone and took pride in finishing on time and within budget. Clients loved her because her commercials had pizzazz without breaking the bank, and so did the account execs, because happy clients made their jobs easier.

Out of the shower, a quick blow-dry, some hot rollers, and her short curly 'do was done. Pat smoked while she applied her executive producer face, carefully accenting her now well-defined cheekbones. Sometimes she still found herself craving buttermilk doughnuts, like Aunt Loretta used to make, or pastrami heroes, especially when the pressure was on, but then she'd immerse herself in work and smoke until the hunger passed.

Pat sat on the end of her bed to pull on panty hose. As far as she was concerned, there was nobody in the shop who could be, should be, promoted, but her.

Althea made group head almost three years ago. The situation had been tense for a while when rumor had it that Tom Reynolds would get the nod over Althea. Pat tiptoed on thin ice during that whole episode. Tom had been her boss, and Pat knew he was a better producer, but Althea had been at CGG longer and she was Pat's friend, so if lines were drawn, she'd side with Althea. They discussed strategy over many a cocktail. Fortunately, Tom surprised everybody and left for LA to produce a flick directed by a college friend.

Pat fastened the clasp on her signature pearl choker. With her first year-end bonus, she splurged on real ones and retired MaRay's fakes to the bergamot tin. Black silk shell, black skinny mini, white-and-black tick-check nipped-waist jacket and skyscraper pumps, then Pat did her twirl in the full-length hall mirror. While she wasn't exactly a swan, she'd learned the secret of good packaging and how to work what she had.

Pat grabbed her keys, her suitcase, and she was out the door by seven-thirty. Althea assured her she had a lock on group head. 'Can't be a soul *but* you,' she said. Supervising other producers would mean headaches to the tenth power, but Pat felt she was ready. She'd see a nice chunk of change in her paycheck, too. *Maybe it'll finally be time to approach my father.*

The hope of adding Turner Hughes's portrait to the gallery of ersatz relatives displayed around her apartment kept Pat motivated, even when she was less than thrilled with the prospect of producing yet another fifteen-second selling extravaganza for a product nobody needed. For as little as Pat thought about her, Verna might as well be dead and buried, but her bogus clan had expanded from the great aunt she 'adopted' in college and now included grandparents and even Dr and Mrs Reid, posed in front of a late-fifties Buick. But she'd ditch the whole crew in a heartbeat for a picture of her father, her real father. Maybe a snapshot of the two of them with his arm around her shoulder. Pat diligently followed his career, kept tabs on The Hughes Companies, and never forgot the proud, stern faces of her ancestors that kept watch from the walls of Hughes House.

Although he made fewer appearances at Republican White House dinners, Turner Hughes remained in the limelight. In addition to Newark, A Hand Up centers had opened in Bridgeport, DC, and Boston. Two months ago she clipped an article about a building in Hell's Kitchen he'd acquired for his first center in New York. It would open in the fall. The timing was flawless.

Her bitterness toward P.J. hadn't kept her from volunteering time at the church where they met. She found it was the perfect way to spend Thanksgiving and Christmas since she had no family demands and didn't want to fall prey to invitations from acquaintances who pitied the holiday lonely. When the new center opened she'd switch her allegiance to A Hand Up and get more involved. With her promotion she might even have enough clout to persuade CGG to produce free public-service ads for the nonprofit agency.

On the cab ride to the office she daydreamed about approaching Turner at his annual Martha's Vineyard affair. Despite yearly invitations from Minnie Littlefield, who seemed determined to fill every moment since Dorothea's passing, Pat hadn't ventured back to the Vineyard because the thought of a social situation that involved Mr or Mrs Peter Jackson made her stomach turn. But she would even risk that torture to talk to her father.

She'd introduce herself, engage him in a witty conversation, and make an offhand suggestion about the ads. He'd give her a business card and tell her to get some ideas to him. She knew she wouldn't work with him directly, but he'd be aware of her professionalism and she'd see to it he was impressed with the results.

Slowly she'd work herself into his sphere, and, when the

time was right, she'd tell him. At first he'd be shocked, but by then he'd know and trust her. She'd be discreet, of course. The last thing she wanted was to embarrass him. Every now and again she'd try on 'Patricia Hughes,' just for size, but she knew that was out of the question, unless of course he offered. Then, maybe, she'd hyphenate. More than anything, though, she wanted him to be proud, and since she wasn't looking for anything but his acceptance and respect, she was sure it would work out – when the time was right.

But that was the future. Right now she had projects at critical stages and she got to the office revved and ready.

She read her assistant's summary of the marketing profile of the 18–35-year-old sports enthusiast for her afternoon red alert meeting with the Tastea team. After years of trying they hadn't made any headway in the sports beverage market, and for the first time in a decade, they were making noises about leaving the agency. They wanted a new, more aggressive image for Sports Quencher, and Creative had some ideas to run by her.

Then she went over her notes and her checklists before her ten-thirty meeting with everybody responsible for the campaign to introduce Adventurer, a new, four-wheel-drive sport utility vehicle. The Adventurer creatives built a campaign around the tag line, 'Engineered to Conquer an All-Terrain Planet.' New car launches were a very big, high-prestige deal, and Pat had worked long hours to devise an around-the-world-in-two-weeks shooting schedule that would capture the car driving over and through swamp, sand, tundra, and Times Square. She still had mosquito bites the size of quarters from the Everglades last week, and she was leaving straight from the office to fly to Alaska, where the Adventurer could plow through snowy mountain passes in July.

'Thought you'd like to see what your friend has to say about you.' Chris Parker slid a memo across Pat's desk, then perched on the chair opposite her, crossed his perfectly creased pant legs, and sipped from a CGG mug.

'I love a man who can dish before coffee break.' Pat shook her head.

'But never before brunch on Sundays.' He gave her a wicked grin.

After the first year Pat realized Chris wasn't a threat, and she actually found him entertaining in a bitchy way. He made producer eventually, but he only did local clothing discounters and supermarkets, nothing national.

'Go on, read it and freak.'

Pat took the paper, expecting a reminder about covering the VCRs in the conference rooms after use, but as she read her brow wrinkled. 'Where the hell did you get this?!'

'I never reveal my sources, but don't thank me. The cat fight will be reward enough.'

The memo from Althea to Lloyd offered her critique of the producers being considered for the group head position. Pat couldn't keep the words in her head, so she read aloud, '"Patricia Reid is a maverick who, while very effective on her own, is not a team player. She has shown skill as a producer, but she has an antagonistic relationship with several key art directors, and her abilities as a manager need further development." I don't believe this shit. Are you sure this is for real?'

'Would I bother you with slanderous falsehoods? Well, possibly, but not this time. I'm afraid Miss Satterfield wrote this little ditty all by herself.' Chris stood. 'I'll leave you to your revenge. Do remember to tell me the gory details.'

Pat headed, memo in hand, straight for Althea's office. She could hear her at lunch day before yesterday, 'I don't

278

know what kinda spell you cast over Lloyd, but when it comes to this promotion the only two words he seems to know are Patricia and Reid.' Pat refused to feel hurt. That would imply she expected more of friendship, and she prided herself on having learned that lesson. She just hated it when somebody thought they got over.

'What's up? You look kinda tense.' Althea plucked a card from her address file.

Pat stood, arms akimbo, the paper dangling at her hip. 'What do you think is holding up the big announcement?' Cool as a breeze she waited to hear what lie Althea had to tell.

'I haven't heard a word. I don't know what you're worryin' about. You're gonna hear before anybody else does.'

'Maybe not. Seems some people don't think I'm ready.'

'You can't live your life worryin' about some people, because they mostly have their own agendas.' Althea leaned back in her chair and propped her hands behind her head.

'I guess you would know, Althea. But since we mavericks like to get our news from the horse's mouth, maybe you could tell me if Zabriski asked you to write this memo, or if you volunteered?' Pat sauntered to the desk and placed the memo in front of her.

Althea didn't break a sweat or miss a beat. 'No harm intended. If I give you a glowing review, Zabriski and the rest of these folks will assume because we're both Black we stick together. It makes my judgment look shaky and won't do you any good either.'

Pat stared at Althea like she had antlers. 'So you're saying you bad-mouthed me because we're both Black and it looks bad if you recommend me for a promotion? That's the biggest load of bullshit I ever heard!'

Althea leaned forward, placing her hands on top of the memo. 'Personally, I hope they give it to you . . .'

'Don't even bother, Althea. Why would I believe anything you say now?'

'Listen, there's only gonna be a few of us with a title beyond secretary . . .' Althea reached for her cigarettes.

'And you figured I wouldn't notice your scissors sticking out of my back because you decided that few shouldn't include me, is that right?'

Althea lit up. 'You give me far too much credit. Zabriski, Greene, Gravitt, they're gonna do exactly what they damn well please . . .'

'Then *you* stay the hell outta my way!' Pat barked.

Althea's eyes narrowed and she blew smoke through her nostrils. 'You know, I got you hired . . .'

'Althea, *I* got me hired, so let's stop right there! My grades! My work! So don't take credit for what you didn't do and don't expect me to play the grateful sidekick, 'cause I'm not! It's a damn good thing I'm *not* in one of your groups. You'd probably have cooked up some shit to get me fired! And you needn't bother speaking to me unless it's unavoidable business, 'cause pleasantries are no longer required or welcome.'

Althea folded her arms on the desk. 'Don't think you scare me, Patricia. I've been threatened worse on the playground in Brooklyn. You should also know, I always won.'

'Your childhood victories don't interest me. This ain't no playground, and I am not playing!' Pat wheeled and left.

Pat closed her office door and sucked all the smoke out of three cigarettes. Whenever she got this angry, she went to Althea to vent. *That's fuckin' hilarious*, but she didn't laugh until she stubbed out her cigarette in the CGG ashtray. *It's probably bugged.*

Pat ordered chicken dill on a roll, a double espresso, and a bag of Milano cookies, and while she waited for delivery tried to remember anything she'd told Althea in confidence that could come back to haunt her. She bitched about Giles all the time, but that wasn't a secret – she argued with him to his face. Tom had recommended her promotion to producer, so if Althea actually told him Pat referred to him as an obnoxious, know-it-all White boy, he probably took it as a compliment. She thought about going straight to Zabriski, but she wasn't supposed to have seen the memo in the first place, and she'd have to explain where she got it. *Besides, what could I say? Althea called me names? That was lame in second grade. My work will stand up for me.*

The Tastea meeting was frantic. The creatives were toying with the idea of building the campaign around high-performance athletes, like marathoners, mountain climbers, and channel swimmers, who walk a little on the wild side. 'Take It to the Limit' was the working title for the spots.

'Michael is committed to the competition, and Tastea is too cheap to sign him anyway,' Giles sneered. He'd let his prematurely gray hair grow long enough for a ponytail, the over forty and still hip hairstyle of choice in advertising. When Pat's assistant nudged her and tapped his watch to remind her the car would be downstairs in fifteen minutes, there was a preliminary list of athletes to pitch. Since Pat's assistant wasn't going on the Alaskan leg of the trek, she left him with instructions to check on their availability and fee range while she was away, then she was out the door.

What the hell am I gonna do if Althea screwed me out of this promotion? Her traveling companions, the Adventurer AD and the director went to sleep after dinner, but Pat was still too angry to sleep on the cross-country flight.

Yes, there were people who had been at CGG longer. Althea put in ten years before she made group head. *That's not my problem. There's a spot open, and I'm ready.* And Pat was ready to finally meet her father, and she counted on the job to help her make that happen, to show him she was somebody he could be proud of. *Althea had probably lied to him, too, or invented some scheme to use him. That's really what happened.* Althea's warning about men like Turner had haunted Pat since her summer internship. Now, as they descended toward Sea-Tac Airport, she dismissed it. *She lied about me. She's just like Verna. She'd lie about anybody if it suited her.*

They caught a connecting flight to Anchorage, then took a private plane practically to the door of their lodge in Chitina, a tiny town at the edge of the Chugach Mountains.

On the first day, Pat spent the morning with the director and the AD, strapped into a four-seater plane the size of a winged sofa, scouting locations. Despite the spectacular beauty of the snow-glazed peaks, Pat stayed focused on finding a large plateau, close to the airstrip so they could helicopter the Adventurer and stunt driver to the location.

After lunch the driver arrived. They showed him the locations and mapped out their shots for the next day. On day two snow squalls kept the crew grounded in the lodge all morning. Periodically the pilot checked in, but the news wasn't encouraging. 'Even if the snow stops, the winds gotta pipe down before we can fly.'

'Swell.' *I don't have time for this!* Bad weather wasn't on her schedule. With each passing minute, Pat's internal mainspring wound tighter, so before it snapped she went to her room to phone the office.

The Tastea account exec bounced off the wall when Pat

told him about the delay. 'I should be there.'

Like your presence would change the freakin' weather! Pat said she'd be in touch.

Pat's assistant had casting info on the jocks for Sports Quencher, but Creative wasn't satisfied they had come up with the right ones to pitch, so they were still looking.

Chris had the serious skinny. 'I don't know if Althea did you in or not, but Zabriski announced the new group head, and it wasn't you.'

Pat hung up and lay, facedown across her bed, feeling like she'd been kicked in the guts with steel-toed boots. *I can just see Althea gloating.* The storm still swirled at three in the afternoon, and Pat reluctantly called the day.

Snow and blustery wind continued the next day. A winter-carnival atmosphere prevailed, but Pat wasn't festive. She saw her budget rise with each falling flake, and there wasn't a thing she could do but wait. After lunch she toyed with calling the shoot and heading back to New York, the next scheduled location. She had permits, insurance, location vans, the works, booked for Sunday, but at the rate they were going, they wouldn't make it. It didn't make dollars or sense to bring everybody back to Alaska either, so she called her assistant back to have him reschedule the New York date, then went looking for the director to discuss the possibility of her going directly from Alaska to New Mexico to prep the full moon in the desert shot.

The next morning the sun finally sparkled and the clean, crisp air tingled in Pat's lungs. The crew plane landed safely on the plateau, but snow had drifted waist-deep in places, and finding a spot for the head-on shot was exasperating. They got some film, but no one felt they had *the* shot.

Pat decided to proceed with the aerial shots the following day. Radio communication between the car and the helicopter faded in and out, so progress was slow, and Pat felt as if she'd been cold for a month. When they finished the aerial work they scouted for another location to reshoot the head-on view. They found a plateau at a higher elevation, and Pat decided they'd do it again in the morning. *If I'm gonna be late, the film's gotta be great.*

The snow on the new bluff was light and powdery, and the angle of the sun created less glare. The director was able to catch the snow flying off the car and make it look electrified. Pat knew this was a winner.

On the return trip, the two-hour layover in Seattle until her New York flight made Pat restless. *I shoulda been in the office today.* Alone in the Executive Club, she sipped coffee, smoked, and stared absentmindedly as another plane raced down the runway and nosed into the sky. Pat worried about making up the lost time, keeping her numbers down. It had all spun out of control, and she had to keep a tight rein from here on.

When this commercial is in the can, I'll make an appointment with Zabriski, get his take on my situation. After sweet mountain air the conditioned stuff felt suffocating. *I don't know what the hell else they expect from me!* But she planned to find out so she could double it.

Unable to thumb through another magazine she marched past the receptionist.

'Will you be back, Miss Reid?'

'Yes. Just stretching my legs.' Pat exited into the buzz of the main terminal, passed newsstands and cocktail lounges, then wandered outside for some fresh air.

A family with a mom, dad, three kids, and a sizable stack of luggage, piled out of an aged station wagon. *If that's not Mr & Mrs America, I don't know who is. And next year, after they see my spots, they'll be climbing out of an Adventurer*.

Dad pulled off to find parking and a maroon Jaguar replaced it at the curb. Pat's eye involuntarily traced the car's sleek exterior. *Damn, that's pretty. One day.*

The driver's door opened. Pat noticed the woman's perfectly coifed pageboy first. No natural force would move a hair out of place. Her azure blue suit complimented her nutmeg skin and drew Pat's eye. *Good TV color. Executive, but not mannish.*

'Mom, look! It's the TV newslady!' The little boy pointed with his cast.

'Shhh. And don't point. It's rude,' his mother cautioned.

Skycaps hunched each other and nodded toward the local celebrity.

Newscaster. Bingo. Pat flicked her cigarette into the street, checked her watch, decided to go back inside. Out of the corner of her eye she saw the brim of a Panama hat dip below the open trunk of the Jag. Just before she walked through the automatic doors the boy squealed, 'Look, Mom! It's Marcus Carter!'

It can't be! Pat wasn't prepared to add Marcus to today's already full plate. She turned to investigate. *Yeah, it's him.* For the briefest instant she could feel the blood pounding in the veins at her temples. *Too much damn coffee.*

The boy wriggled free of Mom and bounced like a Spaldeen in front of Marcus, pleading for an autograph. Marcus ruffled the kid's hair, reached in his blazer pocket for a pen, and signed his cast before Mom claimed him.

He looks like a million dollars. Marcus stood tall and broad like an onyx monument, but more than that he exuded a major-league presence. Pat watched people stop what they were doing and stare.

He turned his attention back to his companion, pulling her to him, whispering in her ear. When he kissed her, he tugged her bottom lip just enough to show they'd shared more than dinner. She giggled behind her hand and gazed wistfully into his eyes. Then he helped her behind the wheel, closed the door, and she drove off.

Pat fished in her pocket, put a cigarette to her lips, flicked the lighter. *Looks like Mr Carter has a long-distance thang.* She noticed the bitter, burning smell first, then the tiny flame at the tip confirmed she had lit the filter. *Damn!* She dropped it and ground it to tobacco dust with her shoe.

A skycap approached Marcus, who had only a garment bag slung over his shoulder.

'Man, can I just shake your hand?'

Marcus grinned and obliged and the skycap walked back to his post with his chest poked out like Marcus had done him proud.

Pat heard people murmur his name or just, 'Cat in the Hat.' Marcus wore a cocky, 'Yeah, I know I'm bad' expression. Then he walked right by Pat, into the terminal. 'Speak,' 'Don't Speak' did a 'heads or tails' flip-flop in her mind before her mature adulthood got the better of her. Hands on hips, she called in a low voice, 'Marcus Garvey Carter.'

Maybe a hitch in his step, but he kept walking, like he hadn't heard. She followed inside and caught up next to him. 'Marcus Garvey Carter, you gonna ig me?'

He stopped, cocked his head in her direction, but nothing registered. Then, 'Holy smokes! Patricia? Is that you calling me by my whole name?' For a split second he looked like he'd seen the Ghost of Christmas Past, but he played it off smoothly.

'I thought it might get your attention since every damn

body calls your name.' Despite her pumps, Marcus towered over her. She eyed the slim gold hoop in his left ear.

'Well I damn sure wouldn't recognize you since you got all fly.' He leaned like he couldn't decide whether to kiss her or shake hands, but a group of swaggering, almost-men toting duffel bags walked by and one called out, 'Hey, Cat, you kicked Mariner ass last night, but you all right!' He straightened, pointed, and nodded, then turned back to Pat.

'You like all that?' Pat fell in beside him, and they continued through the terminal.

'Can't say as I mind. If they don't call my name, I'm not doin' my job.' He looked both ways along the concourse, like he was searching for the emergency exit. His easy manner with strangers seemed lost with an old friend. 'So, ah . . . Seattle must be good to you.'

'I'm passing through. Business.' She noticed people check out their progress and felt uneasy with so many eyes following her. 'Looks like *you* got ties here, though.' Marcus looked puzzled. 'Miss Jaguar Newscaster?'

'A recent acquaintance. My free agent status means I can explore all the options.'

'Uh-huh.' For several steps she couldn't think of what to say. *I talk to strangers all the time. Why is this so hard?* 'So, your mom and dad . . . they still in St Albans?'

It was like the mention of the old neighborhood triggered the emergency warning system in Marcus's head. 'I uh . . . got 'em a place in North Carolina . . . Pamlico Sound. Dad likes to fish . . .' Marcus stiffened, started looking around the terminal. 'Well, it was good seeing you. Keep on keepin' on.' He looked past her eyes, patted her shoulder, and bailed out.

'Yeah, you too,' she said to his back as he glided away.

I'll be damned! This felt worse than their last parting. Now it was like they were complete strangers. *Screw him then!*

When she got back to the lounge the receptionist whispered, 'You know Marcus Carter? The baseball player?' She pointed toward the bar. 'He's in there.'

She meant to go back to her seat by the windows, but her feet took her to the mauve and mirrored bar. A clutch of men in single-breasted corporate uniforms hovered around Marcus, obviously thrilled to be with a genuine sports star. *Everybody eats this up.* She perched on a stool at the far end, ordered a gimlet, and listened to the hero worship.

'Naw, I don't wear the Series ring when I travel. Gets in the way. Besides, that's old. I'm hunting for some new jewelry, even if I have to go to another team to get it.' The men laughed and continued to grill him. A few asked for autographs, for their kids they said.

When the boarding announcement came for her flight, Pat saw Marcus stand, reach into his pocket, and throw a bill on the bar. 'Gentlemen, that's my plane.'

Pat hung back. Part of her was riled up and wanted to confront him, ask why he had left her like she had the plague, but what was the point? One encounter was enough, and she watched Marcus swagger out looking like he expected to be noticed, and, if she wasn't mistaken, the chip was on the shoulder opposite his carry-on.

Marcus was already basking in the attentions of a knot of flight attendants in first class when Pat boarded. She had to slide by them to get to her seat in business class. He never saw her. *They act like it's the Second Coming. He's just a damn jock.*

After they landed Pat told herself to ignore him, but on the ground in New York she still kept Marcus in view. In baggage claim a woman with legs up to her armpits, wearing a leopard print cat suit that scooped to her waist in back and fit her like skin everywhere else, caught sight of Marcus. She tossed her mane of ebony ringlets like the star of a music video, licked her lips, and pounced.

Marcus folded the leopardess into his arms, whispered in her ear, kissed her lips.

Same shit, different dame. He's a star, after all. Pat got a better look at her and realized it was Téa, the model whose feline features graced the cover of every other magazine on the newsstands. Pat headed toward the taxi line, pretending she was not annoyed as she watched Marcus escort Téa to a waiting limo.

In the morning, jet lagged and generally pissed off, Pat stormed around the office like bigfoot. She went over mail and memos, including the official group head announcement, choking back the acid burn in her throat with coffee and a cruller. She checked on the progress in New Mexico, went over the grocery list of athletes her assistant had compiled, then dropped in on Giles.

'That Tour de France guy is okay, but bike racing is not exactly burning down the house in the States. There's still nobody who gives me goose bumps,' he grumbled.

'Tell me again what you're looking for.' She perched at his drawing board and doodled swirls on a sketch pad while she listened.

Giles rocked back in his desk chair and closed his eyes. 'I want a hunk with attitude, big, not stupid. He needs personality and untapped commercial potential, because the client won't spring for an established name. But he's gotta ooze that sweaty, sexy, arrogant thing.'

Don't even think it, Patricia. 'Let me do a bit more research and get back to you.'

Pat plastered on a smile, went to congratulate the new group head, and smoked like a forest fire while he packed to move out of his old office and rubbed salt in her wounds.

She called out for lunch, listened to some voice-over tapes, but no matter how she tried to avoid it, Giles seemed to be spelling M-A-R-C-U-S. *There's gotta be somebody else.* Every time she relived their airport rendezvous she got madder. *He shoulda just kept walking when I called him, even though he wouldn't treat one of his beloved fans like that.* But this was business, and if Marcus was the answer to the Tastea riddle, she had to pursue it because her feelings didn't put two cents in her wallet, and it was her job to keep the client happy.

Perched on the corner of Giles's desk, Pat folded her arms. 'So, how about a big, chiseled, home run-hitting baseball player? World Series ring, single, virile, no scandals I know about. He's got an edge like a razor blade, a good voice, and he appeals to a wide cross section of ages, socioeconomic levels, genders, races. I've seen it with my own eyes. And no prior product commitments to my knowledge.'

'I'm salivating. I wish he played football or basketball . . . more sweat. But if he's active off the field, that'll help.'

Against her better judgment, Pat said she'd have her assistant make inquiries about Marcus's agent and his going rate and marched along the hushed halls toward her office.

'Pat, I'm glad I ran into you.' Lloyd Zabriski, shirt-sleeves rolled to his elbows, appeared behind her. 'I was going to call you this afternoon. We need to talk.' He took a pull from the slim cigar he held between his fingers.

Great, I can hear the shit he's gonna sell me about how being a bridesmaid is an honor, and maybe next time I'll be the bride. At least I can get this over with. She followed him to his office making small talk about the vast Alaskan wilderness. He motioned her to the couch in the sitting area that overlooked St Patrick's and buzzed his secretary to bring in coffee.

Oh, this is gonna be a marathon.

'Pat, you're one of the best hires we've made since I've been with this agency . . .'

Here it comes, the horse manure de jour.

'And we did a lot of very hard thinking when we made our choice for group head . . .'

But it wasn't you, so this is how you can break your ass to impress us next time. She crossed her legs and waited for him to get beyond the apology to the meat of the matter.

'I don't have to tell you the economy took a nosedive last year. Some of our accounts have been hit below the belt, and that means we say ouch. To stay ahead we've had to make some changes.' He took a pull on the cigar, frowned.

What the hell is he saying? He can't be firing me. The smell of the smoke and the thought of unemployment made her dizzy.

'The thing I hear most from clients now is "Lloyd, can you save us some money?"'

The hair on Pat's arms stood up. Not getting the promotion was one thing, but being escorted out the door, that couldn't be happening. She wanted to drag the words out of him.

'As you know, the more we keep production costs down, the more money the client has for his media buys, which is where we make the real money. Are you with me?'

'Absolutely.' *Get to the damn point!*

'What I'm saying is we've created a new position, senior broadcast resources director. As far as we know, we're the first agency to take this approach. The position answers directly to the VP head of Broadcast.'

291

So it's at least on par with group head. Pat steadied her hands on the cushions to keep from falling off the sofa.

'This person would oversee production and Creative with regard to budget. Now, you and I both know that for most of this decade, the more of the client's money we spent, the more they liked it. Kind of a badge of honor. That thinking won't fly now. Our idea is to keep production costs in hand while ensuring the quality we're known for.'

'That person will catch hell from all sides, Lloyd. Producers, group heads, Creative . . . nobody likes a watchdog.' Pat shifted anxiously.

'You've been extremely successful at holding down costs and producing a quality product. I expect some resistance at first, but be assured, we think you can handle it, and we have your back on this. Are you interested?'

Yes! She wanted to shout. *But I can't sit here with a shit-eatin' grin on my face. Be dignified.* 'I'm honored.' *This job will be hell. Everybody'll hate me, but it's a big promotion. Damn, it's a huge promotion. Tough shit on whoever doesn't like it.* 'When do I start?' Pat was so happy, it almost hurt. They discussed salary, which put her above group head, by a healthy margin. *Maybe enough for my Jaguar.* The promotion was effective immediately, but she would complete any projects she had in progress. And since Pat was on her way out of town, Zabriski called a meeting for later that afternoon to make the announcement.

Pat went to lunch with Zabriski and Ted Gravitt, which raised many eyebrows at the elevator. She sailed smoothly through the meal, giving Zabriski suggestions for where he should stay in Paris this October when he took his wife to celebrate their twentieth anniversary. Gravitt peppered her with questions about what his daughter could expect in September, her first semester at Southridge. All the while she really wanted to get back to the office and phone Minnie Littlefield, to say hello and, by the way, find out when Illumination Night would be this summer since she might be able to squeeze a few days on the Vineyard in August. And get herself invited to a certain barbecue at Hughes House.

Stunned murmurs ricocheted around the Rubber Room with the introduction of the new senior broadcast resources director. She received cordial congratulations from the producers, group heads, and creatives who would be subjected to her scrutiny.

Althea, green as a sour grape, left as soon as the meeting was adjourned.

Zabriski also announced that Chris Parker would take over Pat's position.

'Congratulations to us.' Chris clicked Pat's champagne cup. 'Glad they kicked you upstairs. I think I like my spot better, though. You get to cut everybody's goodies. Make us stay at fleabag motels. At least I'll still have friends.'

15

'. . . there's more than one way to skin a skunk.'

'There are almost as many security agents as guests.' Pat handed Minnie Littlefield a glass of lemonade. Minnie, perched on a wooden porch glider, looked fragile to Pat, but she had remained feisty, even after Dorothea died. 'I guess that's what happens when the Vice President says he'll drop by your party.' This year the Hughes annual Illumination Day affair felt as formal as a state dinner. Secret Service had sealed off the perimeter two blocks around the house. Nobody got inside without an invitation and a name on the official list. Pat was Minnie's '. . . and guest.'

Minnie eyeballed the seersuckered sentry posted at the front door of Hughes House. 'This is ludicrous. We've had dignitaries on the island for years. I don't know why he wants that man here in the first place. I must speak to Turner. This party has become a spectacle!'

'Turner's got to stay politically connected because of business, and the last thing you'd want is for the Vice President of the United States to be injured at a Black man's party.'

'Lord, yes. They'd put us all on boats for sure then!' Minnie agreed.

Even though Minnie didn't cotton to the Vice President's

party affiliation, the thought of Turner, her father, playing host to such a prominent figure made Pat swell with pride. She anticipated the arrival of the honored guest as much as anyone, but more to the point she wanted to see Turner, and he hadn't made an appearance yet. Out of the corner of her eye, Pat saw William and Indianola Lewis strolling up the walk and decided to duck into the house to avoid a conversation where P.J.'s name would undoubtedly come up.

'There's too much hot air in there for me. I'll be along later, dear,' Minnie said.

Pat paused at the main stairs to gaze at the portraits. They had stayed so vivid in her mind that she could hardly believe it had been almost a decade since she had last seen them. Just as stern and imposing as before, but this time she felt more secure that she would live up to their challenge. She let her mind wander, to a time when she could trot up these steps and be met by a hug or a kiss on the cheek, what any daughter could expect.

'Can I help you, miss?' The agent, posted at the curve of the banister looked wilted in his dark suit, but he was obviously alert. 'The upstairs quarters are off-limits.'

'Just admiring the pictures. There's a lot of history up there, you know.'

'Yes, ma'am.'

Like he cares. She swung into the dining room, heading straight for the bar for something to quiet her jitters. She assured herself this was no big deal. She'd been introducing herself to strangers since she could remember, but none of them was her father.

Fortified with a gimlet, she entered serious mingling mode, always on the lookout for Turner. She chatted up a bank chairman who had met Hughes at a Colorado symposium for corporate bigwigs. 'He impressed the heck

296

out of me,' he told her. 'Quite a mind.'

A woman she knew by face from the gym turned out to be PR director at a major record label. They promised to get together for more than torture and sweat.

Still no Turner. Pat felt a tap on her shoulder. 'Willie Calloway. What a surprise.' He introduced his wife Janet, a school guidance counselor as Pat checked out his tan double-breasted suit and black silk T-shirt. *He looks almost hip. His wife must dress him.*

'How do you two know each other?' Janet asked.

A goofy grin washed over Willie's face and Pat did her best not to smirk. 'I spent the summer before college here. Your husband was nice enough to show me . . . around.'

Willie had sold the Brooklyn drugstore and now owned three pharmacies in the greater Atlanta area. His parents were retired and sailing wherever the spirit took them. Pat thought Willie and Janet looked happily-ever-after together in a way that made her squeamish. After trading business cards and, fingers crossed, promising to keep in touch, she excused herself and went outside.

Humidity and anticipation dampened the usually lively crowd in the backyard. The hum of conversation barely challenged the trio playing 'It's Only a Paper Moon.' And although the spread was as lavish as before, few people were chowing down.

Pat had just finished debating the merits of a Jaguar with the owner of a Chrysler dealership and gone to the bar for a refill.

'What are you doing here?'

The voice was still rich, but it incited Pat like nails on a chalkboard. 'This is a party. I'm a guest.' It took all of her self-control to keep from bathing P.J. in vodka and lime juice.

'I didn't see your name on the list.' His amber eyes flashed like hazard lights.

'What business is it of yours?' She stepped away from the bar, but he followed. Pat wasn't sure how long her tongue would hold.

'I'm Mr Hughes's assistant. If it concerns him, it concerns me, and I didn't see your name.'

'You *work* for Turner Hughes?' It was inconceivable, like the devil's idea of an April Fool's prank, but this was August and P.J. wasn't laughing. 'So I guess you're living in New York now. It's a good thing Edwina convinced you to take the bar exam there, isn't it?' Pat spoke in an acid whisper.

The corners of P.J.'s mouth thinned into a flat line. 'If you're not an invited guest, I'll have to ask you to leave. If not, I'll call security.'

'You would enjoy that, wouldn't you. Well, I didn't crash the party, P.J. I am the guest of Miss Minnie Littlefield and a Secret Service agent took my name when we arrived. We can go find her if you like.'

P.J. straightened his tie. 'That won't be necessary. Sorry to have bothered you.'

Pat held her glass steady, determined not to give him the satisfaction of knowing how much this twisted her guts. 'And where is your wife? Edwina was never one to miss a party.'

'The twins have chicken pox . . .'

'I see.' A punch couldn't have hurt more.

'Please . . . enjoy yourself.' He shifted to walk away.

'P.J. . . . .' This was the last person on the planet she wanted to talk to, with the possible exception of her mother, but he was Turner's assistant, so her feelings had to stay in her hip pocket. 'Look, you and I have nothing to say to each other, but I'd really like to meet

Turner Hughes. Can you introduce me?'

'Ah . . . today is a little . . . hectic, due to the Vice President's visit.'

'It doesn't have to be long. I have some ideas about promoting A Hand Up . . .'

'There's no promotion budget . . .'

'I'm talking pro bono, P.J. I produce commercials for a living, as you may remember. I'd like to put something together . . .'

'Get that to me in writing.' He peeled a business card from his breast pocket. 'That's handled through the A Hand Up Foundation. I'll see it gets properly routed.'

'Right.' *Into the shredder.*

P.J. disappeared into the house, leaving Pat with a sickening taste in her mouth. She peered at the engraved card in her hand. 'Peter J. Jackson, Executive Assistant to the President.' *Mama or daddy probably got him the job because he didn't pass the damn bar exams.* She crumpled the card and shoved it in her pocket.

I have to find a way around P.J. This wasn't exactly the best time for her to be away from the office. One of Althea's producers was stonewalling big-time over Pat's recommendations for pruning the budget on an insurance company campaign. Staffers at CGG were packing the peanut gallery to see if the new senior broadcast resources director had any real bite, but when Minnie extended the invite, Pat couldn't say no. Her goal was to meet Turner, make sure he heard her name at least once, and to leave a favorable impression for the future. P.J. was going to make that difficult.

Pat decided it was time to check on Minnie, so she went back in the house, got a fresh glass of lemonade, and was at the door when she spied Turner at the top of the landing, a blue blazer draped over his shoulder, hanging from his crooked finger. P.J. followed a few steps behind.

'There you are, you old skunk. I was beginning to think you lured us to this island in the middle of the Atlantic so you could close some deal while no one was looking.' The bank chairman waggled an unlit pipe.

'I am deeply hurt that you would question my hospitality. I will, however, keep that in mind. It's a damn good idea.' He stopped at the last step so he stood a head taller than the audience that gathered around him. P.J. hung on the fringes of the semicircle.

Pat admired the way Turner seemed at ease with all eyes and ears focused on him. *That's what makes him a leader*.

'What do we have to look forward to next? The Hughes Broadcasting System? Then we'll have to hear your opinion about everything all the time,' the banker continued.

'Hughes Broadcasting System has a good ring, but if I said where I was going, you'd trip over yourselves trying to beat me there, so I graciously decline to tell you mothers' sons *what* I might do.' Turner's laugh was as hearty as a slap on the back. 'In all seriousness, does Secretary of the Treasury Turner Hughes sound as good to you as it does to me?'

'So should we conclude it's more than mere coincidence that a presidential candidate will be here this afternoon?' The craggy network journalist arched an eyebrow.

'Not at all. Didn't your mother ever tell you the Lord works in mysterious ways? And while we're on the subject, I just got word the Vice President's helicopter has landed.' Even at a distance, Pat spied his monogram on the breast pocket of the shirt. 'So if you'll excuse me, I'm going to greet my guest, make him feel welcome.' On cue the circle parted and Turner walked toward the door.

This is it. I've got to say something now. As Turner strode

300

past, Pat called out, 'Mr Hughes, Miss Littlefield says she has a bone to pick with you.' Turner stopped. Pat held her breath. He looked her over with eyes that seemed tired, the whites a bloodshot beige. They were set wide and deep. *Like mine.* And once he locked her in his sights they seemed inescapable, yet impossible to read.

'Is that a fact? I don't believe we've had the pleasure. You are . . . ?'

'Patricia Reid.' She fought to keep her voice from shaking. *Does the name mean anything? Does he wonder . . .*

He gripped her hand in a solid shake and every molecule in her body vibrated. Pat had dreamed about this meeting for so long, but this was real, and she wanted to remember it all. She examined his short, square fingers, felt the fine sandpaper coarseness of his palm. *My hands are like his.* Until this moment, she had always wished they were slender and tapered. She was surprised when he let go and his fingers flickered across her open hand.

'Glad to know you. That's what I love about this shindig. Always some new faces.'

'I'm a big admirer of A Hand Up. Teaching self-sufficiency skills speaks to the needs of a lot of people.' *Glad to know me.* She spoke quickly, but she felt like her time was running out. 'I produce TV commercials, and I'd like to propose a public service campaign for the centers.' Pat saw Secret Service agents gathering near the front of the walk.

P.J. appeared at Turner's shoulder, glared at Pat. 'He's here.' Turner buttoned his jacket, reached into the pocket and removed a business card. 'Let me know what you have in mind.' He hustled down the path, but turned back to her. 'And you tell Miss Minnie I'll stop by so she can pick all the bones she wants.'

Pat stared down at the nubby cream card, but P.J.

interrupted. 'Do both of us a favor and find another charity,' he growled, and disappeared inside.

The party perked up as guests positioned themselves for glad-handing and picture-taking with the VP, who, in polo shirt and chinos, was dressed more casually than most in attendance. Turner made a special effort to bring him to meet Miss Littlefield, whose greeting was cordial, but underwhelmed. After a once around the backyard and a great show of rib tasting, the VIPs disappeared behind the closed door of the study.

But none of that mattered to Pat. She already had what she had come for.

That night, after she'd helped Minnie blow out the candles in her fragile paper lanterns and tuck them away for next summer, Pat retired to her tiny bedroom under the eaves and stayed up late, composing a letter to Turner. She looked for just the right tone to convey her pleasure at their meeting and her willingness to get involved with A Hand Up without sounding too eager. *I'll float the public service idea with Zabriski next week.*

Turner's business card, Pat's trophy from her Vineyard expedition, went directly in her Rolodex as soon as she arrived at her office. Her new office. The one with windows. It overlooked short, dingy buildings on the side street, but she got sun from eleven-forty-five to two-fifteen, and Althea didn't have windows. Pat returned ready to chew up and spit out anybody who crossed her. She had a point to prove and a father to impress.

First, Pat had Chris brief her on the status of her old accounts.

'They think the Adventurer spot is the best thing east of Oz, so you can cross that off your list, Dorothy. Or are you the Wicked Witch?' Creative had pitched Marcus as a candidate for Sports Quencher spokesman. 'I hear the

Tastea CEO eats and sleeps baseball. Your friend Carter's got a three-fourteen batting average which won't hurt, and he is one cute item.'

'Forget it, Parker.' Marcus deserved the deal as much as anybody. Pat was just glad she wouldn't be producing the campaign. *It's cleaner this way.*

Then she put on her boxing gloves to duke it out with the troublesome producer in Althea's group. Miss Satterfield hadn't said 'boo,' but Pat knew who her real opponent was.

Pat called the producer to her office, tore holes in the flabby Omicron Insurance campaign budget, and sent him away to revise his figures. That triggered a series of hot phone calls from the AD on the team. Althea took up the argument with Zabriski, but he wasn't moved. The showdown took place in Ted Gravitt's office via speaker phone. Ian Comstock, the creative director, called from his hospital bed, where he was being treated for meningitis, to square off with Zabriski over whether Pat had authority to veto budgets. Since the agency's beginning, no one had constrained Comstock with mere dollars and cents. 'Genius is priceless,' was his line when questioned about exorbitant expenditures, but the market had changed. Gravitt sided with Zabriski and the revised figures, thousands leaner, appeared on Pat's desk, giving her round one.

When she left the office, she was wired, but at home, halfway through her third martini, she was still bouncing off walls and decided it was a perfect time to reorganize her closet. While rummaging through boxes stacked on the floor she ran into her box of mementoes. *I meant to have my diploma framed ages ago.* Tucked in a Con Ed return envelope she found the prom picture Uncle Joe had made her get in with Gayle and Marcus. She knew how

Marcus was doing, but for the first time in a while she wondered about Gayle. *Is she still married to the asshole? What does Vanessa look like? Probably like Gayle did when she was little, with that ponytail bobbing and a thousand dreams for the future.*

Pat fished the olive out of her drink. It was so salty it made her pucker. Back then it seemed impossible they would grow up and drift apart. For half a breath Pat considered calling Gayle, just because. *Get a grip! All this time on my hands is making me soft in the head.* She took the bergamot tin from the bottom of the box, and held Turner's monogrammed cuff link. She rubbed it gently across her cheek as she wondered if he still had the other one. *I just need to shake things up.* And involving herself with A Hand Up was the perfect mixer. Turner hadn't responded yet, so she called The Hughes Companies first thing in the morning, determined to get beyond the secretary.

'I've left several messages, and they haven't been returned,' Pat said.

'Yes, I remember. It's odd that no one called you. Will you hold a moment?'

Pat took deep breaths to slow her pounding heart. Then she heard the click and the pause.

'Patricia, this is P.J. . . .'

'Let's not get into this. I'll leave a message if you're the only one who can help me.'

'You can leave messages from now 'til 1999. They'll end up in my trash can with the rest of them. Your letter went there, too, incidentally.'

'Why are you doing this?'

'It's in both of our best interests . . .'

'No, it's not. I let you confuse your interests with mine once, but not this time . . .'

'Then let me put it another way . . .'

Pat slammed the phone so loud she heard ringing in her ears. *Dammit to hell! He can't do this. It's not right!* But right or wrong he was doing it. *He's afraid I'll find some way to let Turner know what a bastard he is.* P.J. had the means and the motivation to deny her access, for now. *But there's more than one way to skin a skunk.*

Pat continued to carve out a territory and make her presence felt at the agency. She reviewed budget practices with each producer and group head. Her conference with Althea was short and prickly, but Pat got the round two victory and a cheap charge out of requiring Althea to come to her office and pretend to be civil. Pat wrote memos, assessed progress, and skated above the thin, icy crust of resentment that met her suggestions. The pace of her workdays slowed to a more civilized nine-ish to five-ish, but without the need to be at the office early, she hadn't been to the gym regularly either. She had plenty of time for long lunches, but after yet another noontime shopping trip when she couldn't think of anything she really wanted to buy, she realized how much she missed the hectic pace of producing.

Round three started with a flurry of activity from the Omicron shoot. By midafternoon the first day Pat had taken nine phone calls from the Cape May location. The assistant producer claimed hotel arrangements and meal stipends were inadequate. The producer himself phoned in a rage, declaring that the director, one of Pat's standbys, was hopelessly inept. The director's assistant accused the producer of unprofessional behavior and claimed he was trying to sabotage the job. Pat arranged a conference call, and, after a three-way bitch fest, she had ironed out enough wrinkles to permit the work to proceed; but the next morning Zabriski barged into her office.

The Omicron account exec had called him in a panic, demanding the original personnel and production schedule on the commercial be reinstated. It seemed the fragile truce Pat brokered had collapsed, and the client's representative was threatening to suggest to his superiors that they take their business elsewhere.

'I don't care how you handle it, but I want the commercial shot and the client happy! Period!' This was the first time Lloyd had yelled at her. Now it was a fight to the finish.

Pat rented a car, and by the time she got to southern Jersey she was ready to raise her own hell. She took over from the producer, calmed the client's rep, and salvaged the shoot, taking every opportunity to make the producer look like an imbecile. To make sure there were no mishaps in postproduction, Pat handled that, too, and when the finished product received Omicron's seal of approval, the word was that Pat scored a knockdown.

By mid-October, Althea resigned saying she needed to reassess her career goals. Pat skipped the office farewell party, which traveled to a local watering hole and continued into the night. Chris told her the next morning that her name had come up often. 'Let's just say you should check all your packages for ticking.'

Pat didn't care who liked her, she had won. But before Thanksgiving Althea's smiling face appeared in *Adweek* as the director of broadcast at Trafalgar Trace, Los Angeles. LA was the boonies as far as Pat was concerned. *At least there are three thousand miles between us.*

16

'This is business.'

Even though Reggie had tickets, Pat skipped the Thanksgiving week benefit concert that marked the opening of A Hand Up, New York. She suspected P.J. would be running interference, and she'd never get close to Turner. Sure enough, in the next day's papers, she saw a picture of Turner, flanked by the celebrity performers, but in the background, barely visible between Luther and Aretha, stood P.J., smiling thinly.

The Saturday before Christmas Pat volunteered to wrap children's presents at A Hand Up, or AHUP as staffers called it. She just wanted to take a look around, get a feel for the operation before she made a move with the foundation next year.

Pat thought the facility, housed in a five-story, former warehouse, smelled of new plastic, sawdust, and fresh paint. Before the volunteers, mostly corporate women in suits and sneakers, got down to ribbon and wrapping paper, the director guided them on a tour, assisted by Mildred, an enthusiastic new resident, whose sparkly brown eyes and shiny finger waves made her look like a pixie in studded blue denim. Mildred was one of the first class of twelve resident families, forty-eight adults and children in all.

The top two floors were divided into two- and three-bedroom family suites, with all facilities except kitchens. Mildred proudly showed off her apartment. 'This is about two hundred times better than the shithole we were living in . . . pardon my language.' The rooms reminded Pat of dorms – clean, square, and nondescript. Mildred introduced her children, three sons who ranged from junior rapper teen to cartoon-watching preschooler. 'And over there, that's my niece, Darlene. My sister's child.'

The boys sprawled in front of the TV, checking out music videos on TV, but Pat watched Darlene. She appeared to be about nine years old. She sat on a kitchen chair, separate from the others, feet propped on the rung, sad eyes glued to a schoolbook resting on her snack-tray desk. Mildred's voice dropped low. 'Such a shame. My sister was the prettist girl you ever want to see, and no dummy either. She just played herself cheap. Darlene's daddy snapped his fingers, and she up and left that child to follow after him. Momma had Darlene up 'til she was four, but then Momma passed, and she's been with me since. I don't know where my sister is, if she's livin' or dead. Darlene's my little angel, though. Quiet, good grades, I try to get my sons to be more like her.'

She doesn't want to be any trouble! Can't you see it? The group moved on to look at bedrooms, but Pat hung back. *She looks so unhappy.* Without warning Pat got a flash of herself, silent, defiant, and hurt, sitting alone on her bunk at a group home, reading while the other kids played outside. Nobody who knew Pat now would recognize that somber little, too-wise face, but the image sneaked up on her, and she blinked back unexpected tears. Pat used to think she was hiding the hurt so no one would know, but Darlene's sorrow was written all over her face, and Pat realized hers must have been, too.

Pat sidled over to the girl and spoke softly. 'What are you reading?'

Darlene looked up, startled. 'It's about butterflies.'

'You like butterflies?'

'I never saw one for real, only in pictures. I have to do a science report for school, and butterflies reminded me of the ballerinas I saw on TV once. I thought they were pretty.'

Darlene's do-it-yourself braids were unraveling. Pat wanted to fix them, but she kept her hands in her pockets. 'So, you like butterflies and ballerinas. Do you like school?'

'It's okay.' Darlene shrugged. 'I'm new. I don't know anybody yet.'

'I changed schools a lot when I was your age. It's hard, but you'll make new friends.'

'I hope so.' Darlene was all arms and legs, long and tall like a licorice stick.

'Keep up with the old ones, too. Sometimes they're best.' *I didn't, but it's good advice*.

'Say good-bye to the lady now, Darlene. She has to go,' Mildred said.

Pat winked. 'See ya.'

'Bye.' Darlene sighed and went back to her book.

One end of the next floor housed the dining room. Each family was assigned to either a round table or to space at one of the long rectangular ones. The director explained that it was each family's responsibility to send a member to set the table and to get the bowls and platters of food. 'We want it to feel normal, like home, because our aim is to transition families from crisis to self-sufficiency as quickly and smoothly as possible.'

What's normal about a cafeteria for a hundred people? But Pat just ohhhed and ahhed with the group over the sparkling, professional kitchen where meals were prepared and classes in food service would be taught. The day-care center occupied the other end of the floor.

Down from that were two floors of educational facilities, where the residents and eligible nonresidents would receive job training, take classes to prepare for GED exams, and learn the basics of pulling their lives together. Pat peeked into the library and was impressed with the workstations, complete with new personal computers.

The tour ended back in the classroom, where stacks of toys and books waited to be wrapped. *This looks like a classy operation.* As first-rate as she expected from Turner Hughes, and one she would be honored to support. While the women sang carols and wrapped, the director made it clear they needed volunteers in every capacity, from mentors to fund-raisers. Pat left her card and told the director that while her schedule was too unpredictable to volunteer regularly, she had other ideas in mind and would be in touch. That night, though, she couldn't stop thinking about Darlene.

The next day, as Pat bought last-minute Christmas gifts for people at work, she saw a box of pale pink stationery with a butterfly on top. She knew it was right for Darlene. *Nothing big, just a little something.*

Standing in the checkout line, Pat remembered how glad she had been to get Gayle's letters and home-drawn cards with the taped-on dimes. She would have been completely adrift without Gayle, a friend she could tell her thoughts to when nobody else was listening.

Pat included stamps when she wrapped the box, and on the card she wrote, 'I hope these butterflies help carry your letters to your friends.' The next day Pat messengered the package to the AHUP office and figured she'd done her good deed, but at off moments she wondered if Darlene would like her gift, and if the little girl even remembered her.

Christmas Day, with the office upheaval calmed to a dull roar, Pat departed for a week of R&R at a Tucson spa. It was a last-minute decision, but for six months she'd been on a wild ride without a seat belt and figured she'd earned a little paid personal pampering. Besides, between martinis and missed gym classes, she'd picked up a few pounds.

Pat took morning walks past stately saguaro cactus. She enjoyed beautifully designed lo-cal meals and discussed nothing more pressing than the virtues of the seaweed wrap. Alone at the stroke of the New Year, Pat toasted herself with a celery and apricot splash, and flew to New York that afternoon ready to make this the year that changed her life.

First thing back in the office, Pat flipped through her messages. The first one she returned was from the AHUP director. The stationery was a big hit.

'Mildred said Darlene was so happy. It doesn't take a lot to make most of our kids feel special. A little one-on-one attention does wonders. Now, Darlene wants to know if she can write you. I have your card, but I wouldn't give her the address until I asked.'

Pat hesitated. She felt both honored and nervous about getting involved.

'It would mean so much to her,' the director prodded.

Pat saw Darlene's sad eyes. 'Sure. Give her the address.'

Pat's yoga and tofu serenity was out the window by midmorning. Chris was waiting in the agency kitchen when she popped in to get ice cubes for her carrot juice.

'What's the story with this Marcus Carter? Tastea has a bee up their butts about him, but his agent keeps blowing

311

me off.' Chris squeezed a lemon wedge into his mug of decaf.

'What am I supposed to do?' Marcus wasn't on Pat's 'to do' list for the new year.

'I heard you grew up with him. Can't you appeal to his neighborhood loyalty, or at least threaten to tell some juicy secrets to a sleazy tabloid?'

Pat bristled and banged her cup, leaving an orange puddle on the counter. 'Why would you assume that everybody with a little bit of fame has some skeleton they're hiding?' Or a snowy afternoon and a secret Pat still held sacred.

'Put the high horse back in the corral. You know what I mean. Can't you call him or something? Anything. Just let me get him signed. The bicycle racer's contract is in the house. They decided on this woman volleyball player, who also happens to be a model. Her body's about five miles long and she does incredible things for sweat, but I need Carter signed so I can shoot the damned commercial before spring training.'

'I don't have his number. It's not like we're bosom buddies.'

'Talk to his agent,' Christ pleaded, hands pressed together prayerfully. 'The Dodgers just signed him. They want another big bat to go after the World Series again. Personally, I feel you can never have enough big bats. The deal is worth major money, so maybe he's not interested in the pocket change from our commercial, but you gotta try. Tastea may scrap the whole campaign if they can't get him, and need I remind you, you started this.'

Pat abandoned the carrot juice in favor of a diet cola. 'There's gotta be somebody else who can finish it.'

Except she was voted person most likely to reel in the superstar, and in a few days found herself on a plane headed for Curaçao, where Marcus had sailed his yacht.

Sailed his yacht. The farther she went into this, the more bizarre it got.

Over the phone his agent said Marcus hadn't made up his mind if he would do the spot. 'He won't say yes, no, or why, so lots of luck.'

Pat rehearsed her sales pitch on the flight. The product was wholesome. He'd get wider name recognition, which could only help him in his primary career as an athlete and in anything he planned to pursue after he hung up his cleats. And the price was negotiable. How could he turn it down? *This is just business,* she told herself as the cab bounced away from the airport along rutted roads. It was hot, in spite of a constant wind, and sweat ran in thin ribbons down her stomach from bra to panty. *We don't have to be friends. He's signed on the dotted line for many a stranger.*

At the marina Pat strolled into the Neder Cay, where she was supposed to meet Marcus. One wall opened to the sea and the cozy space was cool, dark, and empty, except for the bartender who told her Marcus had gone out on a dive.

'I'm Otto.' Anywhere between twenty-five and fifty, he was golden as the sun and spoke with the crisp clip of Dutch and the dance of the Caribbean.

'Dammit! We had an appointment.' *And Marcus Carter is star trippin' again.* Pat leaned on the bar, feeling prickly as a porcupine.

'Don't be too mad at him. We were afraid we lost him last week.'

'What?' She slid onto a rattan bar stool.

'He took some people out on *Brother's Keeper* . . .'

'He calls the boat *Brother's Keeper?*'

'Ja.' Otto nodded. 'Off Oostpunt. The currents were

devilish, so the party decided not to dive. But Marcus, he musta been feelin' like Neptune out for a swim in his ocean. He went down, by himself mind you.' Otto shook his head. His sandy blond hair was rubber-banded at the nape of his neck in an Afro-puff. 'Do you dive?'

'No.' And she hadn't known Marcus did either.

'Going down by yourself, even on a fair day, is dangerous. Some call it plain foolishness, but he wanted to dive, so he did.' Pat rifled her bag until she found her cigarettes. Otto gave her a light, then put a glass in front of her. 'Welcome to Curaçao.' A few pebble-sized ice cubes floated in a dark rum punch bath.

'Thanks.' She didn't want a drink, but she took a sip to be polite. The bittersweet liquid went down cool, but warmed her to her toes. 'So, what happened?'

'Time pass and then some. No Marcus. The others got worried when they knew his oxygen should be gone and he hadn't surfaced . . .'

'He ran out of oxygen?'

'So they put out an S-O-S and rigged a guide wire so a few of them could go down and look without getting taken by the currents. They were about ready to commend him to the sharks when a radio message came in. A fishing boat dragged him out of the water almost two kilometers south. On his way to Venezuela, I said.'

'Oh my God!' *How could he be so stupid?*

'The man is lucky. By all rights he shoulda been chum. Can I get you a refill?'

Pat had sipped her drink nervously as Otto spoke, and her glass was empty. 'Please.' Otto mixed her drink while Pat watched a yacht back in toward the pier.

'Don't mind me, but you look formal for the marina.' Otto put down her glass.

'This is business.' The coral coatdress was cooler than a

suit, but her pearls felt like a noose and her legs steamed in panty hose. 'And I'd rather not be here.'

'That's not what the other women who come to see him say.' Otto raised his eyebrows, excused himself to wait on a new patron.

The other women! Pat took a big swallow. *That's probably why he's not here now.* She drank and fumed about how unprofessional it was for Marcus to keep her waiting. *I'm here to offer him a deal, he's out on a damn pleasure cruise and the bartender thinks I'm one of his bimbos!* Suddenly her hose had to go. Pat headed for the ladies' room and quickly realized her legs were rubber. She held on to chair backs and well-placed walls until she got there.

What if he had died? Pat pulled down her stockings and chucked them in the trash. *It's stupid. Just stupid!* She looked in the mirror, blotted the shine off her forehead with her palm, and ran a comb through her hair. *Wonder if he's with Ms Newscaster . . . or Téa.*

Pat couldn't sit still any longer, so she claimed her drink, left money on the bar for Otto. She shuffled down the pier, where a party boat had docked. She squinted in the white-bright sunlight, unable to make out more than the silhouette of the man walking toward her.

'Oh, shit! Rich told me I was meeting some woman named Reid, but I didn't think it could be you!' The outline of damp swim briefs darkened Marcus's khaki shorts, his swirling aqua shirt flapped open in the breeze.

'You must be used to people hangin' around until you're good and ready to show up.' Something about Marcus standing there was like a red flag, and Pat felt like El Toro.

'Are you usually this nasty to people you're *supposed* to be trying to impress?' Marcus folded his arms across his chest and cocked his head toward the drink in Pat's other hand. 'It looks like I missed cocktail hour.'

'Listen, Marcus, let's get this over with.'

He paused. 'Aw-ite. We can talk aboard my boat.' Pat followed him down the pier.

'I heard what happened to you last week. Are you crazy or just plain stupid?' The rum was like truth serum. What Pat had been trying not to think, slipped out of her mouth.

'I'm crazy? How much punch did you drink? Otto didn't tell you it makes folks lose their minds, did he?' Marcus laughed, which only stoked her fire. They walked and fussed until he stopped at a sleek, double-decker fiberglass beauty. 'Take your shoes off.'

'What?'

'You can't climb the ladder in heels.' Marcus smirked.

'What's so funny?'

'Life . . . Are you gonna get on, or are you gonna stand here and beat your gums?'

Pat sucked her teeth and walked out of her pumps, leaving them on the dock. 'Fuckin' shoes!' Her dress was too narrow to step out onto the ladder, so she unfastened the bottom two buttons and reluctantly let Marcus steady her arm as she climbed aboard.

'We can talk in the galley.' *Seem like I been fussin' with this woman off and on my whole life.* Marcus led her through the floating living room, furnished with forest green upholstered banquettes, and brass-and-glass cocktail tables. The galley had a laminated oak table and she slid onto a bench while he went to the stove. 'You want coffee?'

'Whatever. What I want to know is, why you left me that way? . . . In Seattle? It was *rude*, Marcus. And mean. I never thought you'd be like that. You may be famous . . .'

Marcus waved a white dish towel. 'Peace! Damn woman! You gon' let me answer?'

She folded her arms on the table and looked at him sternly, if somewhat cross-eyed.

He unlatched the cupboard and got a tin of coffee. 'From April to October it's important to be famous; after that it's a hassle. That's why I come here, for some privacy.'

'Yeah, I bet.'

'Anyway, I musta been preoccupied the day I ran into you. It *was* a surprise you know. In airports and places like that, I'm on my guard. People do some wild-ass stuff.'

'Uh-huh.' The boat rocked in the water, churning the rum in Pat's belly. She put her head down on her arms, but when she closed her eyes she felt the table spin like a forty-five on the hi-fi. 'Marcus . . . I feel sick.'

'You need some air.' He helped her to one of the banquettes, and she stretched out.

The salty breeze eased the bubbling in her guts. *Please. Please don't let me be sick . . .*

The lapping of water slowly came into her consciousness. Pat fingered the blanket tucked under her chin. *Who covered me up?* She wiped a hand across her cheek and felt the sticky track where the drool had seeped from the corner of her mouth. When she opened her eyes, the sky was a hazy purple. *Where am I?* Then she remembered and bolted up.

'I thought Otto's punch put you down for the count.' Marcus looked up from the maps scattered in front of him on the coffee table.

Pat felt like her brains had liquefied. 'I'm so embarrassed. I don't know where to begin apologizing. My behavior was . . . unprofessional.' She licked her fingertip and tried, discreetly, to remove the dried spit trail from her face. *I must look like shit.*

He put his feet up on the table. 'Now, do you want coffee?' Marcus finally let the grin cross his lips.

'I've made a complete fool of myself; I should go.' She

stood and realized she was barefoot. 'Where are my shoes?'

'You mean the ones you left on the pier?'

'Damn,' she muttered.

'Aren't you at least gon' tell me about this commercial?'

'You still wanna hear this?'

'That's why you flew down here, isn't it?'

'Point me to a bathroom, and then we can talk.'

'This is a boat. It's called the head, and it's up toward the bow on the starboard side.'

'Aye, aye.' Pat found the head, spied herself in the mirror. She looked like a shipwreck, and her mouth tasted like bilgewater. *I've never done anything this stupid. Not even close.* But whenever Marcus was involved the world seemed upside down and backwards. She wanted a smoke to settle her nerves, but she remembered he hated cigarettes. *What did I say to him before? What am I going to tell them at the office?*

When she got back, coffee was waiting, and her shoes were next to her seat.

'You can save the sales pitch. Rich explained the offer, and there's nothing wrong with it. I just don't know if it's what I wanna do.'

'Why?' Pat dumped a sugar cube in the mug of coffee.

He shrugged. 'I don't know. Sometimes I feel like it's too much.'

'What's too much?'

'I've been lucky. I got way more than I deserve.'

'What does that mean? You work hard, and you're one of the best at what you do. You should be proud of yourself.'

'Proud. Yeah, right.'

'I'm serious. The team owners must believe you're worth what they pay you. If you don't need the money

318

from the commercial, give it to charity. It's what Dave Winfield does with his foundation. Tastea's gonna pay somebody. It might as well be you. The product's not addictive, doesn't cause cancer or hurt anybody.'

Marcus stared past her, into the night. 'I guess.'

Neither spoke for a while. 'So, what do you do for kicks when you're not tryin' to be shark bait?' She had said all she was going to about business.

He brightened, and the dimple appeared on his cheek. 'Yeah, you had a lot to say about my diving, but I do a little a this, a little a that. Ride horses, water ski, race powerboats . . .'

'Don't you do anything slow?'

'No time. Which reminds me, I do have an engagement this evening.'

'What's her name?' She tried to sound nonchalant, but it still came out testy.

'It's confidential.'

'Fine.' *Why should I care?* Pat gathered her things.

'And I still don't know about this endorsement thing. I'll think about it.'

'Okay. And, Marcus . . .' She rested both hands on his shoulders and shook off a tingle she didn't expect. 'Be careful, will you?'

'Aw-ite.'

By the time Pat got to the agency, Marcus had agreed to the deal. There were a few details to be ironed out, but there was no mention of Pat's unusual negotiating style.

Waiting in her stack of mail was a pink envelope with butterflies on front. The address, written in carefully rounded script, slanted up toward one corner. From the 'Dear Miss Patricia Reid, the nicest and prettiest lady I ever met,' to the 'Very, very, very, very, truly yours,' the letter tugged at an unfamiliar place in Pat's heart. Darlene said she had written two of her friends, and one already wrote back, which made her feel happy. She hoped to see Pat again, but if not, she would always remember her. That night, curled up in bed, Pat wrote back, and she wondered whether Mildred would mind it if Pat took Darlene out sometime, maybe to find some real butterflies or ballerinas.

CGG timed the debut of Marcus's first Sports Quencher spot, a high-speed, high-energy sweatfest, to coincide with his debut as a Los Angeles Dodger. Life-size cutouts of Marcus appeared in stores across the county in conjunction with Tastea's 'Take It to the Limit' T-shirt offer, the preliminary sales figures showed significant movement against the competition, and Pat got an appreciative nod for her role in bringing the pieces together.

And the first two quarters that Pat had been in her new job, production costs showed a significant decline. Zabriski gave her a glowing review, and Pat figured it was a good time to bring up her pet project, the pro bono ads for AHUP. Zabriski asked for figures, which she had on his desk by the next morning, and in a few days he gave her the green light.

Pat wasted no time contacting the AHUP director. She was over the moon and put Pat in contact with the board so the idea could be discussed at their next meeting. Pat had already started preparing a presentation about CGG and what they hoped to do for AHUP when she got the word that the foundation was not interested in public service ads at this time. And Pat smelled skunk.

17

'. . . that was a long time ago.'

1989

'Is she ready?' *Of course not.* Loretta was never ready when Gayle came to pick her up from the hairdresser's.

'Ten minutes more under the dryer. We all ain't lucky like you. Good thing, or I'd be outta business!' Mozelle Jones, the big hipped, silver-haired owner of Mozelle's Beauty Shoppe motioned her to the old brocade sofa in front by the window. 'Take a load off.'

Gayle smiled politely and sat down. *Lucky?* She'd been waiting for her mother at the hairdresser since she was two. Women oozing Shalimar and draped in pastel plastic capes would come over to her carrying their just-delivered, church-sale, fried whiting dinner on a grease-soaked paper plate. 'Umh! Umh! Umh! Lookit this pretty hair.' Then they'd run their fishy fingers over her head. 'Sure is one lucky child!' *Couldn't she be ready just once?* The ancient Mediterranean console TV that sat under a faded Raveen poster played *Wheel of Fortune* in slowly flipping vertical hold, and somebody named Matt was buying an A.

Loretta sat under a domed dryer bonnet, engrossed in the *Amsterdam News*. Mozelle tapped her on the knee, and she looked up, waved to Gayle.

The patron in the front booth, with half a head of just-pressed curls, asked Gayle to buy raffle tickets. She dug in her purse for money, but didn't bother filling in the stubs since a trip to Las Vegas was the last thing she wanted to win. Ramsey hadn't mentioned the ponies, poker, or any other kind of gambling for over a year. Gayle counted her blessings. The smooth patter of a radio DJ came from somewhere in the back, behind the blue sheet strung across a doorway, and competed with Matt, who said he would solve the puzzle.

'So your mother was tellin' us how you all know Marcus Carter.' Mozelle's claims to fame included shampooing Billie Holiday, manicuring Duke Ellington, and turning down 'personal invitations' from the likes of Joe Louis, but she always doubted other people's brushes with celebrity. '*Inside Info* is runnin' some kinda story about him tonight.'

What did Momma dig that up for? 'We went to school together, but that was a long time ago.' Gayle looked at her watch and hoped she sounded casual. She still had to pick Vanessa up from Keisha's. *I don't have time to sit here and watch TV*.

'You and Marcus were more than classmates, and you know it!' Loretta, out from under the dryer, pulled rollers from her hair and dropped them on top of the newspaper in her lap. 'He was your boyfriend! For how long? Shoot, you were always wavin' your hand around showin' off that little ring he gave you and tellin' us you were pre-engaged. Until you met Ramsey, that is.' She moved to Mozelle's styling chair, cradling the curlers.

'Whatever you say, Momma.' Gayle wanted her to get off the topic.

'That boy has been so good to his parents. Soon as he made it big he built 'em a brand-new house in North Carolina. Now he's living way 'cross the country in Hollywood.'

'Malibu, Momma.' Gayle had grown used to her mother's meandering stories since the stroke, but this was getting on her nerves.

'Wherever. Anyway, he's doin' beautiful, in them commercials and all, and you don't see him out with White women on his arm; leastwise he never gets his picture taken with any.' Loretta dropped her voice to a whisper. 'Lord, you know how your daddy loved the Mets, but I rooted for Marcus and the Dodgers to win the pennant this year. We shoulda gone! I know he coulda gotten us tickets.' Loretta bobbed her head so much that Mozelle couldn't do the comb-out. 'They're gonna beat Oakland in the Series, too, mark my words . . .'

'Momma, you have to hold still so Miss Mozelle can . . .'

'Hush, Gayle, the program's comin' on. Mozelle, turn the chair so I can see.' Loretta didn't want to miss a word, so she could add her own embellishments.

Mozelle turned up the volume so everybody in the shop could hear, and the best Gayle could do was grit her teeth and hope the story would be first and short.

'He has it all, chiseled good looks, athletic prowess, fame, and lucrative endorsements, but according to exclusive *Inside Info* sources, LA Dodgers stellar first baseman and hammering hitter, Marcus Carter, may soon be implicated in the tragic shooting death of his brother, Frederick Carter . . .'

Freddy's eighth-grade class picture filled the screen, and Gayle was chilled by a cold blast from her past. *What? What is she saying?*

'Lord, what mess are they fixin' to stir up?' Loretta dropped her head in her hand.

'Carter, "the Cat in the Hat," a high-octane sportsman and very eligible bachelor, first made his mark with the Baltimore Orioles in the early eighties, but the tragic death of his older brother takes us back to 1969, when Marcus was a mere nine-year-old schoolboy. Two decades have passed, but there is no statute of limitations on murder . . .

Murder? There was no murder! What do they mean? Panic silently engulfed Gayle.

The reporter continued. 'NYPD is reportedly working with the DA's office on the investigation.'

What if the police call me? 'I'll be right back.' Gayle headed for the ladies' room to collect herself, but halfway there she stopped, frozen by memory of the chain of events started by another unnecessary bathroom trip. She sat down at an empty dryer.

'Carter declined questions today upon leaving the DA's.' The TV showed Marcus walking down the courthouse steps, eyes forward, jaws clenched like a steel trap, and Gayle knew it was pulsing, like it always did when he got mad.

'We have no comment at this time.' Marcus's attorney spoke. 'I promise this witch-hunt will be over shortly and then Mr Carter will answer your questions. Hopefully by then you'll get back to the real story, the Dodgers' impending victory in the World Series.'

Who would have talked to a reporter? Not Marcus. Pat? She'd never do that. She couldn't, and I never told any . . . Ramsey! The thought chilled Gayle to the bone. *I know he can't stand Marcus, but he wouldn't.*

With a minimum of facts skillfully arranged over well-drawn innuendo the report suggested possible gang or drug involvement in the shooting. 'Carter's chances for another World Series win could be dashed if formal charges are brought . . .'

The beauty shop grand jury hummed with comments on the report. Mozelle talked into the mirror and feathered Loretta's hair with the sharp end of a rattail comb. 'Makes it sound real suspicious, don't it?'

'Freddy found that gun in the garbage and it went off while he was playin' with it. Ain't nothin' more to it than that.' Loretta looked over at Gayle. *My poor baby! They can't put her through this again.* 'I'll tell you why they're picking on him. He's good-looking, rich, and everybody likes him.' Loretta snorted. She wanted to redirect the conversation, sorry she had ever mentioned knowing Marcus. 'Can't let us have nothin' less it comes from them! You know, one of my old Miss Anne's has a sister lives down the road from Gayle. She recognized me at the farmers' market. I was lookin' at the tomatoes. She just knew I had a "situation" up here. Didn't want to believe I could be livin' right in her neighborhood! Her mouth hung open like a barn door when I told her. Couldn't say a word then, except "Oh . . ." Nothin' I tell you. They don't want us to have nothin'. My Joseph used to say . . .'

'Momma, we have to go. 'Nessa's waiting.' She had to get out of here. *Why now? After twenty years? What difference does it make?*

Mozelle stepped on the pedal at the base of the chair, and it sank back to floor level.

'Can you imagine having such a hateful job? Looking for other people's dirty laundry, and if you can't find any, then you claim they must be hidin' it.' Loretta handed Mozelle some folded bills and slid off the seat. 'You ready?'

'Am *I* ready?' Gayle held the door for her mother, then headed for the car. *Ramsey?*

'Are you all right, baby?' Loretta took Gayle's hand.

'I'm fine, Momma.' Her mother's blood pressure couldn't stand for it to be otherwise.

'Lord, what if the police come lookin' to talk to you, and Ramsey finds out?!'

'Momma, nobody's comin' for me, and I have nothing to tell them if they do. You should stop watching that nonsense in the first place.' Gayle unlocked the car. *There's nothing to say. Freddy was already shot by the time I came in the room.*

'Well I guess you're glad you didn't marry Marcus. You'd sure be in the middle of this mess right now.' Loretta climbed in. 'Poor Marcus. What kind of Godforsaken soul would have brought this up now?'

'I don't know, Momma.' Gayle drove in silence, trying to keep from pointing the finger of blame at Ramsey. *It doesn't make any sense.*

Times had been tough. The economy stalled, landscaping was a luxury, and Ramsey was forced to close the Jersey and Connecticut branches of the business. Gayle tried to comfort him, but he came down hard on himself for letting the company grow too fast and get out of his control. Loretta offered to let Ramsey use the money he had invested for her, the profit from selling St Albans, to tide him over, but he said it wouldn't be necessary.

Shopping had been Gayle's pastime, her sport, but Ramsey had stopped gambling for her, so she curtailed her hobby, too. Of course she still bought things for Vanessa, but except for an occasional clearance sale she had stopped shopping for herself, and they hadn't taken a trip since last year. She offered to let the cleaning woman go and suggested they not open the pool this year, but Ramsey said it would look bad, and he wouldn't cut back on things people might notice, like there was anyone paying attention to them now.

After the Derby Day TV incident, Mrs Phillips, Monica's mother, wasted no time getting the story of Ramsey's outburst on the wire. Car pool moms were even more standoffish with Gayle than before. The A-Team now consisted of Vanessa and Keisha, with Monica an occasional visitor, and only at Keisha's house. For the first few weeks kids at school teased Vanessa about UFOs landing in her TV. Several of the girls in her dance class would stare and whisper when she came in, but eventually all that quieted down.

Ramsey wasn't making any big contributions these days, so Gayle's social calendar was nearly empty. Now and then Bessie would have extra seats at his table for some event, but Ramsey liked being the host, not the guest, so they usually didn't go.

Gayle turned the guest room into a makeshift studio and spent a lot of time sketching and painting. She had done a number of watercolors, and even though Vanessa protested she was too old for Ell Crawford and pretended to read the stories only under protest, Gayle kept producing them. She tried to keep Ell Vanessa's contemporary, and sometimes she would catch Vanessa reading her favorites over and over again or sharing them with a friend. As a last-minute decision, Gayle contributed two of the colorful, handmade books to the previous school Christmas Bazaar. She was thrilled when the owner of a local children's store asked if she would consider offering the books through her boutique.

Gayle knew Ramsey was opposed to her working, but this was different. It could be an opportunity to start her own business. But when she finished her sales pitch, Ramsey looked at her like she had suggested they join a nudist colony on Jupiter.

'So folks can say my wife peddles mammy-made junk?' She never mentioned it again.

Gayle hoped he'd turn it around this summer. With the consolidation, Ramsey saved on overhead, and he had a good feeling about a bid he had in on the landscaping and maintenance contract for a brand-new hotel–convention center. 'If that comes through, we'll be sittin' pretty.' *Why would he tell somebody about Marcus? Who would he tell?*

'What would you say if they called you?' Loretta asked as Gayle merged onto the Cross Westchester Expressway.

That I remember that day like it was yesterday. 'Don't be ridiculous, Momma. I wouldn't talk to them.'

'Even to be on TV?'

That it wouldn't have happened if I hadn't . . . 'Momma, I don't want to talk about it. And don't start in with this when we get home.'

Luckily Vanessa got in the car jabbering nonstop. She gave a plié-by-plié description of her part in the upcoming dance recital and gabbed with her grandmother like girlfriends, so Gayle drove in silence.

It was twilight, the moon was not-quite-full, and Gayle knew when she crested the next hill she would see their house. On a night like this, it would be clear and distinct, but even in the dark, its familiar outline was always a friendly greeting. *There it is.* She still said that to herself every time the house came into view. Like maybe the next time it wouldn't be. Even after ten years she sometimes said the same thing about Ramsey. *There he is*, she'd say to herself when she caught sight of him. Like the next time he wouldn't be, either.

Gayle didn't know how much she was hoping Ramsey would be home, until she saw his car wasn't in the driveway. 'I have to go back out. I forgot something,' she said. *I have to ask him if he knows anything about this.*

'Whatcha forget? Can I go too? Please?' Vanessa asked.

'I'll only be a little while. You stay here and look after Gram. Okay? I won't be long, but you can stay up until then.'

'Goody.'

She kissed Vanessa's forehead and felt her heart tug when she realized she didn't need to bend over to do it anymore.

Gayle didn't go to Greener Pastures often. Ramsey's car was parked by the loading dock, surrounded by trucks, trailers, and other equipment, so she knew he was still there. She parked around front, got out, and tried the heavy steel fire door. *This ought to be locked.* Humid air greeted her inside. The thick scent of fertilizer, gasoline, and sick-sweet insecticide always made her feel like she was breathing through a wet washcloth. The ghostly hum of fluorescent lights filled the cavernous warehouse as she picked her way past riding mowers and sacks of grass seed and cedar chips, heading toward the rear. Ramsey's official office, carpeted, appropriately furnished, and accessorized with Gayle's artwork on the walls, was up front, but unless he had an appointment, he preferred his old battered desk in the back, next to the loading dock. He told her he could see what was going on from there.

From far away Gayle couldn't make out the conversation, but she heard Ramsey's chuckle bouncing off the cinder-block walls, loud and hollow, like canned laughter.

'Yeah. I know, but this has gotta hurt 'em, no matter what else happens. You talk to Moses. He'll tell you. They need him at 100 percent or they have no chance.' He sat at a rolltop desk, the phone pressed to his ear. 'I'm lookin' to rake in some mean green.' He looked up and was startled to see Gayle. 'Listen, Bessie, I'll talk to you later. Uh-uh. No problem.'

Okay. She's heard the story already. He figured he'd have to deal with this when he got home, but now was as good a time as any. 'What brings you down here so late? You know I don't want you in this neighborhood after dark.

It's not safe.' He stuffed some papers in the right-hand drawer and stood up.

'Rake in some green from where, Ramsey?'

'I was just on my way home to tell you the good news. I got the Westcenter contract today! Things are looking mighty good, baby. Mighty good!'

'That's great, honey . . . I knew it would work out.' Gayle tried to sound enthusiastic, but it came out lame.

Ramsey pecked her on the cheek, then went to the locker across from his desk and got out his suit coat. He had been wearing khakis and a work shirt when he left this morning, but in case he had to meet with a client or go to a job site unexpectedly, Ramsey always kept extra clothes at work.

'Ramsey?' Gayle spoke to his back. *I don't want to ask him. If he doesn't know anything about it, I don't want to be the one to start the whole Marcus thing again.*

'Huh?' He closed the door, snapped the lock shut, and slipped his jacket on.

Why would he tell? 'Did you . . . have you ever told anybody . . . you remember how you used to go on and on about Marcus and I told you . . . you know . . . about how Freddy got shot?' She knew he was looking at her, but she inspected the milky window behind his desk.

'Yeah, sure I remember.' Ramsey patted his pockets. 'You don't think I could forget a thing so terrible that happened to my Nightingale? Do you?' He removed his keys.

'I guess not. But what I mean is . . . there was a story on TV today . . . about Marcus and Freddy.' Gayle looked down at the toe of her red shoe. *I must own fifteen pairs of red shoes.* 'Did you . . . tell anybody what I told you?' She finally looked at him.

'What? Who would I tell?' His reply was nonchalant.

330

'I'm parked out back, so I'll walk you to your car and lock up on my way out.'

Their footsteps echoed loud and gritty on the painted concrete floor. 'I, I don't know but . . . how did they know that stuff?'

'Whoa!' Ramsey turned to her. 'I don't even know what *stuff* you're talking about. But, hell, you can find out anything about anybody if the right person's diggin'.'

'Ramsey, no one knows about that day but Pat and Marcus and me, and now you. We never told another living soul . . .'

'So you decided that I called up a TV program and told them I knew a dirty secret about Marcus Carter and they said "Great, we'll put it on the air!" Just like that? Because he used to be your boyfriend? Come on, Gayle. You watch too many soap operas.'

When she reached the door Ramsey was holding it open, his hand pressed firmly against the release bar. She hesitated a second then lightly placed her hand on top of his. 'I wasn't accusing you. I love you. It's just that . . .' *It's just that I know you hate Marcus.*

'I'll see you home.'

By the time Gayle got home, she was convinced Ramsey was right. *Of course he is. I probably do watch too many soap operas. What would Ramsey gain by hurting Marcus?*

'It's raining and fifty-three degrees at five-forty-five. Traffic in ten minutes . . . This just in. Beleaguered baseball star Marcus Carter was airlifted to New York Hospital earlier this morning following a motorcycle crash in East Hampton. He is currently undergoing surgery . . .' Pat sat straight up in bed. She could see Marcus lying in the road. *Still, bleeding. Just like Freddy.* '. . . no other vehicles were involved. The motorcycle was registered to supermodel Téa, who is out of town and unavailable for comment . . .' She grasped her knees and rocked herself to quiet the ache.

Ever since Curaçao Pat felt Marcus was cruising for disaster. *So now he's hit pay dirt on a back road! Why the hell does he keep torturing himself?* She angrily flung the covers off and turned on the light. *It's like he won't be satisfied until* . . . When the whole Freddy mess came out she figured he'd let the secret slip during pillow talk with one of his bimbos. *Maybe the reporter. A story is a story.* It was hard to imagine he would actually tell anybody. From that horrible day to this she had never spoken the words aloud, not to another living soul. Now she overheard it being discussed on the street, and people in the agency asked if she knew about the incident. It seemed like sacrilege.

Pat called Marcus's agent for days. When she finally reached Rich, he gave her the standard line, promised to pass her good wishes on to Marcus, which he did, but Marcus wasn't seeing visitors.

'I don't need people tryin' to cheer me up, 'cause I got nothin' to be cheerful about.'

'How about you're alive?' Rich dumped a stack of cards on Marcus's bedside table.

'Don't preach to me, man.' He'd met with premier orthopedists and plastic surgeons. The upshot was he'd need more surgery to repair the damage done to his limbs in his three-hundred-foot slide weighed down by a thousand pounds of motorcycle. Then he could look forward to months of physical therapy. He'd have use of both his arm and his leg, but they told him he shouldn't expect to charge around the bases or hit four-hundred-foot homers. Marcus didn't care what they expected. He knew better than anybody what he could do. Had to do.

Mail and presents accumulated in a corner, unopened.

He watched television all day and most of the night, anything but the news and sports, and kept busy teaching himself to write left-handed, just for now. His request for free weights, so he could exercise his good arm and leg, was vetoed by his doctors, so he had to be content with visualizing himself, lifting weights, swinging a bat, and running, flat out, fast as ever.

A week after the accident Marcus's attorney phoned to let him know he'd been cleared of any culpability in Freddy's death. His legal cloud had been lifted, but it didn't lighten the heavy load in Marcus's heart. He still didn't know why Pat started all this, and it ate him up inside.

The next day nurses and doctors streamed into his room, congratulating him on the Dodgers' five-game World Series win, but Marcus was sullen.

'Why are you so sad? You won.' An aide put Marcus's dinner tray on his table.

'They won. I ain't even started fightin' yet.' But he decided it was time. 'Would you set my phone on the table where I can reach it?'

Marcus punched the keypad, like he intended to punch through to the other side. 'A listing for Comstock Gravitt Greene.' Marcus copied the number in wobbly left-hand print. He had to know.

Pat sent something to the hospital every day, flowers, cards, fruit, notes. The day of the DA's announcement she even walked to the medical center and stared up at the blond brick building, hoping somehow Marcus could feel her vibes. So when he called, she figured it was because he'd finally gotten one of her messages, but he sounded so remote. She chalked it up to pain killers and the enormous burden he'd been dragging around. *Maybe having Freddy's death out in the open will lighten his load*.

The guard posted in front of Marcus's room opened the

door for Pat, who carried a shopping bag full of dinner. Even in a luxury room, it was still hospital food. Inside, the room was dark. Flickering light from the TV cast eerie shadows on Marcus in the bed.

'You awake?' Pat whispered.

He pulled the chain and turned on the light above his bed. 'Are you happy now?'

'What should I be happy about, Marcus?' Pat walked toward the bed.

'Don't come any closer. I can't even look at you.'

'What the hell do you mean?' She sat the bag on the floor, too stunned to hold it.

'You show up outta the past like a damn ghost, talk me into a contract for one of your clients, and for what? So you can inform the whole damn world I shot my brother!'

'No! You *don't* think I had something to do with that *Inside Info* story! I know you have better sense than that.'

'*Don't lie to me!*' Marcus hurled his water pitcher across the room. Pat ducked and it exploded against the wall, splashing her back. 'Was it the money, or do you think I didn't suffer enough?'

'Is something wrong, Mr Carter?' The guard poked his head in the room.

'No . . . Nothing,' Marcus said. The door clicked shut.

Marcus turned his face away from Pat, but she marched to the other side of the bed.

'If I wanted to punish you, Marcus, does it make sense I would get you involved with one of *my* clients? Huh? Do you know how many meetings I've been to about what to do with the Marcus Carter problem? Do you know how hard it is to sit there without yelling that I don't give a shit about how a scandal will affect their market share? That what I'm worried about is you? Then I hear you ran your bike off the road, and I'm thinkin' "did he do it on purpose?" or doesn't he even realize he's acting like he wants to kill himself? Nobody has to punish you, Marcus! You do too good a job yourself!'

'I was *not* trying to kill myself!'

'You coulda fooled me. Last time I saw you, you'd been drifting toward South America without a boat. When you shot the first damn commercial you were taped up from something you sprained or cracked. What have you done since then I don't know about?'

'Just 'cause I like adventure don't mean I'm tryin' to off myself.'

'Don't even try it. You been doin' it since we were kids. You broke so many bones, I don't know how you can walk much less run.'

'So where did the story come from, the damn grave?'

'I don't know.' Pat looked out the window at the red and white lights of cars crawling along the FDR Drive. 'When I heard it, I felt for you the most. It was you stuck in the spotlight. But I felt trapped, too.' She turned to face him. 'If you'll remember, my life changed on that day, too. It's not a memory I care to visit.'

'But I ain't seen Gayle since the day we broke up.'

'And I saw her the year after that, but not since. You don't know where the story came from and neither do I. Maybe Gayle has something to do with it. Maybe there's another source we're not thinking about. We were just kids then, Marcus.' Pat came to the end of his bed. She could see the pain Marcus tried to hide.

'Damn . . .'

'I got pork chops, black-eyed peas, string beans, and sweet potatoes in the bag. You interested in dinner?'

'You cook?'

'You kiddin'?'

'Yeah. They're 'bout to bland me to death.'

Pat perched on the end of the bed while Marcus ate. The meal went slowly. He could pick up the chops by the bone, but he was clumsy with a fork in his left hand. Midway through the meal he put his fork down and laid his hand on the bed.

'Damn, I can't wait to get outta this cast and all these bandages. I'm sick of this bed.'

Pat covered his hand with hers. He stroked her fingers with his thumb and they sat a while without talking. His hands were big with wide, flat nails, and she could feel a scar that traced down from his middle finger almost to his wrist. She'd never felt his hand before, never held it.

'Your dress still wet?'

'A little, but I won't melt. I'm not that sweet.'

'You're lucky it was my left arm. I don't miss with my right.' He smirked, and the dimple dotted his cheek. 'If it's ruined, I'll take care of it.'

'No need. Next time I'll wear a wet suit.'

'No need. Thanks for dinner. Next time I'm buyin'.'

'Gimme a buzz and I'll come hungry.' Pat stood up, and the old awkward space threatened to come between them, but Marcus caught her hand and pulled her to him.

'I apologize for the things I said.' He kissed her hand and laid it on his chest.

Pat leaned down and kissed his cheek. 'See ya.'

18

'. . . don't go in the basement.'

Heart hammering against her ribs, the phone's brittle ring
yanked Gayle from sleep by the scruff of her neck. *Ramsey
knows it scares me to death when he calls in the middle of the
night! Like I don't know he's gonna be late.* She rolled over
and snatched the receiver.

'Yes!' She didn't try to hide her irritation. *Hasn't been
home at a decent hour all week, and when he's here he's been
ugly.*

'Mrs Hilliard?'

The strange voice alarmed her. She turned on the lamp.
It's after five! 'Who is this!'

'I'm calling from Westchester County Hospital . . .'

'Oh my God, what happened?'

'Your husband was brought in a couple of hours ago.
He's . . .'

'*A couple of hours?* Why didn't you call me before now?'
Hands quivering, Gayle carried the phone with her to the
closet.

'Our priority is the patient. He was unconscious when
he was brought in and now that he's stable . . .'

Unconscious! 'What do you mean, stable? Was it a car
accident?' Her brain locked and she stared at the rows of
clothes, trying to figure out what came first. *A bra. I can't*

337

go to the hospital without a bra. She pulled one out of the drawer, then reached for a sweater.

'No. It appears he was mugged or assaulted . . .'

'I'm on my way.' She dropped the phone, finished dressing in a fog, then woke her mother, told her what she knew.

'Get 'Nessa up and ready for school for me.'

'What should I tell her when she asks where you are?'

'I don't know, Momma! Make up something, but don't scare her! I'll call when I can.'

Ramsey had been moved by the time Gayle got to Emergency. She raced through pages of forms presented to her to fill out and sign, then rode upstairs, holding her breath against the fear of what she would find.

When Gayle saw him through the glass door panel she wanted to up and run. *The monitors, the IVs . . . It's just like Daddy . . . but Ramsey won't . . .* Gayle shivered. Ramsey couldn't die. She braced herself, stepped inside.

Ramsey's head was swathed in gauze. His face was swollen and bruised the pulpy red-brown of liver, and stitches held together a gash above his brow. *Who could do this?* Tears seeping down her cheeks, Gayle edged next to his bed, gingerly rested her hand on his bare shoulder. A sheet covered his lower body, but exposed his ribs, which had been taped from waist to armpit. His left arm was in a cast to the elbow. *He looks so helpless.*

Not once in ten years had Gayle entertained the notion that Ramsey might not be able to handle any situation that came up. He was her own personal superhero, who would always save the day. But now she had to be the strong one. Even when her mother had the stroke, Ramsey was there. *I don't know if I can do this.* As she wiped her eyes, shallow, staccato quivers of air trembled past her lips.

The doctor on call, an elfin woman who wore wood-soled

clogs, told Gayle that Ramsey had suffered a concussion and some brain swelling. Gayle felt faint, but she shook off the dizziness and listened. There was no skull fracture, and the doctor expected him to regain consciousness in the next couple of days.

'Days!' Gayle figured he'd be awake and talking in a few hours. Tiny fingers of panic tightened around her throat.

'Could be less, maybe more. When he wakes up, don't be alarmed if he's disoriented, or has some memory loss. Those are common results of head trauma.'

I wanna wake up. This has to be a nightmare . . .

Hour by hour Gayle willed herself through the night, not allowing herself to think of a possibility more than one second ahead of now. And for the next two days she scrutinized Ramsey's every twitch, blink, and groan, desperately afraid to think he might not come to. She watched his IVs like a hawk, and made sure the nurses replaced them on schedule. She sponged him down, held his hand, and talked to him, believing that somehow he could hear her. And every so often, without warning, those tiny fingers would sneak up and squeeze her throat so only tiny shivers of air could escape. She never ventured farther than the cafeteria for a takeout sandwich or the pay phone to answer her mother's questions and quiet her own terror long enough to calm Vanessa's fears as best she could.

'Yes, Momma, they're changing his sheets every day. And I promise to get some rest.'

'Of course he'll be fine, 'Nessa.' *He has to be.* 'No, honey, you can't visit him yet.'

'Soon. I'll be . . . We'll be home soon.' *Won't we?*

When the tall, slender woman with the pale blond buzz cut stopped by Ramsey's room Saturday afternoon, Gayle thought she was a hospital worker until she identified herself as Detective Theresa Stuckey.

'I know this is a bad time. But I have a few questions. I can come back . . .'

'No. It's fine.' Gayle thought the woman was pretty, despite her boring slacks and blazer. *I bet she doesn't dress like this off duty.* Gayle led her to the solarium.

'Did anything strike you as unusual about Friday?' Detective Stuckey took a pen and notepad out of her blazer pocket.

'No. It was a normal day,' Gayle said.

'You weren't a little, I don't know, mad maybe, that he wasn't home by five in the morning? Jeez, my husband still pitches a fit even when he knows I'm on duty.'

'My husband always works late on Fridays. He has a very large business to run.'

Detective Stuckey scribbled on her pad, asked some more questions about Ramsey's habits, hangouts, possible enemies. Gayle didn't know anything that seemed important.

Theresa Stuckey handed Gayle her card. 'If you give me a call when Mr Hilliard . . . ah . . . comes to, I'd appreciate it. My pager number is on the back. Call me anytime. I'd like to talk to him as soon as he feels up to it so we can get this thing wrapped up.'

'Certainly,' Gayle replied.

'Oh, and if you think of anything, no matter how small, you can phone me. You'd be surprised, but sometimes the littlest piece is what helps you put the puzzle together.'

On Monday morning Gayle phoned Greener Pastures, told Mrs Banks what had happened, and asked her to keep things running. 'Ramsey says you know as much about the business as he does. I'm sure it will only be a little while. And, Mrs Banks, thank you.'

Even though he still hadn't regained consciousness by the third day, Ramsey's condition had improved enough to be moved to a semiprivate. When the orderlies got him settled, Gayle stood at the foot of his bed, just watching him breathe. His face wasn't as raw and swollen as it had been that first morning. The cut above his left eyebrow looked puckered and tender, but he was beginning to look like himself again.

Because she needed to hear the sound of hope, Gayle put a positive spin on the news when she called her mother. 'This is a real good sign. He could wake up anytime now.' *But what if he doesn't? What if he stays like this for weeks? What will I do if he doesn't wake up? How would I take care of Vanessa and Momma?* Gayle ventured out to the florist and brought back a vase of white roses to brighten up her own spirits and the dreary room, but terror was never more than a heartbeat away.

Midmorning on Tuesday aides took Ramsey's roommate for tests. He had the bed by the window, so Gayle took advantage of his absence and leaned against the wide sill, letting the Indian summer sunshine streaming through the blinds warm her face. She relaxed that way for a while, watching people come and go, wondering what brought them here. When she turned back, Ramsey's eyelids fluttered. He blinked, then squinted and turned his head away from the light.

'Ramsey? Oh thank God!' She rushed to him, took his hand, and the tiny fingers relaxed their grip around her throat and Gayle could actually breathe. 'You don't know how good it is to see you looking at me.' She touched his hand to her cheek and blinked back a flood of tears. 'I'll ring for the nurse!'

'What day is it?' His voice was weak, like he didn't have enough air in his lungs to push out the words.

'It's Tuesday afternoon. You've been here since they brought you in Friday night.'

'Yeah . . . Friday.' Ramsey's head lolled on the pillow and his lids wavered closed, then reopened. He stared at the wall. 'Friday . . .'

Gayle wanted to ask what happened, but held back because she didn't want to upset him. 'You gave all of us a big scare.'

'Us? Who? . . . Damn!' Ramsey gasped when he shifted his torso.

''Nessa and Momma . . . who else? Be careful, you have cracked ribs and a broken arm!'

'Glad to see you awake.' The nurse stood at the door. 'I'll be back with the doctor.'

'Damn, my head hurts.' When Gayle placed her hand on his forehead he wrinkled his brow. 'Would you stop it?'

The nurse and the clog-wearing doctor marched in. 'Excuse us, Mrs Hilliard. This won't take long.'

Gayle paced the hall during the examination. *He just woke up from a coma. Of course he's grumpy.* After several minutes the nurse beckoned Gayle to return to the room.

'If his vitals stay normal we'll start him on liquids tomorrow. He can probably go home by Thursday, Friday at the latest.' The doctor scribbled on Ramsey's chart, then handed it to the nurse. 'The ribs will have to stay taped, and he'll be in the cast at least six weeks. The stitches can come out next week.' She turned back to Ramsey. 'The nurse will get you up later, and I'll check on you tonight.' With that, she and the nurse left.

'I can't wait to get you home! And as soon as you feel up to it, you'll have to call 'Nessa. She's been so . . .'

'Gayle, where's my ring? I don't feel right without it.'

'They gave it to me a couple of days ago. Here.' Gayle slipped the diamond horseshoe off her middle finger and onto his pinky, then kissed the back of his hand.

Ramsey noticed the flower arrangements on the table. 'Where'd those come from?'

'The plant came from church, the roses are from 'Nessa and me, the arrangement on the end is from Bessie. Wasn't that nice of him? Mrs Banks sent that . . .'

'Bessie? He's been here?'

'No. Nobody's been here but me.' Gayle straightened the covers, sat on the side of the bed. 'Ramsey, what happened? The police asked me questions, but I couldn't help them.'

'I don't know. I was in the back, at my desk . . .'

'I bet you had that door unlocked.'

'Maybe. I don't remember.'

'It's lucky a policeman found you outside by your car. At first they thought you'd been mugged, but you still had your ring, and they said no mugger would have left . . .'

'I already told you I don't know what happened! I'm not gon' talk about this no more! I'm tired.' Ramsey closed his eyes.

Gayle went home that night for the first time since Ramsey had been admitted. Loretta welcomed her with chicken and dumplings, and Gayle wanted to fuss at her mother for cooking. After the time Loretta let the water boil out of a pot of eggs and they exploded all over the kitchen, Gayle made her mother promise not to cook unless she was home to keep an eye on things. But the food tasted so good after days of cello-wrapped sandwiches that Gayle let it slide. The last few days had been an ordeal she wanted to put behind her, and when she dragged up to bed she looked forward to her life returning to normal soon.

Next morning Gayle phoned the hospital, and they reported Ramsey's condition as 'good.' She got Vanessa off to school and started planning his homecoming. She put her mother in charge of making sure Bernice used a little extra elbow grease when she cleaned upstairs in their bedroom, since that would be Ramsey's only territory for a while. While Loretta bird-dogged the housekeeper, Gayle roamed the aisles at the grocery store, choosing fixings for a special dinner. *Maybe veal chops . . . that rice he likes . . . chocolate cherry ice cream.*

Then Gayle hurried home to put away groceries so she could get to the hospital on time. She picked out a blue knit dress Ramsey liked, then went to the bathroom to freshen up. Even with the water on she could hear her mother and Bernice in Vanessa's room, gabbing to beat the band. *Yep. Momma's been helping all right.* The fireplace matches sat next to the toothpaste on the vanity. Gayle carried them back to the den on her way out.

Ramsey was sitting up in bed when she arrived. He stared into space, the newspaper abandoned in his lap. 'You look like a man who's ready to go home!'

Ramsey flinched. 'Don't sneak up on me like that!'

'I'm sorry.' She kissed his cheek and examined the cut above his eye. 'This looks better every day. Here. From 'Nessa.'

Ramsey took the slightly crumpled envelope with 'Daddy' carefully printed in blue marker on the front. 'The cops were here again. Have they been bothering you at home?'

'No. Why would it bother me? I want them to find who did this. You know, 'Nessa made the card herself in art class,' Gayle offered proudly. 'Go on. Open it.'

Lightning bolts streaked across the front, and raindrops fell from gloomy clouds. It read: 'You might be feeling under the weather.' Inside, a smiling sun shone on a rainbow. 'But everything will soon be better! Get well soon, Daddy. Love, 'Nessa.'

'Tell her I said thanks.'

'You can tell her yourself. Tomorrow this time you'll be home.' Gayle propped the card on his tray table so the rainbow faced him. 'Did you remember anything that might help? The police, I mean.'

'I'll tell you like I told them. *I don't know what happened!* If I remember anything, you'll be the first to know,' Ramsey snapped.

'Okay. Okay. Nobody's blaming you.'

'For what? I'm the one in the hospital! And I have to get back to work. Nobody is mindin' my business.'

'Mrs Banks said to tell you everything is copacetic, to use your word. I brought you clothes to wear home.' She hung them in the closet and set his shoes on the floor.

'What happened to the clothes I was wearin'?'

'The police have them, evidence or something. If you'd rather wear something else, tell me and I'll bring it in the morning. Can I get you anything?'

'You can hand me my robe. The doctor says I have to walk, and I'll be damned if I'll parade down the halls in this nightgown!' He sat on the side of the bed, legs dangling, while Gayle helped him into the robe, then eased himself to a standing position.

'Here, let me help . . .'

'I'm goin' to the end of the hall and back. I think I can manage that!'

'I was only trying to . . .' *He's just upset about the attack, that's all.* She held her breath and watched as he inched his way down the corridor, using the wall for support.

When he returned he went directly to sleep and napped while a nurse's aide explained the discharge procedure to Gayle and gave her instructions for his at-home care. Ramsey woke up, and she helped him with his gelatin and broth, then he insisted she leave.

Gayle straightened his covers and held his gaze for a moment. 'I'm so glad you're all right. You really frightened me, Ramsey.'

'You shouldn't have been. It takes more than a few punches to get the best of me.'

'Yeah, yeah, yeah . . . I'll see you bright and early. Love you.' She blew him a kiss.

'What do you mean he's gone?' Gayle yelled at the nurse. 'Where would he go? He was supposed to be discharged at nine! He knew I was coming for him!' Gayle headed for Ramsey's room, followed by the sneakered nurse and a security officer.

'Mrs Hilliard . . . we . . .'

'Have you looked for him? He's probably right in this hospital! What if he's fallen, or he's been hurt?' She stormed into the room, but the bed had been stripped, and there was no sign of him. 'How could he just walk out?!'

'He was a patient, not a prisoner.' The officer shrugged. When Gayle shot him a nasty look, he adopted a more official manner. 'The night nurse said his bed was empty when she made her last rounds before going off duty. That was about six. Roommate didn't hear or see a thing. It's nine-fifteen now.' He tapped a small black notebook with a stubby pencil. 'We've been looking for your husband for over three hours. He isn't here.'

The fingers were back. Gayle felt her chest tighten, and she groped for the chair. 'Did you call the police?' *Something terrible has happened.*

'There's no indication of foul play,' the officer said.

'The man was brought in here on a stretcher because someone beat him up, and the police don't know who! What kind of a hospital is this?'

'Mrs Hilliard? I'm sorry to bother you. I'm from the

346

Billing Office.' A slight, rumpled, middle-aged man whose shirttail hung out of his trousers entered the room.

'What?' *Maybe it's me. I'm losing my mind.*

'I wanted to speak with you before your husband is discharged. Uh . . . you, see, there's been a problem with your insurance.' He rubbed his earlobe between his thumb and forefinger while he talked. 'I spoke with Mr Hilliard yesterday, and he assured me there must be a mix-up of some sort. Promised he would take care of it.' The man adjusted his tie. 'At any rate, he guaranteed his bill would be paid. Could you perhaps . . . ?'

Gayle gaped at the man. 'I have no idea what you're talking about! Of course there's nothing wrong with our insurance! My husband is a well-known businessman in this community. None of this makes any sense.'

'We know who your husband is, Mrs Hilliard. He did the landscaping for our new wing last year. That's why when he assured us the bill would be taken care of we . . . perhaps a check?' He tugged his now reddened earlobe again.

'They've *lost* my husband, and now *you're* talking to me about money? What kind of people are you?' Tears threatened. *I can't cry. Not here.* 'Excuse me.' She brushed past them and went down the hall to the pay phone. *Maybe he went home.* No answer. Gayle had dropped Loretta off at the Red Cross on her way to the hospital, and Vanessa was in school. *He could be upstairs sleeping.* She raced home and searched the house attic to basement, but there was no sign Ramsey had been there.

Gayle phoned Greener Pastures. Mrs Banks hadn't seen him, but his car was gone when she got to work this morning. It had been parked in back since the night Ramsey was found, so she figured Gayle had stopped by for it.

Gone! He's on his way home! I'll give him a piece of my mind for worrying me like this. He should have told me he wanted to leave early. He shouldn't even be driving.

By noon Ramsey hadn't shown up. *Maybe he went to one of the job sites. He was so worried about business.* Gayle called Mrs Banks again.

'No, honey, I haven't talked to him since yesterday.'

'Yesterday?'

'Uh-huh. He wanted to know if I'd done the time cards and cut the payroll checks. I asked him if it was Wednesday.' Mrs Banks laughed. 'I been doin' it every Wednesday for the last twelve years! Takes up my whole day. I tried to get him to pay the guys every other week, but he wouldn't hear it. Said a workingman needed his pay every week. It's easier now that the summer crews are laid off.'

'He didn't say anything else? I'm so worried, Mrs Banks. How could he just walk out of the hospital? He could be hurt. Do you think I should call the police?'

'Maybe. Somebody could have stolen that nice car of his. It's been sittin' out back here for almost a week. Crooks notice things like that.'

Gayle knew Monica's father was the police chief, and she toyed with calling him, but since Ramsey wrecked the TV the Phillipses treated them like escaped lunatics. *Ramsey will have a fit if I give them something else to talk about.* She phoned Detective Stuckey, but she wasn't on duty. The officer she spoke with informed Gayle that Ramsey hadn't been gone long enough to file a missing persons report. He did take her information on the missing car. 'My guess is your husband will be home in a few hours. You know men and their cars.'

Gayle was waiting in the kitchen by the phone when Loretta came in the house fussing. 'The volunteer supervisor told me they only need me one day a week. They already have me counting supplies, like I'm simple or something! Cora dropped me off and she says they . . . oh never mind.' She got a tea bag from the cabinet, dunked it in a cup of water, and put them in the microwave. 'How's Ramsey? He must be glad to be in his own bed! Believe me, I know how they do you in the hospital. Waking you up to give you a sleeping pill!'

'Momma, he's not here.'

'What are you talking about? You didn't let him go to work?'

Gayle told her mother about the morning. 'Vanessa will be home any minute. I don't want to upset her, at least until I hear something, so I'm going to tell her they wouldn't let him come home. I know he'll call me.'

The next morning, Gayle greeted the sun with sleepless eyes. Ramsey hadn't come home, or called, but Mrs Banks did, just before noon. The bank was refusing to cash paychecks because there was no money in the account.

'I made the regular deposit myself, so I called to straighten them out, but they told me the account balance is zero. Isn't Mr Hilliard home yet? You must know where he is. There'll be checks bouncing from here to kingdom come.'

Gayle's hands trembled as she hung up the phone, and the overloaded wires in her brain short-circuited. *What the hell is happening?* That's when she remembered. The pages of names, the columns of numbers, pressing through the pages of Ramsey's notebook like Braille. All that money he gambled away. When the image sneaked up on her, she danced away. *He wouldn't. That was before. I would have seen it.*

By Sunday she was crazy with worry and exhausted from lack of sleep, but she pasted on a confident front to calm her mother and to prevent Vanessa from getting suspicious.

Keisha's invitation for Vanessa to spend the day with her and her mother came like an answered prayer.

'Keisha says she has a surprise to tell me! Tell Daddy I love him!' Vanessa gushed as she kissed Gayle on the cheek. 'See ya!'

Gayle shut the big front door and leaned against it. Loretta was standing there with her arms folded across her chest. 'I know, Momma. Don't say anything.'

'We should go to church. Ask them to pray for Ramsey . . . couldn't hurt . . .'

'I have to stay here in case he calls or comes home. Besides, I would never bring this up in church! Anyway, I have to call the police today.'

'Humph! Don't sound like much of a church to me.'

Gayle listened to the shush-shush of her mother's slippers as she shuffled to the back of the house. *She sounds so old. Dear God, please let Momma and Da . . . Ramsey . . . be all right.*

Before she called the police again, Gayle tried to reach Bessie. As far as she knew he was the only person Ramsey was friendly with. *Maybe he'll know something*. But she didn't leave a message when the answering service picked up.

I can't do this. Her whole life, somebody had taken care of the difficult tasks; now there was nobody but her. Gayle's hand was on the receiver when the phone rang.

'This is Detective Stuckey . . .'

'I was just going to call you.' Gayle was relieved. Somehow it was easier not having to dial the phone.

'I saw the stolen car report when I came in.'

Gayle told Stuckey about the empty business account.

'This is starting to sound like a kidnap.' Stuckey took

notes for the Missing Persons Report. 'Are you sure you can't think of any enemies, rivals, no bad blood with anybody?'

'No! I told you that already. This can't be real!'

'I'll stop by later to get a photograph. You call me immediately if anyone contacts you about ransom. No matter what they say.'

Kidnapped? The idea never crossed Gayle's mind, but now she could think of nothing else. She went upstairs and got the framed eight-by-ten from Ramsey's fortieth birthday that she kept by her bedside. She replayed the last day she saw Ramsey, turning every word he said over in her mind, but nothing stuck out as unusual. Then she scoured the house, not knowing what she was looking for. She scrounged drawers, dug in pockets, rummaged through boxes in the garage, but she found no clue to Ramsey's whereabouts.

There's gotta be something. Gayle called Mrs Banks, apologized for disturbing her Sunday, and asked to meet her at Greener Pastures. She hoped the office might hold an answer, or at the very least something that would help the police.

They used a crowbar to pry open Ramsey's locker. Empty. The warehouse odors mingled with dread, and Gayle felt like she was suffocating. Ramsey's battered rolltop desk loomed in the corner, and they used the crowbar to pop the locks. The drawers bulged with papers. She grabbed stacks of them at random and shuffled through bills, loan documents, second, third, and final notices from creditors and collection agencies, unopened envelopes, letters from banks, each piece a revelation, more frightening than the one before.

'You know, seven – eight months ago he said he thought somebody was tampering with the mail, so he got a post office box. He'd pick up the mail every day or two and bring it in.'

'I . . . I don't understand.' Gayle stared at the pile of papers in front of her and couldn't hold back the tears any longer. *What happened to all the money?* '*I swear to you it's over . . . I promise . . .*' But Gayle sidestepped the thought before it hit her head-on.

'I only saw what mail he gave me. Now that I think about it, he was getting calls from some of our suppliers and the banks. Told me he was looking into expanding the business again.' Mrs Banks tried to comfort Gayle. 'Well, it doesn't look too good right now. But Mr Hilliard was always so fair, he was a real smart businessman and . . .'

'Was? You talk like he's dead!'

'No . . . I mean to say . . .'

'I'll take this stuff home.' The tremble started as Gayle reached for a handful of papers from Ramsey's desk. Before she had a grip on them, her whole body was shaking. *What am I supposed to do?* Gayle sank down in Ramsey's chair.

'I'll tell the boys to take a few days off. Maybe Mr Hilliard will show up by then. Anyway, the busy season is over. You rest a minute, and I'll find a bag to put these in.'

Neither woman spoke while Gayle filled the shopping bag Mrs Banks brought her almost to the top. They walked to the door, and Gayle remembered just a couple of weeks ago, walking this same route, with Ramsey assuring her he had nothing to do with the story about Marcus. Now she didn't know what to think about anything he'd ever said.

The afternoon sun felt mean and cruel to Gayle. Long after Mrs Banks had driven off Gayle sat in her car in front of Greener Pastures, the loaded shopping bag next to her on the passenger seat. She didn't want to go home. Home meant having to explain to her mother and Vanessa. *Explain what? What do I know?*

When Gayle turned onto her street and the house came into view the usual 'there it is' flashed across her mind, but this time she began to sob. She pulled off the road, folded her arms across the steering wheel, and cried until she was drained. *I have to get myself together. I can't let Vanessa and Momma see me like this.*

'You all right?'

The question flung her back in time. *Ramsey? That's the first thing he ever said to me.* She whipped her head around, but when she focused, it was a neighbor from down the road.

Gayle wiped her cheeks on her sleeve, lowered the window. 'Yes. Thanks. I'm fine.'

'Just checking. Take care now.' He touched his hat and quickly returned to his walk.

Vanessa came in an hour later with a long face. 'Keisha's moving to Denver. Her mother got a promotion.'

'That's nice . . .' Gayle answered distractedly.

'It's not nice! It's terrible! I hate it!'

'You can go and visit! Won't that be exciting?' Loretta intervened and launched into the virtues of having friends in faraway places.

Vanessa didn't buy it. 'How's Daddy?' Gayle concocted a story that Ramsey had to go to an out-of-town hospital for a while to help him get better.

Gayle saw her mother's eyebrow arch, but she didn't address her until Vanessa was out of earshot. 'Why get her all riled up, and he shows up tomorrow, whistling and . . .'

'And what if he doesn't?'

'Just give me a little time, Momma. That's all I ask. I promise I'll tell her, if . . . if he doesn't . . . I don't want to talk about it anymore now.'

What if he doesn't? With everyone else asleep, Gayle sat in her bed, surrounded by the papers she had taken from Ramsey's office. It took hours to read them all and put them in chronological order. Some of the documents made sense, others were mumbo jumbo, but together they painted a grim picture.

Over the last couple of years, it looked like Ramsey mixed their personal finances in with the business. *He took a second mortgage on the house to get a business loan?* Gayle couldn't breathe or swallow. *Everything we own is in his name . . .*

Credit cards were delinquent, life and health insurance premiums hadn't been paid in months. *Canceled? That awful man from the hospital was right!* Gayle let the notices from the IRS threatening liens slip out of her hands. She lay for a long time staring at the ceiling and trying to catch her breath. Gayle felt like the girl in the horror movies who ignores the warning 'Don't go in the basement.' Dumb. But she descended another step.

Ramsey had fired both his lawyer and accountant months ago, but he owed them money, too. When she found the bank statements for investment savings, CDs, money market, annuity, she prayed that at least one of them might contain the silver lining she needed. *Momma's money!* But instead she ran smack into a new storm front. Ramsey *had* invested it, but last January he made himself or Greener Pastures, Gayle couldn't tell which, a loan, and from there all of Loretta's money seemed to have disappeared. *When Momma offered to lend . . . he'd already used it!* A scream hovered in her throat, but what bubbled up and out was a low, pleading moan that came from much deeper. *Oh, God help me . . . help us . . .*

Gayle hugged her pillow and rocked. She didn't want to believe he'd been gambling again. *He promised.* 'Learned my lesson.' He said that. *People only get beat up or disappear because of gambling debts in the movies. I would have known if . . .*

But the list of things she didn't know about her own life grew longer, paper by paper. *I know my car is paid for. I didn't even know where he kept the checkbook until now. Checkbook! How much money do I . . .* Gayle sat straight up, grabbed the phone, dialed the twenty-four-hour bank number she used to keep track of her account and waited – $7,219.11. *How long will that last if he doesn't come back? How much is the house note?*

Using the tiny calculator she kept in her purse, Gayle punched in numbers. When she finished she did it again, just to make sure. *If I make just one payment on every bill that's overdue, it will cost more than twice what I have, and that doesn't leave anything to live on now.* When Gayle put on her nightgown, took off her rings, and turned out the light, it was nearly six A.M. She pulled the covers over her head. *What am I gonna do?*

19

'You were my last luck.'

For the next three days, Gayle retreated behind her bedroom door. The phone's sudden ring upset her, so she unplugged it. She refused to talk to police. She ignored reason from her mother, frightened pleas from Vanessa, and the TV was her twenty-four-hour companion.

On the third night, Gayle lapsed into agitated sleep and Ramsey came to her. He stood on the lawn, dressed in pearly white clothes that glowed in the moonless night. And he whistled, faster and faster. Gayle ran circles around him, trying to keep up with his tune. She pulled at his clothes, called his name, but he wouldn't look at her. Then he floated off.

'Ramsey, wait!' Gayle cried out and bolted up, panting. The dream was so real she stumbled out of bed and pulled open the curtains.

Gayle took it as a sign he was coming home. She showered, put on one of his favorite dresses, and by the time Loretta and Vanessa woke up, Gayle had coffee brewing and the breakfast table set. Then she went to help Vanessa get ready for school.

Vanessa looked confused as she came out of her bathroom in her underwear. 'Mommy? You're not sick anymore?'

'No, honey. I'm not sick. Get me your comb and brush.' Gayle eased out the tangles in her daughter's hair. 'I guess your Gram is out of practice on hair combing.'

'Is Daddy gonna die?'

'No, Daddy's not gonna die, 'Nessa. Is that what you think?'

Vanessa nodded slowly. 'He's been in the hospital so long.'

'I think he'll be here soon! Maybe even today!' Gayle secured the end of the French braid with barrettes. 'Now, finish dressing and come get your breakfast.'

When Gayle got to the kitchen, Loretta was at the table, sprinkling sweetener in her coffee. 'Wellsa, you know somethin' I don't?'

'Uh-uh. I just remembered that I can't give up hope.'

'Gayle, you have to be *doin'* something. Hopin' don't make it so.'

'Momma, it'll be all right.' *And Ramsey will be here in time to explain where your money is, so I won't have to.*

In a few minutes Vanessa sauntered in and plunked down in her chair. 'Can't I stay home from school and wait for Daddy, too?' She spooned sugar over corn flakes and bananas and watched her mother.

'You most certainly cannot!'

Vanessa rolled her eyes and played at eating.

'Did you do your homework?' Gayle peered over the rim of her juice glass.

'You haven't *been* caring if I did my homework.' Vanessa bounced the heel of her sneaker indignantly against the chair leg and sloshed her spoon around in her bowl.

'Vanessa stop making a—'

Loretta jumped in. 'Of course she cares, honey. Your

358

mommy hasn't been feelin' so good. But we're sure glad she's better, aren't we?'

Vanessa shoved her bowl away, spilling milk and soggy cereal. 'Yeah . . . I guess so . . .' She snatched her backpack and disappeared out the door.

Openmouthed, Gayle stared after her.

'What do you expect? Her father's nowhere to be found, you hole up in your room and won't talk to her, and she's losing her best friend. Of course the child is upset. You have to be strong, teach her how to be strong.'

'I know. I'll do better. And when Ramsey gets back . . .'

'If you know when that's gonna happen, I wish you'd tell that detective woman who's been callin' every day. She's gettin' on my nerves. Miz Banks left a lot of messages, too.'

'I'll call them both after I clean this mess up.'

'Have you thought about talkin' to a lawyer?' Loretta asked.

'Momma,' Gayle cautioned. *I will not have this conversation.*

'Fine. Have it your own way.' Loretta turned her attention to her coffee.

Mrs Banks was in a hellacious mood when Gayle called. 'Everybody and his brother is calling here, blessin' me out and lookin' for money.'

'Please give him a little time.' Gayle didn't know what else to say.

'Mrs Hilliard, that's all it's gon' be. A little.'

Detective Stuckey apologized for all the questions she had to ask about the money irregularities at Greener Pastures. 'This is a lot like a puzzle. The only way we can solve it is to fill in the blanks.' Bottom line though, she had no leads.

For weeks Gayle maintained her usual routine, keeping

up appearances the way Ramsey always expected. She paid the utility bills from her checking account and ignored Loretta's cautions about spending. 'We have plenty to get by on,' Gayle lied.

When her mother broached the subject of a job, Gayle dismissed it. 'Ramsey doesn't want me to work.' And that was that. Her head promptly went back in the sand.

Once, she came in the empty house and got chills, overwhelmed by the sensation that Ramsey was there. It was like she could feel him, smell his after-shave. 'Ramsey, where are you?' she called. She ran to the den, up to their bedroom. 'How could you just disappear?' She sank onto the bed. *And what would I say if you answered?*

Gayle had to let the housekeeper go. Loretta helped with the cleaning, and items were more out of place than before. Gayle was sure she put her engagement ring in the crystal box on her dresser as usual, but she didn't have the heart to complain when she couldn't find it, especially since more than $80,000 of Loretta's was missing. *It'll turn up*.

Vanessa grew more sullen and withdrawn by the day. Gayle made sure she was clean, fed, and chauffeured, but kept her in the dark about her father.

'Why should I confuse her?' Gayle filed her nails, and Loretta watched TV. Vanessa was in her room doing homework, and Ramsey had been gone five weeks.

Loretta hit the mute button on the remote. 'You know, keeping a secret was the worst mistake your daddy and I made in raising you.'

Gayle looked up from her base coat. She and her mother didn't talk about 'that.' They had made their peace, and one of the provisions of the unspoken treaty was to let it lie. *Why bring this up now?* 'You didn't make a mistake, and I'm not making one either.'

'When you were old enough to understand, you had a right to the truth. Your daddy woulda told you, but I didn't want you or anybody else to know you weren't my blood child.'

'You and Daddy were protecting me. And Vanessa is too young to worry about this.'

'She's already worried! Can't you see she is? What if she hears it from somebody else? You know what happened when you found out the truth. Don't you want to spare your own child from feelin' like that? I wasn't protecting you, baby, I was protecting me. And that's what you're doin' with Vanessa.'

Gayle didn't answer and went back to her nails, her head poked deeper in the sand.

In early November Mrs Banks quit, and the week before Thanksgiving the marshal padlocked Greener Pastures. Almost daily the mail carrier brought sacks of mail forwarded from the business, and Gayle signed for registered letters addressed to Ramsey. She kept them neatly stacked and unopened in a drawer of the break-front.

Bessie called once. 'I'm checkin' on that rusty ol' man of yours. I haven't seen him for a while. He's not still in the hospital?'

'Ah . . . no. He's been kinda busy, Bessie.' She considered telling him, but decided the fewer people who knew, the better.

'Tell him I was asking for him. And you tell him to bring you in here. I haven't seen your lovely face in far too long.'

Days later, Gayle and Vanessa were on the way out when Detective Theresa Stuckey showed up at the back door.

'There's a few things I want to run by you. Is that your

daughter? What a beauty. You'll have your hands full when she gets older.' She smiled at Vanessa, who shot her the 'who are you?' look.

'Thank you,' Gayle said. ''Nessa, go on out and wait for me by the car.' She slunk away with a toss of her ponytail.

'We've established that your husband was a regular at a restaurant in White Plains called Bessie's. Are you familiar with it?' Stuckey looked down at her notes.

'Bessie and Ramsey have been friends for years. We both went to the restaurant.'

'Mrs Hilliard, Bessie Austin runs one of the biggest bookie operations in the state. Controls all the book . . . horses, numbers, and sports action, from Westchester to the Canadian border and then some.' She looked at Gayle, waiting for a response.

Bessie? 'My husband doesn't gamble . . . anymore. He used to, but . . .'

'Mrs Hilliard, Bessie is a powerful and dangerous man. We haven't been able to catch him with his hands dirty, but you should keep your distance. It's very likely that both your husband's assault and disappearance are linked to him.'

'I spoke to Bessie a couple of days ago. He wanted to know how Ramsey was doing . . .' *Bessie couldn't possibly have anything to do with this.*

'I bet. Did you tell him anything?'

'No.'

'This is a little awkward, but our information is telling us Mr Hilliard's . . . ah . . . recent misfortunes are linked to a special betting line Bessie ran for the World Series that went sour. Apparently your husband was involved.'

'I don't know what you're talking about, and I'm sure Ramsey doesn't either.' *Am I?*

'We're talking hundreds of thousands of dollars in

losses. That can make nasty enemies. It boils down to the fact that we're looking for Mr Hilliard, but so are they. I hope we find him first.'

'Who told you Ramsey was involved? They could be making a scapegoat out of him.'

'Mrs Hilliard, let me assure you my interest . . .'

'And if you find him first are you going to bring him home or arrest him?'

'The department wants to get your husband home safely. As far as any connection to Bessie Austin, our sources are reliable. It looks like your husband got in over his head. It happens. We don't plan to charge him, but Austin doesn't forgive or forget. If Mr Hilliard can help us get Austin, it would keep a lot more people out of trouble, including himself. So, if you hear from either one of them, I'd appreciate it if you give me a call.' Detective Stuckey walked down the drive and got in her unmarked car.

Ramsey? Bessie? I don't believe it. It doesn't make sense. Undeterred, Gayle went shopping for ingredients to make Ramsey's favorite Thanksgiving dishes.

That Tuesday the school principal called to tell her Vanessa had been suspended for fighting. When Gayle got there Vanessa was waiting in the office, red-eyed, hair disheveled, a scrape across her cheek. Her blouse was torn, and blood speckled the collar. Gayle felt disconnected, as if this was someone else's problem child, not the daughter who had a fairy-tale room in a dream house.

Gayle minced her way through a very uncomfortable parent-teacher conference. It seems Vanessa had become lackadaisical. She wasn't participating in class, her work was slipping, and now the fight. *Not my child.* Gayle folded her hands in her lap and stared at the chalkboard, her blinders firmly attached to her rose-colored glasses. But when the teacher offered counseling services if there was 'anything going on in the home,' Gayle was momentarily blinded by the harsh glare of reality and it made her mad.

'That won't be necessary,' Gayle answered dryly. She simmered in silence in the car, but by the time she got home she had reached a rolling boil. 'What do you have to say for yourself? Brawling in the halls like a hoodlum!' Vanessa hunkered down in a kitchen chair. 'Your only job is to go to school and get good grades, and you can't even do that! Vanessa Josephine, your father works hard to give you everything! What would your father say?'

Vanessa rolled her eyes and folded her arms across her chest. 'My father couldn't care less, wherever he is. May I be excused?'

'No you may not, young lady! Answer me! Why were you fighting?'

Vanessa fidgeted with the handle of the pepper mill.

Gayle snatched the mill from Vanessa's hands. 'Well?'

She stared down at her hands for several seconds. 'I . . . I . . . Monica said . . .'

'Monica? You were fighting with your friend?'

'She's *not* my friend! Now that Keisha's gone I don't have any friends. Anyway, Monica's a liar!' Vanessa slouched and glared at Gayle. 'She said . . . Daddy's a crazy crook . . . who' – the hard, defiant shell around Vanessa cracked – 'who ran away and left us . . . and I could find him if I wanted to . . . on a wanted poster in the post office!' Vanessa sucked on her bottom lip, and sad, hurt tears spilled down her cheeks.

'You *know* that's not true!' And then Gayle stopped. *She* didn't know if it was true or not. And all Vanessa had to go on was the fractured fable her mother had concocted, because Gayle refused to consider a less than happy ending.

'Oh, baby! I'm so sorry!' Gayle scooped her daughter

into her arms. Vanessa sobbed, and Gayle's own tears dropped silently on Vanessa's hair.

'Mommy . . . I didn't mean to . . .'

'It's okay. This is my fault.' *I was protecting me.* 'Let's get in my bed and talk.'

Vanessa curled her long slender legs under her and settled into the pillows piled against the headboard.

Gayle opened the drapes for the first time in weeks, then sat near the footboard, facing her daughter. Fading afternoon sun streamed across the bed. Gayle looked into Vanessa's puffy eyes and found all the fear and sadness she had spent ten years guarding her against. *I have to tell her the truth.* 'First, don't you ever forget you're the most important thing in the world to me, and I won't ever leave you. Ever . . . Your father has a . . . a sickness . . .'

'Aren't they making him well in the hospital?'

'No, baby, this is something else. It makes him do things we might not understand.'

'Is that why he acts so weird sometimes?'

'Probably. I'm not exactly sure myself.' Gayle explained what had happened as best she could, including the fact they would probably have to move.

'Daddy ran away and left us? With nothing?' Vanessa looked distraught. 'Then he doesn't love us, so I don't love him anymore either.'

'"Nessa, don't talk like that! Your father loves you.' *And I love him 'til it makes me sick of myself.* Gayle didn't want to admit it, but Ramsey still made her dizzy, and whatever he had done, she wanted to know he was safe. They would work it out.

'What are we gonna do now?' Vanessa asked.

Gayle surprised herself. 'First, I'm going to get a job.'

'But you never worked before.'

'I was assistant manager of a store before you were born, young lady.'

'A store?' Vanessa scrunched up her face. 'You mean like at the mall?'

'Yes.'

'Will we really be okay, Mommy?' Vanessa looked up at Gayle.

'Of course. It won't be easy, but we'll be fine.'

Vanessa snuggled down in the pillows and was asleep in minutes. Gayle listened to Vanessa's deep, even breaths and prayed for strength. Ramsey had been their champion. 'Don't Worry, Be Happy.' That was the deal. He kept them worry-free, and she kept him happy. Now he was gone, all she could see were worries, and Vanessa was her responsibility. Alone. She ran her thumb over Vanessa's eyebrows, then covered her with an afghan.

Downstairs Gayle found her mother in the living room reading her *Daily Word*. 'I heard you two, but I thought I'd best leave you to yourselves.'

'I told her, Momma. The truth. It was hard.' Gayle perched on the ottoman at Loretta's feet and put her head in her mother's lap. ''Nessa took it better than I thought.'

Loretta shut her magazine and took off her reading glasses. 'It wasn't so bad 'cause Vanessa already knew, deep inside. Just like I know Ramsey took my money.'

Gayle's head jerked up. 'Momma . . . I . . . He'll . . .'

'You don't have to say it, Gayle. I know. Have for a while now.'

'Oh, Momma, I'm so sorry.'

'Don't be sorry for what you didn't do. I knew you couldn't talk about it, and you are more important to me than money. We'll get by.'

Gayle spoke, her voice muffled by the soft cotton fabric of her mother's housedress. 'Momma . . . when Daddy told me how you got me . . . that my own mother threw me out with the garbage . . . I felt like I must have done something to deserve it. I don't want Vanessa believing that whatever is going on with Ramsey is somehow her fault . . .'

'Look at me.' Loretta lifted Gayle's chin. 'Then you have to make sure she won't. Tell her what she can understand. I expect we're in for some rough times. Vanessa has no idea what sacrifice is. Neither do you for that matter. I'm out of practice, but I haven't completely forgotten. You're gonna need all the help you can get, so don't leave her out.'

'He's not coming back, is he, Momma?'

For Loretta, Gayle was seven years old again, asking if there was really a Santa Claus. No matter how she put it, this truth would hurt. She kissed the center of Gayle's forehead. 'I don't know, baby. Probably not. Looks like his habits got the best of him.'

'You knew? About his gambling . . . you knew that, too?'

'Not at first. Joseph suspected something . . . wasn't sure what. He'd worry himself sick when you went out with Ramsey. I argued with him, said Ramsey was a fine man, mature, responsible. Much better for you than Marcus. He wasn't never more than a step ahead or behind his brother's ghost. I didn't want you mixed up in that craziness.'

'I don't know what I'll do if Ramsey somehow spread that story about Marcus.'

'Ain't nothin' you can do, but learn from your mistakes and do better next time.' Loretta tucked a stray hair behind Gayle's ear. 'I was already living with you by the time I figured out Ramsey had habits, but he took care of you real good, like you always wanted, and Vanessa was growing up so nice, wasn't nothin' to say.'

'I wish I'd known, Momma.'

'You did, Gayle. You didn't want to, but you did. So you squinted until the things you didn't want to see were kinda fuzzy and out of focus. It ain't nothin' new with men and women. We all do it. Anyway, much as I hate to admit it, you're a grown woman. What was going on between you and your husband was your business.'

'Momma . . .' Gayle rested her head on her mother's knees again. 'This is gonna sound stupid, but do you think I'm being punished for what happened to Freddy? Marcus, too. Maybe Pat, for all I know. If we'd all gone home like we were supposed to . . . you know it was my fault. I didn't have to use the bathroom. I didn't . . .'

'It was an accident, Gayle. If anybody was to blame, it was Freddy. He was old enough to know better, so don't let this mess make you start lookin' for extra stuff to blame yourself for. That's a waste of time and energy, and you can't spare neither one.'

Right after rush hour the next morning Gayle drove to the cemetery. She had missed her regular visit with her father while Ramsey was in the hospital, and now more than ever she needed to talk with him and figure out how she was going to make it through.

On the long ride from home Gayle remembered her father's words, his laugh, his big, bony hands, and how she used to think he could lick anybody in the world. As she exited the highway, she wondered what he'd look like now, if . . .

'Haven't seen you in a while.' The florist, a round woman who wore sleeveless shirts year-round, added ferns to the flowers Gayle picked out.

'My time hasn't been my own.' *That's an understatement.*

Gayle bumped over the railroad tracks. She followed the

road into the cemetery, past Serenity Circle, and parked near the evergreen trees that camouflaged the cemetery fence. She got out and surveyed the oddly tranquil panorama of monuments and the skeletons of Japanese maples and elms that would fill in the landscape with reds and greens come spring. Her daddy used to joke, 'They can bury me at the back of the cemetery, but I'ma have the best view.' Tiptoeing across the grass, careful not to step on anybody's grave, she stopped at the bronze plaque that read 'SAUNDERS,' in simple, honest letters.

'Hey, Daddy.' Gayle kissed her fingers and traced them across the smaller letters that spelled out 'Joseph Lemuel.' 'I guess you thought I wasn't coming, but you know I always do.' She lifted the vase hidden in the plaque, always averting her eyes from the empty space that was meant for her mother's name, then walked to the spigot for water.

When she returned she knelt and tore open the paper around the gold and burnt-orange mums. 'There's no point hemming and hawing. You were right about Ramsey.' She arranged the stems one at a time. 'I still don't want to believe he took off like that. Yeah, I know, everybody's not you. You rescued me last time I was abandoned, but some people got cold hearts and ice in their veins . . . I just want to know for sure, so I can stop loving him.'

Gayle fit the vase into the holder. 'I'll get us through this, Daddy. I promise.' With each word she felt stronger, like she always did when she felt her dad with her. 'I made this bed, and I'll figure out a way to sleep in it.' She stood and dusted her knees. 'I'm takin' care of Momma for you, too . . . Daddy, I never thought Ramsey would take money from her.' Her voice cracked, and she looked off in the distance until she could calm herself. Gayle didn't like to cry on these visits. 'Momma's doin' pretty good. Still forgetful, but she remembers things that happened a long time ago, and she tells 'Nessa all about you. I wish you could see how much 'Nessa has grown.' The forlorn hoot of a diesel train seemed to offer a reply. 'I know you're with me all the time, Dad, and I'm glad. I couldn't do this without you . . .'

Thanksgiving dinner was a deliberate break with tradition. The day was rainy and cold, and Vanessa thought they should stay in their pajamas, so they did. Gayle decreed that not one football game would be seen all day. Loretta suggested lasagna, a meal they rarely ate because Ramsey despised it. They ate on snack trays in the den, muddling through anxious moments with tinny laughter, exaggerated politeness, and mock celebration.

Gayle knew this was the last Thanksgiving in her dream house. She wanted to hate Ramsey as much as she hated herself for letting this happen. *Be careful what you ask for* . . . Wherever they were this time next year, she was certain her life had changed forever.

Gayle applied for Christmas jobs, but the response to her eleven-year-old retail experience was a yawn. Even the cash registers were different now. As a last resort she went to one of the anchor stores where she never shopped because she thought the merchandise was tacky. They hired her to work gift wrap, nights and weekends, $4.50 an hour.

Gayle left home in designer dresses which disappeared under a red smock once she clocked in. She would switch from her Italian pumps to the flats stashed in her locker so she could stay on her feet for six hours. When gift wrap wasn't busy, she boxed packages for delivery. Scissors, ribbon, twine, and industrial-sized rolls of paper pricked,

370

nicked, sliced, and gouged her hands. It hurt her to cut her fingernails short, but they broke and got in the way, and soon she stopped even using polish because it was always chipped.

Loretta did laundry and kept the house clean. She offered to take on a couple of days' work a week 'till things pick up,' but Gayle wouldn't have it.

Gayle did her best to tread water, writing checks for the lights, heat, and telephone. One afternoon, desperate for more money, she went through her wardrobe and carted suitcases full of her most expensive clothes to a consignment shop in Greenwich. And she prayed. For Vanessa and her mother to stay well. For strength. For Ramsey to be dead. To find a better job. For a dress to be sold so she could buy Christmas presents. For Ramsey to come back, make it okay again. To win the lottery. For her car to last the winter.

She kept Vanessa's life on an even keel as much as possible, and one of the bright spots of the season came when Gayle and Loretta, swelling with pride, watched Vanessa dance the Snowflake Queen at the annual Christmas recital. Afterward, over celebratory sundaes, Gayle tried to explain to her daughter how different holiday gift giving would be this year. 'It's because of Daddy, isn't it? I hope he never comes back!'

Gayle's efforts to stay afloat were like spit in the ocean. Her bank account sank steadily, with no signs of stopping until it hit bottom, but the week before Christmas she worked sixty-two hours, twenty-two at time and a half. She had already been told she wouldn't be kept on after the holidays, but she justified going over budget on her Christmas shopping by using her store discount to buy a cozy robe for her mother, and Vanessa's first pair of black leather knee boots. The blue turtleneck, covered with big snowflakes, was an afterthought, but Gayle felt it was too perfect to leave.

Gayle was on her way to work when the mail carrier rang her bell on Christmas Eve. She got the usual gut knot and opened the door expecting to sign for another fat envelope with some attorney as the return address. Instead it was a package, wrapped in creased brown paper. She recognized Ramsey's bold script immediately and had barely closed the door before she ripped the paper. *I wish 'Nessa and Momma were home! I knew he wouldn't let Christmas come without a word!*

Rubber bands held the cigar box shut. *He doesn't even smoke.* Gayle's hands trembled so much she put the box on the foyer table to open it. Wads of newspaper padded the top. She smoothed a piece. The *Gloucester Daily Times? Massachusetts?* It was dated December 20. Underneath lay two smudged Greener Pastures envelopes. She tore open the lumpy one and Ramsey's diamond horseshoe fell into her palm. 'Oh my God!' She closed her hand around it. *He never goes anywhere without this.* Gayle leaned against the door for support, but her legs wouldn't hold her, and she slid to a seat on the floor. She could tell there was a letter in the other envelope. *Oh please . . . let it say . . . What? What do I want it to say?*

Gayle felt the fingers at her throat again. She closed her eyes for a second, then ripped it open. The pressure of Ramsey's words indented the lined, tablet paper.

> *Dearest Nightingale,*
> *You'll never know how sorry I am. About everything. But I am. And I can't fix it. I knew that when the money hit my hand after I sold your engagement ring. I walked out of the store, knowing I couldn't get no lower. Didn't want to. Breaking in my own house, stealing*

from my family. Dogs don't do that. I know my ring won't make up for what I took, but it's all I got left, and it won't be no good to me. You were my last luck. I knew it when I first saw you that day, by the side of the road. I looked into your big sparkly eyes. I don't deserve that no more, but they'll be the last things I remember, you can bet on that. The hole got too deep, Gayle, and I can't blame nobody. I dug it myself. I wanted you to know I didn't mean to hurt you, for it to get this bad. I don't know what to say to Vanessa. If she hates me, let her, I earned it. Same goes for your momma. I left my car on a pier in Gloucester, Mass. It's where I stopped driving. By the time you get this, the police should have found it, if it ain't been stolen. Maybe you can sell it for a few dollars. The current here is powerful and that should save you the expense and embarrassment of having to bury me. I am sorry,

> *Ramsey*

Gayle crumpled the note and flung it across the room. That Ramsey had run away, that he had been killed by the same people he owed money, these were thoughts Gayle had a million times. That he would kill himself never entered her mind. *How dare you! Screw up all our lives, not even have the decency to face me! You planned this to arrive right before Christmas. I know you did. So we can think about you every year. I won't have it!*

She sped to police headquarters, looking for Detective Stuckey. Before Gayle found her, Monica's father, the chief of police, recognized her and led her into his office. Gayle showed him the ring and the letter.

'I'll contact the Gloucester Police . . .'

'Whatever you do, I don't want to know about it until December 26.'

'Mrs Hilliard, we might need you to ID . . .'

'If Ramsey is dead, he'll still be dead the day after Christmas. I won't allow this to become Vanessa's holiday nightmare.'

'And if he's not dead?'

'Oh, after this he is to me, whatever happens . . . And, Mr Phillips, I'd appreciate it if you don't talk about this at home. Kids can be cruel, and your Monica's got a big mouth. She's prodded Vanessa into one fight already.'

That night Gayle continued with Christmas Eve as normally as she could. After everyone was asleep, she placed her beautifully wrapped packages under the three-foot artificial tree she had used last year to decorate her booth at the Christmas Bazaar. She looked at her gifts, things that were once run-of-the-mill purchases, taken-for-granted necessities in another life, and angry tears welled up, but she blinked them back, turned out the lights, and went to bed.

In the morning after they opened presents, Gayle made the grits, bacon, and eggs, and Vanessa helped her grandmother make her special buttermilk doughnuts.

'Lord knows I can't remember the last time I made such a pig of myself.' Loretta rubbed her stomach and leaned back in her chair. 'We should see if we can get your momma to eat a bit more. She's looking mighty peaked these days.'

'Trying to keep my girlish figure, Momma.' Gayle got through the day with a pasted-on smile to mask her shifting emotions. By noon the next day Detective Stuckey called. Massachusetts State Police had impounded Ramsey's car. There was no sign of a struggle, and they hadn't recovered a body yet, but for Gayle it was enough. She knew there was no point in pretending Ramsey was coming home. He had bailed out. She had to accept it.

Loretta dabbed at her eyes when Gayle told her. 'Poor troubled soul. I hope he found him some peace.'

Vanessa cried so hard her whole body quivered, and she spoke in anguished bursts. 'I didn't mean I hated him. Maybe he'll come home.'

'No, honey. Your father had a lot of problems, but he loved you very much.' Gayle wasn't sure that was true, but only Vanessa mattered to her now. When she got Vanessa calmed down, Gayle rummaged through her jewelry box and found the gold star, Ramsey's first gift to her. She hung it around her daughter's neck. 'Your father gave this to me a long time ago, but you were his star, too. You have to keep shining for him.'

In three days Ramsey's body still hadn't washed ashore. Stuckey informed her there wasn't much else police could do. The case would remain open, but not active. 'I'll call if anything develops. If you relocate, keep in touch. Sometimes, a year, two years down the road . . . the ocean is funny like that. I'm real sorry about the way this turned out. If there's ever anything I can do, call me.'

Father Pinckney offered to hold a memorial service at the church for Ramsey, but Gayle didn't want to do it.

'Momma, why? There's no point. Nobody will come anyway.'

'You have to let him go. Say good-bye. Close the door and get on with your life.'

Reluctantly, Gayle agreed, then she phoned the bank vice president who signed most of the threatening letters Ramsey received about the house. On New Year's Eve morning she met with the man, who was much younger than she expected. He had coffee brought in, tisk-tisked sympathetically and spoke to Gayle gently, which eased her obvious nervousness, but bottom line she had until the end of February to vacate or risk further legal action. He made the devastating news sound painless, like filling a tooth that had been aching a long time, and when she shook his hand she was still numb, but relieved. She'd start the year with a big, new broom since she had lots of sweeping to do.

And that evening, right before watch night service, the rector officiated a private memorial for Ramsey in a chapel off the nave. Gayle, Vanessa, and Loretta sat in the front row, with Mrs Banks right behind them. Bessie and two men Gayle didn't know came in as the service started and sat in the second to last pew, and Detective Stuckey stood in back, under an arch, next to a short man who held his black Kangol cap solemnly over his heart. He reminded Gayle of a round, pink bullfrog. Vanessa cried like her heart would break. Gayle, arm around her daughter's trembling shoulders, mopped her tears. Gayle didn't cry. In twenty brief minutes it was over.

Mrs Banks left, shaking her head in resigned disbelief. Detective Stuckey pulled Gayle aside and said, 'Austin is outside. Do you want me to walk you to your car?'

'No. He won't bother us.'

The bullfrog and the other strangers were gone. Gayle, Vanessa, and Loretta left by the side entrance to avoid the holiday churchgoers. Bessie waited by his burgundy Rolls, the beaver collar of his overcoat turned up against the wind.

'It's tragic. The man had so much going for him, and to have it end like this . . . seems like some people try to outrun their troubles, but sooner or later it wears 'em down and catches 'em in the end.'

Gayle remembered the first time she saw Bessie, big and bald, decked in a white dinner jacket, tending the door of his restaurant. She was so impressed. Now she wasn't sure if he was friend or enemy, so she nodded mutely.

'You need anything, anything at all, you come to Bessie,

you hear? I'll always be looking out for you.' Bessie kissed her cheek, and his wiry handlebar grazed her face.

It gave Gayle chills.

On day two of the new year she picked a lawyer from the phone book and for a twenty-five-dollar consultation fee found out that for much less money than she expected, she could be divorced in a year, or for no money at all she could wait several and have Ramsey declared dead. She plunked down $200 to get the ball rolling on the divorce.

Driving home, she looked at her hand on the steering wheel. *I sure don't need this ring anymore.* It was such a thrill the day Ramsey bought the diamond and emerald band, the day they were married. Now, she saw it as groceries and the gas bill. At home she gathered her diamond tennis bracelet and a few other pieces. She was going to leave Ramsey's horseshoe. *What for?* She added it to the pile.

For all the fanfare that accompanied the arrival of each velvet box, the sale was cut-and-dried and she received much less money than she expected. She only got $100 for Ramsey's horseshoe. *And he acted like it was such a big deal.* Gold necklaces, bracelets, and earrings were dumped on a scale and weighed like potatoes. All totaled she walked away with $1,100. *I wonder what he got for my engagement ring?*

Next, Gayle resumed the job search, but by February she was still unemployed. On Lincoln's Birthday she interviewed as a receptionist for two young lawyers, recent Wall Street defectors who were setting up a practice. She was braced for the usual brush-off, but they asked her to wait outside, then brought her back and offered her the job. It paid $5.50 an hour to greet clients, make coffee, and answer the phones. She would have six paid holidays, a week's vacation after one year. Health insurance kicked in after she'd been with them six months. They said they liked Gayle because she was more mature than the other applicants. She thought they were kidding. Most of the time, even now, Gayle felt like she was playacting at being a grown-up, but she agreed to start the next day and immediately switched to the real-estate ads to hunt for an apartment. At the end of her second week on the job she found a tiny two-bedroom above a locksmith shop in White Plains.

'This is my room?' Vanessa said when Gayle showed her the alcove off the dining room that would be her bedroom. 'I hate it!' Vanessa stomped down the stairs.

Gayle followed. 'We'll fix it up nice, 'Nessa. Things won't be so bad. You'll see.'

'Can we go home now?' Vanessa leaned against the car.

'Yes. But next week, *this* will be home.'

The movers showed up four hours late with the van already loaded with someone else's stuff. Most of the furniture had gone in the tag sale and it didn't take them long to jam what was left into the truck. Loretta chattered to fill in the awkward silent moments, Vanessa cried, and Gayle wanted to, but as she drove down the hill, away from her dream house for the last time, she didn't look back. What was the point? The dream had died.

They settled into their new neighborhood and the new routine. Gayle arranged for Vanessa to finish the year at her old school even though it meant a forty-minute drive in the morning before work and an after-school program until Gayle picked her up at six. Now Gayle clipped coupons, planned car trips to save gas, and patrolled the apartment turning off lights, but on Saturday mornings Vanessa still had dance class, and after Gayle dropped her off, she went to the coin laundry. And at night, she still dreamed of Ramsey.

Gayle was tired all the time, but somehow each week

they made it through and she felt proud of herself. Then she would look at Vanessa, moody and withdrawn, head bent over her geography book, or catch her mother's lips moving silently as she prayed to Jesus to help see them through, and Gayle would curse Ramsey. Not that she didn't spend an equal number of nights on a pillow soaked with the leftover tears of her solitary pity party. She didn't understand how she could miss Ramsey and hate him at the same time, but both emotions lived side by side, so close she could barely tell them apart.

In April the muffler on Gayle's car dropped off. In early May Vanessa caught a cold that wouldn't go away. Hacking cough, strep throat, ear infection. Doctor bills, tests, prescriptions, and lost pay took a chunk out of what was left of the emergency fund. Again, Loretta volunteered to take on a few days' work, but Gayle had watched her mother get slower, more absent-minded, and saw that her going back to work was out of the question. Instead, Gayle looked for a second job.

Part-time evenings would interfere with getting Vanessa from school. Nights would leave her no time to sleep before going to her full-time job. That left weekends. One of her coworkers from the wrap desk called to tell her they were hiring chambermaids at the new conference center hotel. 'Flexible hours . . . good tips . . .'

Maid? Do I look like I'd be interested in a job like that? Does she think I'm . . . What, Gayle? Somebody who needs work?

Gayle turned into the beautifully landscaped drive that led to Westcenter and remembered how excited Ramsey was when his bid was accepted. This job would turn the tide. She knew that every time she drove past the carefully placed shrubs and flower beds, missing Ramsey would get harder and despising him would come a little easier.

20

'Cat got your tongue?'

If I review one more set of budget figures, I'll die. Pat massaged her neck and reread the thank-you note she'd gotten from Darlene. Pat hadn't found real butterflies, and not exactly ballerinas, but she did take the little girl to a matinee of the Alvin Ailey Dance Company.

Darlene was transfixed from the moment they arrived at Town Hall. 'It looks like a castle,' she said. When the curtain opened she all but exploded. 'They Black!' she exclaimed in as quiet a whisper as she could manage. From then on her eyes were glued to the stage. Afterward, over burgers and fries, Darlene read her *Playbill* aloud, and when Pat dropped her off she got a kiss and a bear hug. 'This is the best day of my life!' she gushed.

At lunch Pat stopped at a pharmacy and picked out a basketful of barrettes, headbands, shampoo, conditioner, hairdressing, and a tortoiseshell comb and brush to send her. Pat waited in line and remembered how warm that hug made her feel. *She keeps the program under her pillow, hoping she'll dream about the dancers.* Darlene had been through a lot, but she still had a wide swatch of curiosity and wonder. Pat had a hard time imagining herself ever so open and sweet, but Darlene reminded her she must have been, once.

When she got back to the office she lit a cigarette and went back to number crunching. There was a meeting on the horizon. *More doom, conflict, and circling the wagons.*

They all knew it was coming, but Gravitt and Greene had not been able to bring themselves to seriously discuss what the agency would do, not if, but when their friend of thirty years and the agency's star innovator died. So, when Ian Comstock, the man most responsible for the agency's signature quirky style, finally lost his battle with AIDS, no one was prepared. The Monday after his memorial service the senior executives woke up to the fact there was no one in the wings with the combination of talent, flare, fire, and good advertising instincts to take over. Giles's relentless crusade garnered him the job, but it was apparent he had lots of growing to do and no grace period to do it in.

And CGG was leaking juicy, status accounts. Pat felt it personally when their Detroit automaker left, taking the Adventurer and its four-wheeled siblings to a rival shop. That was front page *AdAge* news, and speculation about CGG as a takeover target started again.

Each morning Pat dragged into the office looking for her crisis-of-the-day memo, but in her position she felt like a bench warmer, on the team, but unable to score. She longed to be in the production mix again, pasting images together and making deadlines by a nose hair. Pat had a tête-à-tête with Zabriski, told him her talent was being wasted.

'Sit tight. You're doing a great job. We won't lose sight of that,' Zabriski said.

Pat yawned, reached for her cigarette. The tip had gone cold and the inch-long ash dripped into the ashtray. She crushed it, traced it around the other discarded butts. *Damn, have I smoked that many already?*

Her long ski weekend in Vermont with Reggie was

supposed to be a pick-me-up, but she came back early and alone because by Sunday he had danced on her last nerve. Saturday had dawned gray and bitter cold, but Pat made a go of it on the slopes. By the end of the day her fingers felt like swollen sausages ready to explode, her cheeks were so icy they burned, and she had no sensation at all below the ankles.

Sunday started the same way, so when Reggie pulled on his silk thermals, Pat opted out in favor of a Jacuzzi and the fireplace. Reggie wouldn't leave it alone. He cajoled her about how invigorated she'd feel and the fun they'd have getting warm again, then he got petty. 'If I knew you were gonna be like this, I'd have come with somebody else.'

'Keep that in mind for future reference.' Pat closed herself in the bathroom and ran a tub to head off the argument and Reggie slammed out of the chalet.

Snow and sleet brought him in before noon, aggravated and determined to pick a fight. He made snide remarks about CGG's slipping position, he noted the weight Pat had put on. 'Unless you're planning to hibernate, you should get rid of it,' he had said, pinching more than an inch. But the very final straw came when he brought up Marcus.

Pat had left *Newsweek* turned to an article about the pleasures and dangers of riding a motorcycle. Marcus was pictured, and a section of the piece described his injuries and rehab. Reggie picked up the magazine and went off. 'Damn overpaid jock better hope they can piece him together. What's he got, a high-school diploma? At least he can read fan mail and sign checks. Without brawn, he's selling sneakers, instead of wearing them for a living . . .'

'And what are stockbrokers but overpaid sales help? Answer me that, Reggie!' Pat was enraged. 'You could be selling sneakers . . . or french fries for that matter! How dare you assume that because Marcus Carter is an athlete, he's some kind of imbecile!' She read Reggie about how pompous and intolerant he was, things she always knew, but ignored. Suddenly, he struck her as mean, shallow, and she couldn't stand him for one more minute.

Pat emptied her ashtray in the trash. The episode with Reggie meant she was without an escort for the reception next week at the Studio Museum. It would honor Turner Hughes for a large donation to the Harlem institution and announce a match-grant fund-raising drive he would underwrite, equaling all contributions to the museum made in February, Black History Month. As soon as she got word of the event, Pat bought tickets, figuring she'd have a shot at avoiding P.J. and talking to Turner in the museum's intimate galleries. She had to make something happen with her father soon, or it never would.

Pat doodled in the margins of a memo. *I could go alone. I don't need moral support from Reggie or any damn body else . . . or I could ask Marcus.*

Marcus had kept in touch since the accident. After he left the hospital he went to North Carolina to check on his parents and ended up staying for a few months. He phoned Pat once a week or so, just to talk. 'They're getting to me. One's near crazy, the other's blind to it. I'm gonna be in the road, howlin' at cars if I don't get outta here soon.' Pat knew he only meant it halfway, but she worried about the other half.

Three days a week Marcus worked with a physical therapist in Raleigh and trained every day on his own, but he was impatient with his progress. 'Feels like they put some rusty screws from a jar in the basement in my knee. My arm is ugly as sin. It's comin' along, but it still doesn't feel like my arm.' He planned to make spring training.

Often Pat teased him. 'You can quit, marry Téa, and become Mr Supermodel.'

'You outta your mind, too? Must be your damn smoke sticks. Don't get me wrong. Téa's good people, but hangin' with her for too long is like tryin' to live on air alone. After a while I need something substantial.'

Pat was happy to have Marcus back in her life . . . *Just like a brother . . . so what's the big deal about asking him to this thing?* She knew he'd be in town, seeing his doctor, and if she was going to ask, it had to be now, so she stubbed out her unlit cigarette, made the call, and felt giddy in a way she chose not to dwell on when Marcus said he'd be happy to go.

'Does this dress look okay? I should have worn the black one. It makes me look slimmer. I should *be* slimmer.' Pat smoothed the tulip skirt of her red crepe wrap dress. The shawl collar curved down to her waist, where it fastened with two rhinestone buttons.

'Whoa! If I didn't say it before, you look beautiful, Miss Reid.' Marcus leaned closer to her ear. 'You have nothing to worry about in the looks department. Not the way I see it.' He took her hand, gave it a squeeze. 'Let's go get cultured.'

Pat followed him into the Studio Museum's main gallery. She'd been one pulsing nerve ending all day, worried that she wouldn't find a way to talk with Turner. After she dressed for the evening she dug out the bergamot tin and put his monogrammed cuff link in her purse for luck. The warmth of Marcus's hand steadied her, but it sent a charge up her arm that was anything but brotherly. *Get a grip!* A swirling, African rhythm supported the murmur of conversations. Pat surveyed the crowd down-stairs quickly. Marcus led her toward the music, but Pat

385

tapped his shoulder. 'Let's take a swing upstairs first.'

'Are you looking for someone in particular?'

'No . . . Yes . . . It's complicated.'

'Old flame, arch enemy, spy . . . Yeah, Special Agent Reid. It suits you. So, are we gonna be drugged and kidnapped until you tell the secrets?'

'Nothing so intriguing, except in a way it is. I'm not making sense. I'll tell you later.'

'I'll hold you to it.' He winked and walked toward the stairs. Several people acknowledged him, shook hands, including the director, who said she was glad to see him on the mend and hoped he was impressed enough with the museum to become a patron. Marcus seemed at ease. He still favored his right leg, but he looked amazing. He was sharp in a collarless shirt and trousers in jet black, topped by a black-and-cream houndstooth jacket, not at all like a man who almost bought it on a back road a few months ago.

They did a spin around the balcony. No P.J. No Turner.

'I warn you, I don't know word one about art,' Marcus said.

But as they examined paintings and sculptures Pat was impressed with his observations, and when they were done with the artwork on the walls, they took a post at the balcony railing and engaged in people watching, where Marcus really excelled. He pointed to a couple standing in front of a massive canvas.

'See, they're not a regular thing. This is a test date, and the brother is not making headway. He's leaning in, trying to rap, but the sister keeps staring at that painting like the secret of life is on it. Now, my man is kinda good-lookin', so she figured tonight had potential, but she won't even look in his direction, which tells me that what's comin' out of his mouth is not what she had in mind. Damn, she just took two steps away from him. Either he's got stinky breath, or the man can't buy a line. I say he's gonna be doin' a lot of talkin' to her answering machine in the future.'

When Marcus stopped speaking, Pat realized she'd been staring at his lips and she hurriedly looked down into the crowd, just in time to catch Turner's entrance. The museum director hugged him warmly and they huddled in conversation, the nucleus of a small circle who followed their conversation like a tennis match, heads swiveling from one to the other.

'Now there's a man who Jesse Jackson did not have to convince he was somebody.' Marcus looked at Pat and saw her eyes riveted on the scene downstairs. 'Yeah, his momma and daddy made sure he knew his shit didn't stink.'

'Marcus, Turner Hughes heads a huge corporation. The Vice President came to his barbecue. I was there.'

'Is that right? Sounds to me like you're convinced his shit don't stink, too.' Marcus straightened up, folded his arms across his chest.

'What's the matter with you? He's one of the most influential men in the country and he happens to be Black. You should appreciate that.'

'Obviously *you* do.'

'As a matter of fact you're right. He's not just rich. He supports lots of causes, like this museum, which is why we're here in case you forgot.'

'Did you write the press release or just memorize it?'

Pat sucked her teeth. 'I don't see you actin' all humble when folks fall all over you.'

'Aw-ite . . .'

Pat and Marcus listened to opening remarks in huffy

387

silence. It caught Marcus by surprise when the director acknowledged him as one of the honored guests for the evening. He snapped on his public face and waved from the balcony amid enthusiastic applause.

When the attention went back to Turner, Pat whispered to Marcus, 'I guess some of us are just more special than others.' He rolled his eyes.

When Turner stepped to the podium, he yanked down his shirt cuffs and Pat saw the gold disks fastened at his wrists. Knowing she had one just like it in her bag gave her a charge. He spoke in a commanding voice, laced with a dignified Virginia accent. Pat ate up every word. *Marcus can sulk if he wants. I don't know what's eating him about Turner Hughes.*

After the speeches people streamed downstairs and Pat caught sight of P.J., mounting the steps against the tide. *Up jump the devil.* He was heading toward Marcus, so Pat took a step to the side, faced the balcony, and dug in her purse so P.J. wouldn't notice her.

'Marcus Carter, I'm P.J. Jackson. I work with Mr Hughes. He's a big fan, and he'd like to meet you.'

Pat didn't breathe, blink, or move a muscle. *If Marcus goes down, then I can, too. Delivered by humble sycophant, P.J. Jackson.* She wasn't sure which made her happier.

'Ah . . . sure. Pat, are you coming?'

She turned around. 'Absolutely.'

P.J. pressed his lips together, swallowed hard, and looked like he had downed a mouthful of razor blades.

When Marcus introduced them, Pat beamed, shook his hand like she'd never laid eyes on him before, and enjoyed watching P.J. squirm.

Turner eagerly admitted them to his circle, seeming happy to be rescued from seriously appropriate gallery chatter. 'Marcus Carter, glad to know you!' He clamped a hand on Marcus's shoulder, and Pat was surprised to see her father's eyes widen with childlike wonder. When Turner greeted Pat, she searched his face for a glimmer of recognition. She remembered every second of their prior meetings, had lived on them for years, but although he was cordial she knew it was the standard acknowledgment and that she'd be forgotten within seconds of leaving him if she didn't do something. She tucked herself slightly behind Marcus and listened, waiting for an opportunity to jump in.

'We're in a museum tonight, but the way this man strokes a ball, that's art, too,' Turner said. 'I played some tennis coming up in Richmond. Thought I was good 'til Arthur Ashe showed me different. Didn't stop me from dreaming about that Wimbledon trophy. But man, you have done it! Reached the highest rung. The World Series. That must make you feel' – he gave a 'you know what I mean' arch to his eyebrows – 'like a *man!*'

Marcus laughed along with the others. 'I'd be lyin' if I said it wasn't sweet.'

Pat would have given her eyeteeth to hear Turner go on like that about her.

'You must let me know how to contact you. It would be my pleasure to have you to dinner. Do you have a card?'

'Ah no, I don't.'

'Here, you can use this.' Pat handed Marcus one of hers and a pen. While Marcus wrote Pat said, 'I bet you were an aggressive serve and volley kind of tennis player, Mr Hughes.' Pat hadn't played in a while, but she could still talk a good game.

'Mr Hughes was my father. Call me Turner.' He gave Pat a more careful appraisal. 'And I've still been known to charge the net, given the right approach shot. I take it you've played some tennis yourself, Patricia.'

She liked the way her name sounded when he said it. 'I know my way around the court. I'm a baseline player. Patient until my opponent slips up. Then I make my move.'

'You shouldn't tell me too much about your game. It gives me a strategic advantage.'

Both Marcus and P.J. looked daggers at her, but she never noticed.

'And that sounds like a challenge to me, Turner.'

Marcus handed Hughes the card and shoved the pen back at Pat.

'Let me know if you'd like to get together over a bucket of balls. My number at the office is on the other side of that card.' *P.J. can keep me from reaching Turner, but he can't stop Turner from picking up the phone.*

'I'll look forward to it.' He tucked the card in his breast pocket.

They left the gallery shortly after talking with Turner. The car was at Ninety-sixth Street before Marcus spoke. 'Why didn't you just open your legs and ask if he wanted a sniff?'

'Pardon me?' Pat was aware of some frost blowing off Marcus, but she was too busy hoping Turner would call to check out the change in the weather.

'You got what you came for. You were plottin' how to get him your phone number from the time you were hangin' off the balcony, tellin' me how important he is. And he'll get off 'cause he got the digits of a big jock's date, right under his damn nose. Guys try that shit all the time, but most women have the decency to do it behind my back. Damn!'

'It's not what you think.'

'Uh-huh.'

Pat hadn't planned to tell anybody. The situation was

dicey enough without involving another person, but she couldn't let Marcus think what he was thinking. 'He's my father.'

'He's your what?!'

Pat showed Marcus the cuff link, told him her story over sherry in her apartment.

'Do you expect him to open his arms wide and say "Come to me, my child"? That shit happens in the movies. He wasn't lookin' at you like one a his damn kids tonight neither.'

'You read too much into things.'

'Give me credit for being a man. He might like it if you call him daddy, but there ain't nothin' fatherly in that man's mind.'

'You don't understand.' She'd kicked off her shoes, pulled her skirt to her ankles, and clutched her knee to her chest. Now that she'd said it aloud she had to make Marcus see. She'd spent years working, sacrificing, for the chance to make Turner proud, and now she was so close. 'I didn't believe Verna either, but I checked it out. You saw the cuff link.'

'So, does he have any other kids?'

'Two. From his first marriage.'

'The one he dismissed you and your mother for.'

'He didn't know me. He left Verna, and I can't blame him. You remember my so-called mother. The Scotch-swilling, bar hag who disowned me. Would you say "I do" to her?'

'Do you know what she was like back then? Before you? Excuse me for being blunt, but he said "I do" to something. And since you been trackin' the man for years, where are these kids? Have you seen them hangin' with dear old dad? Huh? You got him up on some kinda pedestal, Pat, and you need to be sure he belongs there.

391

That's all I'm sayin'.' Marcus scooted over on the couch and drew her close.

Pat sat still, feeling awkward but somehow happy in the strong curve of his arm. 'I don't even know where she is. And right now I just want my father to be proud of me. That's not so strange. You want it, too.'

'That's different.'

'I don't want his money. I don't need him to help me out. I just want him to see that I turned out all right, not like her.'

'I hope it works out the way you want, but you should be proud of yourself no matter what 'cause he didn't make you who you are. You did.'

Finally she leaned aginst his chest and relaxed into the steady beat of his heart. He kneaded her arm. After a few minutes, she looked up to ask if he wanted another drink and she was so close to his lips, the lips she couldn't keep her eyes away from earlier, that she could feel his breath, and she wanted to breathe it in, feel his mouth against hers. Then she shifted her gaze to his eyes and the ripples started, just under her skin. *Just like it felt in the basement. Patricia, you're making a fool of yourself.* But she couldn't deny the feeling. *I have to stop this. Before we . . . I . . .* She had to say something, just to keep her lips moving. 'Thanks for coming with me, even though I made you mad.'

'I'm not mad. Not now anyway. You're too good a person to set yourself up to get hurt. I couldn't stand for that.' His voice was an intimate whisper that pulled her closer.

'I won't get hurt.' Pat moved to kiss his cheek, just as he turned toward her and she caught the corner of his mouth. She knew if she just tilted her head their lips would meet. So close, but then she pulled away . . . *Like my brother . . .*

'Aw-ite.' He cleared the rasp from his voice. 'One day I'ma figure you out, woman.' He kissed her forehead. 'I oughta go. I got another long day with my physical terrorist, ah I mean therapist, tomorrow. I'll check you later.'

Pat watched him walk down the hall, wanting to ask him to stay, feeling she had no right. Marcus startled her when he turned around.

'Go slow with Turner. Just cause he's blue chip, don't mean he's Dudley Do-Right.'

Pat closed the door, touched the corner of her mouth where his lips had been. *Damn. Why didn't I kiss him? We're both grown now, and nobody's in the way.* She paced the apartment, radiating enough static electricity to make her glow in the dark. In a single evening she had one-upped P.J., gotten her business card in her father's hands, and now Marcus had set her panties on fire. She wanted to call downstairs and have the doorman send him back, but she headed for a nightcap and the Shower Massage instead. *Keep your legs crossed. You just haven't had any for a while. Don't risk a friendship.*

'Did I tell you how much that red dress becomes you? My schedule finds me traveling for much of the next month, so our tennis match will have to wait. Care to join me for dinner? My secretary will call.' Turner's name was signed in a hand Pat was certain was too flowery to be his. The card accompanied a graceful array of alabaster orchids in a ruby red porcelain pot. *He remembers me. What I had on, what we talked about.*

Two days later Marcus phoned her at work. 'I got my reprieve from the glue factory. My doctor says I'm clear for spring training.'

'So soon?'

393

'Soon nothing. I been workin' my ass off, and tonight I'm planning to celebrate with a big juicy medium rare side of beef. Care to join me?'

'Where's Téa?'

'Why do you keep asking me about her? I called *you*. You got a problem with that?'

'No problem.'

'Glad to hear it. I'll pick you up. Before I hit your office, I'll stop in and show those clowns who work on the Tastea commercials that I'm still big, Black, and devilishly good-looking, and tell 'em I'm back in a Dodger's uniform so they don't opt out of my contract.'

'How could they resist?' She could hear his grin over the phone, see that dimple light up his cheek. *It makes perfect sense for us to have dinner. He has to stop by the agency anyway.*

When Pat returned to her office from a meeting, Marcus was waiting for her. She closed the door and turned around into his arms and a short, sweet hello kiss on her lips, like it was their usual greeting. For a moment she was stunned. *What the hell is this? I almost got carried away the last time, but he's . . .*

'Cat got your tongue?' He smiled down at her.

'No . . . uh . . .' Pat felt the fringes of her brain start to sizzle. 'Not yet' – she peered up into his face, the heat from his hands warmed her back, and – 'but he could,' slipped out before she could stop herself.

Then they were in it, clinging together like neither of them ever needed anything so much. When their lips parted Pat had tears in the corners of her eyes. She tugged her jacket down, cleared her throat, and sidestepped to her desk, like she walked that way all the time. 'Make yourself at home, Titanium Man.' She removed her purse from the bottom drawer. 'I'm gonna freshen up.' She could be flip with her desk safely between them.

'That happened because I wanted it to.' Marcus looked directly at her. 'And before you reason it to death, that wasn't just something I do 'cause I'm a man and gotta have it. I meant that kiss especially for you.'

'Marcus, I . . .'

'I've had plenty of time since my accident. I spent a lot of it thinking about you.'

'I don't know what I'm supposed to say.' Pat slipped the strap of her handbag over her shoulder. *I can't stay back here forever.* Tentatively she eased from behind her desk.

'Listen, Pat, when I saw you the other night, well, everything kinda crystallized in my mind, about how special you are and that I want to know you, not just as a friend.'

Pat walked toward the door. *Did it show? Was I that obvious?* 'Marcus, I . . .'

'And this time . . . no guilt, no second thoughts.' He stood in her path.

She looked at her shoes, his shoes, his knees, his face. She bit down on the inside of her cheek, hoping the sharp sensation would ground her. It didn't. 'Uh . . . Okay . . . Marcus . . .' *Speak up. You still know how.* ' . . . I . . . I have to . . . I'll be right back . . .' She felt like an idiot, but she couldn't find any other words.

Marcus stepped aside with a gallant sweep of his arm. 'I'll be waiting.'

Pat stumbled to the ladies' room, tried to put on lipstick, but her hands trembled. No kiss had shaken her so since the one they'd shared when they were kids, and she was unprepared for the dangerous depth of it, or to deal with feelings so strong . . . *For Marcus?* She steadied herself against the sink and forced some air in her lungs. Marcus had just thrown her a long ball from left field, and she didn't know whether to catch it or let it drop. She had to slow her pulse and make room for some perspective, so she adjusted panty hose, combed, powdered, blushed, and lipsticked until she was calmer. *I'll ask him about his stop in the art department. That's safe.* Marcus was seated at her desk when she got back.

'How'd it go in Creative?' *That sounds casual.*

'I don't know what happened or what didn't happen. Before, we were all buddies, now I feel like Frosty the Snowman up there, definitely chilly.'

Pat sensed his distress and wanted to reach out to him. *But maybe this is a retreat.* She found herself stranded somewhere between relief and disappointment. 'Might just be busy. It's a deadline a minute up there. Don't take it personal.' *Good, Pat, good.*

'That's the only way I know how to take it.' He got up. 'I know they think I'm history, but when I start blastin' them balls back into orbit we'll see who's washed up.'

'You need fuel for that.' She started to squeeze his arm, but thought better of it. 'Let's go find that cow you were hankering for.'

In the elevator Pat searched her purse for phantom keys, hoping to dodge the question of hand-holding, or the possibility of feeling hurt if he didn't try. Outside he hailed a cab, took her hand as he helped her inside, and their fingers remained entwined all the way to the restaurant. To Pat, it felt too right to be real. *Marcus?*

Marcus was a regular at the steak house, and they fussed over him like the prodigal had come home. Small talk was as foreign as Sanskrit to Pat tonight, and she strained to pay attention while he laid out his spring training itinerary. She made a great show of sliding her Caesar salad around the plate, but her body poised, on the edge of a meltdown, threatened to override her brain.

'I'm flying out tomorrow to let my folks see me before I head for camp. What's the name of that town where you were born?'

'Swan City. Why?' *What is he talking about that for?*

'It was near the ocean, right? It's gotta be close to my parents' place. I was thinking you might like to visit there sometime.'

'I haven't been back since I left.' Pat played at eating her porterhouse.

'Then it's time.'

'I think time has run out. I don't know a soul, and there's nothing I need to see. Why on earth would I want to go to Swan City?'

'Sometime you don't know what you need 'til you're lookin' at it.'

What is that supposed to mean? She turned down dessert and wondered what would happen when Marcus took her home.

But as soon as she unlocked her door there was no need to wonder anymore. They were in each other's arms, pressed in an embrace that felt like home. After several minutes Marcus came up for air. He unbuttoned her coat, removed it, and hung it on the closet door, followed by his own, then he scooped her up and into his arms.

'Stop! You'll hurt yourself!' Pat laughed and pretended to beat on his chest.

'I doubt that. I can press two or three of you. You are only a tiny morsel.'

They laughed as he swooped her into the living room, backing up at her direction so she could turn on a light. He came in for a smooth landing on the couch, where he pulled her on top of him.

'Now, where were we?'

'Here.' Pat nibbled his bottom lip and they were in it

again, full force. *This is crazy*, but stopping was out of the question. He caressed her body through the silk of her dress, and it was like she'd been waiting for his touch.

Pat fingered his chest, hard beneath his cashmere turtleneck, and she wanted skin against her palm. He kissed her slowly, deeply, and she wanted him to swallow her whole.

'Wait.' Spontaneous passion had gone the way of love beads, and she knew they couldn't continue like this. 'I need to get ready.' Pat kissed his fingers and led him to her bedroom, then doubled back to the bathroom.

In minutes, scented with jasmine and ginger and wrapped in a slinky leopard print robe, condom in her pocket, she joined him. Still dressed, Marcus lay across her bed, propped on his side, fingering the delicate petals of an orchid.

'They're from my fath . . . Turner Hughes.'

And Marcus's face turned to stone. 'You still think it don't mean nothin'.' He sat up.

'I'm sure they're like dandelions to him.' She knelt on the bed, awkward and unsure.

'Yeah. He sends them to the ladies he intends to explore at a later date. It's nothing new. I've done it myself.' Pat didn't answer. 'You ought to tell him what's on your mind.'

'I will. When I'm ready.' She didn't want to discuss Turner right now. 'I want him to get to know me . . . as a person.'

'You're settin' yourself up for somethin' freaky.'

'What's that supposed to mean?' she snapped, her clarity returning.

'I don't need X-ray vision to see what's happening here. I've known you since I was eight, and you ain't never been blind or stupid. It's too late to start actin' like that now.'

She stood, arms akimbo. 'And I have gone through the better part of my life minding my business. I don't all of a sudden need you to mind it for me.'

'Do what you wanna do.'

'I intend to.'

They faced off, the fire of desire turned to anger.

'All of a sudden, I'm feeling tired.' Pat turned her back. 'Really *tired*.'

'Funny how that happens.' Marcus slid to the edge of the bed, slipped on his loafers. 'I need to pack, settle a few things before I leave.'

Pat didn't move for fear a disappointed tear might fall from her eye. 'Good night.'

She sat in the middle of her bed and listened for the door to close. *Damn him!* She punched a pillow, then hugged it to her chest. She felt like she'd been tricked into fessing up to feelings she'd been tiptoeing around for years. *I don't have time for this.* So when he called the next day, she spoke in a monotone, said she'd be in touch, wished him luck.

'I know you think you can handle Hughes, but be careful. He's nothin' to play with.'

'Whatever.' Pat hung up, thinking she'd put her feelings very neatly back in their box, but she smoked half a pack of cigarettes before she could speak to another person.

Two weeks later Pat was summoned to dinner at Turner's office, in an elegant art deco high-rise. In her leather folio she carried the AHUP proposal that P.J. had deep-sixed, and she wore a red bouclé suit, since he thought she looked nice in red. Riding up to the forty-fourth floor she realized she hadn't been so nervous in years. Not for job interviews, client presentations, or dates, because tonight she felt there was so much more on the line.

'Mr Hughes is waiting for you.' His secretary was dressed and jeweled more expensively than a lot of executive women Pat knew.

Turner, in shirtsleeves, feet propped on a massive cherry desk, peered through half glasses at a binder of papers. 'The numbers warrant my participation . . .' He spoke into a microphone. '. . . but at this time I can't risk future political fallout or the appearance of impropriety . . . Patricia! Finally.' He tossed the papers and his glasses on the desk and got up to greet her. 'Just in time to rescue me from this tiresome nonsense.' He strode across the wide room and shook both of Pat's hands.

'I have been boring, even to myself.'

'I doubt you're ever boring. It's good to see you, Turner.' The hello sounded more like a come-on than she intended. *Watch it.*

Turner showed her to a sleek sofa at the far end of the room, then opened a door in the wall unit to reveal a bar. 'You look like you can handle a drink. What do you take?'

'Vodka and tonic.' She perched on the edge of the couch, her folio at her feet.

'I took you for a scotch drinker. Vodka's transparent and watery, got no character.'

'I have plenty of character, regardless of what's in my glass.'

'I presumed as much.' He laughed and handed her a frosty, monogrammed glass. 'To women with spirit.'

Pat raised her glass. *I don't want to play this.* 'You know I actually met you twice before the museum. At your lovely summer home . . .'

'And I let you slip away? Damn, I'm getting too old or too busy, probably both.'

'You had a house full of guests, including the Vice President.'

'That's no excuse. I pride myself on being able to walk and chew gum.' Turner dimmed the lights and sat in the leather armchair across from her.

'Well, you did give me your card.' His direct gaze felt hypnotic, so she let her eyes move around the room to avoid it.

'And you didn't call. I'm disappointed in you, Patricia.'

Pat didn't like hearing those words, even if he wasn't serious. 'Actually, I sent you a proposal about A Hand Up. I didn't get a response, so I assumed you weren't interested.'

'Believe me, I'd have answered whether I was interested in your business proposition or not.' Turner adjusted his crease, crossed his legs, took a swallow of his drink. 'I'll have to monitor my mail more carefully.'

'I brought a copy with me . . .'

'Slow down. We have dinner and a whole evening ahead of us. And the nice thing about this joint is it doesn't close until I say so. Now tell me about Patricia Reid.'

Tell him what's on your mind. She could hear Marcus say it. *Not yet.* Pat skated by with her after-college credentials, preferring to save her history for another time. She didn't want to tell the orphan lie, since she planned to set the record straight.

'I hope you're not one of those joyless, ball-breaking career women.' Turner waved his empty glass. 'Refill?'

'I'm still working on this one. And, yes, I've broken a few to get where I am, but they always had it coming.'

'And I bet you're something to see when you're fired up.' Turner tried to lock her in his sights again.

Pat went to the wall unit and examined the photos and mementos displayed there to diffuse the force field.

'Seems I've heard you're from Virginia originally.'

He got up, rattled around in the ice bucket, and poured another drink. 'Son of Richmond. Firstborn of Turner and Rebecca Hughes. Raised by Rebecca and her mother Elsie. Folks called them Battle Ax and Baby Ax, when they weren't around to hear it, 'cause they were two of the evilest women walking the planet.'

'They probably had to be tough to keep you in line.'

'I was a handful. I won't bother to deny it, but they had meanness to spare.' He took a swallow of scotch as if to rinse a bad taste from his mouth. 'Anyway, that's old, BS.' He sat on the couch next to where Pat had been before.

Light tapping at the door was followed by the entrance of a waiter with a rolling cart who went unobtrusively to work laying two place settings on the table near a window that looked south onto the city. Pat and Turner made social chatter until the waiter served the broccoli bisque and disappeared.

'It seems I've heard you have your eye on a cabinet post.' Pat hit pay dirt. Turner discussed his political aspirations through the salad and into the veal chops. 'Money is no longer the challenge. Once I passed a certain point, making more became inevitable. You have to be the unluckiest son of a bitch in the world or just plain stupid to truly lose a fortune. What's more interesting is power, influence, control.' He said it like an incantation.

'The cabinet is an elite club. How do you get appointed?' Pat was truly fascinated. Turner sounded convinced his dream was attainable.

'I'm sure there's a rule book somewhere, but it wasn't written for a mother's son like me in the first damn place. I've got enough education from the appropriate schools to be in the game. I write big checks at campaign fund-raisers so the party boys know I'm serious and so they feel they at least owe me a chance to say my piece, then I tell them what I want in no uncertain terms. I keep my name on as many lips as I can arrange, know twice as much as the next ten people, give away free advice when asked, show I can make things happen, and keep my nose clean. Sooner or later the president or some flunky with his ear will want to show how fair and forward thinking they are by appointing a Black man to a very visible post, and I can't think of one good reason for it not to be me.'

'I'm impressed.'

'I'm impressive, especially when you get to know me.'

Get back on track. 'I imagine A Hand Up earns you a few integrity points.'

'At least lip service, especially since government social programs are going to be as extinct as the dodo bird.'

'That's where my proposal comes in. I want to offer my expertise and some of Comstock Gravitt Greene's resources to produce some public service announcements that should raise awareness of the program and what it offers.'

'Comstock Gravitt Greene . . .' He wiped his mouth, tossed his napkin across his plate. 'I believe an acquaintance of mine worked there. Althea Satterfield. Do you know of . . .'

'She's no longer with the agency.' Pat had wondered when that would come up. *An acquaintance. He's at least diplomatic.*

'Hmmm. So tell me about these ads you have in mind.' He never missed a beat.

Pat launched into the speech she'd been rehearsing for what seemed like forever, careful to keep it breezy. A 'no skin off my nose' proposition.

'Why are you making me this offer? There are lots of foundations that would do handstands for an offer like this.'

'I'm impressed with the AHUP concept and implementation, and there aren't many foundations run and funded by somebody Black. I liked the package.'

'And what is it you want out of this?' He clasped his hands behind his head.

Pat saw the monogrammed disk at his shirt cuff. *Tell him what's on your mind.* 'To spend somebody's surplus funds and do a little good for people who need it.'

'Are you always so noble?'

'No, but now and then it's good for the soul.'

'Amen.' He leaned forward and reached across the table where Pat's hand rested.

She moved it just before he made contact and got up. 'I'll get you my proposal. It's preliminary, so your input will be helpful.' She headed for her folio.

'You should keep still sometimes.'

'I make it a practice never to be a sitting duck.' She handed him the spiral-bound proposal, but remained standing, admiring the skyline.

'Do you move around this much when you're with Marcus Carter?'

'More. Mind if I smoke?' *Did he really want to check me out just because I was with Marcus?* The waiter came in with coffee, and when she looked at Turner Pat saw he had that relaxed after-dinner glow, and she knew she had to make an exit before he got to the brandy. 'Should I phone next week to see where you want to go with this?'

Turner chuckled. 'I need more people like you working for me, Patricia. I'll read it tonight, in bed. Unless you can think of something else I could be doing there.'

'Nothing more beneficial than keeping the Hughes name on people's lips.'

'Well put. If I'm buying what you're selling, I'll pass it on to P.J. Jackson, my assistant. He's my day-to-day liaison with the AHUP board, so why don't you give him a call tomorrow.' He handed her a card. 'My secretary can put you through.'

Damn! All roads to Turner ran through P.J. eventually. 'Sure.' She checked her watch. 'And I should be leaving.'

'You don't give a man much of a chance to get to know you.'

'On the contrary, I hope you get to know me very well.' She knew immediately it didn't sound the way she meant it. *Tell him what's on your mind.*

'Then you'll have to give me time to find out who you really are, when you're not helping your fellowman.' Turner offered to call her a car, but Pat declined. All she wanted was to get outside. He waited with her until the elevator came. Pat extended her hand. 'Thank you for a lovely evening.'

Turner held it so tightly she almost had to pull it away. 'You are certainly challenging, Patricia. I like a challenge. I'll be in touch.'

When the doors closed Pat leaned against the elevator wall. *He likes a challenge?* The joy she expected was floundering in a sea of uneasiness. *What the hell am I gonna do?*

'You won't leave it alone, will you?' P.J.'s call burned through the phone lines the next day.

'I assume you're calling because Turner Hughes likes my proposal, so let's get this straight. I don't give a shit whether this makes you uncomfortable. And I'm no longer interested in telling the world what a lying snake you were to me. You're Edwina's problem, and unless your spots have changed, you're lying to her now, but that's not my headache.' Pat twisted the phone cord around her fist. 'Don't fuck with me on this, P.J., 'cause it's not about

405

you! If you've got problems with the proposal, I'll work on it, but keep your bullshit to yourself.' She heard him panting like he was about to bust a gusset. When he composed himself he told her it was a go. He'd arrange for her to meet with the AHUP board.

Pat hung up and immediately dialed Zabriski. Over the years, she had collected enough IOUs to put the spots together for close to nothing. Just thinking about the project gave her the old, back-in-the-trenches charge. She needed Zabriski's official blessing and clearance to start the ball rolling on getting the airtime to play the finished ads.

It's finally happening. And all she wanted to do was call Marcus and gloat.

21

'You're my father . . .'

'P.J. told me the board's been praising you to high heaven, Patricia.' Turner's voice crackled over his speaker phone, but Pat strained to hear every precious word.

'That makes my day.' She was in a crappy mood, just back from a meeting in the Rubber Room where Gravitt announced that CGG was seriously considering a buyout offer from Trafalgar Trace. Pat had filed out of the room in a stupor. 'Did P.J. tell you I'll have a sample tape for the next board meeting? If you won't be there, I'll messenger a copy . . .'

'That's why I called. I've got business in DC, so I won't be at the meeting, but on Friday I'm attending the Minority Business Conference at Westcenter. I'm staying 'til Saturday for a workshop. Why don't we meet there? My secretary can reserve you a room, and you'll be my guest at the banquet. We'll find some time to look at that tape.'

Something about the offer didn't sit right with Pat. 'I'm in kind of a pressure situation at work. Seems we're a takeover target.'

'Relax. Enjoy it. Hopefully they'll be as gentle as I am . . . when I take over a company.'

'I appreciate the offer, Turner, but I'm sure you'll be too busy . . .'

'The only time I have is the time I make, and I haven't made much for you. I am very hot on this package you put together. Been bragging about it to some very influential people in Congress. I get a kick out of tellin' them how the private sector gets results while they're still waitin' on a fact-finding study to tell them what any idiot knows. Besides, lady, there'll be folks at the banquet you should meet, unless you have all the contacts you need.'

'You can never have too many phone numbers on file.' Pat always said no when that's what she meant, but she couldn't make the rule apply to Turner Hughes. He was offering her entrée, and she was acting like a scared little girl. *Why do I have such trouble reading him? It's all that nonsense Marcus put in my head.* 'Okay, I'll join you, but I'll have my secretary take care of the room. My expense account can use the workout.'

'That's right! I'll wager you negotiated yourself a pretty nice package to go with that new promotion! I'll congratulate you properly when I see you Friday.'

Pat hung up and sat twirling the phone cord around her finger. It had been a very good year. Zabriski moved to Senior VP, head of Operations, and, true to his word, he orchestrated Pat's elevation to VP, head of Broadcasting. She made sure Turner was sent an announcement. The promotion quadrupled her pressure, but she handled the load and enjoyed the perks. She bought her Jaguar and closed on a two-bedroom co-op the same week. She even planned to scout for a place in Oak Bluffs this August. Turner would probably be on island then, too.

Once P.J. realized Pat wouldn't blow his cover with Turner or Edwina, he cooperated on her proposal for AHUP. Turner spent most of his time managing The Hughes Companies' holdings and politicking for a cabinet post, so overseeing A Hand Up was P.J.'s domain. Pat's

ad campaign would mean a higher profile for the organiz-
ation, a definite plus for him as well as for Turner. Within
a short time Pat had the board's approval to move ahead
with the project, and Pat's ascension to VP gave her the
clout to move her pet project smoothly.

So far Pat's contact with Turner had been minimal, and
she had preferred it that way. She worked her show
and called in favors to make sure the final product was
solid, and now the prize was in sight. And she fantasized
about the moment when she would finally share her secret
with her father, maybe over dinner in Oak Bluffs.

Marcus was wrong about him. Pat played with the
buttons on her phone. *He still hasn't called me back?*

Last month when Pat heard Marcus had reinjured his
arm, she was speechless, but she wasn't surprised.
Everybody tried to tell him it was too soon. From all
accounts his baseball career was over. He had worked so
hard, and, in an instant, it was all gone. She found out he
was in town seeing specialists and left a message at his
hotel. She wanted to lend an ear, encourage him to look
for the next door to open, whatever he needed to keep
going. *What would I do if that happened?* Pat shook off the
thought, grabbed the notes for her next meeting, and told
her secretary she wouldn't be in on Friday.

Pat had planned to get up early Friday to pack, but the
intercom woke her predawn.

'You picked a hell of a time to respond to your
messages! It's four o'clock in the morning in case you
hadn't noticed!' Pat stepped aside to let Marcus in. She
smoothed one hand across her just-woke-up wild hair and
pulled her robe to with the other.

'You want a doughnut?' He brushed past her and
trudged toward the kitchen.

'Maybe the sugar will wake me up.' Pat followed him,

flipped the coffee-maker on, and rummaged through the doughnut bag. 'Any buttermilk ones?'

'Who used to make buttermilk doughnuts when we were kids?'

'Aunt Lor . . . Gayle's mother.'

'How come y'all stopped speaking?'

'You *did not* wake me up to discuss me and Gayle!' She bit into a cruller.

'Look, I'll leave, aw-ite. I shouldn't a come in the first damn . . .'

'Relax. Let's take the doughnuts in the living room. The coffee'll be ready in a minute.' *Maybe he shouldn't have come.*

Marcus sat on the sofa. Pat saw him wince as he moved his arm. 'Does it hurt bad?'

'Naw. It's gettin' better every day,' he protested, and tapped the cast. 'I'll beat this.'

'You wanna talk about it?'

'Ain't nothin' to talk about. It was a bullshit AAA game. The pitcher hung one up where I like 'em and I was aiming for left field. Then "Crack!" I felt my arm snap like a dry tree branch. The California docs told me I could forget baseball. I came here to see my own doctors, but they said the same damn thing. Is that what you want to know?' Marcus stared down at the floor. 'I don't even know what the hell I'm doin' here.'

'I don't either, but you could eat doughnuts in your hotel room. If there's something else on your mind, and you came here to talk, then spit it out.' Pat went to get the coffee.

When she returned Pat saw his jaw working, even in the dim light.

'Shit, Pat . . . You don't get it!'

'Get what? You got hurt, but you were hell-bent on

410

coming back for spring, no matter what anybody said to you. And guess what? You're in a damned cast again. Now the doctor can't piece you together enough to play ball. When will you be satisfied? When you're crippled? Marcus, you won the Series with two different teams. Yeah, you could have had an even brighter career if you weren't injured, but if I had wings I could fly.'

'It's not time yet, can't you see that?' Marcus pounded his fist on his knee.

'How much money do you have to make?'

'It's not the money! I'm not done yet. I have to leave my mark so they won't forget.'

'Forget that Freddy should be where you are? You're the one who can't forget that.'

'He was my brother, and he's dead. I ain't ever gonna forget.' He slid back on the sofa, scrubbed his hand over his chin. 'I hired a car this afternoon, went out to St Albans. I ain't been back since Mom and Pop left. The house is painted different, but there were two boys in the driveway, working on their bikes.' His eyes clouded over a second. 'I wasn't sure I could find your old place, but as soon as I turned down the block I knew. It's all boarded up, graffiti everywhere. You know somethin'? I wanted to burn the place down.'

'Sometimes it seems like it was a hundred years ago, and sometimes it feels like . . .'

'Yesterday. I know. You remember the park by Aqueduct? There was a game going on, so I had the driver stop.' He smiled. 'I had some fun there . . . racing to catch fly balls, digging in that old dented cooler coach used to bring. I'd freeze my arm off tryin' to find the last Orange Crush. I'd brag that I was gonna be better than Roberto Clemente.'

'Marcus, that was Freddy, not you. You didn't even like

411

baseball.' He sucked his teeth, looked away from her, somewhere far beyond the room. 'Sometimes I think this baseball thing is more about him than it is about you.'

'Yeah, well, he didn't get his chance to play 'cause he's six feet under.'

'You didn't put him there.'

'Why am I talkin' about this? You don't know shit about it.' Marcus got up to leave.

'I don't? I was there. I saw the whole thing, probably better than you 'cause I wasn't wrestling. Freddy was wrong for hiding that gun in his bag. Period. It could have gone off and shot Gayle, you, me, somebody on the street, your parents . . .'

'He's the only one dead.'

'And I'm sorry, but I don't think it shoulda been somebody else instead, do you?' Marcus didn't answer. She walked over and stood in front of him. He sidestepped her and headed for the door. 'Haven't you once been mad at him for pulling such a stupid stunt? I have. That shot changed all our lives. Forever. Freddy was old enough to know he should have left that gun where he found it and told somebody about it. He was your brother, you loved him, but *he* did it. Not *you*! And it's time you stopped whipping yourself for it.'

'Somebody's gotta carry the weight.'

'Only the person responsible, and *that's not you*! Freddy woulda called you a chump for taking the rap for what he did. Nobody blames Marcus Carter but Marcus Carter. All your pennants and records aren't gonna change that, as much as you want them to.'

Marcus paused, his hand on the doorknob. 'Look, I just figured you'd understand what I'm goin' through. That you'd be pullin' for me . . .'

'I am pulling for you.'

'You got a funny way of showin' it.'

'It may not be what you want to hear, but I say it the way I see it.'

'You're good at giving advice. You should learn to take it.'

'If you're referring to Turner Hughes, I have that under control.'

'You tell him he's your daddy?'

'Not yet, but . . .'

'Then you don't have nothin' under control.' He opened the door. They stood face-to-face for a moment. 'Later.'

Pat fumed at Marcus all the way to Westcenter. She stood impatiently in the hall waiting while the bellman unlocked her room to the executive floor, handed her the coded key card. He flipped on the light, stepped aside, and she saw the roses, scarlet, with blossoms the size of her fist, arranged in a cut crystal vase. She opened the card. 'Cocktails at six-thirty. Looking forward to the evening. I hope you wear something red.'

Pat had planned to wear a red chiffon dress, but she was glad she'd brought the black beaded one, too . . . or maybe the aubergine sheath. Suits, dresses, shoes, duplicates of everything because she couldn't make up her mind. She tossed them on the spare bed, over chair backs. *What's appropriate attire for introducing yourself to your father?* After a shower she was all shaky thumbs with her hair and makeup, like a divorcée on her first blind date.

By six o'clock she was dressed, but the room was a disaster. She phoned Turner's room. He answered on the first ring. She thanked him for the roses and they arranged to meet at six-twenty in the lounge. 'I like to be early, so I can pick my spot,' he said.

Pat saw him as soon as she walked in. He looked at ease in his tux. Scotch in hand, he leaned against the bar laughing at a story being told by a man who resembled a chocolate chip with legs. Pat detected a hint of disappointment when Turner saw her, dressed in black, not red, but he greeted her with a firm handshake and a wide-open warmth. He introduced her, by her name, company, and title, to his companion, Henry Small, president of a hair-care products lab, who shook her fingertips, and checked out the condition of her hair.

Turner led her to the scenic elevator. 'Perfect timing. Henry could bore the paint off a wall, but his company makes good products. He's drowning in piss-poor distribution, though. I'm trying to buy him out and sell to a hair-care company I know is looking for an ethnic line.'

'Remind me not to play poker with you.'

'I'm very unlucky at cards,' he replied.

Only a handful of guests had arrived, and bartenders bustled with last-minute setups. Turner gave the room a 360-degree once-over and selected a spot by a column just opposite the entryway. Then he snagged a waiter, slipped a fifty in his breast pocket, and had a chat about making sure he and Pat had drinks in their hands as needed.

'You leave nothing to chance.' Pat stepped back. He seemed overpowering up close.

'Not if I can stack the deck in my favor. I treat every party like it's mine. I enjoy it better, and I always feel I'm supposed to enjoy it.' He paused a moment. 'I like your perfume. You know, you always remind me of somebody, but I can't sneak up on who it is.'

'Oh . . .'

'So, tell me . . . this agency merger. Are you on solid ground, or the slippery slope?'

Pat explained the CGG–Trafalgar Trace saga, relieved he had changed the subject.

'My advice is don't get caught between somebody's

414

loyalty and a great big check. They'll knock you out of the way before the ink dries, and they won't stop to say excuse me.'

By the time the waiter returned with their drinks, people streamed in at a steady clip and three-quarters of them stopped first at the column where Turner was holding court. Names rolled off his tongue and he had a clap on the back and a glad word for each one.

Turner introduced Pat to publishers, radio network owners, builders, and importers. While Turner entertained, Pat was at the center of another social circle as she discussed common links with her new acquaintances. She was aware that many were curious about this woman with Turner Hughes, but that was her secret. She'd glance at Turner and think how smooth they were together. They could both chat up anybody and not break a sweat. She was impressed with how far his smarts had gotten him and eager to study at his knee.

'You still not ready to let go of my lazy sack a son-in-law yet? I got the perfect job for that P.J. Got a mop and a bucket with his name on it. You just give me the word.' William Lewis's blue ruffled tuxedo shirt matched his wife Indianola's ample caftan. Pat had to hold back a smirk when Edwina's parents stopped by to say their hellos.

'Bill, you too hard on my man P.J. He's doin' a fine job. A Hand Up has grown so fast that I got him keepin' tabs on all that government rigmarole we have to comply with on our job-training contracts. He's in Cleveland tonight, scoping out a site for a new center.'

'Humph. Whatever he's doin', you must be paying him too much.' Even in the climate-controlled hotel, Indianola wore a sheen of sweat, and her abundant breasts undulated with every word. 'Lord ha'mercy, you shoulda seen the bills he and Edwina had the nerve to ask us to pay. But, you keep those big fat paychecks of his comin', you hear?'

Pat thoroughly enjoyed refreshing the Lewis's memory about her days at Southridge with their daughter. She gave Indianola her card. Sent regards to Edwina.

'I wish Edie had spent less time running man-wild and more time with girls like you. Maybe then she could have seen past the smooth talker she married!'

Maybe not. Pat just smiled.

Turner was on the dais. He had arranged for Pat to sit with Henry Small, and during dinner Pat heard more about good hair habits than she ever wanted to know. She talked to the fuel oil distributor sitting next to her, but his wife wasn't crazy about that. Occasionally she'd look at Turner, wanting to be up there, listening to his stories, basking in his attention.

After speeches and coffee Turner came up behind her chair, put his hands on her shoulders, and whispered in her ear, 'Thanks for baby-sitting.'

Turner's hot breath on her ear gave Pat the creeps.

Henry thanked Turner for the loan of his scintillating dinner companion, then gave Pat his card. She 'forgot' to give him one in exchange.

'Business is officially closed for the day. How about a nightcap?' Turner had looped her arm through his, and they strolled to the elevators. That felt like trouble. On a date it's when she would decide if she was sleeping alone or not. But whatever was going on in Turner's head, she knew this was not a date.

'I'm about done in for the night.' They rode to the lobby in a crowded elevator. Pat stared out at the atrium until they reached 'L.'

'A brandy won't kill you. Don't tell me you're gonna let an old man outrun you.'

'No, it's just that we'll have to get up early to view the tape before your seminar. I've had the hotel reserve a VCR for me, and a conference room.' Pat edged over to the elevators that went to the guest floors and pressed the button.

'You're very intense. My eagle eyes tell me you're extremely tense, too.' He let go of her arm, stepped behind her, and massaged her shoulders. 'But now's the time to relax.'

Pat grew more rigid as Turner kneaded. She slipped his grip and faced him. 'I've just had a long day. And after you see this tape, I'll be able to relax. If you like it, that is.'

Doors opened and Pat hurried into the car, pushed for her floor. Turner followed and pushed every number in between.

'You need to let the feel-good catch up with you.' He looked squinty-eyed and rangy, edging toward her, but then two giggling preteen girls dashed in. They looked back and forth at each other for several floors, then one ran off and the other followed.

Just let me get to my floor. 'What time tomorrow? Eight o'clock?'

Turner eclipsed the space in front of her. 'How about whatever time we wake up?' His lips approached hers in slow motion.

This can't happen! Pat did the first thing that came to mind and started to cough, dry and unstoppably, until the tears ran from her eyes. At her floor she stepped off. 'I've gotta quit smoking.' She blocked the door with her hand. 'What time tomorrow?'

'Eight-thirty. My suite. I'll order breakfast.' He looked peeved.

'Good night.' Pat's pulse throbbed in her temples like she'd dodged a bullet aimed between her eyes. She hurried to her room and fumbled clumsily with the key card. Finally inside, she sat on the bed, trembling so violently she needed two hands to light a cigarette.

She'd never thought of Turner Hughes as a man, only as the father who would welcome her if she could prove herself worthy, but he obviously had other ideas.

What am I gonna do? What seemed simple before was now as clear as mud. Being claimed by her father would make up for years of feeling like a miserable mistake. But she hadn't considered her interest could be misconstrued.

Walking away from the situation wasn't an option. She had entangled herself and a lot of colleagues in AHUP, and she felt obligated to finish the project. *I could complete the commercial and disappear. Nobody's gonna come looking.* But she couldn't let him believe Patricia Reid was a flake. That would be devastating. *I have to tell him. Tomorrow.* That way she could stop ducking his advances and begin with him again. This time with no secrets.

The monogrammed cuff link was in her purse. There was nothing to it, but to do it. She showered a long time, deciding whether to bring it up before or after he watched the tape, rehearsing how she would tell Turner Hughes she was his child. *Does the name Verna Reid ring a bell? Did you ever notice my hands are like yours? You know how you said I remind you of somebody? I know who it is. Why did you let your family run us away?*

She phoned the desk for a wake-up and to have the VCR brought to Turner's room, then she lay awake smoking, and waiting, while morning took its sweet time to dawn.

Portfolio under her arm, cuff link in the pocket of her plum suit, Pat trudged down the hall. *Turner, the truth is, you're my father . . . I'm your daughter . . . Daddy?* No matter how she began or ended, it sounded deranged, the kind of outside nightmare you have when you start sipping at happy hour and pour yourself home when the joint closes. The kind of sick dream that makes you swear you'll stop drinking. At eight-thirty-five Pat knocked on Turner's door.

'It's open!'

She turned the knob, with the weight of her whole life dragging behind her, and stepped into a living room furnished in taupes, tans, and creams as tranquil as a sigh. The only splash of color was a massive array of magenta flowers that filled the mouth of the fireplace. The aroma of coffee surrounded her as soon as she stepped in. Reflected in a wall of mirrors, she saw champagne chilling in a silver cooler next to a dining table, set for two.

'I hope you're a big eater.' Dressed in navy silk pajamas, a glass of champagne in hand, Turner relaxed in an overstuffed chair. 'Champagne or coffee, pick your poison.'

'Coffee for me.' She sat her purse and folder by the table and made a beeline for the pot, to keep him in his seat. 'Have they brought up the VCR yet?'

'No. Which means you have to relax with me until they do.' He patted the ottoman in front of him. 'Why don't you bring those shoulders here and let me work on 'em a while.'

'I don't think that's a good idea.' *I'll have to tell him before the tape.* Turner was clearly starting where he left off.

'You think too damn much. Let me ask you this, have I offended you in any way?'

'No. Not at all.'

'Are you married?' Turner put down his glass and got up.

'No.' She had planned to take control, but Turner was leading this tango.

'A lesbian?'

'No.'

'Some kind of religious zealot?' He slithered in her direction.

'No. It's just . . .'

'Then I guess you're just an old-fashioned cock-teaser. I like that in a woman . . . to a point.' He grabbed her hand before she could move it. 'Let me show you the point.'

'*No!*' She yanked her hand away and edged around the table.

'What kinda crazy shit is this! Act like you never been with a man before!'

'*You're my father, Turner!*' The monumental words were out, and she braced for her world to shift on its axis.

He looked at her a moment, expressionless, then sputtered with spiteful laughter. 'I've been told all kinds of wild-ass stories before, but this beats 'em all.'

'I'm not lying! Verna Reid was my mother.' She shoved the cuff link across the table at him. 'Remember this?'

He picked it up, twirled it between his fingers by the stem. 'I've lost more of these than I can count. It means nothing.' He flicked it on the table, and it rolled to the floor.

'You were registering voters in Swan City, North Carolina. You used to drive her home. She followed you to Richmond . . . She said to tell you, I'm the real mustard seed.'

Turner examined Pat slowly, shaking his head. His eyes had a mean glint. 'Son of a bitch.' He shuffled back to his seat, flopped in the chair, and drained his glass of champagne.

'I wasn't going to tell you like this.' She sank into a chair at the table. 'You didn't give me a choice.' Pat recalled the first time she saw Turner, filling the doorway of Hughes

House on the Vineyard. 'I never blamed you for leaving. Verna didn't care about anybody, including herself. She dumped me as soon as she got the chance. When she told me about you, I vowed to make you proud of me. I'm not like her. I made something of my life.'

Turner propped his head in his hand and smirked. 'Snagged by some thirty-year-old snatch. Ain't this some shit?'

'This isn't a plot. I'm not trying to con you.'

'I know you don't expect me to believe you showed up with Father's Day greetings three damn decades late, looking for my love and devotion? So what's this gonna cost me?'

'What?' The words inflamed her, like she had been struck by lightning.

'You must have a ballpark figure in mind. I could deny this, but then you would probably have your lawyer drag my ass into court ordering blood tests and send out press releases about it. I can see it now. "Another prominent Black man sidelined by his roving penis." I won't have this mess all over the damn newspapers. I can't have a scandal, but you knew that. I admit, you're slick. Nobody's ever blindsided me before . . . So, what's the number?'

'I don't want your money!' Turner's offer fanned the blaze, and Pat's reply burned with an outraged fire.

'Save the high-and-mighty speeches. I heard 'em all from my mother and grandmother. Nothing I ever did was right enough, according to them. They taught me the best way to deal with women is to say what you gotta to get what you want and ignore 'em the rest of the time. You could probably follow in their footsteps quite nicely, but you see, I already have a family . . . A son, damn near thirty-five and never had a job in his life. His crowning achievements are a fine tennis game, a fondness for cocaine, and an even greater fondness for my money. He's a high-class junkie who's been in every over-priced drug rehab in the country! And Daddy's Little Girl?' He got up and yanked the bottle of champagne from its cooler. 'I haven't seen her since she turned twenty-one and came into her trust. But she's a selfish, spoiled, gold-card-wielding, spittin' image of my ex-wife.' He downed half a glass of amber bubbles. 'Oh, yes, I have all the kids I plan to acknowledge.'

Pat stood, swathed in the charred remains of her self-esteem. 'I'll finish the commercial because I started it and because it benefits other people.' She dug in her folio and dropped the videotape on the table. 'Watch it or not. I don't care. Any comments, take them to the board.' There was a knock at the door. Pat gathered her things and sauntered toward it. Hand on the door knob, she stopped. 'Verna warned me years ago that you talked with a silver tongue, but it was forked. She was right.' Pat mustered one last, venom-laced look at her father. He gave her a cavalier half salute and refilled his glass.

Pat yanked open the door, startling the bellman, who had the VCR on a rolling cart. It was all she could do to keep her composure until she got back to her room, but it began to slip away when her key card wouldn't open the door.

'Shit! I hate these damned cards!' she muttered as she rattled the door. 'Money! He asked if I wanted money!?' Pat was desperate to be inside, alone with her shame and despair. 'What the hell is wrong with a key?!' She kicked the door, wanted to rip it off the hinges, and was totally unnerved when someone opened from inside.

'What are you doing in here?' Pat shot through the doorway. She saw the gray-and-pink blur from the corner of her eye and realized it was the maid, but she never looked at her. Pat just wanted her gone. 'I'm checking out! Doesn't anybody in this damned hotel know what they're doing?'

Pat froze near the desk. *'I know you don't expect me to believe you showed up with Father's Day greetings three damn decades late, looking for my love and devotion?'* Turner's smug voice reverbed in her head, and suddenly the red roses he sent reignited her anger. She hurled her folio at the vase and sent it crashing to the floor. That's when she heard the gasp and realized the maid was still in the room. 'Would you leave? . . . *Now!'*

I gotta go home. Pat snatched clothes from the floor and the bed and balled them in her suitcase. She pulled the red chiffon dress off the hanger and wanted to bury her face in it and cry, but the maid was still glued to her spot.

'Are you deaf or just plain stupid? I said get the hell out!' To keep herself from sobbing she continued packing until she heard the dull click of the door closing.

'He thinks he can buy whatever he wants, and that includes people.' Althea Satterfield had told her that about Turner years ago. It angered Pat when she'd heard it, but Althea was as right as Verna had been. 'Damn you! *I hate you!'* Pat sobbed, and the tears flowed from the shattered place in her heart she had hoped her father's love would fill.

Pat rode her staff with a crop and short reins the next week. Turner Hughes had blown up in her face, but she still had control of her career, and she needed to stay focused to maneuver through CGG's looming takeover.

Every person who reported to her was called to account for their decisions. A usually reliable assistant producer lost a director's reel and Pat fired him on the spot. She was a bitch on wheels, but she felt it would get her department through the intense scrutiny.

Soon the sight of Gravitt, Greene, and Zabriski, leading the advance team from Trafalgar Trace Worldwide through the agency became a regular occurrence. The enemy wore ventless Italian suits, spoke with overstarched British accents, and the longer they stayed, the more the acquisition looked like a done deal, and the rumors circulating through the halls of CGG were at least as creative as any commercial the shop had ever produced.

Some of the gossip had everyone at CGG fired and replaced by Trafalgar Trace personnel. Others theorized that key staff would have their brains picked, then get pink slips once their usefulness was exhausted. Clients were restless because Trafalgar handled their direct competition. Chaos was always the norm at CGG, but the office seemed to Pat like a throbbing toothache that wouldn't be soothed until the molar was saved or pulled.

After weeks of uncertainty, Zabriski took Pat to a watering hole across town from the office and told her the merger was a go. He swore her to secrecy, then revealed that Greene was taking his megabucks and retiring and CGG would become Trafalgar, Gravitt, Trace, NY. 'Don't sweat. Changes should be minimal. We'll be an autonomous shop with a global support system. It only gets better from here.'

Pat came in early the morning the official announcement was to be made. When Zabriski called and asked her to come up, she figured it was to go over last-minute details.

'From the first time I met you I knew you had what it took to make it, in this business or any other.'

She felt the vibe. *This isn't good.* 'There's a point here. Why don't you get to it?'

'I wanted this to come from me.'

There was a weighty silence, then she realized what was

happening. 'Son of a bitch! You're telling me I'm fired!'

His lips moved, but the words were out of sync, like a badly dubbed foreign film. 'Trafalgar has someone slated for your position.' Zabriski was almost in tears. 'I did everything I could. You'll have time to negotiate a settlement, and I guarantee it will be a hefty package. I'll see to it. I don't know what else to say.'

'So I was promoted to VP what, to keep me quiet? To keep my crew rowing steady until they were ready to toss me overboard?' *I did everything right, by the book.* Pat couldn't feel her feet on the floor as she stood up. *Be dignified.* 'I'll be gone in an hour.'

'Pat, it's not you. This is politics. You've been a . . .'

She slipped her hands into the pockets of her jacket to keep them from shaking. 'A fine, shining, visible example of forward thinking and affirmative action? Come on, Lloyd, *everything* about my being here is politics! Who are we kidding? I've been good for the CGG image.' Pat turned to leave, but she spun around to face him again. 'So, who is it? Who's my replacement?'

He took his glasses off. 'Althea Satterfield. She's already in from LA.'

'I'll be *damned*!'

In the halls, Pat spoke to no one. She wanted to get her things and leave, before the hoopla started. Before Althea came to claim her office and became HNIC.

Pat's secretary sat at her desk, crying. Pat didn't say a word. She couldn't. She walked into her office to find her desk emptied and her belongings in boxes by the door. A guard waited to escort her out of the building. She had sweat blood for this company, and they were treating her like a criminal.

When she got home, Pat dumped ice cubes in a tumbler, filled it with vodka, and started damage control.

Glad she'd made a habit of keeping a copy of her office Rolodex at home, she called everybody, clients, associates at other agencies, directors, to vent her rage.

Pat got up each morning, burning with the desire for revenge. She made lunch dates with executives at rival shops, who treated her to great meals, but told her they had nothing open at her level. She saw headhunters, arranged a flurry of interviews, but then one night she sat alone, in the dark, in front of the television. She couldn't keep her mind on the programs, but she surfed the channels, dissected the commercials. She found each one sillier, more insulting and annoying than the next. *I've been killing myself to do this for ten years and for what?* She couldn't find one reason that made any sense. Not one she cared about, anyway. She'd even had to pull out of the AHUP project because people who had become involved, to stay on her good side, didn't have to anymore.

Suddenly her world had shrunk to a population of one.

22

'. . . ain't no room for you between
the rock and the hard place.'

'This stuff is worse than spaghetti!' Vanessa turned up her
nose at her plate.

'Sit up in that chair and eat your chili,' Gayle snapped.
For ease and economy she had found that Tuesday's meat
loaf with tomato sauce and spices made Wednesday's
spaghetti. Add some kidney beans, and it was chili con
carne over rice on Thursday.

'You eat good every day.' Loretta patted Vanessa's
hand. 'May not be fancy, but it's good, wholesome food!
Your mommy is doin' the best she can.'

Gayle got up and opened the freezer door for some ice,
so Vanessa and her mother wouldn't see her wiping at
tears. She was dog tired and worked every day to bring
order to their new lives, but she couldn't even relieve the
daily unpleasantness. The time when she could repay her
mother, and restore Vanessa's carefree life, was too far off
to see.

With the freezer open, Gayle lingered, relishing the
frosty cloud that billowed into the steamy kitchen. The
August heat was stifling, and even if the air conditioner in
the living room actually worked, Gayle couldn't afford to
run it. The apartment's puny windows, one to a room,
meant there wasn't enough breeze to move the sheers, so

box fans whirred nonstop. Some evenings she'd come home, and her mother and Vanessa looked so wilted that she felt guilty because she worked in an air-conditioned office all day.

Summer vacation was miserable for Vanessa. She was used to a yard, her friends, riding camp, tennis lessons, and her own pool. Now she sulked and watched TV with her grandmother most days. And when Gayle told her daughter she would enter sixth grade at the school down the block, Vanessa didn't speak to her for a week. Loretta had been right. Vanessa had no idea what sacrifice and hardship were, and she wasn't adjusting well.

Gayle shut the freezer and reclaimed her seat at the table. *How can I tell her there'll be no dance class come September?* She'd registered for two business courses, deciding their future was more dependent on her getting a better job than on Vanessa's improving jeté.

'I'm sorry, Mom. The chili's . . . good.' Vanessa looked at Gayle, then back at her grandmother, who nodded her approval.

Mom? When did it stop being Mommy? 'I'm gonna make a ham this weekend, a real Sunday dinner, when I get off work. Potato salad, fresh string beans, now that'll be good.'

'That Pat sure did love herself some ham! You remember how she'd keep whackin' off hunks.' Loretta grinned. 'She'd put it on a hot dog bun! Girl didn't care, long as she had herself some ham.' She fished the lemon wedge out of her glass of iced tea. 'Yesiree, Gayle, it had to be somebody else you saw in that room. Had to be. Y'all had your spats over the years, and Lord knows you haven't seen each other since Hector was a pup, but she'd never not speak to you. She had her ways, always wanting to be important and all, but . . .'

428

'Ma, I told you it was her, and I told you I don't want to talk about it.' It was weeks since Gayle had come home, foaming at the mouth, after her encounter with Pat at Westcenter. Loretta wouldn't believe it was what it seemed, but Gayle didn't care to dwell on the episode. She knew that if she had run into Pat last year, when she was still hot stuff and could brag about Ramsey landscaping the hotel, she wouldn't have hesitated to make herself known. But Gayle's pride didn't let her say hello that day with a scrub brush in her hand. And give Pat the chance to return that slightly superior pity that Gayle used to feel for her friend sometimes? No, that shoe pinched too much for Gayle to wear.

Loretta sprinkled sugar on the lemon, bit down, smacked her lips, and squeezed her eyes tight. 'Ahhhh . . . my dessert.'

'Momma, there's ice cream if you want dessert.' *Every night she sucks on a stupid piece of lemon.* Gayle figured it was her mother saving money. *Makes me feel guilty as sin.*

'If I wanted ice cream, I'd get some, thank you kindly.' Then, Loretta stacked dirty plates, put them on a shelf in the refrigerator, and went into the living room. Without making a crack, Vanessa moved the dishes to the sink and filled the dishpan full of water.

'By the way, I won't be home for dinner tomorrow.' Gayle watched Vanessa's back for some reaction. 'We just got a big client, an international bank, so Jake and Michelle are taking us all out for dinner. Isn't that nice?'

'Jaaake and Miii-chelle.' Vanessa swayed her narrow hips to the mocking singsong. 'Why should I think it's nice? I'm not going anywhere! And when did you start calling them by their first names?' Without turning around, she dragged a dish rag around a plate.

Gayle had never spanked Vanessa, but right now she

wanted to tan those skinny legs. 'Better be careful. You're not as grown as you think you are!' Vanessa washed with no further comment while Gayle made a bologna sandwich to take for lunch.

She had debated whether to go. Gayle hadn't done anything fun since before Ramsey was in the hospital. Danitha Hemphill, a paralegal at the firm who was one semester away from graduating law school at night, had been on Gayle's case about attending. This afternoon Danitha had cornered her in the conference room. 'Girl, you know it's a four-star restaurant!? And it's *free*! How can you say no?' She brushed her braids behind her wide shoulders. 'They'll work it out of our hides once this bank business starts. Best partake while you're offered. Live large. Get a sitter. That's what I'm doin'. Jamal and Whitney will live. So will Miss 'Nessa.'

Danitha was a 'single mother,' too. Gayle still couldn't wrap her lips around the term, but their kids provided a constant source of conversation about life outside the office.

Sitting in the armchair at the head of the mahogany conference table seemed natural for Danitha. The imposing furniture in the dark-paneled room was intended to dwarf mere mortals, but Danitha, big, square, and strong, carried enough confidence not to be fazed in the least. She twirled around, applied her postlunch lipstick in the beveled mirror behind her, and spoke to Gayle's reflection. 'I'm sorry about your husband and all, but they say life is for the livin'. You'd best be about remembering what livin' is like, girlfriend, 'cause it ain't gonna wait on your feeling-sorry-for-yourself, brown behind.'

Gayle caved in.

'I shouldn't be too late.'

'Uh-huh.' Vanessa kept washing.

'I'll leave Gram some money, and you can order a pizza, okay?'

'Yeah. And maybe if I'm a good little girl, you'll bring me a doggy bag!'

'That's enough! You act like I'm going out to punish you! I'm an adult, and I can go out without your say-so, dammit!' Vanessa paused midplate and glanced over her shoulder at Gayle. She had never heard her mother curse before.

Gayle glared back, and Vanessa returned to her task. 'I didn't make this mess, and I don't know what else to do! I can only fix what I can, and occasionally I deserve to have a good time or at least try. I'm sorry you can't go to your old school with your friends. I'm sorry I can't send you to dance class . . .'

'What?' Vanessa spun around to face her mother. 'What do you mean?'

'I didn't want to tell you like this, 'Nessa. But if we're ever going to get out from under this mess, I have to go back to school, and I'm starting next month. Business English and word processing. I'll be able to get a better job, maybe move up as the firm expands. Anyway, even with the job at the hotel, I can't afford to go to school and pay for your dance classes, too. Besides, I wouldn't be able to get you there or back home because . . .'

'Because? Yeah, because what? Because we live far away from all my friends? Because we live in a dump?' Vanessa glared at her mother. Soapsuds dripped down her arms and dissolved in a puddle at her feet. 'Betcha Daddy ran away 'cause you spent so much money, and that's why we're broke now!'

Gayle grabbed Vanessa's shoulders and shook. 'Don't you ever say "betcha" to me again! Do you hear me! That's why we're in this hellhole today. Because of your daddy's bets!' When Gayle let her go, Vanessa ran into the bathroom and slammed the door.

'Come out this minute!' Gayle shouted above the water Vanessa had turned on full force.

'She'll come out when she's ready. You can't make her, no more'n I coulda made you. She's just as pigheaded as you were, you know. Lordy, your temper. You lost it all when you married Ramsey, though. Became just as meek and mild as you please.'

'Momma, I don't want to talk about me, and I sure don't want to talk about Ramsey! *Vanessa Josephine Hilliard! Come out of that bathroom this instant! Do you hear me?*' Gayle rattled the doorknob.

'I'm sure they can hear you across the street. I'm telling you, the more you yell, the longer she'll stay. Maybe I will have me some ice cream. It'll help me stay cool.'

Two hours later Vanessa emerged from the bathroom, showered, her hair a wet, tangled mess. She had polished her nails, and a lot of her fingertips, bright red, a color she was expressly forbidden to wear. Vanessa sauntered to her bed in the alcove and sat on the side, blowing her handiwork dry, daring Gayle to comment.

Gayle didn't look up from the news. After the weather, she roused Vanessa from her bed, marched her back into the bathroom, handed her the polish remover and some tissues, and stood, arms folded across her chest until the red nails were gone. 'I haven't even decided how to punish you yet, but right now I can't stand to look at you, so go to bed.'

'But Mom . . .'

Gayle held up her hand. 'Don't even speak to me.'

The next morning Vanessa feigned sleep when Gayle kissed her good-bye. *She is my child. Just as stubborn as I was.* Loretta shrugged and shooed Gayle out the door.

As usual, Gayle was the first in the office. Six weeks

after she started, they gave her a set of keys and asked her to open each day. That made her feel important.

Today, like every day, she arrived just before eight, adjusted the thermostat, brewed coffee, neatly stacked magazines in the reception area, and cleared papers from the conference room. Then she checked her appointment book against Jake's and Michelle's to make sure that neither had slipped in a surprise meeting or lunch.

At eight on the dot she retrieved messages from the service and turned on the phones for the day. When the secretaries arrived at eight-thirty, the place was rife with the aroma of Jamaican Blue Mountain. At eight-fifty-nine the associate dashed in and disappeared behind stacks of files. Depending on the day, Jake or Michelle were in the office by nine or they had phoned from their first appointment. Danitha and the other paralegal traipsed in and out all day on a perpetual loop of county offices, courthouses, law libraries, and back to . . .

'Cameron and Ware. Good morning!' Gayle answered the phone. She nodded and smiled as Michelle Ware came in the door, then handed the lawyer her messages.

The rest of the day passed routinely. 'Cameron and Ware . . .' – more coffee, a trip to get pastries for the meeting at ten, then greeting more clients. 'Cameron and Ware . . .' – neatening the conference room postmeeting, picking at her bologna sandwich. 'Cameron and Ware . . .' – calling for copier service, requesting a messenger. 'Cameron and Ware . . .'

A little after four Gayle called home. Vanessa answered, but handed the phone to her grandmother as soon as she recognized Gayle's voice.

'She's fine. Been beating me at crazy eights and hearts all day. We're gonna have our pizza and maybe a surprise for later.'

'What kind of surprise?'

'You'll see. If I told you, it wouldn't be a surprise now, would it?'

'Don't do too much, Momma.'

'Stop worryin' about us. You have yourself a ball, baby!'

The restaurant was even better than Danitha's report. Their party was seated at a long table in the garden, surrounded by trellises thick with flowering vines. Eating out was definitely not in the budget, and Gayle had almost forgotten what it was like. She laughed, easy and carefree. She wasn't Ramsey's wife, she wasn't Vanessa's mother, she was Gayle.

After dinner Jake and Michelle gave their pep talk. They were proud of their coup and the staff that helped make it possible. They promised raises, increased benefits, and called for their continued support in the busy months ahead.

'Dinner was outrageous!' Gayle felt giddy as Danitha pulled off. They'd gone in one car because it was more fun, and they were headed back to the office so Gayle could get hers. 'I'm glad you made me go.'

'And a raise is a helluva lot better than my raspberry torte, and it was *good*! Of course they'll figure a way to tie it to our regular raise.'

'Raise? I hadn't even thought about a raise.'

'Haven't you been here about six months?'

'Almost.'

'Then you got one comin'! Make sure you tell them you're goin' back to school. That kinda shit always makes you look good. They might even offer to pay part of your tuition. "Continuing education makes a more valuable employee blah blah . . ." That is, if you promise not to leave them the minute you finish your classes!'

434

It was almost eleven-thirty when Danitha pulled up next to Gayle's car. They hung out in the parking lot a while, replaying the evening with editorial commentary, but Gayle had to be at Westcenter at six in the morning, so they packed it in. 'Call me when you get home,' Danitha said, then waited until Gayle started her car and drove off.

More money! If I keep the job at the hotel, and figure a way for her to get home, 'Nessa can still have her dance lessons. Gayle yawned and pulled out of the lot. *I bet I can ask one of the other mothers to keep her after class until I can pick her up . . .*

When she rounded the corner, heading toward the apartment, the faint, woody scent of distant smoke seeped in through her closed windows. *Wonder what's burning?* More people lingered in the street than she expected so late. *Folks must be out 'cause it's so hot.* The neighborhood wasn't fancy, but it was respectable and quiet. Sort of like St Albans. *What do I know about who's out this time of night?* Gayle giggled. *It's way past my bedtime!*

She turned onto her street and was met by smoke so strong it burned her eyes. Rivers ran at the curbs and Gayle crawled along the water-slick pavement, scanning the people, some in robes and pajamas, clustered under the hazy glow of the streetlamps.

Where's the fire? She spied police cars blocking the far end of the block and realized the hook and ladder was in front of her building. Silent screams rocketed through Gayle's body. She threw the car into park in the middle of the street and shot out, door wide-open, engine running. *Please don't let it be true! It can't be!!!*

She stumbled a few feet, then stopped, paralyzed by the charred, smoldering skeleton, the remnants of home. The windows, dark, hollow sockets, dripped water like tears. Firefighters, shielded in helmets and protective gear, lounged on axes, folded hoses, took notes, like this was all normal, not the surreal nightmare Gayle had entered.

She clutched herself to keep from falling to pieces and hollered, '*Vanessa!!! Momma!!!*' Gayle searched unfamiliar faces, and screamed her heart out for them.

A patrolman grabbed her by the arms. 'You got a little girl?'

Gayle nodded.

'She's at the hospital. Come on, I'll take ya.'

'Is she . . . ?'

'I don't know how she is. They took her about an hour ago.'

'My . . . my mother. Is she with Vanessa? Is she okay?'

'Sorry, ma'am. That's all I know.'

Gayle rocked and prayed in the back of the squad car, hand over her mouth to muffle the sobs. When they arrived, she searched in a frenzy for the handle. *There aren't any.* She had known it since she was eight. Since Freddy.

'Hold on! Hold on!' The officer opened the door and she took off up the ramp and through the swinging emergency entrance doors.

'Where is she?' Wild-eyed, Gayle grabbed a young man wearing blue scrubs and a disposable shower-cap over his curl. 'My little girl . . . from the fire!' Gayle shoved the startled orderly aside and ran to the desk. 'I have to see her! And my mother! Where are they?'

A motley sea of faces, most of them in shades of brown, turned to see the commotion. Weekends, standing room only was SOP in the Hammond Park Community Hospital emergency room. Gunshot wounds competed with colicky babies and food poisoning. Seniors, dizzy from the heat, lay on gurneys next to teenagers in labor. Tall metal fans noisily circulated hot air, rank with the smell of sweat, vomit, and disinfectant.

'What's the name?' A bulky woman in a pale blue smock came up behind Gayle and laid a calming hand on her shoulder.

'Huh?' Gayle whirled around. 'Vanessa, my daughter's name is Vanessa . . . Hilliard. It couldn't have been long. They said she . . .'

'Pretty little thing? Long pigtails, right?' The woman mopped sweat from her forehead with a brown paper towel.

Fear snatched Gayle's tongue, and she nodded mutely.

'They're workin' on her now. She jumped out a window. Good thing, too, or the smoke woulda got her.' She folded the towel and tucked it under her watchband.

'What about my momma? Older lady, little browner than me, kind of reddish hair. She would have been brought in with my daughter.'

'Oh Lord . . .' The aide turned away, couldn't look Gayle in the eye.

'You have to tell me!' Gayle grabbed the woman's sleeve.

'Doctor'll be with you soon, honey. He'll talk to you about it.'

'Momma!' Gayle's knees buckled. The aide caught her around the waist. 'She can't be . . .' Gayle shook her head frantically, like she didn't hear right. 'You're wrong!'

'I'm sorry, honey.' The woman eased Gayle into an empty chair. 'Just wait here.'

'Momma's gone?' The words were nonsense, gobbledygook. She got up and tottered aimlessly, oblivious to wary glances from those who wondered if she was a nutcase. 'Vanessa?' Gayle trembled violently, and her field of vision shrank to a tiny black dot.

She came to, face-to-face with a doctor who assured her

she was fine, but told her she needed to sign a consent form for Vanessa to have surgery.

'Is she burned real bad?'

He straightened up and took a step back. 'No, that's the least of her problems, but when your daughter jumped she fractured her right femur in two places just above the knee, shattered her right elbow, and dislocated several vertebrae in her lower back. We need to relieve the pressure on her spinal cord.'

Gayle sat up. 'Her spinal cord! Oh my God, she's paralyzed?'

'She seems to have movement and feeling in her extremities so we don't think she's paralyzed, but the sooner we go in, the better. Her X-rays also indicate some bone fragments sliced through part of the surrounding muscle tissue in her thigh. Thankfully the laceration missed the femoral artery, but there's bleeding we need to stop as well.' He took the stethoscope from around his neck and put it in his pocket.

Gayle struggled to digest the doctor's words.

'After the fractures are set, she'll be in a body cast. She's so young and her bones are still growing. We can handle that here, but once she's stable we'll move her down to the city for follow-up at a facility with a state-of-the-art orthopedic unit. Right now, I need you to sign here.' He took a clipboard from the top of a supply cabinet.

'I . . .' Gayle's panic threatened to take over again. *They have to help her, but if I tell them I can't pay . . .* She stared at the forms. *If I had started work sooner, I'd be covered.* But no matter how she counted, she hadn't hit six months yet, and she wasn't insured.

'Is there something else I can explain for you, Mrs Hilliard?'

'I'm sorry. Just tell me again.' *I have to understand.*

Gayle made herself focus on every word as he patiently repeated his explanation. She asked lots of questions before she got to the big one. 'Will she be all right?' She took the clipboard in hand.

'We'll know more after surgery, but barring complications, the outlook is good.'

I need to tell him I can't pay. 'Uh . . . I . . . uh . . .'

'Yes?'

Say it! 'I . . . I . . . don't have any insurance . . . or money . . .'

'A lot of our patients don't. We don't turn anybody away here.'

'Thank you.' Gayle signed by the X. 'Can I see her?'

'I'll have an attendant bring a wheelchair.'

'That'll upset her. I'll walk.'

The doctor helped Gayle down the narrow hallway. She was stunned by how different this hospital was from the shining modern facility where Ramsey had been. She caught her reflection in a darkened window, smoothed her hair, and straightened her dress.

'My mother was brought in here, too. Do you know what happened to her?' She knew it wasn't good, but she had to hear it anyway.

The doctor told Gayle the firefighters had gotten Loretta out before flames engulfed the building, but they couldn't resuscitate her. 'From what I understand, smoke inhalation was most likely the cause of death.'

Death? Gayle choked down the urge to vomit. 'Vanessa doesn't know, does she?' *What am I gonna do?* Her brain screamed, but she got hold of herself. *One thing at a time.*

'No. And it might be best left until after surgery.'

I don't know if I can do this . . . without her . . . Momma! Putting one foot in front of the other required monumental effort, but Gayle followed the doctor down a cluttered corridor.

'Right here. She's sedated, so she might be asleep, at the very least groggy.' The doctor parted the curtain around Vanessa's bed so Gayle could slip through. He mouthed, 'Her mother,' and the nurse who was adjusting Vanessa's IV put an arm around Gayle's shoulder and pulled her close to the bed. Gayle stared in horrified disbelief. Vanessa's whole body was immobilized in what looked like a Styrofoam splint. The skin on her face and the backs of her hands was reddened like she'd been playing in the snow too long.

She's so still. More still than sleep or the pretend sleep of this morning's anger. Gayle reached out, but stopped, her hand poised in midair. 'I don't want to hurt her.'

The nurse guided Gayle until her fingertips met Vanessa's. Remnants of red polish still rimmed Vanessa's cuticles. Her eyes fluttered open, and for the briefest moment the flicker of a smile passed her lips, then she was out again.

She was still sleeping when the orderlies took her up for surgery. Gayle followed alongside the procession, hand resting lightly on Vanessa's good leg until they told her she couldn't go any farther. She wanted to beg them not to take her baby, would have given anything to trade places. Gayle kissed Vanessa's closed eyelids, stepped away, and for a horrible moment wondered if she'd see them open again. *I didn't even want to look at her last night.* She stood, riveted to the spot, unable to move for fear she'd dissolve. Eventually the nurse who had been by Vanessa's bedside came over to Gayle, suggested she go to the cafeteria for coffee. It was going to be a long wait.

The room was half-lit and empty except for the cashier. Gayle took a paper cup from the stack near the coffee urn, filled it, dug some change out of her purse.

'Is that all you havin'?' The woman perched on the edge of a stool was seventy if she was a day. Her slender legs were crossed at the knee and a Barbie-like mule dangled from her bobbing foot. 'You look like you could use some food, baby.'

Baby? She sounds just like . . . Oh, Momma! Gayle barely made it to a table before heavy, gasping sobs erupted from deep inside her. She cried and blamed herself until she was limp. Then the heaving stopped, but a desperate aloneness remained. *I'm nobody's baby anymore.* All she had in the world was in an operating room, and she couldn't do anything to help. She had no family to depend on, no friends to lend support. *I promised to call Danitha! Damn you to hell Ramsey Hilliard!* She cursed him all the way to the phone.

Danitha got to the hospital as soon as she could rouse and dress her kids. Gayle protested. It was five o'clock in the morning, but Danitha was having none of it. 'You shouldn't be by yourself.' After a while Gayle appreciated the distraction of Jamal and Whitney, who came with toys to show her and storybooks they needed to be read. Just Danitha's presence was calming, and when the surgeon came in a little after noon and said Vanessa had done well in surgery, Gayle had a shoulder to cry on.

Then Danitha went into action. First, she whipped out a change purse full of quarters and had Gayle call the hotel to explain she wouldn't be in. Next Danitha had her leave a message on Cameron and Ware's service. 'That'll be the last thing on your mind Monday morning, so now it's done.' Then she went with Gayle to see about Loretta.

The process at the morgue was cut-and-dried. Forms to fill out, and they released the envelope with Loretta's belongings. Gayle couldn't think what was inside until she tore it open. 'Daddy gave her that ring, for their thirty-fifth anniversary, just before he . . .' Danitha just held her until Gayle got it together again. There seemed to be reminders of what used to be and wasn't any more around every corner.

Danitha took a notepad out of the enormous red canvas tote she'd brought with her, and started making lists. Gayle racked her brain to come up with the name of the funeral director who had handled her father. She knew for certain her mother's burial policy was paid up because for the past twenty years Loretta bragged about it. 'When my time comes, all you have to do is make sure they play "His Eye Is on the Sparrow." I like that. Oh, and if Pat could be there to sing it . . .' *Pat.* Thoughts of her were woven through all of Gayle's long-ago yesterdays, but there was no time for that now. She called old Reverend Hobson to get things started, not knowing how she was going to finish it.

'You need to see if there's anything you can salvage at your place before other folks help themselves to it. We should go now, while you've got the time. When Vanessa comes out of recovery she'll need you. Where's your car, downstairs in the lot?'

Gayle hadn't thought about the car since she left it in the middle of her street. After they drove around the neighborhood for an hour looking for the car, Danitha made a note to call the police and report it stolen. Gayle searched through her wallet, found Detective Stuckey's card, and gave Danitha the number. 'She helped me before . . . with Ramsey.'

'Your auto insurance will only give you the book value, but it's something.'

'No theft. I had to drop it . . .'

'After Ramsey died? Damn girl! There ain't no room for

442

you between the rock and the hard place.' They cracked up laughing, which eased the tension for a minute, but when they got out in front of her building it came back with a wallop.

The locksmith store was boarded and padlocked. A wet, blackened sofa, chairs, and mattresses littered the sidewalk, and Gayle could taste the dank, charred smell that emanated from them. After a moment she realized the furniture was hers.

'You can't woulda-shoulda-coulda over it, Gayle. Let's see if there's anything you can use, and get going.'

'What's the point?'

'Maybe there isn't one, but we're here, so let's do it.' Danitha used the promise of ice cream to bribe Jamal into waiting in the car and minding Whitney. She and Gayle slid the saw horse from in front of the door and carefully mounted the dark stairs.

Gayle entered the apartment and wanted to walk right out again. Danitha made her stay. Still in pumps from the night before, Gayle tipped over unidentifiable broken objects underfoot. Danitha guided her to dresser drawers, where Gayle found clothes still intact.

'A couple of washings will take care of the smell.' Danitha pulled a green trash bag out of her tote and stuffed the things in it.

The TV, radios, pot handles, were masses of free-form melted plastic. Wires dangled from the kitchen ceiling. The cabinets by the stove had burned to nothing. Broken dishes, utensils, and blackened cans were scattered all over. And on the floor in front of the scorched stove lay her mother's cast-iron Dutch oven, cracked in pieces.

When Gayle checked in her closet, she was glad Danitha made her come. The green metal footlocker was safe. It contained things she had no place for in the small apartment: family records, photos, Vanessa's baby mementos, art supplies, and all of the Ell Crawford storybooks she had made so lovingly. Things she would have been devastated to lose.

They loaded up the car and headed back to the hospital. 'While you're with Vanessa, I can drop this stuff off wherever you're gonna stay.'

That's when it hit Gayle. She had no place to go. 'I don't know. There's not . . . I don't have . . . any . . .'

'Ain't nobody you can call?'

Gayle shook her head and turned away, ashamed that she lacked something so basic as friends and family. *How did this happen?* Gayle stared out the window. *Is this how it was for Pat?* After Freddy, when Pat was adrift in foster care, Gayle could never really imagine what it was like to have no hope and nobody. She was getting the picture now though. *But I made them find her. She wouldn't even speak to me! How could she do that!*

'Listen, Gayle?' Danitha reached across the seat and rested her hand on Gayle's arm. 'Lord knows I ain't got no room. The kids share one as it is, but you're welcome to my couch for as long as you need it.'

'I couldn't. Thank you, but you don't have to do that . . .'

'Do I look like somebody put a gun to my head? I wanna do it, fool!'

Gayle could see the sincerity in Danitha's face. 'Thanks. I'll stay here tonight, to make sure 'Nessa's all right. We'll talk tomorrow. And Danitha, thanks again for everything.' She opened the car door. 'I want to get a few things out of the footlocker 'Nessa might like.'

Gayle removed sketch pads, charcoal, and the Ell Crawford books, then waved as Danitha drove off in search of the promised ice cream, kids squabbling in the backseat.

'Vanessa's doin' fine,' the charge nurse reported when Gayle got up to pediatrics. 'Her medication has kept her pretty out of it since they brought her down, and that's good because she won't be feeling so great for a while.'

Plaster casts encased her torso and leg, another protected her arm. For the next twenty-four hours, Vanessa awoke only in snatches. Glazed and expressionless, she'd search the room until her watery gaze landed on Gayle.

Nearly choking on fear and guilt, Gayle rested her hand on Vanessa's head and whispered, up close to her ear, 'It's gonna be all right, baby . . .' until she would drift off into a sleep, frequently disturbed by whimpers and twitches. During these episodes Gayle would hold her own breath, until Vanessa's relaxed and resumed its regular rhythm. *How? She must have been so afraid! And where was I? Can it ever be all right again?*

'You gotta get a grip. You can't do her any good like this,' Danitha told Gayle when she showed up the next evening. 'You haven't slept in days, and God only knows if you've eaten. You look like shit. If you're scaring me, imagine how 'Nessa feels when she sees you?'

'I didn't think about . . .'

'Well it's time you did.' The faded murals of clowns and balloons on the old, cracked walls of the solarium tried to put a cheery face on the sadness that haunted the floor. 'The funeral is day after tomorrow. That'll be hard enough, but it's gonna get rougher than that.'

'What are you talking about?'

'Have you applied for Medicaid yet?' Gayle looked horrified. 'Don't look at me like that. Who's gonna pay for this expensive little home away from home?' Danitha made a sweeping gesture with her arm. 'Well?'

'I don't know how I'm going to pay, but . . .'

'You should figure it out . . .'

'Fine. I'll take care of it. Okay?' Gayle snapped.

'What are you gonna do when the time comes for her to leave? Where will you *live*? Eventually you have to *go* someplace. When they say Vanessa can go home, where's that gonna be? What are you planning to do for money?'

'I still have a few hundred dollars left.'

'And none comin' in. That'll last about a minute. I can offer you my couch, my floor, whatever, it's yours for as long as you need it. But money's something I don't have to spare. Between the kids and school, my paycheck's not spread thin. It's damn near transparent!'

'Danitha, I never expected you . . . uh . . . anything like that. You've been so helpful as it is. I'll always be grateful.'

'You're welcome, but let's save the "friend appreciation" speech. All I'm sayin' is I been there, where you are now. Which is exactly nowhere.'

'But . . .'

'But nothin'! Listen, Gayle, when I say I know, believe me, I know.' She paused, absently fingering the leaves of the dusty artificial ficus tree in the corner before continuing, her robust voice quieter than usual. 'If I hadn't grabbed my kids and took off when I did, I'm not sure I'd be here today. I didn't know where I was goin', just that I had to go. I lucked up on a shelter, through one of those toll-free hot lines for abused women. I saw the number on TV at a neighbour's house where I went with the kids the last time he came home crazy and ripped up the house. They helped to get me on assistance and we . . .'

Gayle's mouth fell open. 'Assistance? You mean welfare? Danitha, you're almost finished law school! You were on welfare? I didn't know . . .'

'Well I don't exactly go around braggin' on it. I'm not tryin' to be the welfare poster girl. "From Medicaid to

Legal Aid. What a credit to her people!" Gayle I hated what I had to do, but I had some bad things happen. Things I never planned.'

'But I could never . . . A shelter . . .'

'Don't say it, girl. Never is a long, long time.' Danitha shook her head. 'Look, I had a college degree, no job, two babies, and a husband who loved crack more than us or himself. How do you think I felt?'

'I'm sorry.'

'Sorry, yeah. Sorry ain't shit. I needed some help, just for a little while, until I could get myself together. So will you.'

'It's just that I'm not like . . .'

'Like what? Needy? You got a better idea? Maybe your long-lost rich Aunt Penelope who'll have open arms and lots of space in her mansion for you and 'Nessa? If not, you better get real.'

'I'll think about it.'

'You do that, hear? Call me when you want some sleep.' Danitha got up. 'Oh yeah, the cops haven't found your car. They said they're still lookin', but I wouldn't hold my breath.' She disappeared down the hall.

Gayle went back to Vanessa's room and read her the story about how Ell's magic shoes spirit away a lovelorn Ethiopian princess, forbidden to marry her handsome, but common warrior. The tale, Vanessa's favorite, held her interest almost until the end, but the sandman came before the lovers were wed.

Tears streamed quietly down Gayle's cheeks. All she could think about was Vanessa, snuggled up on her lap, wide-eyed and innocent as she listened to this story the first time in the comfort of her brand-new bedroom. *What have I done to her life?*

Gayle wiped her eyes, then put the book away. Through

447

the open door, she watched for a while, fascinated by the quiet, but constant and well-orchestrated activity around the floor desk across the hall. She took a pad from the shopping bag next to the chair and started to sketch the nurses' station. Drawing used to relax her, but tonight the sleep that had eluded her since the fire seemed to slip even farther from her reach. She was still wide-awake when she finished the drawing. *Maybe I'll give it to them, as a thank you when we leave*. But Ramsey's ridicule of her 'mammy-made junk' flashed through her mind, and she snatched the page from the sketchbook and tossed it in the trash.

For the rest of the night she was dogged by truth Danitha had dropped on her. Gayle had $265.12 left in the bank, no income, no home, and she knew they wouldn't hold either of her jobs forever. *But public assistance?* Loretta's 'You have to be strong, teach her how to be strong,' richocheted through Gayle's mind. She knew her mother meant those words to carry them through the Ramsey ordeal, but Gayle hadn't expected them to be so prophetic.

Next morning, feeling like two cents worth of dirt, Gayle was waiting in front of the office when the hospital social worker came in. It was time to face the inevitable.

As Gayle outlined the last year of her life, the young woman drank coffee, changed from sneakers to her office pumps, and made little tart faces each time she ate one of the grapes from a plastic bag on her desk.

This was the first time Gayle had told the whole riches to rags story. It seemed preposterous, even to her, and she'd lived through it all.

'Do you have any resources available to you?' The social worker was unmoved by the sob story. 'Family? A church? Friends? Anyone who might offer you a place to stay when the time comes?'

Gayle shook her head. 'Nobody.' She knew Mt Moriah or St Phillips, her own church, might have helped, but she was too ashamed to turn to the people she looked down her nose at and too embarrassed to call on those she used to count herself among. 'That's why I'm here.'

'Well, you'll have to start from the beginning.' From dog-eared file folders, she dealt Gayle a stack of Xeroxed sheets, outlining the how-tos of applying for public assistance, Medicaid, and housing.

'We have no place to live. I can't be on a waiting list, not with my daughter.'

'You have to apply for benefits first, then take it from there.'

'My daughter won't be able to walk. We have to have someplace to go the moment she's discharged.'

'And I can't snap my fingers and find an apartment. Do you have any idea how many people have needed a place to live longer than you? You have to wait like everybody else.'

The scolding made Gayle furious, but the anger fueled her through the long hot lines in crowded state offices, the forms with spaces for an address she didn't have, and probing questions asked by workers too busy to be patient. At the end of the day she wasn't sure what she'd accomplished, but it was a start.

Burying her mother was the next hurdle, and Gayle knew she couldn't allow herself to feel the pain, afraid it might take her to a place so desolate and lonely that she would never find the way back, so she shut off that passageway, sealed it tight. *Vanessa needs me. I'll do whatever I have to.*

In the midst of a few mourners who had known her parents and remembered her when she was little, Gayle felt like an observer and not a participant. Sitting in front of the closed bronze casket, she could easily have believed that she had hallucinated the last decade. It didn't happen. Gone. Wiped out, and she could retreat to that narrow slice of time and space between Sunday mornings in Harlem and a tiny, brick-front house in St Albans where she and Pat made plans for being grown. She longed for Pat to help her make sense of this now. *I wasn't around for Daddy's funeral and Pat helped Momma through it. I wasn't around when Pat needed me. It's my own fault she didn't speak. I deserved that.* Vanessa was the best thing to come out of the last ten years. Gayle realized that she couldn't undo her past mistakes, but, whatever it took, she had to be there for her daughter now.

Riding to the cemetery next to Danitha felt strange to Gayle. She was used to driving there alone. When she stood on the hill next to Reverend Hobson, leaves rustled in the dry, hot breeze. *Now these trees will be her view, too.* She watched the undertaker sprinkle a shovelful of earth on the end of the coffin, but Gayle didn't feel the grief or own the sorrow. She couldn't. After Ramsey was gone, love and hate, truth and denial had dueled every day in a battle for her head and heart. She was worn-out, numb to all but nagging guilt because she hadn't been with her daughter or her mother when they needed her most.

After the graveside service Gayle asked for some time alone. She looked off into the brilliant blue afternoon sky, hoping to find the right words written across the horizon, but nothing appeared. She stepped closer and whispered, 'I'm sorry. I never meant for things to go so wrong . . . I love you, Momma. Daddy'll tell you . . . I'm just so sorry . . . for everything.'

Before he drove off, Reverend Hobson beckoned Gayle to his car. She rested her hand on the door, and he covered it with his as he spoke. 'Don't you hesitate to call on us for anything you need. Those are not just puffed-up words, neither. Mt Moriah was your momma and daddy's church home from way before you was born. Now I know you miss 'em, and they can't walk beside you right now, but we're still here for you.'

Gayle nodded, chewing her lip to hold the tears she'd dammed up all day.

When she got back from the cemetery Gayle stopped by the nurses' station and was surprised to see her drawing, rescued from the trash and neatly tacked to a corkboard behind the counter.

'She's been watching the door all afternoon. I think she's waiting for you,' the nurse reported. 'By the way, your drawing is really good.'

'Oh . . . thanks.' Gayle's cheeks burned with embarrassment but she smiled, then headed for Vanessa's door.

'Mommy?' Vanessa's voice was hoarse and barely a whisper.

'I'm here, baby. I'm here.' It was the first time she had uttered more than a whimper since the fire, so to Gayle it was sweet and warm as a baby's kiss. 'They told you I wouldn't be gone long, didn't they? Just had some things I had to do . . .'

'Mommy . . .' Gayle leaned closer so she could hear better. 'The fire . . . I fell asleep . . . It was my fault . . . Gram was makin' me doughnuts. I know she wasn't supposed to . . . but . . . I . . .' Her lashes glistened, shiny with tears.

'No, no, 'Nessa. Hush. It doesn't matter now. You just have to get well.' *Momma's buttermilk doughnuts . . .*

'I was mad at you . . . and . . . I . . .'

'It wasn't your fault.' *Blame me because you're in here and your Gram's gone.*

'Gram? Where's Gram?' Vanessa's face, so full of

defiance a few days ago, now looked sad and pained. 'She didn't . . . get out . . . did she, Mommy? She's . . .'

From somewhere inside the motherplace, Gayle found a quiet reassuring voice. In hushed comforting tones it carried a scalding, painful message, but like cool running water, it helped to soothe the wound as well.

Two long weeks after the fire, Gayle and Vanessa left Hammond Park for the Yorkville Bone Treatment Center in Manhattan.

Gayle never took Danitha up on her offer of a place to sleep. By the time she felt Vanessa was doing well enough to leave overnight, the round-trip train fare from Manhattan to White Plains was more than she could afford. So a new hospital lounge became home, a new ladies' room, Gayle's bath and laundry. The clothes she salvaged fit in two plastic shopping bags, but she only looked forward, because no matter how many times she went over it, the past wouldn't change.

The first week at Yorkville, endless conversations with doctors, physical therapists, and nurses left her exhausted, her head a jumble of medical jargon, confusion, worry. Vanessa would need therapy and a specialized home exercise regimen to ensure she regained her mobility and strength.

Then the job fallout hit. The hotel was first. 'Don't bother to call in anymore.' That was it. A few days later, she got the bad news from Jake Ware. 'We tried, Gayle. We can't hold your position open any longer. It's chaos in here, and with the bank business starting to come in, we can't have chaos. I'm deeply sorry about your mother and your daughter. If you need anything . . .' *My job. I need my job. At least Jake treated me like I'm human.*

After that her days started with bus trips uptown to the

child welfare and the Medicaid office to move her case along. The Housing Authority put her on waiting lists they said could take years.

'I don't have years!' Gayle announced, but it didn't matter. She was so disheartened she just started walking. It was a golden fall afternoon and schoolchildren, frisky after a day of learning in the confines of a classroom, scampered home. Home was such a simple, basic need, like air, and she was starting to suffocate without one. Gayle walked past busy storefronts and rundown buildings, and before she realized where she was, she was standing across from Mt Moriah.

'. . . your momma and daddy can't walk beside you right now, but we're still here for you.' It was like Reverend Hobson's words had brought her there. She had thought she couldn't ask for help, but she had asked everywhere else and no one had any to spare. Vanessa was close to discharge, but Gayle was no closer to an apartment. She remembered how they had helped retrieve Pat from the endless loop of foster homes. Her momma told her they went to Reverend Hobson when Gayle was a baby and he got them baptismal papers and a birth certificate that said she was theirs. *I got nothing to lose by asking.*

Gayle put her false pride in her hip pocket and walked inside. The church secretary directed her to a cluttered office upstairs, presided over by a young woman with dreadlocks down to her waist. Beryl Rawlins heated two mugs of water in the small microwave that served as a bookend and made them tea, then listened to Gayle's saga.

'I put in housing applications everywhere, but nobody is telling me when or where they'll have a place for us. I can't bring Vanessa home to a shelter.'

Beryl thought for a while, bouncing a tea bag in another cup of water. Then she searched through papers in her file cabinet and emerged with a pamphlet. 'This place is pretty new. I haven't sent anyone there yet, but it sounds as if it might work for you.'

Gayle held her breath and prayed as Beryl picked up the phone.

23

'Truthfully, you make hell look good!'

Pat heard the click and whir, watched the message indicator on the answering machine light up. Then she burrowed deeper into the sofa cushions and returned to Sidney Poitier and Tony Curtis on *The Four O'Clock Movie*.

During her first weeks at home she had looked forward to gossipy updates from former colleagues, especially Chris, who was never short of dish. But one day, as she hung on his every word, she felt pitiful and pitiable, the girl parked across the street from her ex's house, watching from the shadows, remembering how it used to be and wondering what's going on inside now.

She raked cold lo mein into her mouth with chopsticks and wiped her chin with her hand. When she realized no one was calling about a job, there was no point answering, so she let the machine earn its keep. Every few days, she held her breath and checked the tape, just in case, but it had been three months, and not a nibble. She washed down noodles with a swig of wine.

Where the hell is she? Marcus hung up. It had taken him a while to work up the appetite for crow, but he'd finally gotten the gumption to tell Pat she was right. Now he couldn't find her. After their last fight he had consulted fifty-'leven doctors, determined to find one to rebuild his arm, but in the end, they all concurred: Give it up.

For weeks, Marcus jetted between New York, LA, and Miami. He partied, acted a fool, and avoided the big, hairy truth: He would never play pro ball again. Period. The end. He insisted to Booker T. it wasn't over yet. Booker tried every way he knew to tell his son all he wanted was for him to be happy, but Marcus was too busy dodging himself to listen.

During an ESPN interview Marcus was asked what he would miss most about baseball. He couldn't answer. He'd arranged his life around the demands of the sport, spring training to fall classic, with the winter reserved for healing wounds. And then it hit him, like a fastball between the eyes. *He never loved the game in the first place.* He put aside his own dreams too long ago to remember them, hoping to shoulder the load of the burden that seemed too much for his parents. But after all his work and sacrifice Freddy was still dead, and, for the first time, Marcus faced his own anger that Freddy had checked out and left him to pick up the pieces.

That's when Marcus started putting his life in order. *His* life, not Freddy's. Baseball had been good to him, but he was ready to move beyond the playing field, so when Rich offered him a piece of the business, Marcus jumped at the deal. Gallagher Professional Management officially became Gallagher & Carter Professional Management on November 15. He'd just moved into his new apartment and already he felt more at home than in either of the sprawling, leased-with-everything houses in Baltimore or LA.

Marcus checked his address book, dialed again, and went out onto the balcony. He didn't like to call Pat at

456

work since he had a big scene with the CGG Tastea team after they dropped him as a spokes. But he'd left messages on her home machine, and she hadn't called him.

'Ms Reid is no longer with CGG. Can someone else help you?'

'No.' *Leave it to Pat. Probably used her promotion to get a better deal somewhere else. Leverage, that's what she'd call it. Maybe she took time off before her next gig.* He watched a runner jog along the Battery Park promenade despite the rainy wind blowing off the Hudson. But he couldn't imagine her not checking for messages. *Is she igging me on purpose?*

A tour boat, lights twinkling around its wide girth, glided downriver. As a kid he'd always wanted to ride the Circle Line. He'd liked boats even then, but Freddy told him only White people hung out on boats. *I bought one anyway.* He still hadn't taken the trip around Manhattan although in three days he was flying to Curaçao to sail *Brother's Keeper* back to Boca for the winter. In Florida he would check out two football prospects, then home for two days, and it was on the road again. Thanksgiving weekend in Michigan, Iowa, and Nebraska, then he'd continue west, meeting coaches and looking at players for two weeks.

Marcus wanted to get the 'I told you so's over with and he was excited about the partnership with Rich and there was nobody he'd rather tell about it. *I'll swing by Pat's before I meet Rich at the Garden. I'll leave a message with her doorman if she's not home.*

The slight man in the gold-trimmed maroon jacket reminded Marcus of a toy soldier. 'Miss Reid said no one is to be sent up.' He spoke with a lisp. 'Hey, wait . . . you're . . . him!'

'In the flesh.' Marcus flashed the 'You can trust me' look.

'You're a friend of Miss Reid?'

'A very old friend. Has she been back long?'

'She hasn't been nowhere to be back from.' He lowered his voice and continued on the QT. 'If it wasn't for deliveries, we woulda thought she was sick or somethin'.'

Weeks indoors? That's not like Pat. Marcus fished a hundred from his pocket, let the doorman see it, then closed his hand around it. 'You ring her. I'll do the talkin'.'

The doorman peeked at Marcus's hand. 'I have to get the dog in 3B.'

'Congratulations.' Marcus held out his hand, the doorman shook it, copped the cash, and went inside, leaving the house phone in the vestibule unattended.

'Yes? What is it?' Pat sounded annoyed when she answered the intercom.

'It's me, Marcus.' Heavy silence. 'Pat? What's up? I been calling you.'

'Listen, Marcus. I don't feel so hot. Another time.'

'Look, I'm not leavin' until you let me up or call the cops. The choice is yours.'

That's when the doorman returned, Pomeranian in tow. 'Can I help you, sir?' he asked as if he'd never seen Marcus before.

'I'm here to see Ms Reid.' Marcus still held the phone.

Pat's voice was muffled as it came over the open line. 'It's okay. Let him up.'

The door was ajar, and cigarette smoke met Marcus as soon as he stepped inside. The apartment was dark except for an erratic flicker of white light. From restless nights in hotel rooms, coming down off nine innings of adrenaline, Marcus knew it was the TV. 'Pat?'

'In here.'

458

He found Pat in the living room, curled into a corner of the sofa.

'Are you sick?' Marcus came around in front of her. *She looks whupped.*

'I guess you could say that. You name it, I'm sick of it.'

'What the hell is wrong with you?' He could see the coffee table littered with takeout menus, empty soda cans, balled-up paper bags, and an overflowing ashtray. The fermented grape scent mixed with stale smoke smelled like a dive bar at closing time.

'I only let you come up so you would leave. I don't intend to play twenty questions. You've seen me. And you know where the door is.' Pat took a sip from her glass.

'Whooaa!' Marcus stepped over a pizza box and took up a position between Pat and the silent television. 'I'm not going anywhere until you tell me something, 'cause this is not standard procedure.' He shoved his hands in his trouser pockets and waited.

Pat aimed the remote control around him and changed channels. She looked up at him like she wished the remote had a button to get rid of him, too.

Marcus didn't budge.

'They fired me.' She looked away. 'Are you happy now?!'

'What do you mean they fired you? I thought you got a promotion!'

'Nice touch, huh?'

'That's some funky stuff.' He sat on the other end of the sofa and hunched forward.

'Life's full of funky stuff you can't do nothin' about.' Pat clicked the remote again.

'I used to think so, but a friend of mine helped me get my head straight.' He reached up and switched on the lamp next to him.

They both squinted in the light. Pat wore gray sweats

and one sock. Her hair looked like free-form steel wool, and the hollows beneath her eyes were deep and dark.

'I'm sure I look like hell, but since I didn't invite you . . .'

'Truthfully, you make hell look good! When was the last time you were out?'

She looked at the soundless set. 'Who cares? I don't have any pressing appointments.'

'A job isn't your life, Pat.'

'It was.' She lit a cigarette and tossed the match at the overflowing ashtray. It landed on the table. Marcus shook his head and put it in the ashtray. 'No antismoking sermon, okay?' She took a long drag. 'I had a neat, prosperous, corporate life. I socialized around it, my so-called friends came from it. Everything I've done for the last ten years was for my career.' *And my father.* But she wasn't ready to talk about that. 'And you know what? It all turned to slime.'

'Okay. Do you want to tell me what happened?'

'Nothing new. I should've seen it coming, but I was blinded by the bullshit.'

'You gonna tell me or keep beatin' yourself up?'

She exhaled a slow stream of smoke and recited the gory details.

'They can't fire you without cause.' He rested his arm on the back of the couch.

Pat smirked. 'They can do any damn thing they want, but technically, I wasn't fired. That was my choice of words. Officially, CGG is now a division of Trafalgar Trace, Worldwide, and I became redundant. I got a lovely golden handshake . . .'

'A what?' Marcus asked.

'My severance package. Oh, they compensated me well after playing me for a fool. I'm not the only casualty. Lloyd Zabriski, the man who hired and fired me, got canned, too.'

'You're good at what you do. You'll find another job.'

'Yeah, I thought so, too. I called the people who said "If you leave CGG, come see us." What I heard was "I'd love to make you an offer, but we're holding the line, especially on Exec Row. Keep in touch." The usual bullshit. I dish it myself. Excuse me, I *used* to.'

'I'm sure you haven't even scratched the surface.'

'I'm not sure I want to. I don't know what the hell I want, which is the first time that's happened since I was a kid and decided I was gonna prove I'm not like Verna.'

'You could start by proving you're among the living. A shower is a good first step.'

'Right.' Pat hunkered deeper into her corner.

'Follow your own advice, hard as that may be. It's your life, get on with it.'

She glowered at him. 'Smart-ass!'

'You had a helluva lot to say to me a few months ago, and you were right. That's why I came by. So you could gloat! I left you messages . . .'

'I know. I didn't feel like talking.'

'Now I *know* you need to get out of here. You always have somethin' to say.'

'Obviously I shoulda been mindin' my business instead of tendin' to yours.'

'Didn't you hear me? I said you were *right!* About baseball, Freddy, absolutely on the money. I needed to make a choice based on what *I* wanted for once. And I did.'

'Congratulations!' Pat snapped. 'Now will you leave me alone?'

'Not a chance. I gotta get you outta here. I know you're dying to hear what I've been doin'. Don't try to deny it.' Marcus grinned and eased back in the sofa, hands behind his head. 'I can see you're burning with curiosity.' That actually got a smile out of her.

'You got tattooed and joined a motorcycle gang? No! No! I got it. You've become a fashion designer and married Téa?!'

'If you don't get your butt off this couch and get ready to go out, I'll throw you in the shower myself. You got 'til ten. One . . . two . . . three . . . four . . .'

'I'm not going anywhere.'

He walked to her end of the sofa. 'Five . . . six . . . seven . . . eight . . .'

Pat crossed her arms and legs, ready for the sit-in.

'Nine . . . ten . . . Okay. Have it your way.'

She knew he'd pick her up if she didn't move. 'Fine! Okay! Okay! Give me twenty minutes.' Pat laughed out loud for the first time in weeks and headed for the bathroom.

Marcus left a 'something's come up' message for Rich, and, twenty minutes later, Pat, hair brushed into a smooth cap, emerged wearing black stirrup pants, a matching tunic, and no makeup. She tugged her black trench coat from a hanger, but Marcus reached past her.

'You're not goin' to a funeral. Wear this one.' He grabbed the red coat next to it.

The rain had stopped, but a damp chill lingered. They strolled down First Avenue, and Pat looked up as the tram crossed the East River. 'I always wanted to do that.'

'Why didn't you?'

'I don't know. Seemed silly, I guess. I never had a reason to go to Roosevelt Island.'

'Maybe you don't need a reason.' He ushered her west at Sixty-first Street.

The tram waggled over the river like a carnival ride, and after the round-trip Pat's spirits seemed a bit brighter.

'There's something I've always wanted to do, too,' Marcus announced.

'What's stopping you?' Pat asked.

'Not a thing.' They raced crosstown and, at the Forty-third Street pier, caught the last tour boat of the day. They stood on the upper deck and sailed toward the glimmering tip of lower Manhattan. Ignoring the tour guide's banter, Marcus explained how Gallagher & Carter was going to become a major player in the sports management business.

Pat envied his enthusiasm for his recruiting trip and the long-range goals he and Rich had laid out. *It's been years since I felt so fired up.* Each promotion at CGG carried her farther from the action, but she still longed for the thrill of a challenge. The bridges floated by overhead unnoticed, Brooklyn, Manhattan, Williamsburg, Queensboro.

Maybe I needed a change. Other than a pinpoint focus on bitterness, she hadn't allowed another perspective on her situation. *Was I even happy? When was the last time I really enjoyed what I was doing? I wanted to succeed. Make* him *proud, and for what?*

'You know, Pat, last time I saw you, you told me things about myself I didn't much care for. My head's kinda hard, so it took a while to sink in, but . . .'

'Before you go on telling me how I was right and all that, I have to come clean, too.' She looked down into the churning water. 'You told me about my . . . fath . . .' The word caught in her throat like a jagged barb. She swallowed hard and lowered her voice 'til it was barely above a whisper. 'Turner Hughes. You were right.' Pat gripped the rail and tears trickled down her cheeks as she told him most of the blistering details of her last meeting with Turner.

Marcus could hardly keep still as he listened. He wanted to hunt Hughes down and jack him up. He wanted to hold Pat tight and take the pain away. She was the strongest woman he knew, yet he had always felt the need to protect her, to make her feel safe. Like that afternoon in the

Saunders basement. He fought his urges and, instead, draped his arm over her shoulders and gave her a gentle squeeze.

Pat lit a cigarette, and, for once, Marcus didn't object. They drifted down the channel between the Jersey Palisades and the Cloisters and were still standing like that when the fog that had wrapped itself around the city like a stole slipped away, and the glittering midtown skyline sparkled in the distance.

'I'm sorry I was right. I wish it coulda been different. I know how much you wanted to be . . . you know . . . like a family.'

'Verna told me the kind of man he was, but why would I believe her?' she said sadly. 'I guess I got what I deserved. He treated me the same way he treated my mother.'

'Maybe you should tell her that.'

'I never knew what to say to her. I know even less now, but it's a moot point 'cause we lost touch almost fifteen years ago.'

Although he wasn't convinced, Marcus decided to back off the Verna issue. 'You need to get away for a while. It would do you good.'

'I thought about it. But I couldn't even get enough steam to look at the *Times* travel section, and I have the paper delivered.'

'Suppose you didn't have to make any plans?'

'Like one of those horrible club things?'

'Club Marcus. But leave out the "horrible" part. Day after tomorrow I'm flying to Curaçao. You remember, home of your favorite rum punch? I'm sailing my boat back to Boca. I figure the trip should be two, maybe three weeks, give or take. Come with me.'

Pat shook her head. 'It sounds great . . . but . . .' *We've almost ruined this friendship more than once. Two weeks on a*

464

boat? We'd be lucky to be speaking to each other when it's over.

'There's a lot of room, if that's what you're worried about. You'll bunk by yourself. No strings. Just sun, the sea, the salt air.'

'I don't know anything about sailing.'

'It's not a sailboat. You were aboard.'

The only thing Pat remembered was passing out. 'I can't, Marcus. Really. But thanks.'

'Don't think you can stand my company for that long?'

'That's not it. But I have to . . .'

'What? You can job hunt when you get back. I bet you can get on my flight.' Pat shook her head. The boat docked with a gentle thump. 'You worried about money?'

'No! I have money. Why do you all always think it's about money!'

'Who all? I just asked a simple question! Damn!'

'I'm sorry . . . It's what he asked me. Turner. How much money I wanted. It's a bad time for me, Marcus. I'm pretty lousy company right now, in case you haven't noticed. Besides, I have no time to prepare for a trip.'

The anonymous tour guide wished the departing passengers a pleasant good night. Pat and Marcus made their way past the terminal and headed toward Tenth Avenue.

'You have two days. It's not like you need a damn evening gown. This isn't a cruise. Dressing for dinner means putting on shoes. Then again it might not.'

'It sounds very nice, Marcus, but it's not a good idea. I'm expecting some calls and . . .'

'It sounds very nice, Marcus!' He mocked her. 'You have to control everything, don't you? Your way or no way. Right, Pat?' He turned to face her. 'It wouldn't kill you to let someone do something for you, not that you *need* anyone. You never have.'

465

He started walking again.

'That's not true, Marcus, I . . .'

'Suit yourself. We'd probably kill each other.' They walked to the corner in silence.

'We're going in opposite directions, let's take separate cabs.' Pat's tone was efficient, like she was leaving a business meeting. She waved at the stream of traffic headed uptown.

'No problem.' A cab screeched to the curb. Marcus opened the passenger door. 'Take the lady wherever she wants.' He handed the driver a fifty-dollar bill.

Before Pat could protest, Marcus crossed the street. The taxi zigzagged in and out of traffic, and she tried to get him out of her mind. *Why do I always say the wrong thing?* Of all the people she had once cared about, or had ever cared for her, only Marcus remained. But instead of leaving her thoughts, Marcus was joined by Verna, Uncle Joe, Gayle, Aunt Loretta, MaRay, Turner. The uninvited guests piled into the taxi and followed her home.

What if he was gone, too? She fell asleep shivering under the blanket of her past, and, when she woke up, Pat was still cold. She lay in bed staring through the open closet door at the dirty clothes that had long ago spilled out of the hamper. She rehashed her conversation with Marcus, trying to find fault with his observations. But she couldn't.

Angry at herself for wallowing in self-pity and disgusted by the condition of her apartment, Pat called her regular cleaning service. She straightened up enough so the place wouldn't scare them away. The rest of the morning she willed the telephone to ring. She wanted Marcus to call and ask her again. This time she'd say yes. But she knew he wouldn't.

24

'Y – e – s!'

At four-twenty-three on the morning Marcus was leaving, Pat gave in and called. 'I'd like to sail with you . . . if the offer still stands.'

'You like it down to the wire, don't you?' His voice was groggy with sleep.

Marcus's flight was booked, but Pat got a seat on a later one. When she arrived at Neder Cay, Marcus was at the bar with Otto. He waved, and she smiled a bit too brightly.

'Care for a rum punch?' he teased. He was going to treat her like always. He decided it was the best way to get the old Pat back, and he missed his sparring partner.

'Club soda for me.' Pat remembered the effects of Otto's potent libation. Marcus's itinerary called for a predawn departure, and she wasn't starting the trip hungover.

Toward sundown they headed to the slip where *Brother's Keeper* was moored.

'I'll show you below. You can stow your stuff,' Marcus said.

Pat followed him past the wheelhouse. 'So this is the living room and kitchen?'

'Saloon and galley. Yep. Your bunk is down these stairs. I'm at the other end.'

Instead of a narrow cot in a tiny room, like she

467

expected, Pat found a cozy cabin with watercolor sea-scapes on the walls. The double bed had a brass headboard, built-in oak drawers provided plenty of storage, and curtains fluttered at the open portholes.

'You have your own head.' He pointed to another door.

'Always.'

Marcus rolled his eyes. 'The head is the bathroom.'

'Right. Whatever . . . A real bedroom! Pretty spiffy for a boy from Queens!'

'Stateroom. It's not the *QE2*, but it'll be home for a while.'

'Tell me something. Are you gonna correct me the whole trip?'

'I'm betting you'll learn quick to keep me from pointing out your mistakes.'

She knew he was right. 'This is so . . . you know. Luxurious. You've done pretty well for yourself, haven't you?' *Like I thought I was doing.*

Marcus saw her face cloud over. 'Anyway, freshen up, or whatever it is you women do, and come up when you're ready. I'm gonna toss a couple of swordfish steaks on the grill. I gotta go over charts and weather reports, so I need to make it an early night.'

'Aye! Aye! Captain!' Pat saluted, and when he left she unpacked, showered, and found Marcus upstairs, taking fish off the grill.

'You look nice.'

Pat fingered the skirt of her purple gauze dress self-consciously. 'Glad you like it. I bought it in three colors, on the way to the airport. I've eaten myself out of most of my clothes, and this hides a multitude of sins.'

'Give yourself some slack.'

'I did.' She patted her hip. 'Twenty-five pounds worth of slack.'

'I think you look good. Kinda like you used to when we were growing up.'

Pat raised her eyebrow.

'Not that I thought you didn't look nice all corporate and pressed for success. That's just not how I think of you.'

She put her hands on her hips.

'I'm steppin' in it for sure now. Why don't I quit while I'm behind? Thought we'd eat out here.' He had set a small table in a corner of the deck.

'I didn't know you could cook, much less navigate this thing. You *can* find Florida?' *And what am I gonna do in the middle of the sea for three weeks while you're looking for it?*

'Gimme a break! This ain't *Gilligan's Island*!'

In fifteen minutes Pat was sampling her swordfish. 'I'm impressed, Carter.'

'Can I quote you?'

'No. But you can quote me on the view. It's beautiful.' The sinking sun left streaks of rose and plum on a sienna sky that was fast turning indigo. *Maybe this is what I need.*

'Just wait. There's nothing like sunrise and sunset at sea. It makes you remember we're not in charge of as much as we think we are.'

Pat wondered if his comment was aimed at her, but she left it alone. After the meal Marcus leaned into the curve of the banquette and put his feet up. Pat took her cigarettes out of her pocket.

'There are three rules for this trip. You can't smoke those funky things below. You can't talk about the good old days at CGG. And as far as the boat is concerned, I'm the boss. You do what I tell you.'

'Okay. I'll only light up outside.' She put a flame to the tip of her cigarette for emphasis. 'Rule number three I guess I have to go along with, but only about the boat. But

469

two? I'll give it a shot, but I can't make promises.'

In trying to be sociable and obey the CGG gag order, Pat was painfully aware that most of her chitchat over the last ten years had been about her work.

Marcus watched Pat as she spoke. Her hands never stopped moving, brushing her dress, smoothing her hair; they flapped like spastic bird wings as she worked to keep the conversation moving. He wanted to tell her to relax, but he knew that would make it worse. After an hour Marcus announced he had work to do if they were going to leave on time.

Pat helped clear the table and went below, glad for the getaway.

Before dawn, they weighed anchor. Marcus had charted what he called the 'easy does it' route that would take them on a leisurely course around the eastern Caribbean, then north through the Atlantic until they reached Boca Raton.

Pat was green around the gills, so she laid low, but with James Brown to keep him company, Marcus stayed 'on the good foot.' On day two she felt less wobbly. They anchored in Grenada at Prickly Bay, found grub in town, and retired early, bushed from the sea air.

In Martinique they docked at Fort-de-France. Marcus dined on blood sausage and conch fricassee. Pat ate bouillabaisse and sampled the local rhum vieux, hoping it would help her calm down. Here she was, surrounded by the most beautiful scenery imaginable, but instead of enjoying herself, she wondered if she was ruining the trip for Marcus.

But he never complained. Occasionally he could coax a smile with a silly story. He dared her into trying her hand at the helm, and when she seemed interested he explained the how or why of sailing. He was giving her time.

A few hours from St Kitts, the afternoon sun was high,

the water calm, and Marcus was at the wheel. He glanced over his shoulder to where Pat lounged on the deck. A book lay open across her lap, but she stared off in the distance, lost in thought.

For weeks Pat's mind would stall when she least expected it. Turner was the usual culprit. She'd see him sneering as he asked how much it would cost him to make her go away. But this time it was the guard posted in her office and the boxes waiting on her desk when she returned from the meeting with Lloyd. *How'd I miss all the signs? 'So busy lookin', you forgot to see.'* Out of the blue Pat heard Gayle's little-girl voice. *Where'd that come from?*

'Hey, come here!' Marcus called.

'What?' Pat jumped, and her book tumbled to the deck.

'Just come here! Quick!'

She joined him on the bridge. 'What is it?'

'Look . . . there!' He pointed at a silvery iridescence vaulted in front of the boat. 'Flying fish!' Another one arced over the bow and splashed into the sea on the starboard side.

'I always thought they were fake. You know, like mermaids.'

'They'd hate to hear you say that! Look at 'em!' Dozens of the wing-finned creatures took flight, and Pat and Marcus marveled at the brilliantly choreographed ballet.

'How do they do that? Know exactly when to jump so it's perfect?' Pat watched in amazement. She'd spent years trying to perfect her own leap. One that would take her soaring into a dazzling future where things fit together neatly. It didn't work.

'They probably don't plan it at all.' The performance was over, and the sea settled back into its random rhythm. 'I think they just stick together. One goes, they all go.'

Pat went back to her seat and buried her head in her

hands. Marcus debated what to do. After a few seconds he eased up on the throttle, and set *Keeper* on auto pilot.

'Life doesn't always work out how you plan it.' He sat next to her, stared at his shoes a minute. 'That not all bad.' He turned to look at her. 'Sometimes it's even for the best.'

'I don't wanna talk about this, Marcus.'

'Well I think you do. You said it yourself. One of us needs to talk . . . poof, the other appears. Think it's an accident? I don't anymore.'

'You don't understand. You have no idea what it feels like to be unwanted! Everybody *loves* Marcus. You were a cute kid, annoying as hell, but cute. You had *two* parents who loved you *and* each other. Do you know how lucky you were? All right, what happened with Freddy was terrible. But even then, you had all the backup in the world. I was a homely, fat, hand-me-down kid. My mother actually lied to keep from claiming me!' She stood, then sat down again. 'Gayle's folks took me in, but I always knew her mother was against it, and I wanted to leave before I wore out my welcome. My first year on the job I got knocked up, and my so-called boyfriend had married a friend of mine behind my back! The only time I ever asked Gayle for anything, she stood me up. And my father! I did everything I could so he'd be proud of me, and that wasn't good enough! I haven't had a damn thing to count on, but my job, and now that's gone! So don't talk to me about what I need, Marcus! You don't know nothin' about it.'

'Okay. You told me some things I didn't know. Let me tell you what I do know . . .'

'I won't talk about this! I've already said too damn much.' Pat got up.

Marcus grabbed her arm. 'Sit down! I'm not through yet.'

'This is not about the damn boat! I'll do what I please!' She wrenched her arm free.

'You gonna hide in your stateroom until we get to Florida?'

'No. Only until we reach a port where I can get a plane!'

'I'll take you to the airport! But you're gonna listen to me.'

'What choice do I have? I'm a captive audience!' Pat folded her arms across her chest and glared. 'I knew this damn trip was a mistake,' she muttered.

'I'll ignore that.' He stepped closer. 'I know you're hurting. You've been treated bad, and I'd do anything I could to change that, but I can't. Neither can you. It's what you told me! We can't undo what's long over. What happened at CGG is lousy luck. You got the short straw. But, tell me if I'm wrong, that shit happens all the time, and you know it ain't personal. I bet you fired people who were doing a good job, because the almighty bottom line said you had to.' Pat glanced away. 'And Turner Hughes is an ass, plain and simple, I don't care how important he's supposed to be. I read him the first time I laid eyes on his pompous, monogrammed-drawers-wearing behind. But he'll get his. One day he'll regret the way he treated you, but it'll be his loss. Don't you know how wonderful you are?'

'Yeah, Oprah's hosting the special.' *He won't make me cry with this sentimental crap.*

'When we were little, I used to think, "Dag, how come she gotta be so smart?"'

'Oh yeah, right.'

'For real.' He looked past her and shook his head. 'The day Freddy was shot, it was you called the police,

473

answered questions. Gayle was screamin' her head off, and I zoned out. You're all the important things, Pat, kind, strong, bright, honest . . .'

'Uh-huh. Me and the damn Girl Scouts!' Pat shot back.

'I usually don't have to wonder what's on your mind 'cause you will speak it! But I always loved that about you. Pat . . . look at me.' She rolled her eyes. 'I've loved . . .'

'Don't, Marcus. We've barked up this tree before . . .'

'It's the tree I want, and I'm tired of yappin' around it. I was jealous of Hughes when we met him at the museum. I thought you had the hots for him. How could you not know, I acted stupid enough.' He rested his hands on her shoulders. 'I can't play this game anymore, Pat. I love you. I guess I have for years.'

'Don't confuse pity with . . .'

'Stop it! It's taken me fifteen damn years to say what I felt in Gayle's basement.'

'You remember that?' Pat never let herself believe it meant anything special to him.

'I tried to forget it. I convinced myself you'd never be interested in a dumb jock. That you were too smart for me.' He pulled her closer. 'You're a real complicated woman, but I love you. If you're not interested, if you don't want me in your life, you'll have to say so.'

Pat felt a tremble from the place only Marcus had ever reached. 'Beautiful women must camp outside your building! What do you want with me after somebody like Téa?'

'Téa was a distraction. But I didn't invite her on this trip. You're the one I want to be with. I think you're beautiful, in every way, and I love you.'

Nobody's said they love me. Not since Gayle, when we were kids. 'You can't, Marcus . . .'

'I can, and I do.' Marcus covered her mouth with his

and they spoke all the pent-up feelings, lip to lip, like the first time, the time neither had forgotten. He held her close when her knees quaked, and, without another word, he eased her onto the deck. She found herself in his kiss, clung to him like her life depended on it, and at this moment, it did.

Marcus disappeared below and returned, ready to love her, in the time it took her to catch her breath. The frenzied urgency of their gropings submitted to the gentle sway of the boat on the swells. Miles from landfall, inhibition peeled away like their clothes. Slowly and seamlessly they stroked, licked, nuzzled, and kneaded. And Pat yielded to him, to the feeling, free to be herself, because Marcus knew her, everything there was to know. And she knew him. Extensions of each other, they shared the touch and the sensation.

Next day they put in at St Kitts, off schedule but on a new course. Playful and teasing like kids, they wandered the streets and shops, then lunched at a restaurant called the Ballahoo and watched people queuing for the ferry to Nevis. With Pat behind the wheel of a rental car and Marcus navigating, they explored the island until almost sunset, when they stopped at Dieppe Bay, left their shoes in the car, and headed toward the shore. Three cows ambled along the black sand, unperturbed by the human intrusion.

'So what do you think?' Marcus asked.

'What's the topic?' Pat walked a little ahead, flirting with the surf.

'Marriage.'

Pat stopped in her tracks. 'They say it's lovely, but I've never given it much thought.'

Marcus spun her around to face him. 'Well think about it now. Will you marry me?'

What did he say? I know I heard wrong. I'm standing on a beach at sunset in the Caribbean and Marcus just asked me what? 'Huh?' was all she could manage.

'Fine. You're gonna make me say it again.' His face was inches from hers. 'Patricia Ellen Reid, will you marry me? Did you understand me this time?'

Pat's head bobbed up and down. 'I . . . I . . . understand . . . But isn't this kinda soon?' The water rushed in and bathed their feet.

'I think it's kinda late. You were so stubborn and contrary, every time I'd get close, you'd run or pick a fight.'

'I did not!' Pat folded her arms across her chest.

'Did so. Anyway, I know I love you, and I want to marry you. It seems pretty simple to me.' Marcus closed the tiny space between them and covered her mouth with his.

Pat wasn't used to feeling out of control, but reason and planning couldn't stand up to the simple truth. *I do love him!* She melted into his chest, and her heart thudded against her ribs, or was it his heart? She couldn't tell, but she knew she was happy. Pat looked into his eyes. 'Yes.'

'Pardon me? I didn't understand you.'

She laughed. 'Y-E-S. Did you get that? Yes, I love you. Yes, I want to marry you.'

He hugged her right off her feet. 'I knew you'd see it my way!'

'Don't get ahead of yourself, Marcus Garvey Carter! Don't you forget the choice was mine!' She tried to scoot away, but he pulled her back and held her face in his hands. 'I'm glad you chose me. Even if you are a pain in my behind!'

Pat felt giddy in love, like the teenager she never was. That night they ate lobster under the star-spangled sky over Frigate Bay, then found their way back to the boat, where they made love on the deck under the yellow moon that felt close enough to touch.

They continued on their journey. During the days, Marcus fussed, and Pat argued. They kissed and laughed at themselves and at each other, like always, only better. At night they'd drift off, bodies pressed tight together, and when they changed positions, they were like the flying fish – one went, the other followed. Somehow, in the middle of the sea, Pat felt grounded and secure.

When they left the Caicos, headed for Grand Bahama, they hit their first bad weather. Wind churned up the sea and cracks of thunder silenced the roar of the waves. From inside the wheelhouse, Marcus steadied *Keeper* as she scudded over the cresting whitecaps. He was surprised when Pat appeared at his elbow, but he handed her a life jacket and started giving orders. She was a quick study and combined with what she had already learned to keep him off her back, she proved a worthy first mate.

They finally left the storm behind in late afternoon. Exhausted and relieved, he adjusted their course, set the autopilot, and they climbed to the flybridge. The water sparkled as the sun shamelessly exposed itself for the first time all day. 'I'm glad you're not scared of lightning anymore.' Marcus grinned and his dimple winked at her. 'And I'm really glad you said yes. But I knew you would!'

'Hold on a minute! We aren't married yet!' Pat started to unbuckle her life vest. 'Can I take this thing off now, Captain?' she asked sarcastically.

'You can take off anything you'd like.'

Pat ignored his aside. 'I've been thinking about this wedding business.' She plopped down in front of the wheel. 'You are a famous person. At least *semi*famous.' She smiled. 'And you know the press loves love. I don't want a big-deal doves and limos show for the world to gawk at. So if we're still on, let's do it simple, and fast. Before I change my mind.'

'That's easy as Zach O.'

'What?'

'Friend of mine. He's a judge in West Palm, retired now. You should see his boat! He's the one who got me into it. Anyway, I know he'd marry us. I'll call him when we get to Nassau. Is there anybody you want to come down?'

Pat thought a moment. *'I'll find you a prince, too. We'll have a double wedding!'* She could see Gayle's ponytail bobbing excitedly. *Jill's in Spain doing a movie. There's nobody I want to invite to my wedding?* 'Not really. I'm sure your friend can scare up two witnesses.'

'How 'bout your mother?'

'Marcus, you *know* I don't know where she is.'

'Maybe it's time you tried to find out. Don't look at me like that. You tried to include your father in your life. It didn't work. Doesn't your mother deserve a chance, too?'

The breeze whipped Pat's hair into spikes she tried in vain to subdue. 'Even if I wanted to, I wouldn't even know where to begin.'

'For starters we can check New York. And lots of times folks go back home to start again. Swan City is pretty close to my parents' place.'

'Maybe I could get past being mad about the way she treated me . . . *maybe* we could learn to understand each other. And *maybe* things are fine just the way they are.' Pat looked out on the ocean. She hadn't laid eyes on her mother since that night in the Easy Street when Verna surprised her with the Turner Hughes story.

'Maybe you won't know 'til you see her. You might not even find her, but you won't know 'til you try.'

478

Maybe she could be surprised again. 'I'll think about it, Marcus. Okay?'

He looked at Pat sitting in the captain's chair. Her brown skin was sunkissed, her hair blew every which way. She looked happy. 'I do love you, you know.'

'Marcus?' Her face turned serious. 'Are you sure?' Because more than anything she needed to be sure because love had never been something she could count on. The boat pitched on a wave, she reached for the grabrail, and he put out his arm.

'I can't give you any ironclad guarantees about the future. You wouldn't believe me if I did. But am I sure I love you? Yes. Am I sure we belong together? Absolutely. Do you make me crazy? Often. But I'm certain I want to be your friend, your partner, your husband. I even got myself a job. Isn't that a respectable married man thing to do?'

'And I'm unemployed, but I don't want you to feel you have to take care of me.'

'Marriage means you take care of each other. You'll figure out what you want to do next. Maybe start your own ad agency, I don't know, but you will, in time. I'll be traveling a lot. But we can handle this. Together I think we can handle anything.'

'We can, huh? When is the first official Gallagher & Carter trip?'

'After Florida I'm back in New York a few days. I leave the day before Thanksgiving . . . big time of the year for sports . . . and I'm on the road almost three weeks.'

'See, you've left me before we're even married!'

'And you're already nagging! You know, except for hospital stays, my parents have never spent a night apart? Amazing, huh?'

'They don't have to worry. Their record will be safe with us!'

'This could count as our honeymoon.' He cut the engine and grinned wickedly.

'What about our first Thanksgiving?' Pat arched an eyebrow.

'I'm feeling very thankful.' He grabbed her hands and pulled her toward the hatch.

The Honorable Zachary Omega Williams was not what Pat expected. The last of fourteen children, his name a declaration there would be no more, grew up on a tenant farm outside Eustis, Florida, and dreamed of playing in the Negro Leagues. Polio sidelined those ambitions. The disease kept him from farmwork, but not from books, and excellent grades were rewarded with scholarships. By the time law school beckoned, his father had been dead six years and his eight surviving siblings had scattered to the four winds. After graduation Williams opened a practice in his hometown, lived in the back of his storefront office, and saved every cent he made. In two years he bought a piece of land near Orlando and moved his eighty-four-year-old mother into a house with her name on the deed.

When his mother died, he held on to the farm out of sentiment until a California company, intent on building an amusement park, made Zachary Williams an offer he couldn't refuse. Williams had done well for a poor crippled colored boy, as he referred to himself, but he never stopped loving baseball and never missed spring training.

Zach O met Marcus in his second rookie season with the Orioles and they became fast friends. He was the first Black man Marcus knew with a boat. Actually a 121-foot yacht, as Marcus later discovered. The fall after he and Gayle broke up, Marcus crewed for Zach on a trip to Bimini, and the friendship hadn't stopped growing since.

Pat and Marcus enjoyed the judge's hospitality, and, three days after their arrival, they stood in front of a gurgling fountain on the palm-fringed terrace of his limestone palazzo. Marcus's mother wasn't well enough to make the trip, so Booker stayed home with her and Marcus promised they'd come for a visit right after the first of the year.

Pat, her hair softly waved, looked radiant and calm in her ivory silk suit. Marcus, handsome in his navy blue suit, held her hand tight as Zach O began the proceedings.

Rather than select rings on the fly, Pat and Marcus had decided to do the do without bands of gold and exchange them as Christmas gifts instead. But at the appropriate time in the ceremony, Marcus surprised her with a sixteenth-century Spanish gold coin he'd found on a dive and had set as a pendant.

The judge remarked on the enduring luster of the doubloon, in spite of the rough seas it had weathered. He told Marcus and Pat they would need to do the same. From beginning to end the wedding was over in less time than it took to scramble two eggs.

25

'. . . ain't nothin' good as an old friend.'

What the hell came over me? Pat stomped through her apartment, slamming doors, trying to imagine packing all of her stuff and moving it. *To my husband's apartment!* **My husband?** *I don't have a damn job, but I have a husband. I must have been out of my mind!*

Pat stayed dizzy with love in the days just after the ceremony. When she and Marcus left Zach O's place, Pat thought it would be fun to tag along on Marcus's football scouting stops, but quickly realized she had no appetite for jock talk or watching barbarians in helmets pound each other into Astroturf. She remembered she didn't get the whole tailgate, big-game ritual when she was in college, and nothing had changed.

At both Florida State and A&M Marcus arranged get-acquainted receptions to meet the athletic staff and their wives. He proudly introduced Pat as his bride. She, too, was proud, watching how confidently he hobnobbed at the packed parties. But when the cocktail talk turned to her, she felt off her mark, anxious for these people to recognize she used to be a powerful decision maker, too. Pat struggled for a simple explanation of her former career, felt lost when she couldn't reel off her future plans, and when one of the alumni, a developer who made big donations to his alma mater, said 'Honey, you can work full time at spending his money,' Pat laughed dryly, but at that moment she felt like a gold digger.

'We both know who you are and what you've done. What does it matter what these people think?' Marcus delivered the pep talk earnestly. Pat knew he meant it, but she hated for people to believe she'd spent her life fishing and finally reeled in a prize catch.

During his three days in New York they tried to tie up loose ends and bring their lives together, but Pat got even more frazzled. They discussed throwing a wedding reception, but she couldn't get beyond the uneasy flutter in her stomach whenever he called her 'Mrs Carter,' which seemed to be his favorite name for her, like she didn't have one before.

Marcus had the bigger apartment, so Pat grudgingly agreed to move to his penthouse for the time being, even though she found lower Manhattan sterile. 'We can take our time finding a place to buy. Maybe in the city. Maybe out of town, someplace with breathing room and space for a swing set,' he said as the locksmith ground each a set of keys to the other's place.

A swing set! Now I'm supposed to stay barefoot and pregnant?

When he offhandedly mentioned he wasn't crazy about her furniture, Pat went off. She was perfectly happy with her furniture, she said, and if he thought she was gonna live with just a couch and a bed, he had another think coming. He apologized, said her furniture was okay, 'for now,' and suggested she could do some decorating while he was away. She informed him she was going to find a job, not shop for curtains. Marcus went for a long walk.

For someone so used to functioning with a committee of one, the sudden shift to 'us' and 'we' wasn't sitting well, especially since Pat felt Marcus had everything to give and all she could do right now was take.

Marcus tried to get Pat to travel with him. 'You can do what you want during the day, and we'll be together every second I'm free because we have a lot to catch up on.'

She wouldn't go. 'This is your show. You don't need me in the way while you run it.'

'But what are you gonna do for Thanksgiving, baby? You're not plannin' to sit in the dark and call out for turkey fried rice, are you?'

'No. I'm not,' Pat answered, even though she would have preferred it. 'For your information I had plans *before* we got hitched.' Pat explained about Darlene at A Hand Up.

'Why does it have to be there?' Marcus scowled. 'What about Turner?'

'Believe me, I wish it was someplace else, too. But he's not involved in day-to-day operations. Come to think of it, he was never at the center unless there was a film crew there to record it. Anyway, Darlene is a special little girl who's had a rough life. I wouldn't disappoint her.' Pat made it sound like she looked forward to the occasion, and she was always happy to see Darlene, but she really wanted to skip the outing and take to her bed until she figured out how she had ended up married to Marcus.

'Darlene's lucky to have someone like you in her corner.'

Pat changed the subject.

The night before Marcus left, Pat staggered to the bathroom at three A.M., half-asleep, and splashed, butt first, into the toilet. She woke him up, wet and mad.

'Don't you look?' He doubled over, laughing.

'I shouldn't have to!' Pat fumed until morning. At breakfast he mentioned the dreaded 'M' word and she about bit his head off. 'I have enough money, thank you! I wouldn't be on the street with a paper cup if you hadn't come along, Marcus.'

Marcus was worried about his long recruiting swing, and his patience was thin as onionskin. 'I'm not tryin' to buy you or your damn love. It was a simple question. If you need money, you can have it, no strings. I was just lookin' out for you.' *Nothin' I say is right!*

Their good-byes were curt and nippy. Pat pecked him on the cheek, and he left for the airport. That's when the doubts joined her for breakfast and stuck around to make her wonder if 'I do' was a colossal mistake.

All the arrangements she made to vacate her place reminded her of the huge leap she had taken with no preparation. She got estimates from movers and realized she'd be living with a man whose habits were foreign to her. She didn't know if he was an early bird or a night owl, if he liked showers or baths, or maybe he liked to haul off and beat the stuffing out of his woman when things weren't going his way. She didn't think so, but how could she be sure? She hadn't been right about much of anything lately.

While filling out a post office change of address form she'd brought home, she was annoyed by the little piles of receipts and loose change scattered on tables and counters all over her apartment. *I'm not Cinderella and this is no damn fairy tale. How did I let him convince me we could live happily ever after? There's no such animal.*

Marcus phoned at least twice a day, always sounding happier than a pig in shit. He reported his progress, discussed his strategy, and told her how much he missed the way she backed her butt into him when they curled up together at night or the way she looked just like the nine-year-old he remembered when she woke up in the morning. Sometimes he made her laugh and she was so happy she ached inside, at others she was just looking for a reason to say, 'Let's call this off, before things get ugly.'

Thanksgiving morning Darlene called, so excited her words slid together. 'You still coming, right? I'm gon' set the table so you sit next to me. Aunt Millie says I can't worry you to death, but I'm not, right? I can't hardly wait 'cause I love Thanksgivin', and you can get to meet my new friend. She's my same age and she used to take dance class, like Alvin Ailey and stuff. She's only been here a little while, but I think we gon' be best friends.'

Darlene was waiting by the sign-in desk when Pat arrived. Darlene's haircombing skills had improved, and she had a neat little ponytail and bangs that framed her eager eyes. She wore jeans and the pink sweater set Pat gave her for her birthday.

'You look pretty, Missy,' Pat said.

Darlene grinned and looked like she would burst. She fished Pat's hand out of her coat pocket and her cigarette pack fell to the floor. 'Miss Pat? Could I say somethin'?'

'Of course.'

'I don't like it that you smoke. It means you gon' die. They told us that in school. I don't want you to die,' she pleaded.

'Does it worry you that much?' Darlene bobbed her head. 'I know I should quit. It's really hard when you've been smoking a long time.'

'You can do anything. I could throw them away for you.' Darlene held up the pack.

Pat was cornered, but she was also moved. 'Okay. I'll try.' She watched Darlene ball up the pack and dart off to put them in the trash.

'Come on!' Darlene tugged at her arm.

Pat thought it was odd there was only one staffer on the

door. Usually there were two. *Must be the holiday. Guess most people go home to their families.* The floors in the halls and elevators looked overdue for a washing, too, but that couldn't be her problem. It was hard enough being in the building. Even after the commercial fell through the AHUP director urged her to stay involved. 'Funding is tight these days. We could use a person with your drive,' she had said. Pat made excuses about being busy with her job hunt, but once Darlene and her family were out of the center, she was never going back.

'My friend just went upstairs to get her momma. She's a real nice girl. She in a bad mood a lot, but she just got outta the hospital when she came here and her arm and leg still ain't right yet, so I guess it hurts sometimes.'

The dining hall smelled like carrots and canned gravy to Pat. *Floor needs mopping here, too,* but drawings and collages done by the children decorated the walls. The room hummed with kid energy like a gymnasium, and the line of families heading for their seats was bisected by the servers, who rushed by with platters of sliced turkey and bowls of mashed potatoes.

'Dinner won't be like it used to be at Nana's. I miss her sweet potatoes, but we gon' have cranberry sauce.' Darlene twirled around to emphasize how good that was.

Pat saw Mildred standing by the table and waving, and she waved back. Darlene saw her, too, but made a beeline toward the long tables across the room.

'Hey, girl! What you doin' sittin' down? Where's your momma?'

Despite a smile, something about this child looked depressed to Pat. *She's here, isn't she? Who knows why?* Hair cascaded down her back and the striped polo shirt she wore seemed loose, like it was bought to grow into or maybe handed down.

'I couldn't carry the tray so Mom went to get it.' She looked at Pat, sizing her up like she was used to grown-ups. 'Hello. My name is . . .'

'Wait! I'm gon' introduce you if you give me a chance.' Darlene let go of Pat's hand and in her best etiquette said, 'Miss Patricia, this is my new girlfriend Vanessa. Vanessa, this is my grown-up friend, Miss Patricia.'

'Pleased to meet you.' Pat held out her hand and Vanessa reached out to shake it. The movement seemed stiff, awkward. *Vanessa . . . Funny. She's about the right age.*

'Here comes your momma,' Darlene announced.

Pat turned to look and the room noise dropped away. Her heart thumped wildly, sending a deafening rush through her ears as she stared into the face of a ghost. Gayle's long hair was chopped off to the jaw, and gray strands salted the pepper. She had always been slender, but now she looked gaunt and faded, a shadow, not the vibrant woman Pat last saw. *It can't be!* 'Gayle?' Pat sputtered. She took two steps, then froze.

Gayle stood rod straight, holding her tray of institutional bounty. 'You can stop staring and go on about your business. You didn't want to know me before. Kicked me out of your room. Don't bother speaking now.' Gayle's lips curled around the bitter words like she'd practiced, hoping for a chance to say them out loud.

Pat was speechless. Sure she remembered the day she put Gayle out of her apartment and out of her life. Pat spent years trying to forget the hours she waited for Gayle at that clinic, finally dragging herself home, drained and bleeding. Gayle finally showed up, dressed sharp as new folding money, sparkling with jewelry and youthful beauty. 'I tried,' she had said, expecting to be forgiven. 'I *kept* my baby,' she had said when she wasn't. If Gayle had reached in and torn out Pat's heart, it couldn't have hurt any worse and Pat had despised her for that. But this woman barely resembled the Gayle she had known. She looked old and the kind of weary that sleep alone won't cure. *What happened?*

'Mo-om!'

'Vanessa, hush and move that glass so I can set this tray down.'

The children looked at each other, baffled.

'Gayle, that was ten years ago. I was mad and hurt and . . .'

'You know I'm not talking about ten years ago. Just this summer, you looked me dead in my face and ordered me out, like I was a mangy dog or something . . .'

'What are you talkin' about?' There were plenty of times Pat wondered about her. But those moments always ended with an image of Gayle updating her wardrobe and making a lovely home for her family. Living in a shelter never made the list of possibilities.

'Don't deny it, Pat. You ignored me and it hurt, like it was supposed to, but I deserved that, so why don't we call it even? I apologize for leaving you alone that day. I didn't do it on purpose. I know you needed me, and I wasn't there. Okay? Satisfied? I would have said it then if you let me, but . . .'

'Listen to me. I never saw you this summer. What room?'

'This is quite a festive crowd we have for the first Thanksgiving here at A Hand Up, New York.' The reverend stood in the center of the room. His smile gave him chipmunk cheeks that made him look too young to be ordained. 'I'd say we're all about ready to take part in the giving thanks and to partake in this joyous Thanksgiving repast, so if you would all take your seats, we can get under way.'

'Darlene, honey, you should get to your table. You don't want Aunt Millie to come looking for you.' Gayle turned her back and sat down.

Pat decided it was better to pursue this after the meal. 'Let's go, Darlene.'

'You know Miss Gayle?' Darlene whispered, trying to make sense of what she had seen.

'From a long time ago.'

'But you pretended you didn't know her?'

'No. I'd never do that.' Pat was somewhere outside herself, looking in.

'She musta made a mistake and thought it was you. Just tell her after dinner. It'll be okay.' Darlene looked satisfied with her conclusion.

The reverend blessed everybody including the farmers, 'Who raised the gorgeous, nourishing food we are about to receive.'

Gayle is living in a shelter! How is that possible?

Dinner seemed endless. Pat had to make herself stop staring at Gayle's back across the room. Fortunately, Mildred was so happy to have the company of another adult at her table, Pat didn't have to say much to stimulate conversation. 'How are your classes going? You're taking word processing and business accounting, right?'

'Supposed to be. I thought this place was gon' be so different. And it's okay as far as shelters go. Better than those roach motels they make you stay in.' Mildred turned briefly to her sons. 'Stop mixin' up your cranberry sauce and potatoes. And you! Don't let me catch you kickin' your brother under the table again, you hear me?' Darlene ate her turkey, wearing her 'Aren't I being good?' face and listening intently to the grown-up conversation.

'Where was I . . .'

'Here is better than the roach motels.' Darlene refreshed her aunt's memory.

'Thank you, angel. Anyway, when we first got here you could set your watch by how things got done. Meals on time, teachers in class, sweep the floors, bip, bip, bip. But now, shoot, the teachers are here like every other day. The computers are sittin' up there, but no teacher, no touch. You can't learn that stuff unless you practice it.'

Whatever little bit of Pat's brain that wasn't focused on Gayle thought this sounded odd. Mildred went on to tell her how the training for nonresidents hadn't started yet. 'First they said June, then September. Now they sayin' January, but the story is stale. My friend Xenia keeps askin' me about it, and I can't tell her nothin' new. But at least I gave that big shot who they say started this place two earfuls of me.'

'What?' Pat was only half-listening, but the 'big shot' got her attention.

'Oh yeah. He came down here, big and black as he wanna be, with his ole hound-dog eyes, showin' some muckety-muck from Washington around. He was pattin' people on the head like we were all his "good lil' chir'en." Shoot, I told him if this is the best hand up he can give, he best keep it in his pocket. He was none too happy with me, but I got a tongue and two lips and I must speak up. He says he gon' look into it, but at least he can't say nobody told him.'

Turner. It used to be that he mattered, but not anymore. What mattered now was figuring out what Gayle was talking about.

Mildred laid her knife and fork delicately across her plate. 'Anyway, my father moved back to Gulfport, Mississippi, where his people are from. I been thinkin' about movin', me and the kids, and startin' over. Never thought I'd say that, but it might be the best thing.' When the table was cleared and it was time for a dessert, Darlene went to get the tray of spice cake and ice cream for her family and Pat saw Vanessa walk slowly, painfully, toward the service counter.

'Excuse me, Mildred. I need to talk to . . . an old friend.'

'Livin' here? Life sure can mess with you, can't it?' Mildred replied.

Pat walked to Gayle's table. 'Is there a place we can talk?'

'There's no need. Some things can't be fixed. I learned that the hard way.' Gayle brushed at the hair that used to lie on her shoulders, seemed startled it wasn't there.

'Hear me out. This won't take long.' Vanessa was on her way back to the table, and Pat waved Darlene over. 'Would it be okay with your aunt if Vanessa had dessert with you?'

'Sure.' She winked at Pat as they walked away.

Gayle sucked her teeth and, without looking at Pat, got up and led the way to one of the day-care rooms down the hall. And there they stood. They'd traveled by different paths, each with heavy baggage to shoulder, but they arrived at the crossroads together.

'Gayle, I don't know who you saw, but it wasn't me.' For so long Pat had viewed Gayle through a lens distorted by anger, colored by hurt, but looking at her straight on Pat realized there was more to what they had shared than that. For the first time in years she felt the strong pull of their shared past.

'I may have lost everything else, but my eyesight is still good.' Gayle recited chapter and verse of the morning at Westcenter that had been branded in her memory.

Pat sank to the red, preschool tabletop. 'You're right

. . . It was me.' She looked directly in Gayle's eyes, searching for that place where they used to tell each other the truth without even speaking. 'But I swear on my life I didn't see you.'

'You didn't *want* to see me. Just admit it and we can go our separate ways.' *'Cause I didn't realize 'til now how bad I miss you and I can't take this much longer.*

'No . . . Not our separate ways. Not again . . . I had just come from meeting my father . . .'

'Your father?' Gayle's harsh demeanor was softened by the impact of Pat's words.

Pat nodded. 'And he basically told me to go to hell. When I got to my room, I couldn't see or hear anything but what he said to me. I wish I had seen you, but I just couldn't.'

Voices and the clatter of plates and forks from down the hall filled the void as each adjusted her view of now, based on a new understanding of then.

'You found your father? And he said that?' Gayle spoke quietly.

Pat nodded and brushed at the tear that dripped onto her skirt. They were silent again. Pat looked up. 'Gayle, what happened? I mean, what are you doing here?'

'The short version? Ramsey was a gambler, I was blind and dumb. So busy lookin' I forgot to see. Remember we used to say that? Anyway, he lost it all then ran off and killed himself, just before last Christmas.'

'I'm so sorry.' Pat cringed, feeling Gayle's pain.

'We kinda had life pieced together, Momma and Vanessa and me. I was working as a receptionist and at the hotel, but then there was the fire. Vanessa was hurt real bad, and Momma . . .' Gayle's voice cracked and her fragile composure dissolved. 'I lost Momma.' Telling Pat, who had eaten those buttermilk doughnuts around the kitchen table, brought home the enormous ache she hadn't made time to feel.

'Aunt Loretta?' The shock of sadness brought Pat to her feet. Tentatively, they reunited in a hug that felt familiar and long overdue. As they clung to each other and cried, time and space fell away, and they were in front of the house in St Albans the day Pat came to stay.

'I love you, Patty.'

'I love you, too.'

Each remembered, but neither said a word. They held on to each other a long time, each one comforted and comforter. When they finally let go, both felt sheepish after the outburst. Gayle found folded brown paper towels stacked by the teacher's desk. She took one to dry her eyes and handed one to Pat.

'I have to get back,' Gayle said.

'Before Vanessa and Darlene come looking for us.' More composed now, Pat explained how she met Darlene. 'You'll stay with me. There's a sofa bed in the second bedroom, but it can easily fit two twins. It'll be crowded, but there's a separate bath and . . .' *Marcus.*

'Hold it. I can't let you do that.'

'Why the hell not?' *Marcus that's why!* 'I got a place, you need one.' They walked against the wave of residents leaving the feast. *Who do I tell first? I'll figure it out. Stop thinking and keep talking.* 'This isn't bad, but I know you're tired of life without a kitchen. You can still come here for whatever classes you're taking.'

'It's hardly worth the carfare. They're not teaching me much.'

When she and Gayle entered the dining hall again the boys had already gone, but the two girls and Mildred were watching the door.

At the table Gayle said, 'Happy Thanksgiving, Mildred.

Vanessa, I want you to meet somebody special to me.'

'Like your best friend?' Darlene was all into this story.

'It's *so* nice y'all found each other,' Mildred said. 'My daddy used to say, "ain't nothin' good as an old friend."'

'Vanessa, you remember me talking about Pat? We grew up together.'

'The same Pat you said dissed you on your job?'

'We straightened all that out. Say hello to your Aunt Pat.'

'You don't have any brothers or sisters, so she can't be my aunt.' Vanessa wasn't buying into the warm and fuzzy moment.

Gayle said good night to Mildred and Pat apologized to Darlene for leaving so abruptly, but Darlene didn't mind. She held Pat's hand as they all walked to the elevator.

'Now that you have Miss Gayle and Vanessa, you won't forget me, right?'

'I'll never, ever forget you, Darlene.' Pat hugged her and promised to call tomorrow.

Gayle's apartment was on the floor below Mildred's, and it looked pretty much the same, except Gayle's walls were covered with artwork. There were portraits of her mother and father and one of her and Vanessa together, all copied from photographs. A delicate watercolor of a formal garden hung over the donated sofa.

'This looks like Paris,' Pat said.

'Central Park. I'd go for a breather while Vanessa was in the hospital here in the city.'

'Reminds me of when I lived with you . . . our room, with your drawings all over the walls. You still have any of them?'

'What didn't get thrown away got burned up. I never missed them until too late.'

Vanessa, nightgown in hand, closed herself in the bathroom.

'She's so miserable. Her whole life changed almost overnight. I don't know if it'll ever be the same, but I can't even say the worst is over because I'm afraid to.'

'Look, move in with me and take all the time you need to get yourself together.' *I have to tell her. How am I supposed to say that of all the people in the world, I married Marcus?*

'We'd be in the way.' Gayle perched on the sofa, hands clasped in her lap.

'We've shared tighter spots. We'll manage.' Pat sat next to her. 'Gayle, I need to . . .' *I didn't think I'd ever see her again.* 'I uh . . . need to know where Vanessa goes to school.' *I have almost three weeks to tell both of them.*

'She's been on home study, but in two weeks she's supposed to start at an elementary school not far from here.'

'Fine. We'll get her registered near my place. It's perfect.'

'I don't know. We haven't lived together in a long time, and we haven't exactly been . . .'

'Close? That's true, but I can't leave you here! I know what it's like living in an institution. It's not a home. I know your mom wasn't exactly crazy about me being there . . .'

'Momma just . . .'

'Don't apologize. She took me in anyway, and I love her for it.' Pat put a hand over Gayle's. 'You'll be on your feet again, but for now, my place is yours.'

Vanessa came out of the bathroom. Her red plaid gown came down to the floor and had long sleeves that covered her arms to the wrist.

Gayle and Pat exchanged a long, deep gaze, then Gayle turned to her daughter. 'Vanessa, Aunt Pat has offered to let us live with her.'

'Great. That'll be five moves since January, counting hospitals, and we still don't have our own house,' Vanessa blurted.

'And I don't know when we will, but I want to get us an apartment. Real soon. If we move with Aunt Pat now, we can get you enrolled in school over there and you won't have to change again,' Gayle said.

'Whatever. I'm going to bed.' Vanessa went in her room and closed the door.

'It's like this every day. Nothing I do makes it better. I know she's spoiled, but she's had such a terrible year.'

'I'm coming for you tomorrow. She'll poke out her lips and be mad for a while, but she'll get over it.'

'Saturday. I'll never be ready tomorrow.'

'Saturday then.'

'I don't know how to . . .'

'No need. Get some rest. You've got packing to do.'

When Pat got home she surveyed her apartment to see what needed rearranging. Finding Gayle at A Hand Up like that was a shock to her system. In the middle of yanking used-to-fit clothes out of the guest closet, she noticed her message light flashing.

'How's my baby . . . ? I had a whole heap of football and too much dry-ass turkey. Who likes turkey anyway . . .'

Shit. What the hell am I gonna tell him? I know we just got married, but while you were away I found Gayle and invited her to move in. You don't mind, do you, honey? What a stupid name. Why would anybody decide to call a grown man 'honey'? She fixed a drink and examined her options, one at a time. *I can't tell Gayle we're married before she moves in. She'll never leave AHUP, and she's got to get out of there. What if she still loves him?* Pat remembered watching them kiss in front of the house. *I'm supposed to move in with Marcus, anyway, so they can have this place to themselves for a while. That makes sense, doesn't it?*

Pat hemmed and hawed about calling Marcus back and came down on the haw side. She was still trying to digest the horror story Gayle had served up to her. *Gayle should be in a corner somewhere babbling and drooling. How did she stand it?*

Besides, Marcus knows how close we were growing up. I lived in Gayle's house. He'll understand I have to do this. She fingered the coin around her neck. *What's he gonna say? You oughta leave her there? He wouldn't come out of his mouth with any stuff like that.*

Pat got a pack of cigarettes from the carton in the kitchen. *Tomorrow. I'll quit tomorrow.* She snatched the phone book and looked up 'M' for mattress. *I'll tell him tomorrow. No, too busy. I won't have a sane moment for a conversation like this, and he'll be just as crazy, since he said this is a big football weekend. Games and parties around the clock. Shit! Next week.*

Another cigarette and she started a list. *Have the super move the sofa bed from the back room to her storage room in the basement. Get twin beds and linen.* She remembered how Uncle Joe and Aunt Loretta got her a new bed and she and Gayle both got new matching sheets and bedspreads. She never let anybody know, but that had meant a lot. *When I move in with Marcus, Gayle will have my room and Vanessa will have an extra bed for company. Maybe Darlene can sleep over since they've become friends. It'll be good for both of them.*

Marcus called early Friday. He was checking out of his hotel to catch a flight from Lansing to Iowa City. Tomorrow he'd leave for Nebraska. He'd had good talks with two offensive linesmen and a running back so far and was excited about his prospects. 'But I sure do miss you, woman.'

When she heard his voice she realized she missed him, too. She talked about Thanksgiving next year and how she hoped they'd spend it together. She talked about only liking the dark meat on turkey, anything to avoid mentioning the specifics of yesterday. 'Maybe I'll have a surprise for you when you get back.' She knew she shouldn't have said it the moment it came out. At best it was a pretty sick joke, but she just didn't know how she would tell him about Gayle over the phone and was glad to have time to develop a strategy.

Pat spent the day shopping and organizing. By evening mattresses were delivered and set up, beds made with white eyelet sheets and dust ruffles and finished off with down comforters. She had a fleeting moment when she thought of calling the movers and having them pack her stuff and take it down to Marcus's place and out of the way, but she decided she wanted to spend time with Gayle first. They had a lot of ground to cover. *I'll get a fresh start in the new year. New apartment, new husband, new life. I'll find the right job*. It sounded good if she didn't think about it for long. Otherwise, it made her nauseous.

Just as in her producing days, Pat overlooked no detail, other than answering the annoying little voice that wondered what would happen if Marcus and Gayle didn't get along? And what would happen if they did?

'Are you sure this is a good idea?' Gayle asked that evening when Pat called to check in. 'If we stay on here, it doesn't mean you and I have to be strangers again.'

'You two are the closest people I have to family.' *Well, not exactly. Marcus is my family now, too . . .* 'I just wish we'd found each other sooner.'

When she hung up, Pat felt like she was hovering between Gayle and Marcus, juggling switchblades. If she didn't catch them just right, somebody was gonna bleed.

26

'. . . sometimes, when you gamble you lose everything!'

'This place is beautiful, Pat.' Gayle put the last shopping bags in the second bedroom. 'And this room. You didn't have to do all this.'

'My pleasure.' Pat sat on the foot of a twin bed. The move didn't take long. She hired a station wagon from a car service, and they were done in one trip. The hardest part was leaving Darlene. Pat promised Vanessa she could call, and that Darlene could come soon for a sleepover, but she still looked crushed as they drove off. 'The closet and dresser are empty. There are storage bins under the beds. Let me know if you need more space. We'll find it.'

'There's plenty of room for our stuff. We'll unpack right now.' Gayle was mortified when she caught the doorman looking askance as she stood in the hall amid her collection of odd bags and boxes. The sooner they were empty, the sooner she could throw them away.

'All you can see from this window is another building!' Vanessa peeked through the blinds. 'And I have to share a room with you?!'

''Nessa! You make it sound like punishment. We'll have our own refrigerator again.' *Nothing is yours, except what's in those bags, Gayle.* 'I mean Aunt Pat will let us put things in her refrigerator.'

501

'You were right the first time,' Pat said.

'Which means we can decide what we want to eat and when we want to eat it, like Friday night chocolate chip sundaes. I never thought I'd look forward to scrambling an egg.' Gayle almost lost it, but she held back her tears. She had to help Vanessa cope with this transition. *'Be strong for her.'*

'How do they expect people to live in rooms this small. In our real house the rooms were twice as big as this, maybe three times.' Vanessa plunked down on the bed opposite Pat, conspicuously unimpressed.

'Don't let me hear one more complaint from you. Aunt Pat didn't have to invite us here,' Gayle snapped. *I don't want her to think I raised a monster.* Vanessa folded her arms across her chest in under-protest silence. 'Make yourself useful. Put your clothes away.'

'I don't know where they go.'

'You always tell me you're a big girl. Figure it out.'

'My leg hurts,' Vanessa whined.

'Then you need to stay here and rest until you feel better, then put your clothes away. I'm going to the kitchen.'

Vanessa flung herself on the bed and faced the wall as Pat and Gayle left the room.

'She's not usually so rude.' Gayle leaned against the kitchen counter.

'I understand. She's had one shock after the other. Now she's living with this strange lady you say is her aunt. It could put you in a bad mood. What can I get you?' Pat asked

'Just point me to the teakettle,' Gayle said.

'I don't own one. I drink coffee all the time, but the pots are right behind you . . .'

'Never mind . . .'

502

'Gayle, it's no trouble. Boil the water and I think I have tea bags hidden in one of these drawers, courtesy of Chinese takeout.'

'No, really, it's fine. I just said tea to say something.'

'Okay, the first rule is, nothing is a problem. I'll give you the easy sleazy tour of the apartment, but if you don't see what you need, look for it, like you would at home.' Pat reached for a saucepan, ran water, and put it on to boil. *I sound like Marcus, with my rule number one.* 'Is she in pain often?' Pat asked.

'More than she should be. Sometimes she uses it to get attention or to punish me, but she's still got a lot of problems. I'm working on getting her treatment. Everything is so much harder now. But hey, we have an address. A ritzy one at that. And we are not your responsibility. I'm sure you've got a job that keeps you running. Are you still in advertising?' Gayle opened a cabinet door. 'Cups?'

'Over there.' Pat pointed. 'I was. Now I'm a displaced executive.' Pat told her the CGG story in a nutshell.

'Why didn't you tell me?! You don't need us here. You've got problems of your own to deal with.' Gayle poured hot water in her cup. *I don't know the first thing about what's going on in your life, and I've plunked myself down in the middle. I should know better.*

'Tell you the truth, I'm takin' a breather. I've been killing myself, and I'm not sure what for. They gave me a generous kiss-off. That gives me time to figure out what I want to do next.' *What I really need to figure out is how I'm gonna tell Marcus about you.*

'It's their loss. You were always so smart. You'll find an even better job.' Gayle scanned the countertops. She had a hundred questions, about the father Pat found and what she'd been doing for the last ten years. *But Pat could be sometimey, kinda private. And right now I don't even*

503

know where the sugar is. 'Sugar?'

'Where is my head?' Pat reached around the chrome canisters and handed Gayle the sugar bowl. *That's Aunt Loretta's ring she's wearing.* Pat wanted to know about the fire and what happened with Ramsey. *She probably doesn't want to answer a lot of questions about that.*

An obvious silence filled the kitchen as Gayle sipped her tea, and Pat watched.

Finally Pat spoke up. 'Why don't I show you around?' Pots, pans, utensils in the kitchen. Pat was at the supermarket when it opened and there was more food in the refrigerator than there had been since she'd lived there. Before they continued, Gayle insisted on washing out the pot she boiled water in.

'Just leave it.'

'No trouble.' *I don't want to be any trouble to her.*

Linen closet, toilet paper, soap, shampoo. 'Use what you need. That's what it's here for,' Pat instructed. Gayle nodded.

TV, VCR, and stereo lessons. Pat showed Gayle the ins and outs of chez Reid, then got two sets of keys out of her purse, Gayle's on a silver ring, Vanessa's on a pink heart.

'You're so together.' Gayle closed the keys in her palm. *And I'm all in pieces.* On the one hand, she was overjoyed at running into Pat. It was like getting a part of her life back. She'd be able to say, 'Remember the time when . . .' and know that somebody else lived it, too. But Pat was also the only person who knew what Gayle had started out with. And how far she had sunk. 'I'm gonna check on 'Nessa. You do whatever you were planning. Don't let us hold you up.'

'You're not. I'll rustle up lunch.'

'Don't go to any trouble,' Gayle said.

'Soup and sandwiches. I can handle it.'

'Oh, and Pat, I have a girlfriend I used to work with, Danitha. I called to let her know I was moving and said I'd let her know the phone number. I don't have many folks to call these days, but I can give you a little toward the phone bill if you . . .'

'Forget it! You let me worry about the bills.' *And how I'm gonna keep you from picking up Marcus on the phone.*

Pat wanted to sit in the bedroom with Gayle and Vanessa and talk while they worked, but she fixed lunch and pretended not to hear them arguing.

'I don't wanna call her Aunt Pat. I don't even know her, and you said she hasn't seen me since I was a baby!'

Lunch was strained. Pat had fixed hot roast beef on rolls and beef barley soup. Vanessa wasn't interested in either.

'Since when don't you like roast beef?' Gayle asked, incredulous.

'What would you rather have?' Pat asked.

'There's not a thing wrong with her lunch.'

'Maybe she just wants something else. I wasn't thinking. I should have asked. So, Vanessa, what would you like?'

'Peanut butter and jelly,' Vanessa announced.

'Whole wheat toast okay?'

'Yes,' she said.

'Yes, thank you,' Gayle corrected.

Vanessa mumbled the magic words.

'Coming right up.' When Pat put the plate in front of her she said, 'Since we're just getting to know each other, you can figure out what you want to call me. Miss Reid is more formal than I can stand, so that leaves Aunt Pat or just plain Pat. You make up your mind.'

'Patricia! She is still a little girl.'

'Times have changed.' Pat bit into her sandwich.

'Maybe too much.'

505

The days that followed were pretty much the same. Pat and Gayle ran neck and neck for Miss Congeniality, and Vanessa held her own as Pitiful Pearl.

Fortunately, Marcus had no time to call until late at night, after Pat was already in bed. She would pick up in half a ring.

'Been waiting for me, huh.' He told her about his stint in Provo, Utah, to check out a junior who looked like a Heisman hopeful for his senior year. 'I leave for Seattle in the morning. How's my surprise?'

'Still surprising,' was the only thing she could think of to say.

'Maybe I'll have one for you, too,' he said.

After Gayle returned from walking Vanessa to her new school, she found Pat weeding through old magazines.

'Do you mind if I hang a few things up on the bedroom walls?'

'Of course not. You really should get those framed eventually. They're beautiful.'

'I don't know about all that. It's just what I do to keep my hands occupied and my head from rolling off my shoulders.'

'Seriously. There's gotta be a way for you to earn a living with your talent. I'm sure you'd like it better than word processing.' Pat tossed a magazine on the discard pile.

'I don't have any formal training. What should I do, take one of those correspondence courses from the back of a magazine? You know, "If you can draw Skippy, you can be an artist." That won't do anything to help me pay my bills.'

'I don't know, but there has to be a way to market yourself,' Pat said.

'I think you've got advertising on the brain.'

'Trust me, when it comes right down to it, everything is marketing. I've been thinking about commissioning one.'

'A pity painting.'

'Not pity, just pretty. Anyway, you need a hand hangin' those pictures?'

'If you're not busy.'

'Do I look busy?'

Gayle removed her artwork from between pieces of cardboard she'd taped around them so they wouldn't get bent. 'I like having the one of Momma and Daddy around. It keeps me company in between visits.'

'You still go to the cemetery every month?'

'Mostly. When I was working two jobs it was hard getting there on the day I like, Daddy's birth date. I missed a couple of months with Vanessa in the hospital, too, but she was better this month, so I went. I hadn't checked on Momma's engraving 'til then.' She taped her mother and father above the head of her bed. 'Without my car I had to take the railroad, but it's not a bad ride. There's a stop right there, and it gives me time to think. It's funny, I haven't felt like I could talk to Ramsey. I sure can't go visit him out in the middle of the ocean.'

Pat wasn't sure what to say. 'The landscape would look good over the bureau.'

After they secured the painting Gayle looked at it, wistfully. 'This one's okay, but the things I love the most I did for Vanessa when she was little.'

'Did you lose those, too?'

'Fortunately, they survived.' Gayle moved the lace tablecloth she used to camouflage the banged-up foot-locker and took out the stack of Ell Crawford Books. Underneath was Vanessa's baby picture with her bronzed shoes. 'She'll probably fuss, but I love this picture. It was

Ramsey's favourite, too.' Gayle set it on the bureau and handed Pat the books.

'These are amazing.' Pat lay on her stomach on Vanessa's bed and paged through the storybooks. 'You wrote the stories and illustrated them and everything?!'

'I used to love doing it. Just to see Vanessa's little eyes sparkle and have her ask me a million questions about how the magic shoes worked. She used to enjoy them so much. I know, it's hard to believe she ever liked anything based on the way she's been acting, but she was such a happy little kid.' Gayle lay on the bed, looking up at the ceiling.

Pat continued reading the books.

'I sold a few of them at a Christmas Bazaar once . . . Even had a boutique owner ask me to do more for her shop.'

'Did you?'

'No. Ramsey didn't think it was a good idea. Mammy-made junk he called them.'

'Are you serious? What did you think about that?'

'I didn't. I always left the thinking to him. See where that got me . . .' Gayle sat up abruptly. 'Where's the grocery store? I thought I'd fry some chicken for dinner. Vanessa loves it. I haven't made any in a long time. Unless you had something else in mind.'

'Home-fried chicken? I can't remember the last time I had any.' Pat rolled up on one elbow. 'And you gotta have collards and corn bread to go with it.'

'And dirty rice and candied yams, maybe a pineapple upside-down cake for dessert . . .'

'Stop! I give! Let's go.'

They went to three stores before they found greens they liked, but when they got everything home, the cooking commenced.

'I can handle this, Pat. You don't have to . . .'

'You can't cook food like this by yourself. It ain't right. Besides, I don't remember the last time I cooked in here. My neighbors will think somebody new moved in!' Pat pulled a brand-new chef's apron from the drawer and threw one to Gayle.

Pat picked greens, washed the chicken, and chopped onions, celery, garlic, peppers while Gayle started the cake, then put the greens on to cook. It didn't take long for the aromas to make the house smell the way Sunday dinner used to.

'Remember when Aunt Loretta would put us out on the back steps with a gigantic bowl of string beans to snap. We really thought we were working hard,' Pat said.

'Peas were worse. We'd be shelling for days and still only have enough for two people. Then Daddy would grab a handful and eat 'em raw. It used to make me so mad!' Gayle wiped flour off her hands and started cracking eggs. 'Momma used to cook like this every week . . . make rolls from scratch. And most of it done before we went to church.'

'I don't know how she did it, but my favorite was when she baked a ham . . .'

'Daddy would slice the skin off and make cracklin'.'

'I used to couldn't wait to cut off a hunk . . .'

'And slap it in a frankfurter bun so you could sneak it up to our room.'

'The bread didn't matter. It was the meat, honey!' Pat waved a celery stalk for emphasis.

They laughed, openmouthed belly laughs that seemed fed by the luscious aromas.

'Momma was talkin' about you and your ham eating . . . the night before she died.'

Conversation stopped for a bit, but the space was filled with the hiss of simmering pots, steam rattling their lids, a knife clacking on the cutting board, and the dull slap of the wooden spoon against the sides of a glass bowl full of batter.

Pat put a scrubbed yam on the drain board. 'What happened to Aunt Loretta in the fire? Did she suffer much?'

'I have prayed every day since then that she didn't.' Gayle seasoned, stirred, and related what happened, from the first stroke to the last, fiery night.

Pat was through chopping onions, but she wiped tears from her cheeks with the back of her hand. 'I don't even know what to say.'

'There's nothing to say. I know what you mean.'

Gayle left to retrieve Vanessa from school and the kitchen smells that met her at the door seemed to improve even her mood. She did her homework without complaint and then, a week late by the calendar, they sat down to a gut-busting, gravy-sopping feast. Once, Vanessa even asked, 'Please pass the rice, Pat,' which at least meant she was trying out a name. Vanessa had managed not to call her anything up to that point.

Mealtime talk went back to everyday life, Vanessa's new teacher, and the best times for Gayle to use the laundry room. But the frosty climate had moderated at least into the temperate zone, and comments were punctuated by lip smacking and satisfied sighs.

After dessert they all rolled into Pat's bed to watch 'A Charlie Brown Christmas,' because they were too stuffed to sit up. Vanessa soon fell asleep and Gayle and Pat crept into the other bedroom. They took up their respective spots on the twin beds.

'Tell me what happened when you found your father.'

The Verna-Turner saga required sherry. Pat glossed over the part Marcus had played in her eventual introduction.

'I don't care how much money he has, he must be a pathetic man.' Gayle leaned back into the pillows she had propped against the wall. 'And if he was like that with his flesh and blood, imagine what he was like with your mother.'

'Probably twice as nasty. I'm not sure if I can ever be objective about Verna, though.' Pat took a sip of sherry, noticed Gayle absentmindedly looking at her hands while she listened. 'I always wondered why she hated me so much, and I guess I can see how that could happen. It doesn't do diddly to change the way she made me feel. But then I know how you can do things you regret when you're old enough to be grown, and still too young to see what's happening until it's too late.'

'Tell me about it,' Gayle said.

'I was scared I'd be like her after the whole mess happened with P.J. . . . I couldn't put a kid through that . . . I still wonder if I made a mistake.'

'I shoulda been there to help you figure it out, or hold your hand . . . Whatever you needed. After Ramsey left . . . died, I realized a lot of things about myself. A lot of them I don't like very much. I wish I could have seen that before.' Gayle looked over at Pat.

'I know.' Each let her thoughts settle into place, and after a while Pat said, 'There's nail polish and files and stuff in my bathroom closet . . . If you want it.'

'My hands look like I've been walkin' on 'em.' Gayle went out and came back with the manicure tools, polish, and two old magazines to lean on.

'There's red in there.' Pat always thought of Gayle with red nails.

'It's a little too spicy for me right now. I'll start with clear and work my way up.' Gayle winked and started filing.

511

'You know, I've been thinking, ever since you showed me those storybooks . . .'

'Is that what I smelled?'

'Yep. Fried brain!'

'I'll pass, thank you!'

'Seriously, those stories are great, the pictures are wonderful . . . what would you say if I asked you to go into business with me, publishing Ell Crawford's adventures.' Pat sat cross-legged on the bed.

'That I'll get you two aspirin. You should stay in bed 'til the fever breaks,' Gayle said.

'It's not as crazy as it sounds. This year I've spent a lot of time looking for books for Darlene, and there's not a lot to choose from for little Black girls, or boys for that matter.' Pat's voice gained momentum with excitement. 'There's a need, and I was thinking Ell Crawford is the beginning of a way to fill it.'

'I don't have two cents to rub together, Pat!'

'I do. You've already created a product. Do you think you could come up with more adventures?'

'Sure, but . . .'

'Great. I think mail order is the way to go. We could start with Ell Crawford books. Maybe dolls next, and down the line who knows, maybe a Saturday morning cartoon . . .'

'Whoa! You're talking about lots of money. How can we do this?' Gayle asked.

'On a shoestring to start. I don't know the publishing business per se, but I do know how to get things produced. I was always good at coming in under budget, so I figure I can do the same for us. I'm sure I can scare up a few people to give us free advice,' Pat replied.

'You can't risk your money on something this crazy!'

'Why is it crazy? If a big publisher did it, we'd say they

had vision and rush to the store to buy it. Besides, I'd rather put my money to work than leave it in the bank for my old age. I expect I have a few good years left to earn more. If this doesn't work, I'll go back to being an employee, but I haven't been jazzed by much of anything since I was canned. It's worth the gamble.'

'You say it like it's a joke, Patricia. Sometimes, when you gamble you lose everything!' Gayle snapped.

'Bad choice of words. I apologize. I'm just saying that I think it's a fabulous idea, one worth investigating. Will you at least think about it?' Pat asked.

Gayle shaped the tips of two more nails. 'You're crazy . . . but I'll think about it.'

They continued to talk, sprawled on their twin beds, filling in the years. Gayle finished up the second coat of polish on her pinkie and said, 'So, I know you haven't spent all your time in this great big pretty apartment by your lonesome.'

'More than I care to remember.' *I don't like where this is going.*

'Hello! It's me you're talkin' to. There musta been at least one man, in all these years, who rocked your world. Who made the cool, calm, and collected Patricia Reid see double and speak in tongues? I mean, as much as I hate to admit it, I still love Ramsey.'

'You what?'

'I know it's crazy. I hate him for what he did. He was moody, demanding, he stole, lied, and deserted us. My mother is dead. My daughter could have been, but sometimes, late at night, he comes over me like a fever, and I miss him . . . Oooh, girl, I miss him. Let me tell you how bad it is. If he walked in that door right now, and he said, "Nightingale, I came back for you," I'm afraid I'd have to tie myself to this bed to keep from going.'

'I'd get rope, chains, locks, a pit bull, and a shotgun. Whatever it took to keep you here 'til you came to your right mind.'

'And I appreciate that, but come on, Pat. Wasn't there ever anybody you were crazy about? I mean cuckoo crazy?'

Here's the opening. Just walk through it. Pat paused, like she was thinking. 'I was like that with P.J. And didn't I make a fool of myself?' *Not yet. We just got on the right foot.*

'What about now. Who's making your toes curl and your heart happy?'

'Well . . . There is somebody . . .'

'I knew it! Had to be! I want name, age, place of birth, occupation, all the vitals. Lay 'em.' Gayle counted off the stats on her just-dry fingertips.

'It's too soon to talk. I don't wanna jinx it.' *She's not ready . . . I'm not either. Early next week, while Vanessa's in school, before we get too far into this project. I'll tell her. If she accepts it, good. If not, I'll move downtown, she can stay here until she straightens out her life, and we'll each go our separate ways.*

'My unscientific gut tells me Ell Crawford appeals to girls ages four to eight.' Pat poured more hot water into Gayle's mug.

'That sounds right.' Gayle sat on the living-room floor with her sketch pad open on the coffee table. She doodled as she spoke. 'Before Vanessa got so grown I had this idea about the magic shoes taking Ell into space.' Vanessa was tucked in bed, and after days of brainstorming, Gayle felt good taking her artwork seriously for the first time in her life.

'I like it. After all, we have Mae Jemison.' Pat poured a third after-dinner cup of coffee and pinched another hunk of pineapple upside-down cake. She'd thrown out the rest of the carton of cigarettes, and if she wasn't going to smoke, she had to do something. She was going great guns on their publishing empire. They had come up with names; Heritage Publishing, Kuumba Press, and Reid, Saunders, Inc. emerged on the top of the list. Pat had already spent hours in the library researching mail order businesses, publishing, and licensing, and she'd set up a meeting with an attorney she knew to discuss incorporation.

Gayle sketched the outline of Ell and twirled a lock of hair around her finger. Early in the week Pat talked her into a trip to the hairdresser. He added shape to Gayle's whacked-off 'do and gave her layers around the face for softness, but she kept the gray. 'I earned every one of them,' she had said.

'I found this article about how a mother from Texas turned a purple dinosaur into an empire. Let me get it.' Pat ducked into her bedroom.

The jingle of key in lock startled Gayle. She sprang to her feet.

'Mrs Carter?! Surprise delivery for you!' Marcus closed the door, put down his bag.

What? Gayle stepped into the hall.

'Uh-oh. Excuse me.' Marcus was startled by the stranger. 'That's the trouble with surprises. They can backfire on you. I'm . . .'

'*Marcus?*' All Gayle could do was gawk. He looked just like he did the last time she saw him, on TV, leaving the DA's office. He was bigger than she remembered, but the last time they actually came face-to-face was in her parents' house, the day he and Ramsey squared off. Marcus was taller than Ramsey even then. That day was awkward, but in a way she had been relieved. To this day she hadn't missed Marcus, ached for him, the way you

515

miss a lover who's gone, the way she missed Ramsey.

Marcus searched her face for a clue to who she was and how she knew him.

Pat came into the hall. 'Oh damn!' They both turned to her.

'Mrs Carter?! You and Marcus are *married?!*' Gayle felt like she had looked the wrong way, stepped off the curb, and been hit by a truck.

'Gayle, I was gonna tell . . .'

'*Gayle?*' Marcus looked dumbstruck. 'Were you gonna tell me, Pat? Or is this the surprise you were talkin' about?'

'What are you doing here? You weren't supposed to be home until next week.' Pat felt the situation sliding out of her hands.

'Am I supposed to make an appointment to come home? I didn't think it was necessary *after* we were married. Rich was called away, and I have to cover for him. I *thought* you'd be happy to see me.'

Marcus and Pat scowled at each other, with Gayle wedged in between, like the referee at a prizefight, but she didn't know the rules for this contest. She was obviously missing a lot of important information, and the best thing she could do was get out of the way before they started swinging.

'I'll leave you two alone.' Gayle slipped past Pat and escaped to her bedroom.

Arms folded across his chest, Marcus tapped his foot on the floor. 'You mind tellin' me what's goin' on here?'

Hands on hips Pat replied, 'Don't stand there like you think you're my father. I don't answer to him, and I'm certainly not answering to you.'

'Like your father? What is that supposed to mean? I'm *not* your father. I'm not *like* your father. But I *am* your husband . . .'

'And if you think I'm gonna consult with you before I *breathe*, you can forget it. Gayle and her daughter were living in a shelter. I couldn't leave them there!'

'You mean they're living here?'

'I didn't have a chance to tell you.'

'I talked to you every night! What do you mean you didn't have a chance?!'

'I know you didn't expect me to ask your permission.'

'Permission!? Ain't nobody said nothin' about permission. You damn sure coulda talked to me about it! What? Is her husband here, too? Maybe we can go on a double date? Yeah. I ain't seen him since we almost came to blows in the Saunders front hall!'

'He's dead, Marcus. And you said none of that mattered to you anymore!'

'I said we shouldn't a been married. I didn't say I wanted her livin' in my house!'

'Your house?! Keys don't make it your house!'

'It's gon' be like that, huh? Here I was thinkin' that bein' married made *ours*. That's the way it was where I grew up. If I was interested in *yours* and *mine*, I'd a stayed single!'

'Well maybe you should have!'

'Don't think that can't be arranged.' Marcus's jaw was clenched, and he was breathing like an angry bull.

Pat glared back. *He can't come in here, thinking he can run my life*.

'Oh, you got nothin' to say now, so I guess that's the way you want it!'

'I guess!' *I knew this was a mistake!*

'Bet.' He tossed his keys on the hall table. 'I'm outta here.'

27

'Maybe we can all be friends and maybe we can't.'

'How could you not tell me?' Gayle came out of the bedroom where she'd retreated while the fight was raging.

'This isn't your business, Gayle.' Pat sat on the sofa hugging a throw pillow.

'How could you not tell him I was here?'

'We didn't wake Vanessa?'

'No.' Gayle perched on the arm of the couch. 'And you're right. It isn't my business. So, first thing in the morning, we're outta here. We shouldn't have come in the first place.'

'Yes, you should have. What the hell is wrong with him? Was I supposed to leave you and Vanessa . . . like I didn't know you? If Marcus can't accept it, tough.'

'You should've told him. Nothing's worse in a marriage than secrets. Look at me.'

'It wasn't a secret . . . I was going to tell him. But obviously I've made one *huge* mistake. If he thinks I have to ask his permission to do every little thing, just because we're married, he's got another think comin'!' Pat jumped up and snatched her handbag from the chair by the door. 'I need a damn cigarette.'

'You quit. Remember? And you *know* inviting us to live here is not a little thing! I asked you the other day if there was a somebody in your life. You said, "It's too soon!" *Too soon? You're married to the man!* If my head is spinning 'cause you forgot to mention that the "somebody" was Marcus, can you imagine how he feels finding me here?'

'The time was never right. I wanted to tell you, but I didn't know how you would take it. You and Marcus were . . . I mean, I know it was over years ago, but what was I supposed to say? "I'm sorry to hear about all your troubles, Gayle. Come live with me and my husband. And by the way, he's your old boyfriend"?' Pat dumped the contents of her bag on the coffee table.

'Why didn't you tell *him?* That's who called late at night, isn't it? You had the chance.'

'I thought I'd have more time to figure out the best way to tell both of you. He was supposed to be gone another week yet.' She dropped the purse on the floor. 'He'd call full of news about his trip. I never found the right moment. We just did this stupid marriage thing a few weeks ago, and he's been away most of that. I don't even feel married, whatever that is.' Pat headed for the hall. 'There's gotta be a cigarette here!'

Gayle followed. 'You know, I heard about Marcus getting married. *Inside Info,* that was it. I went to get Vanessa and Mildred had it on, but I left as soon as I heard his name. I didn't want an excuse to be thinking "what if it was me?" 'cause I know that's just me feeling sorry for myself. I've had a lot of practice lately. I guess I shoulda watched!'

Pat rummaged through the drawer in the hall table and avoided eye contact with Gayle. 'I didn't think I'd ever see you again, and Marcus hadn't seen you in years. As far as either of us knew, you were a happy housewife in Westchester or wherever . . . Dammit! I can't believe there's not a cigarette here!'

'Even if I had been around, what would that change? Would you feel any different?'

'I . . . I don't know. I'm not even sure I know how I feel.'

'You married him. You have to feel something!'

'I don't know, Gayle! We always had a connection, I guess. Even way back . . . then. But it wasn't like . . . you know . . . I didn't like him like *that* when you two . . . I'm babbling, aren't I?'

'Listen, Marcus and I had our little thing because we did. We were kids! We didn't know anything. You remember way back in the beginning, I had the crush on Freddy. Marcus was just another dumb boy in our class, but I put up with him because he was Freddy's little brother.' Gayle talked to Pat's reflection in the hall mirror. 'When I said I didn't want to know about him getting married, it wasn't because I still loved him. I don't know if I ever did. We probably should have been just friends.' Gayle turned and looked straight at Pat. 'What it boils down to is, do you love him? Doesn't this sound crazy? I'm the one asking if *you* love Marcus.'

'Love doesn't make him my boss!' Her frantic search for cigarettes moved on to the coats in the hall closet.

'That's what this is really about, isn't it, Pat?'

'I don't need him to . . .'

'You never needed anybody, did you? I needed my parents. I needed you. I needed Ramsey, dumb as that seems. I need Vanessa. But you never needed one single solitary soul, did you? Needing someone makes you human, Pat, not weak.'

'It makes you vulnerable. You get hurt. Trust me. I been there.' Pat slammed the closet door and leaned against it.

'How do you think Marcus feels now? You don't think

he's hurt? You invited us to live here, and not only didn't you ask his opinion, you didn't even consider it! Even if you had a dog, you'd think about how he'd feel before you brought a cat home, wouldn't you?'

'That doesn't give him the right . . .' Pat sank to the floor. Gayle sat down beside her.

'He has every right, Pat. Every right. We're gonna leave.'

'And go where? The armory? Your place at the center is long gone. You have to stay here. I want you to stay.'

'What about what Marcus wants? He's your husband, Pat. I know you thought I was nuts to marry Ramsey, but I loved him, and I wanted to make him happy. I think he wanted to make me happy, too, but it got lost . . . in all the secrets he kept.'

'But you didn't know Ramsey was sick.'

They sat side by side on the floor, their legs stretched across the hall.

'Maybe if I'd paid more attention to us and less to our precious image, I would've seen we had problems. I don't know if I could've helped him, but at least I'd've faced what was going on . . . before it exploded. My marriage was a disaster, but that doesn't mean I had the wrong idea, just that I had the wrong person . . . I don't think you have the wrong person.'

'He's so hard-headed!' Pat coiled a stray piece of string around her finger.

'You're no slouch in the hard-head department! Remember, if anybody knew you when, it's me.' Gayle found a peppermint in her robe pocket. 'You want this?'

'Yeah.' Pat tore off the wrapper and sucked the candy, inhaling the mint like it was a menthol 100. 'I can't let you leave. When I had nowhere to go, y'all gave me a home. You *belong* here. And what about Vanessa? You know she needs physical therapy.'

522

'Look, Pat, we found each other again, and nothing will change that, but I won't get in the way of you and Marcus. Call him. Tell him we're leaving. Tell him you're sorry.'

'I don't know, Gayle.' Pat yawned. 'It's late. I can't make much sense now.'

The phone rang and Marcus strained to focus on his watch. *Who in the hell is calling me at six-thirty on a Saturday morning? The week since the fight had been filled with restless days, followed by sleepless nights.* He'd only dozed off two hours ago. 'Yeah?'

'Sorry to disturb you.' Pat's hand trembled when she dialed his number. Now she tried to keep her voice from doing the same.

Marcus scrambled to sit up on the sofa, like he didn't want her to know that's where he'd been sleeping. 'I was up.'

'I need a favor. Well not for me exactly, so that might help you consider it.'

'What's that supposed to mean?'

'Never mind. Sorry.'

'Are you?'

'Will you help me or not, Marcus?'

'I can't answer that until you tell me what you want.'

'It's Vanessa.'

'Who?'

'Gayle's daughter. I didn't get to tell you what happened to them, but Vanessa got hurt pretty badly jumping from a window during the fire last August.'

'What fire?'

'The one where Gayle's mother died and they lost whatever they had left that Ramsey hadn't already lost gambling. That's how they ended up at the shelter. I'd

523

have told you if you hadn't jumped down my throat, telling me how wrong I was.'

'I am very sorry about Gayle's misfortunes, but get to the point.'

'The point is Vanessa's doctors haven't done a bad job, but I think your team at ISI could make a big difference.'

'It's the Institute for *Sports* Injuries. I don't think falling out a window qualifies.'

'You know as well as I do they fix broken jocks whether they fell off a ladder cleaning the gutter or got trampled by a whole football team.'

'So?'

'So I know they can help a little girl.' There was a pause. Pat wanted to reach through the line and touch him.

'I don't know.'

'What don't you know? Forget about Gayle, forget about *us*, we're not the issue. She's a little girl, Marcus!'

'Yeah, right. I'll think about it, okay? How she's gonna pay for this?'

'If they take her as a patient, I'll pay the bill.'

'I see.'

'See what, Marcus?'

'You've adopted both of 'em, huh?'

'You seem to have forgotten that if it hadn't been for Gayle and her family, who knows where I'd be today.'

'I haven't forgotten. I just think you would have made it to the top no matter what. Remember, you're the one who likes to fly solo.'

'I have to go, Marcus.'

He told her he'd be in Philadelphia most of the week. Gave her the name of the hotel. 'Not that it matters to you.'

'If you won't help, don't keep me waiting. I'll need to find somebody who will.'

Pat hung up and fell back into her pillows. She'd been planning the call for two days, and since five this morning she'd been trying to anticipate what he would say, rehearsing her replies. Hoping something would break the ice.

But now it was over. She had talked to him, and nothing was any different.

How can I choose between him and Gayle? How?

All week Pat had avoided making a choice. She steered Gayle away from conversation about Marcus and focused on their new venture. Pat lost herself in creating detailed projections for their business plan. She got estimates from printers, worked out a preliminary timetable and the beginnings of a budget. Then she tried to pull Gayle into her frenzy, insisting she come up with at least a dozen new story ideas, the sooner the better.

But despite her attempt to fill every second, Marcus still crept into her thoughts. Those warm afternoons aboard *Keeper* would float through her mind before she could drown them out with work. In unguarded moments she'd hear him say, 'I love you. I guess I have for years,' and have to shake off the tingle that shot through her body. *I love you, too.* She would force herself back to the task at hand.

When Pat finally recovered from her early morning phone call enough to drag out of bed, Vanessa was sitting on the sofa, watching cartoons. Her bad leg was propped on a pillow. 'Good morning.' Vanessa never looked away from the screen. 'Whatcha watching?'

'Nothing.' She flicked off the remote and got up.

'You don't have to . . .' Pat found herself talking to Vanessa's back as she limped down the hall. Pat had decided not to mention she'd asked Marcus to help Vanessa until he said yes. Even then Pat expected a knock-down-drag-out getting Gayle to accept it. She found Gayle in the kitchen sipping tea and poring over the want ads.

'You giving up on our business?'

'Dreams are fine, Pat, but I gotta have a paycheck, *now*. Putting my life back together is not your responsibility.'

'I didn't say it was. Besides, nobody's hiring this time of year.' Pat took a carton of orange juice from the refrigerator.

'This is hard for me to ask . . . If you could lend me enough to get a place. Nothing fancy. We could go back to Mt Vernon. I could try to get my old job back. At least they'll give me a good recommendation.'

'I'll help any way I can, but don't give up on Ell Crawford. We haven't even tried yet.'

'Speaking of trying, have you tried apologizing to Marcus yet?'

'Why?' Pat poured a glass of juice.

'Because the longer you avoid each other, the harder it's gonna be. Don't use Vanessa and me to forget your own life needs tending to.'

'Thank you for those words of wisdom. I promise I'll talk to Marcus.' Pat crossed her heart the way they did when they were kids.

Gayle lay awake that night. Despite the perky act she could see that Pat was hurting. She had only seen Pat and Marcus together arguing, but in her heart she felt they were right for each other. *I gotta do something! I let her down the last time, I won't do it again.*

Since the fire Gayle had been too overwhelmed to make plans. Getting through each day took all her energy. When she tried to look ahead it felt as if she had so far to travel just to get back to square one that she couldn't bring herself to take the first step, until now.

526

She didn't have it all figured out by morning, but she had come up with a way to proceed. *Take small steps. Baby ones if necessary, but find a way to keep moving forward. It's better than standing still.*

The young man struggled with groceries, but he smiled and propped the door open for Gayle with his foot. *Good. I can get upstairs.* She found out where he lived from the address book Pat kept on the desk in her bedroom. On the top floor Gayle took a deep breath in front of PH-C and pressed the buzzer.

'Just a sec.' She heard rustling, footsteps, then the lock clicked.

'I know I'm the last person you want to see, Marcus.'

'You're right.' He leaned against the partially open door. He was barefoot and his T-shirt was half-tucked into his rumpled jeans.

'Hear me out. Please.'

'You shouldn't be here. This ain't your business.'

'Of course it is. If I hadn't been around, none of this would have happened.' Gayle squeezed the strap of her shoulder bag. *Small steps.* 'Are we gonna have this conversation in the hall or can I come in?'

'Suit yourself.' Marcus stepped aside, and she walked past him, but didn't go any farther than the foyer. *She's so skinny.* Her tweed coat looked two sizes too big.

Gayle started straight in. 'I didn't know about you and Pat. Not until you showed up. I wouldn't have been there if I knew. And I'm sorry.' She shifted the purse on her shoulder. 'But maybe I can help fix it. Marcus, Pat shoulda told you . . .'

'Pat's a big girl; she knows where I am if she wants to talk.'

'She'd probably kill me if she knew I came down here.'

'Then maybe you should go. Or is this part of the plan to get me to help?' He folded his arms across his chest. 'You don't have to go through this little routine. I'm gonna do it.'

'Do what?'

'I'll make the arrangements first thing in the morning. They'll take her, don't worry. So you can stop the act.'

'Who'll take who?'

'Come on, Gayle.'

'What are you talking about?'

He studied her face, but couldn't read anything but worry. 'Pat didn't tell you? She asked me to have my orthopedic team take a look at uh . . . your daughter?'

'No. She did not.' Gayle dropped her head a minute, then looked up again. 'And thank you, but no thank you. I didn't come here to ask you for help.'

'But Pat said your little girl was . . .'

'I'll talk to Pat when I get back. That's between me and her. But now I need to talk to you. We were friends once, so maybe for old times' sake you'll let me say what I came to. Then I'll go.' She waited for an answer. 'I'm barely hanging on here, Marcus. Give me a break. Please?'

'Yeah. Aw-ite.' He walked into the living room, gathered up the Sunday papers strewn across the sofa and floor. 'You may as well sit.'

Gayle sat at the very edge of the couch, playing with her knit gloves. 'Pat is wrong. She should have told you Vanessa and I were there. But she was trying to do a good thing, Marcus. I really believe she didn't know how to tell you, or me for that matter. But don't hold her responsible because of what happened between you and me.'

'This has nothing to do with it, Gayle.' Marcus stood in front of the fireplace.

'No? I have a lot to apologize for. I shouldn't have tried

528

to trap you into marrying me, Marcus. And I treated you really terrible that Sunday you stopped by and Ramsey showed up. You deserved better. I was young and stupid and, truth be told, I was tripping on it a little. What I did to you was bad, but it probably saved us from a bigger mistake.' A flicker of a smile crossed her face. 'Think about it.'

'Gayle, I'm not holdin' a grudge . . .'

She held up her hand. 'Let me finish. All these years I've known that if I hadn't pretended I had to go to the bathroom so I could delay having to take my lousy report card home, Freddy wouldn't be dead. Don't you know that's why we hooked up in the first place? We didn't choose each other, Marcus. We got all tied up in that horrible afternoon. We didn't know what else to do, so we stayed together.'

Marcus moved to the window across the room. A few aimless snowflakes drifted by. 'None of us were to blame for what happened to Freddy. It took me years to see that.'

'I've made a mess of my life and other people's, too. I can't let that happen with you and Pat. Not because of me.' She shoved the gloves into her pocket. 'There's another thing I have to tell you.' She took a deep breath. 'It was my fault the story about Freddy got out.'

Marcus whipped around. 'You're the one who told?'

'I told Ramsey. He was my husband. It just came up one day. But I swear I never told that TV show anything. A detective told me it had to do with Ramsey's gambling. I don't understand exactly how. I do know he never got over the fact that I used to go with the famous, rich Marcus Carter. The bigger you got, the madder it made him. He couldn't seem to accept that I loved him.' Gayle's voice trailed off. 'I never thought he would do a thing like that.

But it seems he did a lot of things I didn't think he was capable of.'

'Do you know what I went through behind that?' Marcus snapped.

'I would've done anything to stop him if I had known. You have to believe me.'

'He's dead?'

'Yes.' Gayle walked over to Marcus. 'I am so sorry. For Freddy, and Ramsey. And I'm sorry for landing smack in the middle of your new life.'

'Yeah, well. . .'

'Marcus, I can't stand your pity, and I don't deserve your sympathy. Whatever you have to say, say it to Pat. Vanessa and I will move as soon as we can find a place to go. Maybe we can all be friends and maybe we can't. But don't let this ruin what you and Pat have going. Enough has been ruined already.' Tentatively, she placed her hand on his arm, then moved it away. 'We both know how stubborn Pat is, especially if she's scared, which we also know she'll never admit. And the more hurt she is, the more stubborn she gets.'

He was quiet for a moment. *How can I love her if she won't let me?*

'You have to try. I think Pat shuts the door herself, before it gets slammed in her face. That's kinda what happened with us.' Gayle put on her gloves. 'At least say you'll think about it?' She moved toward the door.

'Yeah. Okay. I will.' He followed her into the hall. 'Take Vanessa to my doctors. I'd like to help.'

'Marcus, I . . .'

'Can we make a deal?'

She smiled. 'Okay. I'll *think* about it.'

On the subway ride uptown Gayle wondered if her visit did any good. She pulled the new help wanted section out

530

of her purse, and found the pickings slimmer than last week, but she made a mental note to call Cameron and Ware in the morning and ask for a recommendation. *And maybe I'll apply at employment agencies, too. Even if they don't have openings now, I'll be on file for the start of the year. Just keep taking little steps.*

'Your mother didn't say where she was going or when she'd be back?' Pat was still half-asleep when Gayle knocked and asked Pat to keep an eye on Vanessa.

'No.' Vanessa hunched over the dining-room table reading Pat's new Kwanza book. A partially done jigsaw puzzle of a mountain scene lay in front of her.

'Do you usually celebrate Kwanza?'

'No.'

'Would you like to this year?'

Vanessa shrugged her shoulders and kept reading.

Pat turned to walk away, then came back. 'You know you're making all this extra hard, on yourself, your mother, and on me. Why?'

Vanessa closed the book, picked up a puzzle piece, but didn't open her mouth.

'We're all doing the best we can under pretty rotten circumstances, but you don't seem to want to help.'

Vanessa rolled her eyes and twirled the puzzle piece.

'I'm talking to you, Vanessa!' Pat felt her anger rising.

'So.' She jammed the piece in place and pounded it with her fist.

'So I know your mother taught you better. And if *she* didn't, your grandmother did! I'm an adult. You are not.' Pat pulled out a chair and sat across from her. 'Vanessa, I know how much your life has changed in the last year. I know it's hard.'

'You don't know anything!' Vanessa shoved the puzzle

away. 'You have everything. You never lived in a shelter and your father didn't . . . didn't . . .'

'I guess your mother didn't tell you much about me, did she?' Vanessa stared at her. 'Neither one of my folks wanted me. My grandmother took me in, but she died when I was five . . .' Pat filled her in on the details Gayle had omitted. 'So, however nice you think my life is now, it hasn't always been like this. It wouldn't be like this now if it weren't for your mother . . . and your grandparents. I'm sorry you never knew your grandfather. I called him Uncle Joe, and he was very special.'

Vanessa traced the shapes of the puzzle pieces with her finger. 'Then I wish he had been around instead of my father. It's all his fault. Since he left us, only bad things have happened!'

'It won't always be this bad.'

'Yes, it will! My gram's never coming back. My leg's not getting any better.'

'It may take a while, but your leg will improve.' Pat wanted to tell Vanessa about ISI, but she still hadn't heard from Marcus.

Vanessa whacked her thigh. 'Kids make fun of me.'

'Darlene never made fun of you, did she?' Pat propped an elbow on the table.

'That's different. She's my friend. I used to have lots of friends. I used to have lots of clothes. I used to have lots of fun. I miss the way we used to be.'

'Your life will never be exactly like it was, but it won't always be this hard. I promise you that.' Pat rubbed the spot where Vanessa had slapped her leg. 'But you have to help your mother. She's doing all she can, but you have to get rid of that chip on your shoulder.'

'I don't have . . .'

'Yes, you do. This is hard, I know that. But you're a big

girl, almost a teenager. You know your mother didn't do this on purpose. It's not her fault. It's not your fault, either. I know that what your father did hurts, but you can't take out your anger toward him on the one person you know loves you. It's not fair.' *It isn't fair, is it, Patricia?*

Vanessa looked at Pat and sighed.

'Okay. End of lecture.' She got up.

'Uh . . . I . . . we learned about Kwanza in school last year. If you want, I could tell you what I remember.'

Pat sat back down. 'I'm all ears.'

Vanessa and Pat had three quarters of the puzzle together when Gayle got back. They all finished it after dinner.

When Gayle tucked Vanessa in she got the biggest goodnight hug she'd had in a while, then came out to talk with Pat.

Deep breath, one foot forward. Gayle told Pat about her visit with Marcus. 'Don't get mad . . . 'cause you're no better. You can talk to him about Vanessa's problems, behind my back, I might add, but you won't talk about your own, but that's all I'm gonna say on it because, as you've both so accurately pointed out, it's not my business.'

'Did Marcus act like he missed me?'

'Why don't you call and ask him? Better yet, go see him. It's easier to talk face-to-face.'

'He'll be in Philly for a week. A basketball clinic or something for high-school kids.'

'He wants to work it out, Pat.'

'I . . . I don't know.'

'Now who's being hard-headed?' Gayle let it drop and outlined her plan to spend the next several days canvassing employment agencies. She even figured she'd try a temp agency. Maybe she could get a few days here and there, anything to tide her over and help her feel like she was making progress.

'I'm not giving up on Ell. That'll be my other job, the one to grow on, and it's the one I love, so I'll keep doing it. But I'd still like that loan. Funny, I was looking for a place to live last January, too.' *No steps backward, Gayle. January. A new year. A better year.*

28

'What comes around.'

Last year Ramsey was gone. This year it's Christmas without you, Momma. Wind whipped the bare trees in the deserted cemetery and the gray sky threatened. Gayle burrowed deeper into her coat as she stood before her parents' graves.

And so much has changed since this time last month. But Pat is back! Isn't that wonderful. You were right, Momma. It wasn't like it seemed in the hotel. We're getting reacquainted, but in a funny way having her around makes life feel more . . . normal. She wanted to come today, but I told her next time. I need to be alone, to catch my breath.

Pat insisted Gayle take the car. The whole ride out, Gayle stayed cautiously to the right and five miles under the speed limit. Pat said not to worry, but she couldn't help it. *Not with the kind of luck I've had this year.* She glanced over her shoulder and checked on the silver Jag parked by the towering evergreens that hid the iron fence.

I hope we've turned the corner, 'Nessa and me. The holidays will be rough. But we're gonna pick out a tree tonight. Pat's taking 'Nessa shopping for ornaments after school. Vanessa wants to celebrate Kwanza this year, too, so we invited her friend Darlene and her family, and my friend Danitha and her kids. I want Pat and Danitha to meet. They'll like each other.

Vanessa's new physical therapist says she'll be dancing in no time. One day I'll find a way to repay Marcus. Icy spikes of rain sliced the cold air.

What am I gonna do about Pat and Marcus? They have to come to their senses! Marcus was in Philly, but this time, Pat wasn't getting any late-night phone calls. *She's afraid to admit he matters, but if she keeps this act up for long, he'll be gone.*

The rain picked up. Gayle shivered and held her purse over her head. *I'm gonna go. I love you both very much. Thank you for loving me. I was lucky.*

Gayle trotted to the car. She pressed the alarm remote while she still had a distance to run, so she could just duck inside. The lights blinked and she heard the whistle. It sounded different. *Who knows how many tunes this thing sings.* She swung open the door.

'Nightingale.'

The voice pierced Gayle's skin like a million flaming needles, and the air in her lungs turned to stone. Her head snapped in the direction of the voice, toward the evergreen trees. She saw nothing. *It's the pressure. Just get in the car.* Then the pine boughs rustled. And she saw him. He wore an ashy blue parka and a black knit cap, pulled down to his eyebrows. A scrappy beard obscured his face. *Get in and drive out of here.*

'Baby, it's me.'

Gayle backed away from the car, away from him. '*Don't you come near me, Ramsey!*' Her shriek echoed in the empty graveyard.

'I had to do it, Gayle.'

'*Momma's dead and my baby coulda been, too! Don't tell me you had to!*' Molten anger erupted.

'They woulda killed me!'

'*I wish they had! Then I could pretend you loved us. Don't come any closer!*'

536

'You don't mean that. You gotta listen to me!' Ramsey lunged and caught her around the waist, pressed her against the fender.

Gayle, soaked with sleet and sweat, wrenched her body around and pounded him with her fists. '*I hate you!*' She clawed at his face, her nails gouging his skin. '*I hate you!*' She sobbed.

Ramsey finally caught her fists. Pressed them to his cheeks. 'There ain't nothing you can say or do that I don't deserve a hundred times over.' Blood trickled from a gash below his left eye, like a tear. 'Gimme a chance to explain. Please.'

Gayle gasped for air. 'Why, Ramsey? Why'd you do it?'

He kissed her fists and led her toward the open car door. That's when the fear set in. Gayle realized she was in a cemetery, struggling with a dead man.

'Let go of me!' She wrestled, started to scream.

Ramsey snatched her and clamped a hand over her mouth. 'I won't hurt you! I could never do that! I swear! Just hear me out!' Ramsey's voice was still as smooth as butter.

Gayle stopped fighting, fell silent. Ramsey let her go. She straightened up, panting, eyes wide with rage. They faced each other, dripping in the pouring rain.

'Five minutes. After that I won't bother you again if that's what you want.'

Gayle swept wet hair off her face. Ramsey's expression, his whole demeanor, looked pitiful, defeated. He seemed so . . . *Old. I never thought he'd look so old.* 'Five minutes. That's it!' Gayle slipped into the driver's seat, popped open the door, and Ramsey sat down. The pitty-pat of rain pelted the car roof.

'Gayle, I messed up bad . . .'

'Is that what you came here to tell me?! If it is, I already

537

know that!' She focused on the water washing over the windshield in sheets.

'You look like you doin' okay.'

'Looks was all that *ever* mattered to you. If you're talkin' about the car, it belongs to a friend. A friend who found Vanessa and me living in a shelter! You left us buried in your . . . in your *shit* Ramsey! I'm still trying to clean it up!'

'You don't know . . .'

'That's right! I don't. You made sure of that!'

'They were gonna hurt you or Vanessa to get to me. I couldn't let that happen!'

'Who is *they?* Who was gonna do this?'

'It doesn't matter.'

'Don't you *dare* tell me what matters! I've been stuck in the middle of this for more than a year. I have a right to know what it is!'

Ramsey fiddled with the ties at the hem of his parka. 'I owed a lot of money . . .'

'Why? Your horse drop dead again? You bet on the wrong team? You swore to me on your *knees* you'd stop. And I *trusted* you!' She gripped the wheel, furious at him and at herself. 'Who, Ramsey?' He reached for her hand, but she jerked it away. '*Who?*'

'Bessie . . . I got in too deep . . .'

'You told about Marcus, didn't you? Answer me!'

Ramsey nodded.

'How stupid could I be? I *let* you lie to me. I didn't want to *believe* you could be so low. And you have the *nerve* to tell me you pretended to be dead to protect us?!'

'I think about you and Vanessa day and night. It's all I have to keep me going.'

'Thinkin' about us obviously wasn't enough to keep you from gambling!'

'I did, baby. I quit, for a while. But I already owed so much. I thought I could . . .'

'*Shut up!* You did what you wanted, and the only person you thought about was you!'

Ramsey hung his head, slipped his cap off, and dropped it in his lap. 'You're right. I can't say nothin' for myself.' He looked at her again. 'And sorry won't begin to make it right. I told myself you were better off thinkin' I was dead, but I had to see you. I had to find out if you and Vanessa were all right. I didn't even know where you were. This is the only place I knew to come. I remembered you went every month, same date, like clockwork, and I knew you'd make it here if you were able. I didn't know about your mother.'

'You stole from her! She worked hard every day. And she trusted you, but then so did I!' Gayle turned to him. 'I loved you, Ramsey! How could you do this?!'

'Let me make it up to you . . .'

'You *can't* make this up! Not to me, not to your child. Vanessa jumped out a window to save herself from the fire that killed my mother.'

'Oh no . . . I didn't . . .' He buried his face in his hands.

'None of this would have happened if it hadn't been for you and your lying and scheming! How can you possibly make that up?!'

Thunder rolled in the distance. 'I'ma have to live with that the rest of my life. But at least let me try and do something right.' Ramsey reached under his jacket to his pants pocket. 'I been scraping by, pickin' up odd jobs, livin' in a flophouse . . . none of that matters.' He handed her a roll of bills with a rubber band doubled around the middle.

'I don't want your money! What is it this time. Football? Poker?'

539

'Naw. I swear! I worked for this. Fifteen hundred dollars. Please take it. For Vanessa. It's nothing compared to what I took, but let me help you what little I can.'

Gayle turned away, stared out the windshield. *I could move with that money . . . be out of Pat and Marcus's way . . .*

'Nightingale, I loved you more than anything in my whole life, and what I did was so wrong I can't ever hope you'll forgive me, but let me help . . . I owe you that much.'

His outstretched hand was ashy, his nails chipped and dirty. *Ramsey's hands never looked like that.* When she took the roll their fingers touched and a charge shot up her arm.

'I'm gonna leave now. I'm headed out of state for a while. It's safer for me far away. I don't know when I can come back . . . Give Vanessa a hug. You'll know it's from me.'

She paused. 'All right.'

Ramsey opened the door, closed it back. 'I shouldn't ask you for nothin', but . . . you know the picture of Vanessa . . . the one with her bronze baby shoes?'

'Yeah?'

'Do you still have it?'

'Yeah?'

'It would mean a lot if you'd give it to me. You know it was always my favorite.'

What am I gonna tell Vanessa? I broke it. Her daddy asked me for it?

'It's been so lonely. That's not your problem, but I'm tryin' to straighten myself out. Every time I'd look at that picture, see those little bitty shoes, it would remind me why.'

'How am I supposed to get it to you? Parcel Post?'

'If you would bring it . . . it wouldn't be safe for me to

come to you. And I don't want Vanessa to see me yet . . . I'm gonna catch a bus tonight.'

This is crazy, Gayle.

'You could meet me at Fortieth Street, near Twelfth Avenue, by the old Greyhound terminal . . . I'll pick it up, get on my bus, and I won't bother you no more. Not 'til I'm straight . . . Maybe then . . .'

He looks so . . . sad. 'I'll bring the picture. Don't talk to me about then.'

'Seven-thirty. I won't keep you waiting. You never even have to get out of the car.' Ramsey opened the door and got out. 'Thank you, Nightingale.'

When he left, Gayle realized she was drenched to her skin, freezing cold, and her head was pounding. She wrestled with herself the whole drive home. *I won't go . . . He looked so bad . . . I don't owe him anything . . .*

When she got to the apartment Vanessa and Pat were still out. Pat had left a note on the refrigerator. 'Don't cook. We'll bring dinner.'

Gayle got out of her clothes, into her robe, and wrapped a bath towel around her damp hair. She was grateful she'd have time to pull herself together. She put the rolled-up bills in the dresser, under her panties, got the photo, and sat on her bed with it in her lap, a hand on each small bronze shoe. *Why should I do this? I love this picture, too, and I have so little left . . . from then. But I do have her. If it'll make a difference . . . if it'll help him. Maybe, down the road . . . if he straightens himself out. Don't be stupid, Gayle!* Her head ached and she still didn't know what to do. She glanced at the clock. *Three-thirty.*

The frame tucked under her arm, Gayle went in search of aspirin. She found a bottle in the medicine cabinet and fumbled with the childproof cap. The picture slipped and crashed to the floor. Glass shattered, the bottom popped off the bronze base and crisp hundred-dollar bills skittered across the white tiles, a green carpet at her feet.

Gayle went stone-cold. *'It's been so lonely . . .'* Ramsey's voice rang in her head. *'Liar!'* she spit the word in a hostile whisper, and whatever feelings she had left for Ramsey curdled into bitter hate. Gayle perched on the side of the tub. Her hands shook as she scooped the money into the lap of her robe and carried it to her bed.

'I loved you more than anything in my whole life.' 'Bastard!' Gayle counted. Her rage grew as the piles mounted. When she finished she had 570 hundred-dollar bills. *All this time there was $57,000 under my nose! This is why he came back. And I was gonna give it to him . . . because he said he loved me! He knew I would do it!* The realization made her sick.

I always did what Ramsey wanted, and all he ever cared about was Ramsey. Gayle got dressed, reattached the bottom to the base with instant glue. *Look what he did to Marcus. And he didn't fake suicide to save Vanessa and me. He did it to save his own cowardly behind.* She searched the apartment, found a CGG interoffice envelope, and stuffed the cash inside.

And for what? His gambling? It's sick. He's sick. You won't get your way this time, Ramsey Hilliard. Everybody's had to pay for your mistakes but you. Gayle wrote Pat a note, wrapped the frame in a towel, put it in a shopping bag. Then she got the card from her wallet and dialed. 'Theresa Stuckey, please. Tell her it's Gayle Hilliard.'

After a short pause she came on the line. 'I've been wondering how you were doing.'

'Detective, is it a crime to fake your own death?'

'My favorites are the painted glass balls.' Pat carried three shopping bags full of lights and tree decorations.

'I like the angel best! She's sooo pretty. Almost pretty as Mom.' Vanessa carried her books in a backpack, and carefully balanced the bag with her chicken parmigiana.

'You're right. She does.'

'I have a note for you,' the doorman said as they walked into the lobby.

Gayle's writing was on the envelope. 'Drop it in here.' Pat held out a shopping bag.

'Hey, she's not home.' When Vanessa opened the door the apartment was dark.

'I'll read the note in a minute. The hall light is on the . . .'

'I know!' Vanessa flipped the switch. 'I do live here!' She smiled at Pat, then hustled in the kitchen with the food. 'I'll set the table,' she shouted.

'You start your homework. I'll set the table.' Pat hung up her coat and set her bags down in the living room.

'I hope she gets home soon so we can go get a tree.'

'Maybe the tree will have to be tomorrow. By the time we finish dinner it'll be time for you to get ready for bed.' Pat was looking forward to the tree, too. She hadn't put one up since she'd been on her own.

'Aaaawwww . . .' Vanessa came back, peeling off her coat.

'Aaaawwww, there'll be trees left tomorrow.' She kissed Vanessa on the forehead and pointed her toward her room. 'To the books.' It had been a good day. She had lunch with an attorney friend who gave her several options for setting up a corporation and promised to check out copyright procedures. They'd meet again, after the holidays, this time with Gayle. After that Pat retrieved Vanessa from school so there was no downtime to think about Marcus. She plodded toward her bedroom for slippers.

What's this? The bulging manila envelope lay at the foot of her bed. Pat unlooped the string and lifted the flap. 'What the hell . . . !' She closed it quickly.

'You call me, Pat?'

'No. I'm talkin' to myself.' *The note . . . where did this money come from? Where's Gayle?* She dug the note from the shopping bag and took it to the bathroom to read.

I'll explain this all later. What you need to know now is Ramsey is alive. He came to the cemetery. There's an envelope on your bed with $58,500.00 in it. I have your car. I'm meeting Ramsey at 7:30. I'm okay, don't worry. But if anything happens, take care of Vanessa. I love you. Gayle.

Pat's legs started to shake. *Ramsey at the cemetery? She's gone to meet him!?* Terror gripped her throat in a choke hold. Pat couldn't think. *What am I gonna do?* Panicky tears welled up in her eyes. *He'll hurt her, I know it!*

'Pat . . . What did Mommy say in the note?'

Pat cleared her throat to find her voice. 'Just a minute.' She flushed the toilet, threw cold water on her face. *Get a grip! You have to talk to this child. And say what?*

She stuck her head in Vanessa's room and hoped she didn't look like she felt. 'She said she went for a drive and she won't be too late.' *It's ten to seven. What's too late?*

'She took my baby picture with her. That's really weird.'

'Maybe she wanted your company.' *Why did she take that?*

'You sure she's all right?' Vanessa sounded edgy.

'Sure I'm sure.' *Please let her be all right!* 'Ready for your dinner?'

'I'll wait for Mommy, okay?'

Pat nodded. She turned on the TV in the kitchen for noise. *I have to talk to somebody. I'll lose my mind . . . Please don't let him do anything to her.* Before she knew what she was doing Pat had dialed information and was asking the number for Marcus's hotel in Philly. His room phone rang and rang, then the operator came back on the line. 'Mr Carter isn't in. Would you like to leave a message?'

'No. I'll call back.' *Where is he? Where is she? What am I gonna do?*

Gayle turned from Twelfth Avenue onto Fortieth Street. The block, slick with an oily sheen from the rain early in the day, looked like it was lit with a fifty-watt bulb. Detective Stuckey told her to park in front of the abandoned redbrick building. The dilapidated bus station, windowless and deserted, loomed across the street.

She parked, cut the lights, but kept the engine running. It's seven-twenty-five. He said he wouldn't keep me waiting. Stuckey said she'd be there, with NYPD backup. 'Don't worry if you don't see us. We'll see you,' the detective had said. Gayle checked the rearview, side view, and in front in a regular circuit. Fraud. The detective told her Ramsey would be charged with fraud for faking suicide. *He's been guilty of fraud for longer than that.*

Gayle had moments of doubt as she drove around the city, parking where she could, killing time until her rendezvous with Ramsey. How she had enjoyed his flash and cash, the jewelry, the houses, the trips. *I was bought and paid for like everything else. It was so easy. No scrimping, no penny-pinching. I had everything I wanted, and I didn't have to work like Momma. I got somebody to take care of me, he got somebody he could control. No lip, no back talk. How many times in ten years did I say, 'Yes, Ramsey,' even when I didn't mean it?* But Ramsey told her bald-faced lies.

Her momma was still dead, he put Vanessa in jeopardy, and now he was trying to get over one last time. Gayle wasn't having it. *He made this bed . . .*

The knock on the passenger side window nearly sent Gayle through the roof. Then she saw the blue parka. She fumbled with the console until she lowered the window.

'I knew I could count on you.' Ramsey bent down and leaned against the door.

Gayle got a flash of the first time she'd laid eyes on Ramsey, bending down by her car on the side of the road. Right now it was all she could do to keep from throwing the car into gear and running over him. She handed him the bag. 'Here. I'll miss this.'

'Not as much as I'll miss you.'

'I gotta go, Ramsey.'

'You stay sweet, Nightingale.' He blew her a kiss, started to back away.

'Police! Hold it right there, Hilliard!'

Stuckey, gun drawn, stepped from the shadows. Ramsey bolted toward Twelfth Avenue. The detective was on his heels when they disappeared around the corner.

Gayle waited, hand clamped over her mouth to keep her teeth from chattering. It felt like an hour, but in less than five minutes Stuckey jogged up to the car.

'Lost him.' Still panting from the chase, her breath floated in white puffs. 'By the docks. Does he know where you're staying?'

'No.'

'Good. Go home. I'll keep lookin'. He can't get far. I'll be in touch. If you need me, call my beeper. I'll be on an undercover assignment indefinitely. There's no point leaving a message.' Stuckey watched Gayle drive off, then walked around the corner and rapped the back door of a black panel van. 'It's me.' The door opened, and Stuckey climbed inside.

'She's gone. I said he got away. I'll call her after.' The driver pulled off as soon as Theresa Stuckey closed the door.

Ramsey lay on the floor, hands, feet, and mouth taped. He sucked air through his nostrils in jagged wheezes. Two men sat on the floor next to him. One pointed a gun at Ramsey's head.

'What was that shit he said about money in a picture frame?' Theresa squatted, her back against the side of the van, bracing against the movement.

'Ain't nothin' in there but dust.' Moses slipped his Kangol back and ran his fat pink hand over his nappy yellow hair. 'It wouldn'ta saved his ass anyway 'cause it ain't about the money anymore. Bessie wants to make an example since he tried to skip out. It's pretty easy since the man's dead already. You sure y'all through with this case?'

'I told you, we closed the books months ago. Nobody cares.' Stuckey blew on her cupped hands and Ramsey squirmed on the floor.

'His wife don't suspect nothin'?'

'Naw. And I don't wanna know any more about it. I delivered him. Gimme my money and the picture and let me off at the light. It wouldn't look good for an officer of the law to be seen with you crooks.' Stuckey laughed and glanced inside the envelope Moses handed her. 'As always, tell Bessie I enjoy the rewards of doing business with him . . . and, Moses, make it clean.'

Pat raced to the door as soon as she heard it rattle. 'You had me scared to death,' she whispered. She threw her arms around Gayle and the tears came in a flood of relief.

Gayle hadn't found her tongue or her tears yet, but they rocked in each other's arms.

'Mom, wait'll you see all the stuff we got! We couldn't get a tree 'cause you weren't home, but we can go tomorrow, right?'

Pat wiped her face on Gayle's coat sleeve before she turned around.

Later, with Vanessa in bed, Gayle told Pat the events of the day.

'Aren't you worried Ramsey will come lookin' for you?'

'Not really. When he opens that picture he'll know I'm on to him. Whether the police find him or not, he won't be back. He won't have the nerve. I just don't know what to tell Vanessa.'

'That you broke the frame and took it to try and get it fixed. My guess is she's so busy right now that she'll forget about it. As for the rest of it, what can you say that won't make her hate her father more than she already does?'

'I don't want to keep secrets from her, but I don't think she's ready for this.'

'As long as you don't think she's in danger, hold on to the story. Tell her when the time is right. You might want to skip the cemetery for a while . . . You know, when I got your note I was out of my mind thinkin' something terrible would happen to you.'

'I know the note was crazy. I didn't know what else to say.'

'And if you *ever* leave me a note like that again, I will string you up by your ankles!' They both laughed. 'But while I was out of my mind waiting to hear from you, I realized what's important, who I can't live without. Who I love. You and Vanessa are on that list. But there's somebody I need to ask to forgive me for being pigheaded and just plain wrong.'

'I know he will.'

'So if you and 'Nessa will be all right here tonight, I've gotta drive to Philly.'

'You go on, girl.'

Pat drove as fast as she figured she could get away with, feeling that every extra minute was a minute longer than she could stand to wait. Every so often, without realizing it, she'd reach up and finger the doubloon. It was just before three when Pat parked the car. Wide-awake and wired, she stopped at the desk. 'MynameisPatriciaReid-Carter.' *Slow down.* 'I'm meeting my husband Marcus Carter.' She wiped sweaty palms on her coat, while the sleepy-eyed clerk called his room, hoping Marcus wouldn't send her away.

'Room 2412, Mrs Reid-Carter. The elevator's down the hall to your left.'

What will I say? She paced the elevator, like her steps would make it go faster. *When I read Gayle's note I was confused and afraid. Without even thinking I called you. And when you weren't there I got a flash of how my life would be if you weren't in it.* She watched the numbers light up. Nine . . . Ten . . . Eleven . . . *I was wrong not to ask you about Gayle. I'm scared. Afraid you're too good to be true.* Seventeen . . . Eighteen . . . Nineteen. *I want you in my life. I want to be your wife. Please give me that chance.* She was out as soon as the doors opened, and when she saw Marcus, standing in his doorway, she started to run. 'Marcus! I love you.' She flung her arms around his neck and he pulled her to him. 'I'm sorry. I apologize.'

'And I accept, if and only if . . .'

'If what?'

'If you'll relax and let me love you back.'

'I do . . . I will . . . yes!'

Marcus smiled and drew her into the room. 'Mrs Reid-Carter, huh?'

'How's she doin'?' Marcus asked when Pat hung up. They had just come up to the room from a romantic dinner in the hotel restaurant.

'Better. The detective stopped by with Vanessa's baby picture. Seems Ramsey dropped it while he was running, but he's still missing. She told Gayle word on the street is Bessie's people got to Ramsey, but they don't have any evidence yet.'

'They coulda got him or he could be in Hong Kong by now. Or Vegas.' Marcus dropped his jacket over the chair arm.

'This is the second Christmas in a row she's heard about Ramsey being dead. This has to be torture.' Pat sat on the foot of the bed.

'There's nothin' for her to do now but keep on keepin' on.' Marcus sat next to her.

'That's pretty much what she said. She's planning to write the police chief. He's the father of one of Vanessa's little friends. Anyway, she wants to tell him how helpful this Detective Stuckey has been. Then she says she's finished with it.'

'It's a damn shame.' Marcus reached for the remote on the dresser, flicked on the TV. 'I need to catch the sports . . . business, you know.' He grinned and nuzzled her neck. 'Nightcap?'

'How about champagne? To celebrate our new wedding bands.'

'Comin' right up!' Marcus called room service.

In no time the setup arrived, and Marcus made a ceremony of presenting and uncorking the bottle and filling two flutes with the vintage bubbly.

Marcus was about to make a toast when he noticed that Pat's eyes were glued to the television. Turner Hughes stood behind a bank of microphones.

'Millionaire businessman Turner Hughes held a press conference today at the Manhattan headquarters of The Hughes Companies to announce he will cooperate with federal officials in their probe of fiscal irregularities at A Hand Up, the charitable foundation Hughes established. It's too early to tell whether the investigation will take him out of contention for a cabinet post.'

'You really wanna see this clown?' Marcus asked. Pat nodded and kept watching.

'I intend to aid prosecutors in every way I can to root out corruption in these centers. I will not allow the greed of one individual to tarnish the noble efforts of many fine people.' Turner was smooth as ever.

The scene shifted to the courthouse steps. 'Foundation Director Peter Jackson declined comment as he surrendered at Manhattan Federal Court. He is accused of skimming more than a quarter of a million dollars from foundation coffers.' To Pat, P.J. looked ill, and Edwina, following behind him, appeared supremely pissed off.

Marcus eyed Pat to gauge her reaction.

She chuckled. 'Sometimes you really do get to see it.'

'What?'

Pat raised her glass. 'What comes around.'

29

'. . . together like this . . .'

The presents this Christmas weren't as important as being together. Everybody ate too much at dinner and Gayle, Pat, and Marcus told stories that started, 'Do you remember the time . . .' and ended in raucous laughter. Vanessa looked from one to the other skeptically. 'You all didn't really do that, did you?' she asked.

'Cross my heart,' Pat answered, and Gayle and Marcus crossed theirs, too.

The next day was the first day of Kwanza, and more people were in Pat's apartment at once than had ever been there, but it felt like family, not a crowd. Danitha had finished her final semester of law school and was already cramming for the bar exam. She and Pat hit it off instantly, which made Gayle feel good. Mildred and the kids were moving to Gulfport during semester break. 'Bein' together like this is so nice,' she said. 'I'm proud to know you folks, and y'all have to come down and visit. We got some pretty beaches.'

While Vanessa taught the girls ballet positions in the bedroom, Danitha's son and Mildred's boys attached themselves to Marcus. They tested their strength against his, asked a million questions about his pro ball career, and he made them promise always to do their best in school.

The Kwanza ceremony began with Marcus reading the seven principles of the celebration. Then Mildred, who admitted to being the oldest one there, had the honor of lighting the first candle. Vanessa recited a poem she had written about her grandmother, and each child talked about what family meant to them. Darlene summed it up when she stood in the middle of the living room, hands clasped in front of her, and said, 'Family's not just a regular mother and father. It's all the people who care about you.' She smiled directly at Pat.

With the celebrating done, packing became the business at hand. Gayle spent the rest of the week helping Pat get ready for the move to Marcus's apartment.

'Your storage bin is empty.' Marcus set the last box on top of the stack in the hall. 'Vanessa and I might be a little late. I'll take her for lunch after her therapy, if that's all right with you, Momma.'

'Fine with me, Uncle Marcus.' Gayle propped her arm on the stack of boxes near the door.

'You ready, Miss Vee?' Marcus called. He turned to Pat. 'You need anything from the outside world?'

'Not a thing.' Pat stretched up on her tiptoes, and Marcus kissed her.

'Oooh, they're kissing.' Vanessa came down the hall.

'They're supposed to. You get your coat,' Gayle said.

Marcus already had it off the hanger. He held it for Vanessa, then they were out the door.

'You think they'll be all right?' Pat peeled the cellophane from a candy cane she'd snatched from the tree.

'Marcus and Vanessa? She'd follow him to the moon, or didn't you notice? Vanessa's having her first crush.' Gayle winked.

'On Marcus? You're kidding. And I was worried about

how they'd get along.' Pat dragged on her candy like it was a cigarette.

'It was nice of him to take her to physical therapy.'

'His idea. Now that he's "Uncle Marcus," he wants to get to know her. And he figured he could be kind of a cheerleader, since he knows what she's going through.' Pat looked at the boxes Marcus had brought up, all of them labeled 'personal.' 'I haven't opened these since I've been here, and I don't have a clue what's inside. I guess I should see if they're worth moving again.'

They sliced through the yellowed tape on the top box and found a stash of textbooks. The next one contained old report cards and term papers from Southridge and Princeton. Gayle removed a manila envelope which was tucked in a yearbook. Inside she found the picture of the two of them she had drawn from an Easter Sunday photo her dad had taken.

'How did you end up with this?' Gayle held up the brittle drawing. 'It used to be . . .'

'Taped to the wall, between our beds. Can you believe those outfits? Girl, we actually thought we were fly! I look like a mailbox in that blue dress.'

'No you don't! Well, now that you mention it . . .'

Pat laughed and whacked Gayle with the empty envelope. 'We did look happy, though. You know, you could draw even way back then. I'm so glad we're gonna publish Ell Crawford.'

'*Try* to. I still think we're crazy.'

'That'll be our secret. I won't tell if you won't.' Pat reached to the bottom of the box and pulled out a twisted orange plastic lanyard. Two keys dangled from the metal loop. 'I didn't know I still had this. You made it for me, at camp.'

'Are those the keys . . .'

'Yep.' She wrapped the cord around her hand. 'Maybe it's time to get rid of them.' One by one, Pat removed the keys and dropped them in the trash can. 'Life is funny . . .' A buzz from the lobby interrupted her. 'It's too early for Marcus and Vanessa; besides, they don't need to buzz.' Pat picked up the intercom. 'Yes? Who? Damn.' She covered the receiver, closed her eyes, and bit down on her candy cane. 'Just a minute.'

'Who is it?' Gayle asked.

'Turner Hughes.'

'After how he treated you he has the nerve to show up at your door! Tell him to get lost.'

Pat paused. 'This is my turf. And I wanna hear what he could possibly have to say to me.' She took a deep breath. 'Send him up.'

'I'm right here if you need me. Okay?' Gayle squeezed Pat's arm.

Pat nodded, and Gayle reluctantly disappeared down the hall.

When her doorbell rang Pat yanked it open. 'What the hell do you want?!'

Turner looked stunned but quickly regained his composure. 'I regret the way I behaved the last time I saw you. May I come in?'

Pat held her ground in the doorway. 'You have the floor. Speak.'

'When you came to my room in Westcenter, I had very specific ideas about where I wanted to go. You're a dynamic, vibrant woman. Those are qualities I find appealing. I'm not a subtle man. If you ask her, your mother will tell you that. Finding out you are my child was most definitely not on my agenda.' His tone was deliberate, his voice controlled.

Pat didn't respond.

556

'I don't suppose you can imagine my shock. Thirty years is a long time by any yardstick. Did I pledge my devotion to your mother when we were together? It's likely. I say a lot of things I don't mean to get my way. I always have. But you made an impression on me. One I couldn't dismiss. Look, I couldn't please my parents, I didn't respect my wife, and I don't like my kids. It's not a nice family portrait, but it's the truth.' His left eyebrow twitched as he spoke, but he never took his eyes off hers.

Pat met his gaze head-on.

'When you told me I was your father, it was as if you were accusing me of something, and I had to deny it. As you may have heard, I've recently been accused of many things I haven't done, and it's made me think about what I *have* done over the years. Most of it is beyond repair. I can't claim any credit for how you turned out, but our brief association left me feeling that I would like to have known you. You obviously weren't handed every damn thing on a platter. You worked hard. You've got backbone. I appreciate and respect that.' He paused.

Pat was not moved. 'You're saying this to say what?'

'At this point I don't know what I have to offer you as a parent, but I'd consider it an honor if you'd give me a chance to try.'

'That's a lovely speech. What a pity there's not a microphone in sight.'

'I'm sorry you think that, but I understand why you would. I have no ulterior motive, and I haven't been diagnosed with a fatal disease, so I'm not here to clear my conscience before I die.'

'Fine. So what you want is a little forgiveness? Glad Tidings, Happy New Year, see you 'round?'

'That's not what I meant, Patricia. And I don't expect you to give me an answer right now.'

'That's good, because you won't get one.' Pat pulled herself up tall. 'From the moment I found out you were my father, my goal was to make you proud. But what you taught me that day was I had to be proud of myself first. I don't know whether you fit in my life anymore. I know where you are . . . if and when I decide.'

'Understood. Thank you for letting me say my piece. And by the way, best wishes on your marriage.'

She nodded. 'Bye Turner,' and calmly closed the door.

Gayle materialized at her side. 'Are you all right?'

'I don't know.' Pat paced a figure eight. 'I'm a grown woman and my long-lost daddy wants to be in my life. I've got boxes up to my eyeballs. I barely remember my new phone number. How am I supposed to feel?'

'However you do. Come on.' She took Pat's hand. 'Let's sit down. I cleared a spot.' Gayle led the way to her bedroom, and each plopped down on a twin bed. 'Whatever you feel, you feel. You'll figure it out. But it takes time.'

'I've spent so much time, and energy, denying what I felt. Hell, I denied I even had feelings!' Pat hugged a pillow. 'Now I have more feelings than I know what to do with.'

'Since my life went to hell on the express track, my feelings about nearly everything have changed.'

Pat stretched out on the bed, hands behind her head. 'Yeah, but that doesn't change what happened to you, does it?'

'No, but feelings change *you*.' Gayle flopped onto her stomach. 'Lord, Patty . . . we used to stay up talking half the night. Remember?'

'And your mother would come in and make us stop yakking and go to sleep? How could I forget?'

Bleached winter sun filtered through the curtains, and,

for the rest of the afternoon, they talked about then, and now. For the first time the past they shared met the women they had become, and once again their dreams for the future included each other.

Dear Reader,

Reading a book can be a little like taking a vacation trip. In the beginning you look forward to new experiences, excitement, and some fun. If you've had a good time, the end comes too soon; you feel better than you did before you went away, and you can't wait to tell your friends all about it. We hope that's how you feel about Tryin', and thanks for spending your time with us.

Our aim was to make Pat and Gayle feel real, like friends we've known, or maybe even like women we've been ourselves. Most of us have at least one 'soul sister,' a friend we love, trust, and rely on like family. There's no special day to honor these deep, vital relationships (like the friendship the two of us share . . . it's how we can write fiction together), so we tried to celebrate it in this story.

We hope to make the sights, smells, conversations, and situations in Tryin' feel familiar and honest. Please let us know if we've succeeded. We're hard at work on our next book and would like to hear how you felt about Tryin' To Sleep In The Bed You Made. You can write us at:

DeBerry Grant
P.O. Box 5224
Kendall Park, NJ 08824
USA
E-mail: TRYINSLEEP @aol.com

Sleep well,